## Praise for *Smile and Look Pretty*

"Readers will cheer Pellegrino's shattering of the glass ceiling in this fast-paced, millennial-centric, you-go-girl novel about workplace empowerment."
—*Library Journal*, **starred review**

"*Smile and Look Pretty* is *9 to 5* for the Instagram generation— a darkly funny and bitingly modern tale of friends banding together to stand up for what's right. As a former assistant myself, I couldn't stop nodding with recognition and cheering on its richly drawn cast."
—**Andrea Bartz, bestselling author of** *The Herd*

"A sharp, funny, and incredibly relevant tale of young women taking their power back—a *9 to 5* for the digital age."
—**Susan Fowler, author of** *Whistleblower*

"*Smile and Look Pretty* is a timely, page-turning battle cry that will make you want to call your friends and change the world. Bad bosses, prepare to quake in your boots."
—**Laura Hankin, author of** *Happy & You Know It*

Also by Amanda Pellegrino

*Smile and Look Pretty*

AMANDA PELLEGRINO

# THE SOCIAL CLIMBER

PARK
ROW
BOOKS

PARK™
ROW
BOOKS™

Recycling programs
for this product may
not exist in your area.

ISBN-13: 978-0-7783-8702-2

The Social Climber

Park Row Books
22 Adelaide St. West, 41st Floor
Toronto, Ontario M5H 4E3, Canada
ParkRowBooks.com
BookClubbish.com

**Printed in U.S.A.**

*For mom and dad.*

# THE SOCIAL CLIMBER

*The most unsettling thing about a gunshot in the woods isn't the echo, the metallic ping that reverberates through the spines of trees and leaves, but rather the peaceful silence that follows.*

# PART ONE

# ONE

**I FORCE MY** eyes open and lie back onto a thin, sweat-stained towel, which has fallen, in inconvenient heaps, atop a thick sweat-stained mat. The time between the final vinyasa and the bong of the culturally appropriated bell by a white woman named Feather is always my least favorite part of the class. It's when you're meant to lie still, silent, attempting to empty your mind and focus on breathing in the dense air, thick with privilege and millennial body odor. It makes me feel sick. I refuse to be the first to leave so I lie in wait, falling into a sort of sleep paralysis, sweat worming down my neck, my eyes twitching with each unused moment as the to-do list in my head spins like a whirlpool, forever sucking me back in until I inevitably drown.

I truly hate yoga.

My Apple Watch vibrates on my professionally tanned wrist, no doubt reacting to my lowering heart rate, asking if I'm finished and want to see my results. We're not supposed to bring technology into the yoga studios—there are offensively low-budget signs Scotch-taped to each heavy door, advising us to "gift" ourselves "screenless meditation"—but no one obliges. What's the point of burning 359 calories if you don't get an itemized receipt in return—if a tree falls in the forest and all that. There's a vulnerability that comes from existing without awareness of what's happening beyond these four purportedly calming off-white walls that for me is more distracting than a slick glance at a vibrating wrist during Downward Dog and choosing to actively ignore it. I'm the one throwing down three hundred and fifty dollars a month to be here. I can do what I want.

During the warm-up—why yoga needs a warm-up, I'll never understand—I received two calls from an unknown number, which has been running circles in my mind ever since. Generally, I don't answer unknown numbers; if it's anything other than a spam call about insurance for my nonexistent car, they'll leave a voice mail and I'll have ample time to prepare before returning. No one likes a surprise. But it always provokes curiosity. Especially when I've been expecting a call, and I'm stuck in this dull room thinking about it.

There was also a text from Graham asking what I wanted to order for dinner. Sundays are his cheat days, and it will take everything in me to respond *whatever you want, babe*, instead of demanding a hulking, bloody Angus burger on greasy ciabatta bread with sweet potato fries and onion rings and a pickle so thick and juicy it will take more than two bites to shove down my throat. But I don't get cheat days—and honestly, the weekend before your wedding should render the concept irrelevant to both parties—so I'll order a salad, pick off anything even remotely resembling a carb, and ask for oil and vinegar on the side.

Nothing could seem less appetizing as I sit in a pool of my own sweat, running on only lemon water and a chocolate RXBAR.

I could feel Feather closing in on me like a dreadlocked panther in the way you can sense someone undressing you with their eyes from across a dimly lit bar.

"I'm going to move your leg," she whispers in my ear, so close I can feel the baby hairs on her forehead scratching my eyelid. She likes to "perform stretches," she calls it, gliding from person to person before she bongs the final bell, gently telling everyone to get the hell out. She's not my favorite instructor, but I like that she course-corrects your poses and stretches you by telling, not asking. Touching without permission.

Ten fingers coil around my calf, gently folding my leg in half and bringing my knee to my nose. I want her to push harder, press the entire weight of her body on top of me until my hip dislocates. But to my disappointment, she relaxes, and I am able to take yet another breath.

The bun plastered to the top of my head forces my neck into an uncomfortable angle, so once Feather is optimally distracted stretching another self-proclaimed yogi, I shift to the right, resting my cheek on the damp towel, and sliver my eyes open. The woman two inches beside me has long brown hair threaded into a choppy braid and a small bicycle tattooed to the nape of her neck. I'd fixated on her a few times during class—the way her skin softened below her sports bra, how the excess pinched together on each side during Triangle Pose but held its shape in a plank. The way some coarse dark hair poked out from her shorts during Happy Baby. I never thought I'd be the kind of person to work out in a sports bra—or take part in any fad-based exercise cult in the first place—but here I am, just like her, in an overpriced Lululemon set picked fresh for the season like summer tomatoes in the Hamptons.

The woman's eyes open and she smiles, idly, when she sees I'm looking at her. Her teeth are yellowed in that way everyone's are, but her forehead holds not one wrinkle. She's paid good money to look like she's never worried about anything in her life. My first instinct is to avert my eyes, but instead I smile back. I've learned that's what you're supposed to do. Then she closes her eyes again, just as Feather tolls the last bell, finally relieving me from this compulsory calm.

Rather than follow the herd of half naked four-packs to the showers, I make my way down the mood-lit hallway to drop my damp towel into the linen collection basket. Then I move into the mat section, attempting to clean mine with an unidentifiable substance simply labeled "mat cleaner" in that half-assed way one cleans knowing someone else will come in and do a better job shortly.

A petite and stout woman in bleach-white scrubs appears from a room across the hall, like a ghost. I think it's the laundry room, which we're not supposed to know exists. All that stuff is meant to happen in the shadows, when classes are in session so they can maintain the secret that there are women who aren't twenty-eight, five foot eleven, and a size two who exist in the world without paying hundreds of dollars to try and change themselves. There's an image to uphold here, after all.

I watch her approach the dirty towels, replace the full basket with an empty one, and then wheel the full basket back down the hall, a crease in her too-tight scrubs forming on her underwear line as she walks away. She probably had to buy brand-new, crisp white panties for this job. I'm shocked management doesn't require something a little more seamless.

In the lobby, I grab my sneakers from the cubby near the front desk. My black APLs beetle from the other swanky and vague "performance shoes" because of their pristine condition: stark white soles, untattered knit heel. The same shade of blackest black as my leggings and the fitted sweatshirt I pulled over my head when class ended. I've found the state of someone's shoes in Manhattan implies the state of their bank account.

I peel my phone out of the shoe and scroll through the notifications as I slip them on: links from Lena with last-minute centerpiece ideas (as if the wedding hasn't been planned to the last, tiniest detail for months, if not years); Graham's dinner question; emails from Kiley, our office assistant, confirming my meetings tomorrow; and, of course, a voice mail from the unknown number.

As soon as I push through the glass studio doors and onto a particularly bustling Amsterdam Avenue, I feel a chill from my bones outward. It's unseasonably cold for October, a time when New York City usually sees an additional week or two of summer and everyone walks around in sundresses and shorts, denouncing global warming skeptics while drinking rosé at tables set up on the sidewalks. But after burning calories in a ninety-two-degree room for sixty minutes, it feels like the tundra.

There are hot yoga studios on the Upper East Side, the closest just five blocks from his—well, *our*—72nd Street apartment. But two years ago, I chose this one, 2.2 miles across the Park. Initially, it was a way to encourage Graham to explore the neighborhood—"meet me for coffee after yoga and we can walk around"—so that maybe he'd want to look into apartments up there, in the buildings occupied by Tina Fey and Jerry Seinfeld and other new money New Yorkers. But his Upper East Side roots are dug too deep for swaying, so I gave up that battle and now use my studio's location as an excuse to get an extra four-mile run in a few days a week. In anticipation of the size two gown (in traditional sizing, I refuse to acknowledge wedding sizes) that will be sewn onto my body in approximately one hundred and thirty-two hours, I've been gradually upping the ante, adding fifty calories to my daily active burn goal every few weeks, which has landed me now at a whopping eight hundred and fifty a day, a feat that's forced me into two- or three-a-days to pull off.

I fix my AirPods into my ears and play the voice mail as I wait for the light on the corner to change, bouncing up and down on my toes in that performative way joggers do to ensure everyone knows we're not just wearing pricey athleisure, we're actual athletes, a step above the rest.

When the woman's voice comes into my ear, friendly but firm, I stop.

"Hi, this is Sarah Keens with the *New York Times*'s Vows column, looking for Eliza Bennet. We received the submission for your upcoming wedding and would love to cover it. Please give me a call when you have a moment to talk about some details."

Check.

I play the message two more times, listening carefully to each word and memorizing her phone number as I make my way closer to the Park. I had been confident when I submitted the form eight weeks ago that it would be enthusiastically accepted. Barring today, I'd read the Vows section every Sunday since our engagement, studying each entry like gospel, memorizing the quirky meet-cutes, the successful second attempts at love, the spontaneous elopements, until I knew exactly how to pitch *us*.

First, the cliché hook: my name lends itself to potboiler headlines without even trying. *Eliza Bennet Marries Real-Life Darcy.* People eat that shit up.

Second, the tragic line: everyone loves a Little Orphan Annie who got herself out and up.

Third, the aspirational sinker: I have worked very hard to be exactly how women envision themselves in their perfect lives. No matter how hard you try to fight it, the life you thought you'd have when you were eight is still what you want. Engaged to someone with a high-six-figure income; living in a prewar luxury building that's exploding with natural light and professionally decorated with just enough accent pieces to claim a coherent "style"; and working a glossy job in public relations wearing heels and pencil skirts with the impressive (though entirely meaningless) title Director of Communications. I am what every woman hopes for, and every man wants. And look, she's done it by thirty. Some people my age are still getting blackout drunk on a Friday night and hooking up with strangers who drop their condoms on the floor when they're done, leaving you to scavenge for it in the morning like a rat in a Central Park garbage can.

Not me.

I glide across the Park, replaying the voice mail in my head as I push my fastest mile time in years. That was the last potential hitch in the wedding plans, the last box left unchecked. The last thing that could have potentially tainted the otherwise perfect day. Now there is very little left to do but return the call, and wait.

I make my way past the Mall and the Bethesda Terrace Arcade, where at least two couples are taking engagement photos at all times, until I land on the corner of 72nd Street and Fifth Avenue, satisfyingly out of breath, to start my cooldown. My version of a runner's high is nearly indistinguishable from that of an addict's. I'm fully addicted. To the alertness; to the acute feeling of your own cells shrinking exactly where you want them to; to the knowledge that, if I weren't getting married next weekend, I've worked out so much today that I could come home and binge, standing in the cool light of the open fridge, clawing at leftovers until I could throw up, feeling absolutely nothing.

There's also a power in seeing everyone watch as I pass: I'm too thin to be obviously running for weight loss, and too fast for this to merely be a two-mile jaunt to fill my government-suggested movement necessity for the day. I'm a runner now. I run.

"You're going to run until you disappear," Danny, our uniformed doorman, exclaims when he sees me approaching. My strongest appetite is for comments like this: *you're so thin, you're going to disappear; if you turn to the side, you'll disappear; you're going to run until you disappear.*

Sometimes I want nothing more than to do exactly that.

"T-minus six days," I say as he holds the door open and follows me into the lobby. Normally I revel in walking in before men, knowing they're scoping out my ass, the way my hips move in my jeans, hoping my dress blows just the right amount to see a little bit more. But not Danny. He's either gay or superabundantly dedicated to whomever that gold ring on his left hand ties him to. Or both. Meanwhile, Graham's eyes can't stay away from a woman with grabbable hair or a girl with an innocent face.

When we first started dating I was the girl he looked at that way, but after a few months, when the honeymoon phase wore off, I could see his gaze escape mine and linger on other women for longer than a passing glance. Once, we'd played hooky from work, faking dentist appointments for an early fuck and breakfast at Bluestone Lane on 90th and Fifth. A group of girls from the Catholic high school nearby passed in their plaid skirts, made mini by rolling at the waist until you could practically see the virginity they all so desperately wanted to lose. I watched him watch them, stare at their poreless faces, skin as tight as rubber bands, then look between their legs with a ferocity I'd never seen on him before. But I wasn't bothered by it. I didn't really think twice, if I'm being honest. I've spent entire yoga classes oscillating between the protruding crotch on the hot trainee and the bulbous tits waterfalling out of Feather's sports bra. Attraction is a primal, biological instinct. Refusing that would be like refusing something as basic as hunger or thirst. Right?

But that confidence comes with knowing that Graham would never act on it. He loves me too much. I'm his perfect woman. I made sure of it.

Pressing the elevator button for the twenty-fourth floor has given me immense satisfaction since the day I moved in. We're penthouse-adjacent: all the benefits of the top, without actually reaching the peak. I'm too young to be so high that there's nowhere to go but down. Though it does serve as a constant reminder of how fragile this life is. And how far there is to fall if the bubble ever pops.

I can hear the television as soon as I step out of the elevator and into our small semiprivate lobby. There are two apartments this lobby serves, but the other has been vacant since I've lived here, so it's basically just ours. Graham never locks the door and cites this as one of his reasons. I hate it. He argues that's why we have a doorman and cameras, so we never have to worry about carrying around keys. But if someone wanted to get in to steal our laptops or hide under our beds and murder us, they'd find a way. And it would be made much easier if the door is unlocked.

"Out here," he yells, as if I'd have trouble finding him in our twenty-three hundred square feet. That's the point of an open living space, one of the things I loved about this apartment when I first saw it. That I can see him, or know where he is, from basically everywhere, indoors and out. People can't surprise you that way—can't sneak up on you when you're pulling a French fry out of the garbage at three in the morning—if you always know where they are.

I dead-bolt the door behind me and walk through the foyer and into the living room, surprised to find it empty as the television is blasting, a woman in a tight dress pattering on about a football game to no audience. I reach for the remote and turn it off, though the white noise seems to linger. Through the glass double doors, I can spot Graham outside. First just his black-socked feet twisted on top of the glass coffee table. Then, as I move across the living room and closer to our terrace, the rest of him, slouched on the outdoor sectional, a late-afternoon O'Doul's in his hand.

"Did I leave that on?" he asks, staring at the outdoor television mounted on the brick column in the corner, showing the same objectively hot woman describing a "play" with football terms she seems surprisingly versed in. I guess that's the point.

He doesn't care about the answer to his question, so I don't give him one.

Graham looks exactly like you'd expect someone who rowed at Yale to look. He's tall, broad, with thick brown hair that will, based on his maternal genes, stay that way until he's at least sixty-five. He has striking blue eyes, the kind I used to admire on nameless teen stars in the *Cosmo* magazines I'd steal from the grocery store when I was a kid. He's a Ken doll of a man, but with a high-power finance job and a wardrobe that consists of only business-to-business-casual, Under Armour running gear, and soft T-shirts from general stores and self-proclaimed "fine dining" restaurants in his hometown.

I don't know how he can concentrate on the television out here. I always find myself too distracted by the views. Especially as the sun begins to set over the Park.

I perch on the edge of the coffee table and rest my hands on his calves.

"How was it?" he asks, not bothering to make eye contact to talk, but leaning forward to plant a kiss on my cheek.

I shrug. *"Transformative."*

He generally laughs about yoga in a way I'd find condescending if I didn't agree with him. But he's learned to shut up about it considering I'd never be able to get my leg into that position he likes were it not for my yoga practice.

"Guess what," I say, patting the top of his legs until I've stolen his attention from Ms. Blonde *Quarterback Hustle*. "The *Times* wants to cover the wedding. They just called me."

He's surprised, cocks his head to the side, raises his eyebrows. "That's great," he says, flatly. He was never as excited about the possibility of the Vows article as I was. He's skeptical of a journalist and a photographer lurking in the shadows of our ceremony and reception. *They're always looking for an angle*, he said when I first mentioned I'd applied, palaver taken straight from his conservative father's mouth. *They already have an angle*, I told him. *The wedding is the angle.*

"I'm excited," I say, a hint for him not to ruin it for me.

He finally smiles, his nose slightly unsymmetrical, apparently from a fight in college. "Have you told my mom?"

"Not yet. I want to call them back first. Make sure it's official."

"She'll be happy."

"I think so." Truthfully, she'll be thrilled. She might even let a smile escape those thin Hermès Red–stained lips. Only if her Botox allows it, of course. "You want another one?" I ask, nodding at the beer no longer sweating in his hand. He doesn't drink. At least, not *often*. He's only had a couple drinks the entire time I've known him. *Partied too hard in college*, he joked when I asked why. But he still likes the tradition of it.

"Sure," he says. "You joining me?" I stand and make my way around the couch to the outdoor bar, always stocked regardless of season, weather, or the fact that he's mostly sober and I'm mostly dieting.

"Maybe after my shower," I say, pulling another bottle from the fridge. He knows that's a noncommittal, non–wet blanket attempt to say no. I'm not even officially allowed croutons on this diet, so he'd never expect me to actually have a beer. Especially one that won't get me drunk.

I do crave a glass of wine though, more than brie with figs or dark chocolate or a frothy latte. I have wet dreams about a smooth cabernet cascading down my throat, coating it in a thick purple paste that won't go away no matter how many times I lean over the toilet and push the sharp side of my toothbrush into my tonsils.

I nearly start touching myself in the shower at the thought.

Until the bathroom door slides open with a squeak and Graham overtakes the doorway. If he were only a few inches taller, he'd have to bend at the neck to cross all the dramatic archways that give this apartment the character he pays so much for.

I press my hand against the glass, leaving a momentary handprint in the steam before wiping it away. He leans a shoulder on the doorway and smiles now that my face and my breasts are clear in his view.

"You're so fucking beautiful," he exhales. Every time he sees me naked, he reacts like it's the first time. The awe, the amazement, the general excitement all straight men have when there's a naked woman in front of them. But his comes with a kind of reverence; like I'm a statue carved only for him. Which isn't entirely wrong.

"You come in here just to watch?" I ask, scratching shampoo into my scalp but moving my hips back and forth to make it sexy.

"An added benefit." He laughs. "I was thinking the diner again?"

He's sweet. We've ordered from the diner on Lexington every cheat day since I started outwardly acknowledging this wedding diet. All he ever wants is pad Thai and veggie spring rolls, but this man has pretended to crave a Reuben with potato wedges for the last eight weeks so that there's some lettuce-based option on the menu for me.

"I'll do the green salad again," I say quickly, before I have a chance to change my mind. Just the thought of potato wedges makes my stomach ache for something so greasy I have to wash my hands and the corners of my mouth after eating.

He nods and then watches me for a long time as I wash out my hair and slip on the black exfoliating gloves that make me feel like an intruder in my own shower. I love scrubbing my skin with these. It's like I can feel every single pore.

"I'm going to personally feed you seven cheeseburgers when we get back next week."

I laugh, letting the warm water run into my mouth and then spitting it onto my toes. "I can't wait," I say, knowing it will never happen. Diets don't end. They just get rebranded into "lifestyle changes" and "wellness" and "clean eating." Whoever does their PR is a genius and a billionaire.

By the time I finish in the shower and stand in the center of the bathroom, my toes tangled in the white shag rug, meticulously moisturizing every inch of my skin with white goo *proven to reduce the look of wrinkles*, our buzzer goes off. Before Danny's voice can materialize over the speaker system, Graham says, "Let him up," and stomps to the door. He walks like he's angry at our downstairs neighbors. Luckily, they're nearly ninety and almost never turn on their hearing aids.

I throw on one of Graham's sweatshirts and leggings and walk outside just as he appears with our plates—he insists on plating takeout, a flaw I've learned to accept—and places them on the coffee table.

Once the sun begins to fall behind the buildings across the Park, a timer automatically turns on the fairy lights drizzled onto the ivy-covered wrought iron banister that surrounds our terrace. I love knowing there are people my age, twenty-four floors below us, who look up from the sidewalk to see the lights and smoke from the custom brick fireplace and think: *What a life it must be up there.*

When Graham is sufficiently distracted by the football game, I finally pick up the phone and dial the number I'd been running through my head all afternoon. It's been three hours since Sarah Keens left that chirpy message and, considering how desperately I'd been waiting for the call, even *I'm* shocked it's taken me this long to return it.

But I like to tempt fate. You do it without realizing. Stand a little too close to the yellow edge of the subway platform, unaware of the mental state of the commuters around you. Shove a shoulder into a slow walker on the sidewalk without knowing whether there's a weapon in his pocket and he's been eager for an excuse to use it. Wait to call the *Times* back, knowing they could very well move onto the next, more interesting, more beautiful, wealthier couple anytime.

While this might seem like a low-stakes tempting, it's not. This could be the most important piece of the wedding. What kind of elite event isn't covered in an elite newspaper? And this, I can guarantee, will be an elite event. Between the location and the flowers, the dresses and the views, the attendees and the family I'm marrying into, my wedding will be talked about for years. And now it will be immortalized in the pages of the *New York Times.* An event for the entire world to read.

This is the last piece of my puzzle. The final lock in the chain between me and my life plan. The last thing I needed before I could take my first deep breath in five years, knowing very soon I'd be able to start the rest of my life. The post-five-year-plan life. Just one hundred and twenty-nine hours to go.

# TWO

I ARRIVED AT college in a state I'd now describe as Poor European Backpacker: two tattered duffel bags in hand, greasy hair, Tevas with a taped-on sole, the doe-eyed wonder of someone truly believing she's embarking on a transformative adventure. I had no concept of what college was supposed to look like before I got there, but somehow Covenant University was exactly what I imagined: large, bright green quads lined with orange and yellow tulips in front of redbrick buildings crawling with gnarled ivy and endless opportunity.

The students, in their button-downs and pearls; the teachers, in their sweater vests and chinos; the staff, in their white-and-beige uniforms. Everything I saw represented college. And college represented freedom.

I checked in with a group of students in matching green polo shirts, received two thick folders welcoming me to my future, and was told to make my way to Willits Hall, where I'd be living for the next year.

I moused around the campus, scanning the scene like a trespasser anticipating getting shot down at any moment. When

I reached Willits's open glass doors, I heard a woman scream "Howdy" and I stopped short, staring at the lanky body that appeared in the building's lobby like I was a deer in headlights, waiting to see if her intentions were good or if she was going to run me over for the venison.

"How are ya?" She waved me inside and I approached slowly. She was also in a green polo shirt, a gold LU embroidered above her pointy nipples.

"I'm good," I said, dragging my bags across the bright lobby and toward the fold-up table she'd covered in a pressed gold cloth and even more stacked folders.

"Welcome to Covenant!" She spoke exclusively in exclamation points, employing a kind of genuine glee I'd never experienced before, and her entire body seemed to pulse with the same enthusiasm. "I'm Brigid! Let me check you in and then we'll get you all settled into your new home!" She beckoned me closer to the table. "What's your name?"

"…Elizabeth," I remembered after a brief brain freeze.

She smiled kindly. "I'm going to need more than that. We've got a lot of Elizabeths this year. Must have been something in the holy water." She laughed at her own joke without any reservations.

I watched pleasantly until she was finished. "Elizabeth Bennet."

She gasped. "Like *Pride and Prejudice*!" I nodded slowly and faked a smile. This was the first of what would prove to be an utterly endless number of times I would hear this reference upon saying my name. I'd never read the book or heard of the author and when I tried to check it out of the Covenant University library later that week, I learned it was banned. "That's so cool," Brigid continued. *"Iconic."* She tapped her black marker down the line of female names until she found mine and pressed the felt tip into the E, crossing it out until it disappeared altogether.

"Follow me!"

She plucked one folder from each stack on the table and started down the hallway as another student entered. She had brown hair in two thin braids that stopped abruptly at her collarbone, and she stood smiling, flanked by an older man in khakis and an older woman in a floral sundress. I had no idea parents came to this kind of thing. Mine certainly wouldn't have.

My room, like all dorms, I learned, was a rectangular container made of linoleum and beige cinder blocks, with a heavy non-slam door and a sprinkle of fluorescent lighting to ensure you wanted to spend as little time inside as possible. You know the saying: nothing good happens to unsupervised preadults behind closed doors. On opposite sides of the only window were two slightly lofted beds and three-drawer dressers tucked underneath. Near the door where Brigid stood, flailing her arms with decor suggestions, were two desks and two chairs; and on a long concrete wall between two short armoires was a sink and a medicine cabinet mirror.

"Which one's mine?" I asked, interrupting something she was saying about peel-and-stick dry-erase calendars. The only word I recognized was *calendar*, which I now acknowledge as a blessing considering how tacky anything *peel-and-stick* is.

"Well, you got here first, so you get to choose!" she said. "So lucky!" She walked farther into the room, tugging on each naked mattress, opening and closing shaky drawers, looking out the tall window. "I'd take this one, if I were you," she said, gently placing the folders atop the bed on the right. "In the other one, you'll get the sunrise straight to your face in the morning."

I nodded and joined her on that side. I would have accepted

whatever she said, but I appreciated the thought she put into it. She seemed to actually care.

"I've got to get back to it, but..." She lined the three folders on the blue plastic mattress cover, taking care to ensure each corner perfectly aligned with the next, and pointed to them. "You should skim these while you're unpacking—they've got your class list, campus maps, mass schedules, and other stuff." She picked up the thinnest folder—labeled *The Covenant Code*—and handed it to me. "I'd focus on this if you have time. It's what we'll be talking about tonight. We have our first dorm meeting at seven in the common room, which it mentions in there." She tapped the top of a different folder.

"Thanks," I said, pressing it against my chest as she turned to exit. I wanted to ask another question, one hundred questions, to keep her there. Keep someone telling me what I was supposed to do. But she had the door open and was standing in the threshold before I could come up with even one.

"See you later!" The door closed after her, fitting into its base with a low thud, leaving me in the room alone.

I looked down at the folder in my hands. *The Covenant Code: How to Succeed at Life, at Covenant, and at the Pursuit of Pure Happiness.*

An hour later, there was a firm knock on the door and I froze, sitting on my bed, all my things still in the hand-me-down bags slumped in the center of the room like garbage on its way to the dump. Seconds after, I heard the jangle of keys and then the door swung open, faster than I ever thought something that heavy could move.

Since the day I decided to attend Covenant and live on campus, I'd pictured my roommate, the built-in friend you get on your first day, the partner you have for orientation and convocation and freshman classes. I'd stay up at night, staring at the chipping paint on my bedroom's bubbling ceiling, and pray that it would be someone different from me. Someone who wasn't homeschooled. Someone who wore clothes from the mall and watched movies and chewed bubble gum. Someone I could watch and learn from: about school and books and also about boyfriends and vodka and kissing. I spent eighteen years missing out; now was my chance to make that up.

"Hey," she said as she entered, the first person I'd encountered that day with the temperament of a normal human. I slid off the bed and my shoes landed on the fake tile floor with a slap.

Everything about her was perfect.

"I'm, um, Elizabeth," I said nervously, already kicking myself for bungling every introduction I'd had so far that day.

"Right," she said, looking past my outstretched hand toward my khakis, frayed and permanently dirt-stained at the cuffs, and then my shirt, a white Aéropostale tee I'd secretly thrifted and hid under my bed at home specifically for this day. "I'm Ruthie."

She was tall and thin like Brigid but, unlike Brigid, she had boobs and hips that started growing in puberty and hadn't stopped since. I'd taken one of those *What's Your Body Type?* quizzes in a stolen *Seventeen* magazine—mine was "athletic with stubborn baby fat"—and I didn't think the hourglass option was real until that moment. She was as gorgeous as Angelina Jolie and looked like she'd be named Britney or Courtney, not Ruthie. Ruthie was the name of the stray cat my brother and I found in the barn a few years ago, not a beautiful eighteen-year-old with brown hair straight out of a shampoo ad.

She lugged her blue floral duffel—I had yet to be introduced to the immediately recognizable paisley that is Vera Bradley—onto the bed opposite mine. She was wearing new jeans, you could still see the two dots at the lower back from the haphazard tug of the tag, and a shirt that smelled like the Victoria's Secret perfume insert that had once been left in our PO Box by accident.

Ruthie was exactly what I needed.

"I've got some more stuff. I'll be right back."

"Need help?" I asked, seeking something, anything, to do. I was already bored and desperate for school to start—classes, dinners, parties with red cups: this new world I could dive into headfirst.

"I've got it," she said halfway out the door. I was suddenly ashamed of how few things I'd brought—how few things I even *owned* to bring.

The door closed slowly and I stared at her colorful bag on the bed. I wondered what kind of exciting things were inside—did her mother take her on a shopping trip before dropping her off? Did her father send her with things to read? Did her best friend give her a charm bracelet? Poking out of the side pocket was a digital camera. Maybe she was studying photography or art.

Four trips later and I'd watched her haul a pink plastic cabinet, a mini fridge with a microwave affixed to the top, and three more suitcases, one of which she pointed to and said "shoes." Meanwhile, I'd fit all my clothes comfortably into two of the three drawers, hung up my only four dresses, and attempted to make my bed with the yellowed twin XL sheets that had been sewn just for me. I had cried for two days when I learned that college mattresses weren't traditionally sized. The plan had been for me to bring my brother's childhood set—white-and-blue-striped sheets with a red comforter. But when *Elizabeth's College Checklist* came in the mail from Covenant, detailing the excessive list of everything I could possibly need for my freshman year, including specialty twin XL sheets, I had my first of many realizations that this world was not built for people like me.

Ruthie walked over to the refrigerator/microwave combo I'd never seen before and leaned on it. Then, she surveyed the room, eventually pinching her lips together like she was struggling with something. "What do you think about feng shui-ing this shit?"

My eyes must have bulged out of my face, judging by the raised-eyebrow look she'd given me. I'd never heard anyone curse so casually before. My brother once yelled that word when he hammered his finger while fixing the janky porch steps. My parents made him sit with a green bar of Dial in his mouth for ten minutes before they'd give him any ice to soothe the swelling knuckle on his pointer.

"Sorry," she said, with a shrug and a coy smile. "I forgot you can get in trouble for that here."

Ruthie was *exactly* what I needed.

"I won't tell if you don't," I responded. We were quiet for a long time, just looking at each other, scoping out exactly what this relationship was going to be. I didn't know this yet, but that was the most important thing I could have said in that moment. Covenant U ran on a code far more precious than honor, and alliances forged on the first day were the most difficult to break.

Ruthie and I were almost the last to arrive to the seven-o'clock meeting that night. For fifteen minutes the alarm in my head went off, reminding me I was supposed to be somewhere I wasn't. *If we're not early, we're late*, my mother had always whispered to herself as she corralled five dirty kids in their Sunday bests into the van for church. But Ruthie said she had to figure out something to wear, so I agreed, claiming I needed to change my outfit, too.

"I like your shirt," she said, her face an inch from her behind-the-door mirror as she applied a thin black paste in a line above her eyelashes. "Don't change that. But you can borrow some jeans if you want…"

She slid the bottom dresser drawer open with her foot, inviting me to choose from not one, not two, but five different pairs, neatly folded in a pristine row. A light blue one, a dark blue one, a dark gray one, one with a lot of buttons at the waist, and one that got super tight at the ankle. My father never let me wear jeans. He said women's denim is the thread of the Devil, only for promiscuous girls with arm tattoos. But Ruthie didn't have any tattoos—as far as I could tell, at least—so I pulled the dark blue ones out and stood there awkwardly holding them, realizing I didn't have a bathroom in which I could lock the door and get changed.

"Don't worry, I'm not looking," Ruthie said, sensing my deliberation. "I shared a room with my stepsister for years. You'll get used to it."

I moved to my side of the room, where my bed met the wall and turned around, quickly pulling my pants off and slipping into hers. They were snug in the way my clothes would get as a kid, until my mother could convince my father to let us go to the thrift store for something new. They were probably one size too small, but I could still button them.

I moved to the mirror and stood behind Ruthie to see how I looked. I didn't feel any different in denim. I didn't feel more promiscuous or less godly. I felt the same.

"Those are tricky, but when you suck in, they'll fit fine," Ruthie said, eyeing me through the mirror.

"When I what?" I asked.

She turned around, closing the cap on the long black eye pen, and looked at me with one eyebrow raised. "Suck in," she repeated. "Like…" She stood up straight, pushed her shoulders back, and slowly her stomach receded into itself like a wave on the shore. "Like that. Suck it in."

I did as she said and lost an inch off my stomach. I don't understand where it went, or how my organs handled getting squished together, but the jeans fit much better after. "You do this all the time? How do you breathe?"

She laughed, entertained by my naivety. "*Everyone* does this all the time..."

I haven't stopped sucking in since.

She waved another black makeup object at me. "Do you want some?" she asked. "I can do it for you, if you—"

I said yes before she even finished the question. I'd never worn makeup before. My only experience with makeup had been watching my mother swipe blush—which she concocted herself from some combination of beetroot powder and cornstarch—across her hollow cheekbones before church on Sundays. My father didn't think women should be attracting attention to themselves in that way, so my mother hid in her closet for this ritual each week.

When Ruthie was finished swiping black stuff on both my eyelashes, she pulled back and smiled. "You look super cute," she said, capping the brush and carefully putting it into the makeup bag on her bed that was the same colors and pattern as her duffel. She wiggled into white sneakers and I slipped back into my Tevas. "I'm definitely going to need to borrow that necklace," she added. I reached for it without thinking, maybe to tuck it into my shirt, maybe to rip it off my neck and hand it over to her right there.

My mother gave it to me before I left. She told me to hide it inside my bra and leave it there until my father and his greenish truck had dropped me off on the base of campus and turned toward home. I stood beside the Covenant University welcome sign, my bags stacked next to me, and pulled the gold chain from under my shirt, dangling off of which was this thin piece of gold-painted something—an old flattened coin, perhaps—

my initials scratched into it in my mother's cursive. A cross delicately drawn on the back.

Ruthie looked at the two of us in the mirror. "Let's do this thing," she said, pulling the door open quickly. I followed her before I could change my mind. Before I could wipe off the makeup and change back into my pants and pack my things and trek back home. Ruthie had an immediate confidence about her—like merely being in her presence made you more self-sufficient, more accepting of your own decisions. At least, that's how I felt. I felt invincible in her jeans and her makeup and her direction. Maybe with Ruthie I really was.

I followed her through the wide archway and into the second-floor common room, sneaking in and taking a seat in the back, behind the crowd. Sixty students scattered around the square linoleum space—squished on couches, leaning on walls, perched on windowsills. They were all different. A girl with dark curly hair sat in the corner, her hair puffing up around her face as she leaned back into the wall. A girl with skinny legs sat crisscrossed on the floor like a pretzel, next to a girl scanning the Covenant Code like she was afraid we were about to be quizzed.

Brigid entered just seconds after us and made her way to the front of the room like Pastor Ryan during the procession at my hometown church. She was still in her green polo shirt, but it was a little more wrinkled and a little less tucked than it had been a few hours ago.

"You guys excited to be here?" She clapped her hands together, which made me jump.

She was received by an unenthusiastic smattering of *yeah*s. "Well, that won't do!" she said, through a smile so wide it looked like it could rip right through her cheeks to her temples. "I'm going to ask again, and now I want you to yell so loud the guys in McKinley Hall next door can hear you! Ready!" She took a long pause there, as if she sincerely needed to give everyone time to prepare themselves. "Are y'all excited to be here!"

The room erupted with hoots and hollers; *woohoo*s that could have pierced the glass windows. I opened my mouth to join them but before I did, Ruthie caught my eye, opting to simply clap and nod. So I shut my mouth and did the same.

"Well, *we* are *so* excited for y'all to be here," she continued once everyone calmed down. "We've been waiting all summer!" Behind her were two other women: a brunette with unbelievably long eyelashes, and a woman with black hair and a dirty white rope bracelet hanging off her thin wrist. "You all know me. I'm Brigid. I'm the head RA here in Willits Hall. This is Marie and Lucy, my two second-in-commands." They both smiled and waved, but the brunette seemed bitter about it.

I leaned an inch closer to Ruthie, our shoulders nearly touching. "What's an RA?" I whispered, as Brigid pattered on, explaining how each RA has a *very specific role here at Covenant University.*

"They're narcs," Ruthie whispered back, staring at them with the kind of slitted eyes of someone burned.

"We're so excited to talk to y'all about the Covenant Code! It's really the thing that sets our school, and our community, apart. It's probably part of the reason you chose Covenant over all your other prospects. It's a really special part of our identity, and it's such an honor to introduce more people to our special way of life here." She paused, again, but this time it seemed like she was waiting for applause or something. When none came, she glanced behind her at Lucy—or Marie, I missed who was who—and then back to the crowd. "So, if everyone can open your folders, we'll get started!"

Brigid joked that the rules of the Covenant Code were written in stone on the back of the Ten Commandments and, for a second, it seemed like she genuinely believed it.

She opened to the first page and started reading. "'Students are responsible for memorizing and following the Covenant Code. Students are also responsible to notify Resident Assistants'—" she looked up and smiled "—that's us—'of anything they believe to be a violation of the Covenant Code by other students. Intentionally not reporting a violation is, itself, a violation. The university reserves the right to adjust this document, formally or informally, at any time to ensure fairness and a homogenized university environment.'" She paused and glanced at us. "Everybody got that?" The room nodded in unison, and I did, too.

"Great," she continued. "Now, while this is by no means contractual, all members of the community are asked to profess our maxim. You guys see it?" She waited a beat and Ruthie's nail-bitten finger, the cuticles mauled to crusty red nubs, moved to the last line of the page, bolded and italicized at the bottom.

I'd already memorized this. Months ago. It was the only reason my parents allowed me to go to college. I didn't choose Covenant; Covenant was my only option. It was the only college I applied to because it was the only one my parents would approve of. The only college whose modernity and forward thinking wouldn't scare them because there was none of that here. The only college that would convince them I'd get the exact same education they'd been giving me through homeschooling all these years. Now that I was here, out of my parents' house, I could do whatever I wanted—be whomever I wanted. I just needed to get here first. And now I needed to stay. So I memorized the mantra. Because you have to know the rules to successfully break them.

Brigid held her right hand, palm up, like she was singing at the podium at church, and everyone followed, reciting the sentence like a prayer, filling the entire room with the chant.

"I have a responsibility to protect our community from corruption and harm, to promote and defend the righteous standards of our community, and to personally confront those who do not."

I *needed* to stay.

The meeting ended when pizza and salads were delivered, and Brigid lost everyone's attention to the smell of cheesy sauce wafting through the small room. Ruthie and I didn't even consider the soggy arugula when grabbing a slice each, thick and warm in our fingers, and plopping them onto paper plates so thin they could hardly hold the weight of the grease.

I followed Ruthie toward the windows where, according to her, we could see everyone, and everyone could see us. As the room filled with the sound of mouth-full conversations, I brought the slice to my face, letting the warmth radiate up my nose. It smelled like what I imagined New York City smelled like—greasy, primal, completely addictive. I'd never had pizza before, and I savored each beautiful bite.

Ruthie surveyed the room, observing who was talking to whom and for how long. It's funny how like gravitates toward like. Before you know it, you're surrounded by people just like you—good or bad. The girl with dark curly hair was talking to someone in a track T-shirt similar to her own. The girl with the skinny legs sat on the couch with two others, each stabbing fistfuls of greens with their plastic forks. If I hadn't met Ruthie, I'd probably be walking toward the two girls in the corner, standing an awkward distance apart, glancing at the Covenant Code and successfully avoiding eye contact with anyone. I immediately understood that would be me if it weren't for Ruthie.

She motioned toward the center of the room, where a group of girls stood in Abercrombie shirts and the same white sneakers with a red stripe as Ruthie's. "They look fun," she said. Before I could agree, Ruthie started toward them, leaving her half-eaten pizza on the windowsill behind us.

"I'm Ruthie," I could hear her say. She had a way of introducing herself that made you feel like it was your pleasure to meet her. She made you feel important, special; like what you said and did mattered. Even from the first hello. "This is my roommate—" She looked to her right, surprised that I wasn't standing beside her. I pushed off the windowsill and took a deep breath, then sucked in just like I was taught and walked to her, trying to ignore the blush growing on my cheeks. "Elizabeth," she introduced me, without skipping a beat.

I marveled at how easy it was for Ruthie to make friends— a handshake, a wave, a nod, that's all it took for her to start a conversation. I was less jealous of her ease and more jealous of everyone else; the people who got to meet her. Because everyone immediately loved Ruthie.

But I loved her more.

That night, Ruthie and I were lying in our beds, relishing the dark silence that comes after a busy day. Curfew was midnight, but we had our lights out by 11:30 p.m. just in case. I was on my side, my back to the window in our newly feng shui-ed room, staring at the streak of light creeping in from under the door, unmoving, unrelenting.

I could see the lump of Ruthie's body snug under her brandnew white floral duvet. She said she spent months picking it out—creating a vision board for what she wanted her college dorm to look like. The *vibe* she wanted to go for. I wondered if I fit that. If I was the roommate she expected. If me and my yellowed dresses and mismatched sheets and grease-stained hair were what she wanted. Or if I was the human version of my khakis, something she'd want to quickly swap out for something fancier.

"What do you want to do?" she whispered. I heard her sheets shuffle as she moved. "Like, with your life?"

I had no idea. I didn't know how I fit into the real world—the world outside my parents' house and our church. Up until today, I didn't have a choice about what to do with the rest of my life. Once I turned eighteen, my parents would start looking for a husband for me. Once I was married, I'd become his wife. I'd do whatever he said. I had no idea who I was outside of that house. But I was excited to figure it out.

"What do *you* want to be?" I asked, hoping she wouldn't turn the question back around.

"I want to move to New York City—" she began. I could hear the awe in her voice. I imagined it sounded very similar to the way I talked about college. "Live in Soho or Greenwich Village in a tiny apartment where the shower is in the kitchen and just visit galleries and museums and art street fairs and go to the opera and see off-Broadway plays every single day."

"That sounds amazing," I said. I'd been so focused on getting here I hadn't considered where I'd go or what I'd do after. Getting here was a feat in itself. I knew I wasn't going home, but maybe Ruthie and I could go to New York City together. Maybe I could do those things with her.

"I don't know what I want," I admitted. "I haven't figured it out yet."

"That's okay," Ruthie said. "That's what you're here for. To find your purpose."

It was then I decided I wanted to be whatever Ruthie wanted. Following her to New York City would be my purpose. I would mold myself to fit whatever shape of a roommate she'd etched into her vision board all those months ago. I would become just like her.

I heard the hallway fire door open, then close with a dramatic and unsatisfied huff and we both rolled over, knowing better than to whisper anymore. A few soft footsteps dully echoed in the hall from the entrance all the way down to the other end. Then, just outside our door, two Mary Janes fractured the light like knives. Standing, unmoving, listening in just as I was listening out.

I felt watched. I held my breath. Even as I knew no one could penetrate these concrete walls, it still felt like they could. Like Ruthie's earlier curse violation, and my violation of not reporting her violation, were somehow notched on the outside of our door in a symbol only the RAs could decipher. *Look out for these two*, it would read. *They're trouble.*

Just as the shadow moved away, and I heard the hallway door whisper closed, I rolled to face the window, looking out on the woods behind campus. It was black and quiet. Not even the trees made a sound.

Until, through the darkness, I heard it: a tinny ping so faint, at first I thought I made it up. That I was inventing sounds of home to lull myself to sleep. On a farm with brothers, you were never that far away from a gunshot. They'd set up an entire shooting range in the back corner of the property, with targets painted onto bales of hay and, once they got more advanced, old cans hanging from wrangled tree branches.

The soft ping rang out again.

Then again.

Then, finally, silence.

# THREE

I WORK IN an office of all women. Twenty-two of them. From the cofounders—Brittany and Ashleigh, who as college roommates decided on a whim with Daddy's money that their sophomoric passion for PR bested their inexperience and warranted them being their own bosses—to Kiley, our sprightly office assistant who graduated from Stanford five months ago with that illusive degree in communications. As Women in the Workplace or whatever, I'm supposed to think it's incredible; that the Brit & Ash Agency has been built from nothing and is now changing the game for women in communications everywhere. Really, it's barely more than two unprofessional bullshitters with perfect bodies and big tits convincing old men to trust their vague "public relations needs" with us. Because what looks better for your boring business than a bunch of hot young women parading it around as important.

The whole thing is ridiculous.

To the untrained eye, it seems like a perfect place to work. There's an old-school popcorn machine crackling 24/7 behind the reception desk, a neon sign reads "You Better Work Bitch," a line from Britney Spears's unforgettable classic, and a chalkboard wall boasts Polaroids showcasing a month's worth of Outfit of the Days, determined by the cofounders themselves. Add to that the fully stocked kombucha fridge, the FriYay happy hours, and *The Home Edit*–level rainbow-organized snack pantry, you might forget that you're expected to work eighty-hour weeks for a midlevel salary with no dental.

I recognized the truth behind this PR facade the second I arrived for my interview. Popcorn is the biggest snack offering because it's a weight-loss-friendly food; "You Better Work Bitch" isn't a cultish motto but an expectation: work even when you don't need to and lean into it; the Outfit of the Day board isn't only a sexist workplace bonding activity, but also a way for you to feel constantly judged by who you're wearing and how well it fits you. All three of these things serve to brilliantly establish Brit and Ash's powerful influence: they tell us what to eat, what to do, and what to wear. But they do it with a giggle and a smile so you don't question the overflowing condescension. *How can someone so pretty be so mean?*

If you put a group of professionally tanned and blown-out women in Alice + Olivia pencil skirts and four-inch Celine heels in a room together, it's not a means to a feminist revolution, but a way to ensure you never want to work with women again.

On top of that, as if we needed to give everyone another reason to hate our half of the species: everyone over thirty synchs up. I'm sure I'm not supposed to reveal this age-old secret, but it's true. The kids are stuffed with diaphragms and IUDs, but for everyone even remotely close to starting a family, for about fifteen days a month discarded tampons overflow from the bathroom's garbage. Because of this, four women in the office are currently pregnant, all due within two months, all about to cash in on that six-month, full-pay maternity leave

Brit and Ash hoped their "You Better Work Bitch" mindset would keep anyone from redeeming.

Rebecca, a five-foot-eleven blonde who isn't afraid of four-inch heels, stands in front of the neon sign, mocking it with her protruding basketball of a belly as she adjusts the blue bow in her hair and thanks everyone for the gift: a Bugaboo stroller that costs more than my first apartment. She's a little bitter that her office shower fell on a Monday, which gives me immeasurable satisfaction as I sit on the edge of a too-low couch watching her dance around the conference room like a fucking ballerina, singing "ah ah ah" anytime someone tries to stick a blue bow onto her cashmere sweater.

Weddings trump pregnancies in this group, which is why all my planning has overshadowed hers. Weddings enter you into a new class; a club of women with shiny accessories proving to the world that we're lovable, while we show off our newly plural life: *we* finally found a contractor, *our* friend works there, *we* watched that episode last night. Babies, however, bring you down at least three notches until you can brag about their accomplishments. Even then, no one wants to talk about them as much as you do.

"This little nugget says thanks, too," Rebecca continues, pulling the loose sweater taut around her belly, like we'd forget she is pregnant if she didn't remind us. "My little Halloween baby is very excited to meet you all soon." Everyone *ooh*s and *aah*s but the silence between her sentences reveals how little that sentiment is reciprocated. Another thing: Who the fuck wants a Halloween birthday—destined for themed parties every year for the rest of your life?

For most of the shower, I'd been focused on Kiley, our office assistant. She's a petite girl with mousy brown hair and some freshman fifteen still lingering in her cheeks. She sits in that familiar way everyone has at one point: arms crossed gingerly over her stomach, a subconscious attempt to hide what everyone knows is there. I've been watching her stare at the orange and black cookies on the conference table, decorated with Rebecca's unborn son's monogram: SMM (the third, obviously). The entire table is covered in other expensively decorated and on-theme processed sugar—doughnut holes with orange filling and brown sprinkles, cake pops shaped like spiders, Rice Krispies Treats topped with sugar ghosts—but Kiley's only got eyes for the cookies.

I'm willing her to take one; be the first to open the gates of processed sugar hell. It just takes one to reach forward and grab something, then all the pregnant ladies will dive in, then everyone else will feel like they're allowed. They'll call it "nibbling," the cute, pathetic way women are supposed to eat. I won't take anything. Politely say, *I'm good, thank you*, when someone inevitably holds out the tray and offers. But part of me wishes I could stay late tonight, claim to be *just finishing up before I leave*. Then, once everyone's gone, I'd descend upon the box of doughnuts, shoving them into my mouth two at a time, leaving a couple for the cleaning ladies as a thank-you for scrubbing down the toilet I'd immediately rush to throw up in.

"This is the fucking worst," Lena whispers in my ear from behind, breaking me out of my obsessive stare at Kiley. "What, she couldn't buy herself a fucking stroller? Her dad's a vice chairman at Goldman and her husband's on his way there. Why am *I* shelling out two hundred dollars so her nanny can walk her kid around SoHo comfortably?"

She speaks slowly, with the rhythm of someone you'd expect to be wielding a gold-handed cigarette holder, taking puffs in between syllables for emphasis. Everything Lena does is slow, calculated. She's never rushed. Never caught off guard. She's as level as a plank and nothing affects her.

"I'm waiting for someone to bring up the wedding," I whisper back. "I think she'll throw the stroller out the window if another person asks me what the weather's like in Vermont this time of year."

Lena was the only one invited to the wedding, no one else from work. One of the many benefits of having it in Vermont, at Graham's childhood home. I didn't want to invite her—I didn't want to invite anyone—but my soon-to-be husband, in all his childish naivety, thought it was "bad luck" not to invite the woman who kind of introduced us.

Lena is also a director of communications (a title so meaningless, there are two of us). At thirty-two, her saddest and most admirable trait is that she still shows up to work hungover, though with perfect hair and pristine makeup. It's really just the added glow of a one-night stand that gives her away.

We spend another ten minutes going around the room guessing the weight of Rebecca's baby. Part of me hopes the baby is super fucking ugly, in that way you do when two really hot people get together. As if even natural selection knows a person with genes as ridiculously lucky as this has no choice but to be an asshole, so it intervenes early, gives him a pointy chin or a left-leaning dick.

When it comes to the "guess the melted candy that looks like shit in these diapers" portion of the afternoon, Lena and I graciously bail. There are enough twenty-three-year-olds in the room staring at Rebecca, equally jealous and thankful it's not them, that we could sneak away nearly unnoticed. Rebecca was getting the attention she needed from a group of women basking in the fact that they were, for a nine-month period, hotter than her.

Lena follows me out of the conference room, past the row of empty desks, each displaying the small orange pumpkins gifted to us by Brittany and Ashleigh, and into my office in the back. She sits down on the couch as I plop into my chair behind the desk.

"So, I've been wondering," she begins, "what *is* the weather in Vermont like this time of year?"

"Who fucking cares. That's what tents and heat lamps are for." I jerk the mouse on my Brit & Ash Agency mousepad until my computer awakens with a bright light. Did I mention a professional photo of our fearless leaders posing in front of the "You Better Work Bitch" sign is suggested as everyone's computer background?

I pull a Post-it off the right corner of my computer screen and type its letters into the password box. They make us change our password every sixty days like we work for the goddamn CIA, not a PR firm that proffers for designers. After four separate occasions where I had to call Australian Chad in IT because I got locked out, I finally decided to keep it there, out in the open, where everyone, including me, could find it.

"What are you doing tonight?" I ask, expectant. "Want to come to a thing with me?"

"Depends on what kind of thing," Lena responds.

"Drinks with the Vows writer?"

She bumps to the edge of the couch, her bony knees the only part of her legs still touching. "Oh shit, you got it?"

"They called yesterday," I say with a shrug, as if it didn't matter either way. "They're sending a writer and photographer up to Vermont, so now I have to make sure there's room for them somewhere."

"Please." She leans back, reaching her right hand in front of her to admire her perfectly polished nude nails. "I'm sure you've had a room booked for them since you sent in the application."

She knows me well.

"Le Coucou at seven thirty?"

She nods. She'd show up anywhere I told her to.

"You have everything you need to handle the Wright pitch next week?" I ask.

"For their project in Sonoma? Yeah, Prude and Stash out there have it all under control."

I look behind her, out my glass wall toward the conference room across the floor where the girls she's referring to—one who couldn't wear higher cut shirts if she tried and one whose mother really should have given her a lesson on waxing her Italian upper lip—sit and stare admiringly at our blushing mom-to-be.

"You really have to stop calling them that," I tell her.

"I'd never say it to their faces."

"That doesn't make it better."

"Doesn't it, though?" She shrugs, apparently deciding her nails are as perfect as she expected them to be, and drops her hands into her lap, looking up at me. "We've got everything for all your pitches and all your press releases and all your clients. We've got you covered. You have nothing to worry about."

I check in like I care, but I don't, and Lena knows that.

"I should just quit, and you can take over all of my clients," I threaten. "Why am I even here?"

She stands, her colorful midi-skirt falling into place around her, and begins walking out the door. "You're about to marry a man richer than God. I have no idea why you're here. I ask myself that every day." She stops in the glass threshold and looks at me in a way I could only describe as *fondly.* "I'd love to drink on the *New York Times*'s dime. See you there."

She waves me off as she makes her way to the office next door, leaving me with only my thoughts and the earsplitting sounds of adult recess happening across the way.

The only personal item I have in my office is a picture of

Graham and me, in a simple silver frame. His sister-in-law, Veronica, took it when we were in Vermont for Christmas two years ago. Veronica loves photos. Especially the ones that make her high school boyfriends jealous. The ones where she's cradling her son in their coordinating outfits. The ones where she's drinking colorful cocktails on a rooftop with her hot and botoxed girlfriends. The ones where she's laughing, leaning into her charming husband, Reed. The Brother.

For this photo, we were all sitting around the firepit after dinner, under blankets and heat lamps, drinking mulled wine. We were newly engaged; Veronica and Reed carried Henry's baby monitor around like it was their only lifeline to mankind. Even though everyone knew their nanny, Rose, would be the first (and only) person to settle a sound from Henry's crib, Veronica and Reed jumped with each coo for show. *They're such great parents. See? See!*

My future mother-in-law was, again, telling the story of the night she met my future father-in-law, as she does any time she has one too many vodka martinis.

"Should we tell them about the night *we* met?" Graham whispered, his breath warm on my neck. I felt the heat of his hand as it moved dangerously up my leg under the blanket.

"I think... I think we save that for after we've made it official and there's a document keeping them from disowning me," I responded, struggling to get the words out as his hand continued on its path toward my zipper.

"Yeah?" He twisted his fingers around the copper circle and undid the button easily as we both stared forward. Through the fire, his parents' faces were blurred as they began to tag-team the story, attempting to finish each other's sentences in a way that would be endearing had they gotten any of them right. Or if they actually liked each other.

He slid his thick hand into my underwear and I moved a

little farther down the couch, resting my feet on the firepit's stone base and bending my knees so no one could see our movements under the blanket. I couldn't say anything and risk it coming out as a series of breathless moans, so I kept my mouth shut, resting my head on Graham's shoulder and breathing into him as his fingers moved.

That's when Veronica appeared in front of the fire out of nowhere, phone pointed toward us like a gun, flash already on. We froze and she smiled slyly for a beat before tilting her head and saying, "You guys look so cute. Let me get a pic." She adjusted the angle. "It's perfect for your wedding slideshow," she added. "Smile," she said, and I could have sworn I saw her wink.

We looked into the camera and obeyed, my breath still catching, his fingers still in my jeans. And it became my favorite photo of us. The one on our wedding website. The one on the back of our save-the-dates. The one that looks perfect but hides our dirty little secret.

I take the frame in my hands and look closely at us one last time: his elated smile, my flushed cheeks, the light of the fire creating a natural glow around us. As I pack my things and initiate my Out of Office, I slip the frame into my purse, next to my notebook and the fraying copy of Gillian Flynn's *Gone Girl* I'd read at least ten times. I lift from my office chair and step behind it, tucking it neatly under the fingerprint-less glass desk, and then I look at my space: a sleeping computer, a Post-it with the password, a white pencil holder home to three black BICs. A gifted pumpkin one day away from rotting.

That's it. The absolute bare minimum.

I wave at Lena as I walk past her office—"Seven thirty, Le Coucou." She's on the phone and offers me a head nod in return. *I'll be there*, she mouths.

Then I stop outside the glass-walled conference room, peeking my head through the doorway to not take up *too much* of everyone's attention.

"I'm headed out," I say, watching Rebecca lose as much of the color from her face as possible when it's covered in expensive fake tan, as all the girls turn toward me.

"Congratulations!" They all start cheering, bringing their hands to their hearts, as if my joy is their joy.

"Send us pictures!" someone in the front yells, I can't see who.

"Can't wait to hear all about it!" Kiley exclaims, her lips stained slightly black from the icing on the cookie she's scarfed down since I last saw her.

I smile around the room, meeting a few people's eyes, and finally land on Rebecca, front and center, now with jeans covered in blue bows. "Congrats, Bec. Can't wait to meet the little dude. Sorry I have to bail early."

She takes a deep breath and smiles so slowly it's as if each centimeter of emotion is exhausting for her to muster. "I'm *so* happy for you," she says back, cradling her belly with her left hand. Her engagement ring is nowhere near as impressive as mine. There's at least a carat's difference. Maybe one and a half.

"See you Monday!" they echo as I walk away, leaving the office, and my desk, as empty as it was when I arrived nearly five years ago.

I don't respond. They'll figure it out eventually.

# FOUR

---

> **One-Point Violations\*\***
> **(may include a $15 fine):**
>
> Late to convocation (1 additional point for each additional 10 minutes late)
>
> Late for curfew (5 additional points for each additional 30 minutes late)
>
> *\*\*Any further 1-point violations (no fine) are up to the sole discretion of the Resident Assistant, including but not limited to: untoward behavior, untoward language, untoward association.*

**THE HALLWAYS OF** Willits Hall—and all the other dorms, I assumed—were as bleak as our bedrooms. Cinder block walls painted a harsh light yellow. Gray carpets worn so thin you could see where the stitch met the backing. A cross loomed above each and every heavy metal door. It felt like ghosts lived here. Not that I believed in ghosts. But if I did, this is definitely where they'd haunt.

The only thing that attempted to offset the general air of

dreariness of the dorms were the dry-erase boards. Two days after we moved in, Brigid knocked on our door, offering an overzealous smile and a fistful of colorful markers, and asked us to pick one that *represented our best self*, whatever that meant.

Ruthie grabbed green and I chose pink, to which Brigid proudly responded, "Perfect complementary colors, great job, ladies!" From the floor, she lifted a recently bleached dry-erase board, a piece of thin black tape sectioning it off into four quadrants. On the top and bottom right, she wrote Ruthie's name, and on the top and bottom left, mine.

"What are these for?" Ruthie asked.

"They're our logs," Brigid said. She held the finished board up to the wall beside our door and hung it on a protruding nail I hadn't realized was there. "Your violation log and your scale log. Just keeps everyone on the same page. God loves transparency!"

"That's what they say," Ruthie muttered.

Brigid wrote *0* in the top two boxes underneath our names, then motioned for us to follow. All the other girls from our wing were standing outside their doors, too, watching Brigid as she moved toward the end of the hallway, where a strange machine was waiting. I'd seen something like it before in the women's bathroom of the church. A small pedestal to stand on, a tall metal rod, a few knobs at the top I would move back and forth while I waited for my mother to finish peeing.

Everyone looked at one another, equally confused, and I couldn't tell if they also didn't know what the machine was for, or if they knew but didn't understand why it was there.

Brigid cleared her throat. "Covenant University focuses on mind—giving you the best liberal arts education; soul—bringing you closer to God and all that is true and good; and, equally as important, *body*. 1 Corinthians says, 'Your body is a temple of the Holy Spirit within you, whom you have from

God...so glorify God in your body.'" She paused for a moment, to make sure we were understanding her, taking it all in. "Every week, we'll meet here as a group and we'll check in. We'll check in with your minds to make sure everyone's classes are going well; with your souls, that you are obeying and understanding the rules that help us live good Christian lives; and with your bodies, to make sure you are glorifying God and making all your diet and fitness choices through Him, with Him, and in Him."

She snapped the cap off the pen in her hand and looked at us, her smile again threatening to permanently get stuck that way. She pointed the pen toward the machine. A scale, I realized. "Line up, ladies." She giggled. "This will be so fun!"

When we were finished and everyone trudged back to their rooms, the boards had been updated.

0 and 128 for Ruthie. Next to *Weekly Goal*, Brigid simply put a bubbly smiley face.

0 and 152 for me. In my *Weekly Goal*, Brigid wrote *5!!!* (the exclamation points, hers) and added a *You Got This* sticker.

The system of violations was, I found, the most difficult thing to learn at Covenant. While the rules of the student handbook seemed firm and finite—spelled out in the Covenant Code in detail so acute you'd understand what you were doing wrong and the punishment you'd receive in the same bullet point—the violations were seemingly as arbitrarily created and enforced as my parents' rules at home. Terrifying at first, but once you understand how to outsmart them you realize how little effort it took in the first place.

We had a lot of rules growing up, and I spent a long time not questioning any of them. Mostly because they were all formed out of the three basic principles—poverty, chastity, obedience—that I had been taught since the day I was born.

I didn't know any better or any *other* way. So I did what my parents told me to do.

Throughout the years, my parents also formed the habit of publicizing their punishments. A slap across William's face for talking back. A night without dinner for Elin after staying out too late. Two days behind a locked bedroom door for Adam after being caught with a playing card that had a naked woman on it. The punishments only got worse as my brothers got larger, stronger, smarter.

But I grew up thinking I knew everything. I studied—hard. I followed every single rule. I watched my brothers carefully and learned how to *not* do what they did. I knew how to mow the grass and clean the troughs, and also how to tend to the sourdough starter and tell if a squash in the garden is ripe enough to pick. I knew the Bible back and forth, and sometimes after dinner my father would perch me on a chair and question me in front of my brothers, like I was the biblical encyclopedia he always wanted. When I was little, I thought I knew everything.

I didn't realize my family was different from others until I was eleven. It was the first time I was allowed off the farm besides to go to church: to accompany my mother to the grocery store. She had hurt her back and right shoulder in a fight with my father and couldn't even open the oven herself. There was no chance she could push a cart or pull bags of rice from the shelf without making a scene. Before we left, my father examined my clothes—loose hand-me-down corduroy pants held at my waist with some thick leftover rope; a long-sleeved white shirt squished beneath a too-small navy sweater. I wasn't used to wearing shoes. I was uncomfortable, too hot and too cold at the same time, and everything felt itchy against my skin, like there were invisible bugs all over my body. I couldn't stop fidgeting. But I didn't care. I was going somewhere.

At the grocery store, my mother told me to keep my head down and my mouth shut, which was impossibly difficult to do in a new place, seeing new things for the first time. I snuck a few glances here and there—a woman in tight blue pants (jeans, I later learned) and a red sweater standing in line with a cardboard box called Bud Light; a girl my age with short yellow hair asking her mother for a book of stickers: "If you get me this, then I'll have something to do at Kevin's soccer game and I won't complain, not even once"—but it wasn't until we were at the checkout counter, transferring our haul from the wiry cart onto the moldy black conveyor belt when my mother realized she'd forgotten pinto beans.

She looked up and down the grocery store, then let out a deep sigh. "Stay with the cart," she told me. "Don't move."

When I looked up—my mother now gone—a magazine was an inch away from my face. *Cosmopolitan*. Staring back at me was a brunette in a blue polka-dot bra and underwear, her curly hair blowing in the wind, her eyes huge and outlined in black-and-blue makeup. Her belly button was long, unlike mine, which squinted when I sat down.

This woman did not look like me or my mother. None of the women on the covers did. Their big eyes, long torsos, wind-swept hair. There were no lines around their eyes. No red acne scars on their chins. No itchy fabric hanging over their makeshift belts. Is this what beautiful was supposed to look like? And, if so…how?

I was mesmerized. I couldn't believe real women looked like that. Maybe one day I could look like that. That's when I saw the headline tucked under my thumb: *Your Period: All the Questions You're Too Afraid to Ask* was bolded on a pink background.

It may as well have been written specifically for me. I was spotting at the time, but I didn't know it. I thought I was dying. I thought I was slowly bleeding out like Jesus on the cross. It was my penance for something. Or maybe I was eliminating the sins of the world one blood-coated pair of underwear at a time.

It wasn't until I saw that headline that I realized I had my period, a word I only recognized because I heard Lucy Gibbons whisper it to her mother after she attended a church session called "The Role of a Woman" that you were allowed to attend when you turned thirteen, apparently the acceptable age to start menstruating in the eyes of the church.

In that moment, I devoured every other headline I could see. *White Lies Every Guy Tells Their Girl. Thirty Days until Your Best Abs Ever. Deep Sex: What Is Vaginismus and What Our Experts Recommend. New Facts about Your Va-Jeen! Ten Workouts to Burn Off That Donut—FAST! The Hottest Hair Trends This Summer. Should the Drinking Age Be Eighteen?*

There was so much I didn't know. So many questions I didn't understand and answers I never could have come up with. It was then that I realized how small my world was. Before I knew what I was doing, I'd slipped the magazine into the waist of my pants, pulling my shirt loose over it. Then I grabbed another and did the same. I loosened the belt a little bit, found a third, and stuffed it into my pants just seconds before my mother came back, rushing to the conveyer belt to continue with the groceries.

Accompanying my mother to the grocery store became my newest chore, and shoplifting magazines my new favorite hobby. *Cosmopolitan. Seventeen. Teen Vogue. Glamour. Self. Lucky. InStyle. People.* One by one, each magazine made its way into my pants, then under my mattress until I knew I had a moment to myself; until I could open its pages in the dark and read it cover to cover with more vigor than I'd ever read the Bible.

I treated the magazines like another homeschool course,

one I could only teach myself. It was everything I had been missing—opening up my world to things like sex and style and exercise, to trends and boys and celebrities; things my parents never would have taught me. It's also where I learned about college. Not from *Cosmopolitan*—though the idea did first show up there, in a column about "how to protect yourself from party rape *and* the freshman fifteen"—but in a local newspaper tucked within the magazine's glossy pages. In my haste to not get caught, I didn't notice until I got home that I had accidentally grabbed *The Weekly Woodchucker* along with my magazines. Right before I threw it out, I noticed an advertisement on the back: *Apply To Covenant—Where Christian Leaders Are Made.*

When I told my parents I wanted to go to college, they reacted as I imagined they would, by detailing all the reasons why I shouldn't go. Massive debt, authoritarian schedules, wavering morals. My mother lingered on that last point, looking at me with her gray braided head cocked to the right, her fiery brown eyes thin and leery. I was their only daughter and that made my parents suspicious of everything I did. My motivation for traditional schooling was no exception.

*I* filled out the application. *I* worked with my homeschool curriculum office to submit my transcript. *I* applied for FASFA and scholarships. And when the oversized envelope from Covenant University appeared in my PO Box, like water in the desert, I convinced them I needed to go by showcasing the honest, decent, *Christian* education I could get. A curriculum formed by people who shared their beliefs and who, like my parents, strived to create the next generation of good Christians.

At least, that's what I told them.

Because I knew Covenant could do that. I knew Covenant required weekly convocation. I knew Covenant had a code of conduct more complex than the bridges and tunnels in New York City. I knew Covenant would keep my parents' cross snug around my neck. If I let it.

But I also knew people like the ones in these magazines existed there. In-betweeners.

People like Ruthie.

Ruthie and her family went to church—an unofficial requirement for admission at Covenant—but she didn't *pray*. There's a difference. She didn't start each day on her knees thanking God for waking her up, and each night asking him to do the same tomorrow. She never spent one Saturday a month with her church's teen group, standing outside the fancy grocery store in town, asking people, "What's your relationship with Jesus Christ?" only to be hurriedly waved away or smiled at with pity.

Ruthie was everything these magazines told me I needed to be. And now Ruthie was my roommate and friend, my ticket to learning how to live in the real world. How to get out and never go back.

For the first month on campus, I followed Ruthie around like a shadow. She was tan from her summer working as a lifeguard and the boys seemed to like that based on how many of them stared at her while we walked from the dining hall's entrance to our table, so I snuck to the CVS in town and started slathering myself in Jergens Natural Glow after every shower until my sheets were stained brown and our room perpetually smelled like sunscreen. Ruthie used the school's "look good for God" mantra as an excuse to never leave the dorm without mascara and blush, so I never left the dorm without mascara and blush. Ruthie ate a ham-and-cheese sandwich and chocolate Froyo for dinner, I ate a ham-and-cheese sandwich and chocolate Froyo for dinner.

Ruthie carried a camera around with her everywhere, snapping photos of ivy spiraling up the side of our dorm, of students piling into the dining hall, of me laughing at something she'd said. Then she'd print them in the library and hang them one by one on the cement walls of our room.

"Let me take a picture of *you*," I said once at dinner.

She shook her head and pulled the camera back. "A true artist is behind the camera, not in front of it," she said. I didn't think she was giving herself enough credit. She was a much prettier subject than anything she took pictures of.

By the end of the month, I'd lost a disappointing one pound, but I was more like Ruthie by the day and had memorized all of her stories the same way I did with the magazines. Stories of sneaking out of her second-floor window in high school to go to parties in the parking lot of a 7-Eleven; of sipping six-dollar vodka mixed with pomegranate-flavored Crystal Light hidden in Poland Spring water bottles; of kissing her older brother's friends and almost getting fingered in the back seat of a light gray Toyota. She was worldly and beautiful—the epitome of the person I wanted to become. As long as Ruthie was friends with me, I would know everything.

Once we realized the purpose of the white boards next to everyone's door, Ruthie and I made a habit of going on what we called Violation Rotations. After dinner but before curfew, we'd walk up and down the halls of Willits, and Ruthie would count all the newest violations.

"Fresh meat," Ruthie said as she beelined toward the postcard taped to 609's door, the Dean's Office coat of arms branded to the top. In the body of the note, meant to be kept "for your records" was a handwritten violation, detailing what you did, the date you were caught, and how many points you have received. Brigid's bubbly cursive made the whole thing worse, like she was mocking you while punishing you. In the bottom right-hand corner was a small box where your violation total was scribbled in red. It never refreshed. It carried over until graduation. If you made it that far.

"Her second time late for curfew this week," Ruthie said, her eyes flickering with suspicion as she put the postcard back. "What are you doing out so late, missy?" she asked more to herself than to me.

While Ruthie peeked at the points—counted what Margaret in 515 got for watching *Mean Girls* in her room, and what Rachel in 102 received for being tardy for convocation—I stared at the other numbers. The log of our weigh-ins. Most girls were closer to me than to Ruthie, and Ruthie seemed to be the only one receiving affirmations instead of goalposts each week.

*I can do better*, I thought. *I can be like Ruthie.*

"I still can't believe all of this is just on the wall for everyone to see," Ruthie said outside 805, Christina and Jane, who got caught wearing inappropriately tight and short outfits last night. "Where were you guys headed?" she asked under her breath again.

"It's public to be a warning," I said, focusing not on the violation but on Christina's plus-one-pound change this week. Don't do what she did. Don't let everyone know you're failing.

"I think…" Ruthie began, flipping over their postcard again, showing me the violation, bringing my focus out of my own head. "If you pay enough attention," she continued, "it's less of a warning and more of a guide on how to not get caught."

Ruthie collected and hoarded this information, and it wasn't until then that I knew why. She was scouting—who was being careless, who was fearless, who was in the pocket of Brigid and the RAs, who was worth looking into a little further. She was shadowing others in the way I was shadowing her.

I found it ironic that we called them points, like in a game. One big, manipulative game. Only here, the more points you have, the more you stand to lose. Brigid may have run Willits Hall like a better-fed and better-dressed women's prison, but she was just following the guidelines of the entire school. Where one is presumed guilty (and *untoward*) until proven innocent. Or until graduation. Because, we'd later learn, it was impossible for women to prove any kind of innocence.

Later that night we sat in our beds, using our phones as flashlights after curfew. We looked like kids trying to be spooky, underlighting our faces, creating unnatural shadows.

"If we're going to party at this school, we're going to do it right," Ruthie mouthed into the light. We learned early on, during one of our very first Violation Rotations, that if Brigid heard even a peep coming from your room after lights-out—a light switch flicking, a page turning, a bottle of water being squeezed—you'd wake up to a violation on your door the next morning. So we became masters at lipreading. We honed our craft until it became second nature. Until we'd be sitting at dinner, talking for half an hour before realizing we'd only been moving our lips. Our first loophole of many.

"Kids are getting in trouble for it," she continued. "So it exists. We just need to figure out how to get invited…"

Ruthie had been determined since the day we met to go to a party. I figured maybe it was a phase; maybe if I kept her entertained enough, if I filled our evenings with movies and games, she'd realize there are other things to do here that don't involve getting enough violations that could send me home. I needed to make it the full four years, so I'd never have to go back. I didn't have other options like Ruthie.

"That's all we need. An invite or a hint or *something*—"

"That's all *you* need," I interrupted. Ruthie looked up,

squinting through the flashlight. "I—I don't know, Ruthie. I can't get caught at a party," I said. "If I get sent home, that's it for me. I'm done. I'll never get out."

"We're not going to get caught!"

"You don't know that. You just said other people have been. I don't know if that's worth it to me—"

"I didn't come to college to sit in my dorm and play cards or whatever every night. That's not the college experience. The whole point is to do things—to drink and dance and date. To...*to have sex*," she said, out loud.

Our heads bolted toward the door. I wasn't sure what the violation was for *talking about* sex, but *having* premarital sex was impossible to come back from—in every way, I guess. I wasn't afraid of sex because of all the reasons I was told to be—that I would descend straight to the fiery gates, that I'd get an STD and *then* get sent straight to the fiery gates, that I'd get an STD and pregnant and it would hurt and I'd bleed and no one would want to marry my impure body and *then* get sent to the fiery gates.

I was afraid of sex because of the violations.

Big things like that are often covered by multiple violations and you better believe they give you all of them. Premarital sex? Well, you were inappropriately dressed (five points) + you entered, or allowed someone to enter, the residence of a person of the opposite sex (ten points) + you deceived (ten points) + you participated in inappropriate contact with the opposite sex (twenty points) + you created a disruption to the community (twenty points). They'll also probably throw in a couple bonus violations like late for curfew (one point), falsification of information (twenty points), failure to identify oneself (twenty points). And next thing you know, you're expelled, paying the school almost a thousand dollars in violation fines, and living on the farm with your parents going on chaperoned dates with an older man they've arranged for you to marry in exchange for a few farm animals.

"Why did you come here?" I finally asked, after a few seconds of silence. "Why didn't you go to a normal school?"

Ruthie sat up straighter, her head resting on the wall behind her. "My stepdad thinks I'm a fuckup," she said. "He's from all *this*—" she waved her arms around "—and he thought it would be good for me. Some discipline or whatever." She got quiet and looked down at her hands, nails bitten down to their core. "I'm not a fuckup. I'm just not like his other kids…"

Ruthie didn't talk about her home life much, which I appreciated because I didn't want to talk about mine. Everything I could possibly say about my parents or siblings would only add to the arrow over my head—the loud, neon, pulsing arrow that told everyone around me that I was different, that I wasn't like them. But I guess Ruthie had a little arrow over her head, too.

She rubbed her eyes before she looked up, a redness forming on her cheeks. "We need to experience things, Elizabeth. You wanted so badly to get out, well, you're out. If you don't do anything with it, then what's the point?"

She wasn't wrong. I also came to college to do all those things. To put all my magazine knowledge to the test. But a party still scared me. It felt like another easy way to get one hundred points and expelled—how could a party possibly be planned *on* campus? It seemed like a ticking time bomb. A risk I didn't want to take just yet. We had four years. There was no need to rush it.

Right?

After my first weigh-in, I started jogging. Well, it was more like walking with an occasional gallop if no one was looking. I'd never exercised before. My father didn't think it was something a woman should do. Working out meant you wanted your body to look a certain way and, by wanting your body to look a certain way, that meant you wanted people to look at your body in the first place. But they had an entirely different approach at Covenant.

The weight was not coming off fast, no more than one pound a week, if I was lucky, but it was happening slowly. The weekly weigh-ins, at first embarrassing and awkward, full of shame and void of eye contact, had morphed into something more competitive. Girls pretending to be encouraging and helpful, smiling as you walked the plank to the scale. But you were only praised when you lost the most of the hall that week. And everyone salivated for those claps.

A bigger motivator for me was that Ruthie's clothes started fitting me better. The halo of fat around my belly that stuck out above her jeans was slowly shrinking, which opened up her entire closet to me. I hadn't touched my old khakis in weeks.

During one of my "jogs," I stopped behind the football stadium, on the edge of the wooded area, at the top of a long and shallow staircase flanked by overgrown weeds and the flowers you blow and make a wish on. I bent over and tried to catch my breath, my hands desperately clutching my knees. It was pathetic how little I could go before feeling like my chest was closing in on me. I hated every second of it.

"Um, hi—" a deep voice echoed in the trees, forcing from me a scream so shrill I wasn't sure it had actually come out of my mouth.

I spun around, out of breath and shaking, as a man appeared from behind a thick tree that was white and peeling and leafless. His eyes were wide and his hands up—*I'm innocent*. He was here first, I guess.

He was tall and lanky, his saggy brown hair highlighting his long face and drooping features, like gravity had an extra-hard hold on him. He was wearing jeans and a plaid button-down and as sure as I was that I'd never seen him before, he looked familiar in that way everyone on campus could—like we'd probably passed each other on the grounds one hundred times without noticing.

"Sorry," he mumbled. I didn't respond. I tried to slow my breathing, not make it known how scared I was, but the air was so cold going into my nose and down to my lungs that it made me cough. He backed up a few steps. "There's never anyone back here, so we, um…" He trailed off as four people appeared behind him, static, like they weren't sure they could trust me. I didn't recognize the two guys—dressed in jeans and button-downs just like every other man in this school. But the girls I knew. I'd seen them before, but I didn't know where. Or why.

From behind his back, the guy closest to me pulled a lit cigarette. "We come here to smoke," he said, sticking it between his lips, breathing in deeply, waiting a moment before the smoke started waterfalling from his mouth, dense and white. The others stepped two feet closer to me, their eyes squinting, skeptical, like if I turned to run, they'd attack and pin me to the ground until I promised to keep my mouth shut.

He reached his hand toward me, the cigarette between his thumb and forefinger. "You want some?"

I'd never smoked in my life—I was never offered the opportunity, and then vowed I would never after *Seventeen* magazine partnered with the American Cancer Society to sell *Kiss Me, I Don't Smoke* T-shirts. I'd never seen a cigarette until I saw a pile of orange butts in the dirt next to the sugarhouse. I picked one up, felt the damp paper shred in my fingers, then dropped it when William appeared behind me and said, "Tell and you're dead," in a kind of whisper that gave me chills even thinking about it ten years later.

But this cigarette didn't smell the way my brother smelled that day, his breath burning against my ear with the threat. This smelled like skunk, familiar but I couldn't place why.

I could feel them all looking at me and I knew my decision would determine how they viewed me forever. It wasn't so much peer pressure as it was opportunity. I'd never been given the opportunity to smoke, but God did I want to try. They'd clearly been doing this here for months and, look at them, still alive, no Devil in sight.

I stepped forward and took it in my fingers, suddenly remembering why the skunky smell was so familiar—it wasn't a cigarette, it was weed. Surprisingly, that made me want to try it more.

He put the joint between my lips and held it there as I took a deep breath, quickly flipping through the Rolodex of magazine articles in my brain until I found the one I was looking for: a letter to the editor in *Cosmo*. Take a deep breath, let the smoke seep into your lungs and your esophagus. Do not swallow. Then let it out slowly to avoid coughing.

When I finished, he nodded, one side of his mouth lifted into an impressed smile, as he took the joint back and put it in his mouth. I liked the idea that we both tasted the same thing, our lips against the same paper. It was the second closest thing to sex I'd ever done.

The whole group of them seemed to relax, but that was easy to do as the bank of knowledge just became equal; I had something on them, but they had something on me now. We were partners in crime.

"I should get back to it," I said, motioning up the hill.

"We come here every once in a while," one of the girls in the back said. There was something about her hair—the dark straight bob—that I couldn't quite get out of my head. "If you're ever around and want to join us again..."

"Don't tell anyone," the other girl said, backing away. "If you tell, we tell."

I watched them disappear into the forest, then stared at the trees for a while after they were gone. I was waiting to be punished. To be struck by lightning or visited by the Devil or shamed by Jesus. Maybe I was just adding to the list of reasons Saint Peter will reject me at the pearly gates, but for now, on Earth, I was starting to think nothing was quite as bad as I'd been taught.

Then I threw up right there on my own shoes.

When I got back to Willits, I was rejuvenated. Maybe it was the excitement of getting away with something, maybe it was the weed, maybe I was getting better at running. Either way, when I sprung our door open, ready to tell Ruthie all about it, I was shocked to see our room was empty.

I checked my cell phone, which I'd left charging on my desk while I worked out, and saw a text from Ruthie: grabbed dinner with some kids from class. see you later.

My stomach fell. We always ate dinner together. It felt like I messed up. Like this simple text might be the start to it all. Like I might be losing her.

That night, I was lying in bed in the dark. It was ten minutes to curfew but Ruthie wasn't back yet and I had started planning for what I would do—how I would prove myself by covering for her. I could say she's in the bathroom. That she's not feeling well and needed some fresh air. I could bat my eyes and smile and Brigid would believe me. As much as I didn't want to be, I was just like her. I was very believable.

I rolled around when I heard keys jostling in our door, pretending I was asleep. With two minutes to spare, Ruthie walked in. She attempted to be quiet, to find her pajamas, her toothbrush, her glasses case, but she wasn't. It bothered me at first—if I were really sleeping this would be very annoying—

until I saw some movement out the window. I leaned in closer, tried to get my eyes to separate darkness from objects, until, somehow, I recognized it: the two girls from the forest, snaking between the trees. Camouflaged by the darkness, their limbs blended in with the trees, moving leafless, lifeless, with the light wind. If I didn't recognize them, I'd assume I was dreaming. But there they were, heading away from the dorm, and disappearing into the night.

For the next few days, I listened to the campus gossip carefully, waiting to hear about two girls who were defending themselves to the Student Court of Appeals for sneaking out after curfew to drink and smoke and dance and have sex and do all the other things I realized I also went to college to experience. I did extra Violation Rotations, looking for something that would have exposed them. But there was nothing. They didn't get caught.

So neither would we.

"I found our party group," I finally told Ruthie as we were getting ready for bed one night. "We got that invite you wanted."

# FIVE

**WHEN I GOT** home from work, Graham was in his office, the second bedroom we'd "eventually turn into a nursery." Though the timeline on *eventually* remains unspecified. He doesn't like anyone in his office. I could count on one hand the number of times I'd entered, and in two of those instances, I had to distract him from kicking me out with an elaborate fantasy of fucking at his desk at work with his assistant in the next room. "Take this image to your real office," I'd said, pushing my tits together. I didn't have much sway in the matter. Technically, *I* moved into *his* apartment. It's not ours. As of right now, he was allowed to tell me I was banned from a room I wasn't paying for.

I knock on the office door twice, giving him ample time to finish whatever he's doing—sometimes I like to imagine he's eating SkinnyPop and watching *Keeping Up with the Kardashians* or *Selling Sunset*, reminding himself why old money is better than new money.

As I wait for him to answer, I glance into our bedroom across the hallway. Graham's suitcase is lying open and empty on the floor. He refuses to throw out that old suitcase and I hate it—it's covered in stickers from his study abroad days, each one representing another exotic exploit: the Visca Barça jersey, a reminder of the dark-haired twenty-two-year-old who rolled her Rs around his dick in the back of a five-story club; the red phone booth, a relic of the uptight blonde wearing thick foundation who smeared her over-lined lips while telling him she wanted to try it up the ass.

Maybe I'll accidentally destroy it before we leave. Clip the zipper or something simple.

"Come in," he calls, and I push the heavy door open. He looks exhausted, his hair standing up in the places he must have run his hands through it. Purple bags had formed under his eyes that are in no way wedding acceptable. I will not have him standing beside me in *New York Times* Vows pictures looking like he's given up.

"You're home early," he says.

I walk into the room slowly, like someone approaching a stray dog, ensuring I mean no harm, I won't snoop, I'm just saying hello. The room is dark by design; the only window behind Graham's wooden desk faces the building's airshaft and lets in the morning light for only about two hours during peak summer months. But he leans into the vibe. The heather-and-brass drum chandelier is always dimmed to the point of being useless, and the smoked-glass table lamp is more for form than function. I believe he thinks it makes him seem more academic, more cerebral. Probably richer, too. As if the framed diploma from Yale and the mortgage-less Upper East Side apartment didn't do those things for him.

"Did you finish packing?" I ask, moseying toward his desk.

"We had an emergency at work," he says. "But I'll do it tonight."

"What are you not going to forget?"

He feigns hesitation. Then winks. "My suit."

"Because…"

"That would be a *catastrophe*," he quotes the line I've told him at least eight times since we decided to have a spurious destination wedding. (Though, *real* destination weddings involve resorts in the Maldives, not… *Vermont*.)

He pushes away from his desk to make room for me to amble onto his lap and see, firsthand, that I had not, in fact, interrupted a raucous afternoon of KarJenner madness.

"Lena and I are getting drinks with the *New York Times* person tonight."

"Right…" The left side of his lip lifts slightly in contempt. Graham does not like Lena. To be honest, most of the time *I* don't really like Lena. Being gay, hot, half-Black, and third-generation rich has afforded her the luxury of an extraordinarily bland personality. She's inherently more interesting than anyone she surrounds herself with, without really being more interesting at all. It's a disappointing dynamic for anyone who meets her expecting the depth of conversation to verge beyond the surface. Which is the basis of most of Graham's disdain. Though it's not as if he's personally profound himself.

"Are you sure I don't need to be there?" he asks.

When I returned Sarah Keens's call last night and she asked for this *very last-minute* meeting to "get to know us" she did request we both attend—spouting something about how meeting both of us in person helps shape the tone of the article or something. I didn't see why this preinterview was necessary—they had all our information from the application, and the real meat of the story was going to be the ceremony. But she insisted and I knew Graham's aversion toward Sarah's perceived intrusion would be blatantly obvious on his overly emotive face, so I told her he was traveling—"So close to the wedding?" she asked, disapproving. "Boys will be boys!" I responded, a statement that puts a virtual end to any male criticism despite being a male criticism in itself. And then he was cordially un-invited, so Lena took his place.

Plus, Lena had been begging me to get dinner all week—despite seeing me at work every single day—so I was killing two birds with one 2003 vintage.

"If she has any questions for you, I'm sure she'll find you at the wedding," I say. "I think Lena's going to ask at dinner if she can bring her new girlfriend."

"She's dating someone?"

"Apparently. She described herself as *smitten* and you know how infrequently Lena uses fluff words."

He nods, no doubt picturing the kind of ethnically am-biguous leggy model Lena would date. She has a reputation with them. Front row at Tom Ford during Fashion Week and somehow *she* manages to catch *their* eye. "Can she bring her?"

"Of course. She's basically my maid of honor. She gets a plus-one even this late in the game," I answer. "Though, your mother may feel otherwise."

He flinches in his seat. Anytime anyone brings up his mother, his defense goes up. If he wasn't fucking me, I wouldn't be surprised if he eventually started fucking her, they're so obsessed with each other. "Why?" he asks. "She doesn't have a problem with gays. She's been to a gay wedding."

I nod and resist the urge to let out a big, fat, disappointed breath. "Not because Lena's gay," I say, my head shaking at his denseness. "Because we've already put together the table assignments."

"Oh." He lets out a low laugh. "Right." Yet another notch on the *how oblivious to wedding planning can Graham be* tally. "I'll pack while you're at dinner," he offers, resting his chin on my shoulder. "I promise I'll be done by the time you get back."

I lean over and give him a kiss. I know that's what he's looking for. "That's what you said about work today…"

"Well that…that was a lie." He laughs. "Blatant and rude and I deeply apologize for leading you astray." He wraps his arms around my waist and squeezes, pressing deeper and deeper into my rib cage until I can't breathe. I don't want him to stop.

"You look good, you know," he says, before loosening up his grip, his hands wandering toward my breasts before I shake him off.

"If you actually pack, maybe I'll treat you to something special when I get home…" Slowly, I push myself off his lap and let my dress fall into place, but not before giving him a nice view of the legs I pay good money to be tanned and hairless.

"Ugh," he gripes, his head falling back against the tall leather chair. "Fine."

"We're leaving tomorrow, babe," I say, moving toward the door. "You have to do it eventually." I stop in the doorway. "Unless you're having cold feet?"

His eyes thin. "First off, the plane leaves when we tell it to leave," he says, genuinely oblivious to the pretention in his voice. Then, he pulls his legs up, resting his bare feet on the desk and crossing his ankles. He studies them, staring as he clenches and unclenches his long toes. "Second…they're toasty, thank you very much."

I laugh as I close the door, but the second the latch bolt clicks into place my smile is gone.

# SIX

**AS A CHILD,** every year when Halloween came around, while other kids wore colorful masks and red capes, old sheets with holes for eyes, while their parents shuttled them from house to house—in neighborhoods far too hilly and separated to walk—while they filled up pillowcases with chocolate and candy I'd never been allowed to touch before, my brothers and I sat around the kitchen table bowing our heads in prayer. Halloween was a satanic, sinful day, filled with temptations and overindulgence, and we prayed for the souls of the children encouraged to participate by their shameful and irresponsible parents. My parents hung up a cross on the front porch where everyone else's plastic skeletons or light-up pumpkins would be, which scared parents and children away from the farm faster than if we offered a bowl of homemade raisins.

I'd only ever heard of Hell Houses before. When I was very young, fliers would sprinkle the doorstep of our church each year, just as much a sign of the beginning of autumn as leaves falling off the trees. My parents considered taking us once— a different way to pray and become aware of the temptations around us—but after consulting with our pastor, they decided it wasn't a good idea. Or they were told as much. The next year, the leaflets were destroyed as soon as they hit the speckled pavement.

Covenant's Hell House was a forty-year tradition that started when Dr. Felix Chastain, the school's founder, president, and pastor, who insisted on being referred to by his full name and title whenever addressed publicly or privately, wanted to use the holiday as a teaching experience—a way for students to participate in and experience the college-specific temptations that could send you straight to, well, hell. When graphic posters showcasing horned red devils dripping in bedazzled blood started popping up on bulletin boards around campus, I was intrigued. I wanted to know what my parents and hometown pastor felt such vehement hatred toward; what got them heated enough to dedicate entire dinners and sermons to debunking the devilish practice.

Ruthie was uninterested at first, which tempered my own excitement. "Isn't it just a haunted house?" she asked. "What's the big deal?" I tried to tell her Hell Houses were different, they were... *Christian,* but I didn't know how to say that without molding her disinterest into disgust. Then we'd never go. It didn't take long for her to hear through the gossip channels I had an apparent inability to connect to that there was always an after-party. A post–Hell House Hell House, for students, by students, where they *hand out* drinks and mandate costumes, instead of telling you you'll go to hell for both.

Until this point, Ruthie and I found any excuse in the book to meander behind the stadium to the steps where I had made new midjog marijuana friends. I'd drag Ruthie on my jogs—which were getting better and easier with each added mile until it became a routine. We also realized it was the perfect excuse. Should we get caught wandering in the woods all we had to do was quote Dr. Felix Chastain—"You have to look good to feel good."—and we'd be golden. Once a day, sometimes twice, we'd jog up the hill and around the stadium until we found the steps. We'd stand at the top, exactly where I was when I saw them last, and wait, listening for movement in the forest, occasionally faking a cough or a sneeze to make sure, if they were deep in the trees, they'd know we were waiting for them. Ruthie even went so far once as to bring a tiny bottle of Smirnoff she'd snuck from her parents' liquor cabinet and hid in her underwear drawer waiting for the perfect moment to use it. I'd figured that would be at our first party but, no, it was while we stood in the woods pretending to sneeze.

But we never saw them. We came home disappointed every time. I was starting to think I imagined them—maybe they didn't exist, maybe I never smoked weed, maybe I was in such a state of jogging exhaustion that I was hallucinating. And Ruthie started thinking that, too. So, to compensate, she started focusing on this alleged post–Hell House Hell House party.

"You found our first party group, now I'll find our second," she said generously, placating me and my seemingly imaginary friends.

The Hell House opened at 3:00 p.m. on Halloween day—a little early, Ruthie and I thought, to have the potential sin scared out of you. It felt more appropriate, and scary, after the sun went down, so we happily waited until seven thirty to join the line of students, which, by that point, wrapped around the whole of the McMahon science building where the events were held. Weeks were spent turning the building into this spooky show, affected classes were moved or canceled, and more security guarded the entrance than any other part of campus.

While we waited, I thought about the fliers I saw as a kid. I was excited to experience something my parents didn't approve of yet was endorsed by the university. I guess it's more about the way you interpret the rules, rather than the rules themselves.

"I don't know why I'm nervous," Ruthie said, laughing and jumping in place like an athlete prerace. "This is going to be so fun."

I wasn't sure *fun* was how I'd describe it, but I could be wrong.

When we finally reached the steps of the building, the main security guard, a burly man with a boyish face like Matt Damon's when he was on *People*'s Sexiest Man Alive cover, gave us the same "one second" finger my mother used when we were asking her questions while she measured flour or sugar for baking.

"Go ahead," he finally said, pulling the heavy wooden door open and motioning for us to walk inside.

Once the door closed behind us, it was dark. Not just lights-off-at-night dark, but the kind of dark where you can feel your pupils expanding, desperately grasping for any hint of light they can find just to spatially orient your brain, to make your feet know there's a floor and your arms know there are walls.

We followed the pack of students in front of us, inching around the perimeter of the room, waiting for instruction on what we were supposed to be doing, seeing.

A light in the corner flashed, sending everyone flying in the opposite direction, the whiteness stinging my eyes even when I closed them. Then, impossibly loud music came on, the kind that seemed to thump inside my ears. Purple, blue, and green lights started flashing around the room like an out-of-control disco ball. Boys and girls—*student actors*—crowded into the scene in front of us, dancing, shaking their hips and butts, touching each other, moving in tandem. A few of them took sips from red plastic cups. A few pretended to smoke unlit cigarettes. On a table meant to be the bar was a line of white powder and some credit cards. A boy, tall and chubby, leaned over the bar and, with a rolled-up dollar bill, sniffed some powder into his nose. Then, as he walked back toward the dance floor, he collapsed and started shaking, the white powder bubbling from his mouth now. Everyone else was too drunk to notice him dying.

Darkness as we followed the crowd into the next room.

A scream, a flash, another scream. When the light turned back on, so bright and fluorescent I had to turn away, a girl, younger than me, was lying limp on a hospital bed, her legs up in stirrups, blood everywhere. On everything. On the bed between her legs, on her hospital gown, on the walls. It dropped onto the floor in thick red clots. A man in a white coat sat at the end of the bed, holding a long metal piece of equipment, a speculum, also covered in blood.

Then, again, darkness.

We were led, next, into a dorm room, identical to any of ours—the same yellow wood furniture, the same plastic-covered mattress. A girl stood on her desk chair in the center of the room, staring at us, unmoving. Behind her, the bedsheets were disoriented and there were dozens of used condoms and wrappers on the floor. The lights turned off and a gunshot and the feeling of water spraying on my face and then in the light, she was on the floor, blood and brain goop that kind of looked like guacamole all over the room.

Darkness.

Then, a voice came over the loudspeaker, crackly and distant, sending goose bumps up my arm. I squeezed Ruthie's hand so hard she had to ask me to stop.

"If you died today..." a voice said slowly, echoey, like a heartbeat in your ears. "Do you know where you'd go?"

I had to get out of there. I dropped Ruthie's hand and walked in whatever direction I could find, grasping the air in search of a wall or a path or anything that could lead me outside. I felt like I couldn't breathe, like the darkness and the voices were closing in on me and if I didn't get outside it would completely take me over. *Do you know where you'd go?* echoed in my head until I pushed through an emergency exit covered in black felt and the cool October air slapped me in the face.

I didn't know where I'd go. I didn't know where I'd want to go.

The last thing I heard before I bolted out of there was a laugh, loud and triumphant. It had sounded like Ruthie.

Outside, I was shocked to see how bright it was in the darkness. The campus lights were blinding, covering everything in sight. A way to convince you you're safer here than you really are.

I kept walking, behind the McMahon science building

turned Hell House, around the corner, down one path, then another. I was sweating through my shirt.

"Elizabeth!"

My hands were shaking.

"Elizabeth!"

My temples felt like someone was squeezing them as close together as possible. The back of my throat was raw from screams I didn't even realize had escaped.

"Elizabeth!" I felt someone grab my arm and pull me back, and when I turned around it was Ruthie. "I've been calling you. Are you okay?"

There was so much blood. That was all I could see when I blinked. So much blood.

"We have to go to the stadium," Ruthie said, trying to tug me back up there. "This fucked-up thing isn't over."

I couldn't move. I couldn't breathe.

*Do you know where you'd go?*

"You, again..." It was the same deep voice as before but this time it didn't scare me. When I looked up, there they were, at the top of the staircase, again appearing from the trees like they were part of the forest themselves.

Ruthie moved toward them quickly, then slowed herself down once she realized how obviously excited she seemed.

They weren't only smoking this time, also passing a Poland Spring bottle around, wincing as the liquid passed their lips. I knew there wasn't water in that bottle.

I'd been drunk before. Once by accident, then on purpose. I knew my father hid bottles of moonshine around the house and in the barn—on the top shelf of the pantry, behind the stack of broken rakes in the shed, inside the old brick fireplace that no longer worked—and I found a bottle under the sink in the hall bathroom when I was looking for hydrogen peroxide. It was in a blue glass canister, which made it look like it could be mouthwash. When I took a sip, it tasted like what I imagined mouthwash would if you swallowed an entire bottle in one gulp, accompanied by the same burning sensation in your throat and ears and eyes. I started coughing and threw up into the sink. I watched my orange bile circle the drain until there was nothing left. Then I shut and locked the bathroom door and did it again. I kept it down the second time.

"I know you," Ruthie said, to herself more than me. She took a step forward, toward the two girls. "You're in Willits?"

*That's* where I recognized them from. I was impressed Ruthie could get it so quickly. They were at orientation. They were the ones sitting on the floor next to each other, scanning the Covenant Code in the same fashion I had, afraid we'd be quizzed or given a violation if we didn't have a certain passage memorized.

The blonde one came forward, her hair in a long braid. She had thick dirty-blond eyelashes that made her big brown eyes stand out on her freckled face.

"Yeah. 108," she said. "They call me Catherine." Even the way she introduced herself was rebellious. Who says it like that?

"Ruthie," she said. "We're in 314."

"I'm Elizabeth," I added.

The one with the dark bob joined her roommate, her eyes friendly but removed, like she didn't want to get too close or too comfortable without knowing more about us first. "Annie," she said, quietly. If you weren't attentively listening, you wouldn't have heard it. Maybe that was her first test.

"We'll see you around," Annie said, finished with the conversation before we realized it was over. She started making her way down the steps toward the woods. Toward the campus's edge, the area that was dark and shadowy and no doubt camera-free.

To Ruthie's disappointment, the rest of them followed, except the lanky guy, the one who gave me the joint last time. He stood there looking at us. It wasn't until later that night I realized he wasn't looking at us, he was looking at me. Only me.

"You don't look like the type that would find a place on campus to smoke," I said as he lingered. I wanted to keep him around longer. The more he stared at me, the more I stared back. And the more I started to feel hot on my cheeks, my neck, between my legs.

"Neither do you," he said. He started backing away, only to lose his balance on the edge of a step, tipping backwards until he caught himself, his thick boot stomping back on concrete. "These fucking steps," he said, tapping his joint against the air in an attempt to recover from his embarrassment.

I'd never seen stairs like these before: the tread was at least two feet, but the rise was only five or six inches.

He kicked the step, rustling the edge of an anthill. "These stairs have a lot of nicknames," he said. "Did you know that?" He looked up at Ruthie and me like he was waiting for an answer even though he knew we wouldn't have one.

"The smoking steps?" I toyed.

He smiled at the thought. Clever. "That's one of them. At least to us. They don't really teach you that here, but you learn." He stuck the joint into his mouth and bent at the knees, watching the ants frantically evacuate the home he'd just crumbled. "They're also called the Rape Steps."

I suddenly realized how cold I was. I was shaking, the sheen of sweat on my face—from fear—making it even worse.

"Why?" I asked, stepping closer to him like a dare. Why would he bring that up? And why did I like it?

He jolted to his feet and I knocked backwards, tripping over two steps before grabbing the edge of a tree and standing up straight. Ruthie didn't move. She stood a foot away from him, stoic, making a point. *You don't scare us.*

He looked at us blankly, like whatever was in that water bottle was finally setting in. "Apparently, the way they're built—shallow and long like that—it benefits a girl's gait but not a guy's." He jumped up suddenly, landing on my step with a thud that seemed to echo around us. "Rumor has it, they were made special so girls could outrun rapists." He let out a laugh. "Or anyone trying to chase them, I guess. Regardless of intent."

His dark eyes were so close to mine, I could differentiate between his brown iris and the black pupil. He didn't move so neither did we. But I wanted to run.

The edges of his lips curled up, then went flat again as he raised the joint to his mouth and puffed. "It's also possible they were built in the eighteenth century and made this way so horses could easily climb them," he said, laughing to himself. "I guess we'll never know, huh?"

He began descending the stairs backwards, still looking at me, his brown eyes like a black hole I was getting closer and closer to, unable to pull away from even though I realized it was deadly.

"We're hanging out here tonight," he said. "You should come."

"Sure," Ruthie said quickly, quitting on the post–Hell House Hell House before we had even been invited.

"Okay," I said.

He smiled at me—"Good"—then disappeared into the trees.

As Ruthie and I started walking back up the hill toward the stadium, we could hear Dr. Felix Chastain beginning his post–Hell House speech inside the stadium where we were supposed to be.

"Welcome to salvation," Dr. Felix Chastain's voice echoed into the forest. "Be not afraid," he began, pausing perfectly.

"*Fear not* and *be not afraid*, and such, are the most repeated phrases in the Bible. By telling us not to be afraid, what God is really saying is that there are things out there to fear. The Lord our God is with us to protect us from temptation and from the Devil himself, but the Devil is out there, in so many ways. He's in every bar. He's in every sip of alcohol. He's in every inappropriate sexual relationship and every dance party and every profane word, and improper thought and immoral feeling. He's all around us, tempting us every single day. Those scenes you witnessed today—they're real and happening everywhere.

"Be not afraid," he repeated. "For God is with you," he finished, a sentiment I'd been force-fed my entire life. "We want you to know that here, at Covenant, *we* are also with you." He paused. "We look out for one another here. We are together in our pursuit of a holy life. We will teach and protect each other. We are one another's strength and might. We are together wherever we go. We have your back. Be. Not. Afraid."

His voice faded as Ruthie and I continued toward our dorms, the stadium shrinking behind us. Ruthie entwined her arm with mine and I leaned my head on her shoulder as we walked in step together.

They didn't have our backs here. Maybe God still did, but even that I'd started to question. The one thing I knew for sure was the only person I could trust here was Ruthie. Ruthie and me.

And I loved it.

We arrived at the woods at 10:01 p.m. We didn't want to be late and risk missing any aspect of our first party, no matter how inconsequential. We were in. We'd made it.

We figured they were testing us tonight, whetting their palates to the concept of introducing two more people to their group. But we were also testing them. If they were truly able to navigate so far under the radar that they could drink and smoke on campus without getting caught, then we'd dip our toe in the water tonight. Let them know they can trust us. But not give them too much ammo against us if they decide they can't.

We pushed out of Willits's front doors and into the darkness probably playing it too cool; walking slowly, casually, toward our fate as if we were just walking to get a midnight snack in the dining hall. Ruthie started moving toward the quad, but I grabbed her arm, remembering that night I saw Catherine and Annie sneaking out.

"Let's go the back way," I told her, figuring if that's how they did it, that's how we should do it, too. As we made our way around our dorm, forming into the same shadows I saw Catherine and Annie disappear into, I looked behind me, for a brief moment, and wondered if anyone in there was watching us the way I had been watching them. Would they tell? Or would they want to join us?

We walked through the cold forest, the bitter chill sat at ground level all the time, the evergreens too plush to ever let it out, until we found the stone wall surrounding campus. There were rumors that Dr. Felix Chastain had the perimeter of the grounds blessed by a pastor prior to breaking ground on the first building. While the pastor was saying his prayers, Dr. Felix Chastain followed him, dropping stones on his path to lay the groundwork for a wall to separate the blessed land from the unblessed land; to make sure everyone knew that on this side of the wall lived purity, and on the other side of the wall was more temptation than we'd ever know.

We were fifteen minutes into the forest before we started hearing noises, the whispers of laughter, the crackle of crisp fall leaves under boots.

"Hello?" Ruthie said, cautiously, though we hadn't broken

any rules yet. We had two hours before we were technically doing anything wrong. Right now we were just two students going for a walk. If we found anyone other than Catherine, Annie, and their guy friends, that's exactly what we'd say.

"You made it." The guy who invited us, Timothy, we learned shortly after, approached, his face a soft gold from the light on the end of the joint in his mouth. He seemed surprised, but happy to see us; to see me.

"Thanks for the invite," Ruthie said. I was too busy looking at Timothy's face, distracted by the way the fire made his eyes glow.

A few steps farther into the woods and a small patch of clearing opened up before us, just large enough for a green-and-gold picnic blanket, stolen (or so Timothy would claim) from Covenant's bookstore. I could understand why they came here. The trees were so thick around us, there was no way we'd ever be found or heard. It was the perfect spot.

Catherine, Annie, and their two other friends, Nicholas and Andrew, looked up when we arrived and smiled, though they also seemed surprised to see us, as if we hadn't been given an invitation. Maybe Timothy hadn't consulted with the rest of the group first.

The whole thing was trippy, a term I learned from *Cosmo* that felt appropriate for me to use here, as everyone was getting high. Everything about the way they looked directly contradicted the behavior I was witnessing. The joint hung limply from Annie's lips as she fixed her hair, a prim dark bob held back by a white floral headband I'd seen people attach a veil to during mass. Catherine was wearing a long paisley dress that looked like she might have sewn it herself while pressing her beer can's ring back and forth and reciting the alphabet, a game to find her next potential hookup. Nicholas's moppy blond hair and broad shoulders only seemed to highlight the two-inch golden cross hanging from his neck as he laughed about that time he hooked up with a girl who wore braces—"nearly ripped my tongue right off." And Andrew had his balding head parted in what one might already consider a comb-over, while he created a pyramid with all the empty beer cans.

They were the last people I'd expect to see here, which I guess was how they got away with it all.

Timothy instructed us to sit down and we did, joining everyone in a circle around the school's logo on the picnic blanket, in a pejorative hot seat. He lifted the joint toward me, and I was about to take it before Ruthie nudged my ribs so hard I let out an unattractive grunt.

"What?" I asked. I'd done it before, I'd assured her on the way there. I wasn't as innocent as I'd seemed.

"We're just drinking," she said. "We have to be back by midnight. Brigid will smell the weed but not the vodka."

That was a valid point I'd forgotten about. We'd always planned to be back by curfew, so we were only breaking a certain number of rules in one night, but I hadn't considered the state we'd be in when we returned. We couldn't be so inebriated that if we ran into Brigid in the hallway she'd be able to tell.

"You should probably sit upwind, then," Catherine said, standing with Annie to switch spots with us. Once she sat down, leaning onto the tree stump behind her to get comfortable, she added, "The key to sneaking in after curfew is that you have to sneak out, too." I could see Ruthie taking a mental note for next time. "Make sure your name is on that sign-in sheet so Brigid doesn't think twice."

"Thanks," Ruthie said.

"You'll get the hang of it."

Andrew passed us two blue cans, freezing my fingertips the second I touched them. They didn't even have a cooler; the air was doing all the work. I slipped my nail under the ring and pulled. The satisfying pop seemed to echo through the forest as it gave and opened, a layer of foam slowly crawling out. I'd never had beer before. Just hard liquor.

"Any other tips?" Ruthie asked, taking her first sip.

Catherine and Annie exchanged a look, no doubt deciding how much they wanted to tell us; how many of their strongly held secrets they wanted to divulge.

"Make friends on the first floor," Annie joked, motioning toward Catherine and herself. "So you have a window you can sneak into."

"And don't dress for a college party in the movies. If you're spotted sneaking back in and you're wearing a skirt that doesn't cover your knees, no one will believe your excuse."

"And have an excuse ready. You needed some air. You work late in the dining hall. Something."

Ruthie and I listened carefully, noting each piece of advice. Use the sign-in sheet to our advantage. Make Brigid your friend, not your enemy. Even the tiniest violation gets Brigid's attention.

I watched as Ruthie's smile got wider and wider the more we engaged, the more friendly the group of us became. She knew better than to bring her camera here, especially on our first time—that's when it goes from recording memories to recording evidence—but I could tell she was taking pictures of everything with her mind. She was too happy to ever let herself forget all the details.

"The thing is," Catherine said, white smoke snaking out of her mouth with each syllable, "if you want to break their rules—or break their system entirely—you have to blend in. To break their rules, you have to become one of them."

# SEVEN

**NEW YORK TIMES** Sarah had managed to make a reservation at Le Coucou, a place famous for their bite-sized entrees and the ego boost forged when sauntering past the catastrophic line its walk-ins only policy forms outside. I guess touting the *New York Times* had multiple benefits.

The hostess, ostensibly fresh and young in her oversized wiry glasses and blown-out light brown hair, walks me through the dining room into the back where Lena sits next to a large factory window looking out onto the dimming Lafayette Street.

Lena and I had met nearly five years ago, when I first moved to New York. I was a barely functioning twenty-four-year-old who expertly maneuvered her way into a job at Brit & Ash with exactly one thing in mind: meeting people like Lena so I could become someone like Lena. It's times like this—seeing her sitting there like a painting, light grazing cheekbones so pronounced they don't need contouring, the red lip she sports every day without ever smudging, smiling slightly once she sees me—that I realize I did it. I became one of her.

"Hi, gorgeous," I say when I reach our table.

She turns toward me slowly, taking her time. "I ordered a bottle of the sauv blanc." She flicks her wrist toward one of the empty chairs across from her.

"You know I'm not drinking until the wedding," I say, lowering onto the seat. I attach my purse to the horned edge of the chair—Goyard bucket bags never touch the floor—and pull the napkin off the silver charger plate, gently covering my lap.

"You have to put on a show, hun. No one wants to write about another bride on another wedding diet."

"I guess I can nurse one glass," I say, instinctively, looking toward the back of the restaurant, where a dark hallway inevitably leads to a dimly lit bathroom. I always find the bathroom. Knowing its proximity eases me while I eat. Not that I'd ever do *that* in such a public place.

The waiter appears then, silently presenting a sweating bottle to Lena, who offers a nearly imperceptible nod of approval. All her movements are like that: nearly imperceptible, highly calculated. That's where I learned it.

"Should we wait for Sarah?" I ask, as the waiter performatively opens the bottle, twisting it this way and that in his arm like a kid showing off how much he just learned to bench.

"You're probably right," she says, a hint of disappointment in her tone, before turning to the waiter. "We have someone else coming," she explains with a squint, like she's unsure he understands. He nods and corks the bottle, gently fitting it into the silver ice bucket adjacent to our oversized two-top. Another thing I learned from Lena? Don't apologize.

After a month at Brit & Ash, I was waiting at my desk for my direct report at the time to leave; she was a mousy woman named Hilary whose hair was just as thin as the veil around her "well-intentioned" insults and she never left before 8:00 p.m., which meant I never left before 8:05. Being busy is something only New Yorkers and liberal arts students think is cool. *Busy* translates into *important* and in a city of eight million you hold tight to things that make you feel like you matter.

At seven o'clock, Lena moseyed toward my desk—she'd been there a year longer than I had, and her boss actually had a social life, unlike Hilary.

She pressed her hands on the edge of my desk, leaning forward and looking both ways like she was about to spill a secret worthy of DeuxMoi. "Want to get a drink?" she asked, shimmying her shoulders at the offer. "There's a new bar opening in SoHo. A friend from college is the mixologist and there's a soft opening tonight." I glanced behind me at Hilary, slumped behind her computer, so close to it her pores were reflecting the blue light.

Lena followed my gaze and let out a disgruntled huff. "It's not your fault she hates her husband and never wants to go home. *You* shouldn't have to suffer."

She was right. And she was right about a lot of other things as we slowly became friends. Lena isn't easily impressed, but I knew if I kneaded her enough she'd become exactly what I needed her to be. And she was.

Lena adjusts herself at the wooden table, sitting up straighter than she already had been. "Before she gets here," Lena begins, drifting forward, the thin white silk of her top hugging her braless breasts. "I have a question."

I knew she was going to ask. I feign obliviousness well, all those years of practice really paid off, and I smile at her kindly, openly, like a friend you can *say anything to*. She started dating her girlfriend—I'm sure they're using that word already—three months ago. I knew when we received her RSVP, which had been addressed to Ms. Lena Cunningham and Guest and returned as Ms. Lena Cunningham, that she was going to eventually find a woman to bring. It was a waste of everyone's time to pretend Lena, *this Lena*, wasn't going to show up with a model on her arm to my conservative fiancé's family's home, wearing something my future mother-in-law would comment looked "modern," which to her meant "tawdry" or "wanton" or just plain "ugly."

"I'd like to bring my girlfriend to the wedding," she says. In typical Lena fashion, it wasn't so much a question as a statement, one for me to approve or disapprove but, by the way she was looking at me—eyes wide, half her mouth lifted in a smile—there is no way I can say no, and she knows it. "Shocking, I know," she continues. "I, too, didn't think I was a bring-the-girlfriend-to-a-wedding kind of person. But this girl tells me I am, so I believe her."

"What's her name?" I ask, flattening the napkin on my lap.

"Jess." The word drifts through her lips, lingering on the slithery sss like some ASMR podcast. The bartender from my engagement party. Perfect.

"Of course she can come." I brush off her nonexistent trepidation with a smile and a flick of my hand. "I already like her."

"Do you need to check with G?" she asks. I swallow my hatred for when she calls him that. She has this strange obsession with him—every glance in his direction more loving than anything I could offer. It's platonic, almost sisterly, but it annoys me nonetheless. It's a stab to the rib cage with a blunt knife, a subtle reminder that she knew him first.

"Nope," I offer, flatly, without explanation. Taking back my upper hand.

To our right, the hostess appears, pointing a petite woman toward our table.

I brush Lena off and take a deep breath, remembering my story—*our* story—and how much Sarah is going to swoon when she hears it, like a little girl watching a rom-com. Because that's what Graham and I are: a real-life *You've Got Mail*.

"Sarah?" I stand and Lena follows as she approaches with

an outstretched hand. I immediately notice her skin, poreless and wrinkle-less. If only one-hundred-and-twenty-five-
dollar creams could do to me what her genetics have done
for free. She looks even more petite up close, drowning in
an oversized gray plaid blazer and skinny jeans. Shouldn't she
know that no one wears skinny jeans anymore? Doesn't she
read her own style section?

"Ms. Bennet." She clears her throat as she sits, like she's a
little out of breath. "Or should I say Mrs. Walker?"

I offer a tight-lipped smile. You'd think progressive women
like her would stop assuming progressive women like me will
automatically take our husbands' last names. I'd had this fight
with Graham too many times to count but, of course, I won—
"my body my choice" and all that. He didn't have much of a
leg to stand on. And, practically speaking, it eliminates a lot
of unnecessary paperwork.

"She's keeping her name," Lena says, defensive, spreading
her feminist tail feathers like a peacock during courting season.
"I'm Lena. Maid of honor," she adds, a title she's given herself
without any of the traditionally associated work. They shake
and sit across from each other, Lena smiling kindly but ready
to pounce like a boxer the second the bell goes off.

"Thank you so much for meeting me," Sarah says. "I know
this is very last minute. I'm sorry your fiancé couldn't make it."

"He's sorry, too." I frown, shaking my head. "I'll make
sure you can catch him on the big day and he can answer any
lingering questions."

She digs into a tote bag larger than her torso. "That would
be great, thank you," she says, distracted, pulling it onto her
lap, sifting through it until—"Eureka!"—she pulls out a black
Moleskine notebook, the pages wrinkled and browned from
months of coffee spills. She drops the tote onto the floor without a second glance to make sure nothing fell out.

The waiter appears next to the patient bottle. "Ready?" he asks Lena, who nods toward her glass, shoving off any dramatic tasting.

"We ordered a bottle of wine," I explain. "A little prewedding thing. I hope you'll join us."

Sarah's eyes go wide, like an eighteen-year-old getting into a club for the first time with her brand-new fake ID. "I'd love a glass, thank you!"

Once the long-stemmed goblets are filled, and Lena forces a cheer "to Vows," which is embarrassing but just corny enough to get a chuckle from Sarah, she opens her notebook, uncaps a pen, and begins.

"First, I'll say—" Sarah sits stick-straight in her chair, as if a nun slipped a ruler down the back of her wrinkled white button-down. "You're impossible to google, Eliza Bennet."

"I know," I say, shrugging, letting out a short laugh, as if it was so charming of her to bring up. As if it wasn't intentional. Or, at least, an invaluable coincidence. "What can I say—I moonlight as an eighteenth-century millennial."

Sarah's head falls back as she lets out the longest and most unattractive guffaw I've ever heard. Something that would come out of a bird as it was being shot down. Lena and I share a look: Did *that* really come out of *her*?

"I love that," she says, once she catches her breath. "So funny." She scribbles in her notebook, then puts the cap of the pen in her mouth, biting down. "Let's start with how you met," she says, teeming with excitement. She either really loves her job or is incredible at faking it.

"I can answer this one," Lena cuts in. "I introduced them."

"Oh, I *love* that."

Lena takes a long sip, expertly drawing out Sarah's anticipation. She knows how to keep the attention on her when she's not the main event. I play along with this game every time Lena brings it up. Yes, Graham and Lena went to Yale together—though they had different classes and different social groups. Yes, on that day she shimmied to my desk to ask me to get drinks, Graham was also at the bar, downing bourbon as if it weren't a Tuesday. And yes, she did say, "Oh shit, is that Graham Walker," so loud when she spotted him that we had no choice but to go over. But I would hardly call it an introduction, in the ordinary sense of the word. It was more that we were all in the right place at the right time.

"Well, isn't that an adorable story," Sarah gushes, scribbling the last of Lena's exposition into her notebook. "And now you're the MOH. I *love* that."

Sarah loves a lot of things.

"Did you know right away?" Sarah asks me. Lena visibly slouches now that she's no longer the focus of the conversation.

"I did," I say, slowly, pretending to think about it, as if I hadn't had this answer prepared since the day I pressed Submit on the application. "The second I saw him, I knew he was the person I'd been looking for."

Sarah puts her hand over her heart and then writes my line down in her notebook, underlines it, and then surrounds it with a bold box. That's what you call being quotable.

"I *love* that," she says, managing to emphasize each syllable equally. "Now, he went to Yale and you went to—"

"—Brown," I finish. The Ivy Package, essential to any *New York Times* Vows coverage. You couldn't be a future Walker if you didn't go to the kind of school you don't have to explain.

She nods, scribbling little check marks along different lines in her notebook. "Yes, of course. We've got all that in with our fact-checkers now." I swallow the sip of sauv blanc sitting over my tongue with nary a flinch and set my glass back on the table. The fact-checkers will come back empty-handed, all their i's dotted, their t's crossed. *Someone* named Elizabeth Bennet went there. *Someone.*

"And you work at—actually…" Her pen hovers over a question mark at the bottom of the page, like she is tempting herself, until it lands with a thud. "Before we get into that…can you give me some details about your parents? All you included in the application were their names."

I reach for the stem of my wineglass before stopping myself, letting my fingers linger on its base, twirl the sip or two left. It would be in bad taste to take a sip after this question; it might reveal my hand.

"They passed away. A long time ago."

I can feel Lena sitting between us and looking at me, but I stare straight at Sarah. She is nodding, uncomfortable. She clearly needs more information, but I don't give her anything. Any questions she wanted answered, she needed to ask. I am no fool to the old journalistic tactic of leaving long silences for your interviewee to fill with nonsense they'll eventually regret. I'm not afraid of silence.

"What did they do for a living?" she asks.

"I don't know," I say, slowly. Letting her think about it before continuing. "I never really knew them, and the family I lived with after—my aunt, until she got sick, blood cancer—she never really talked about them. I was on my own pretty early on." Being rich, with non-divorced parents of an acceptable age, and growing up in SoHo when it was still teeming with artists and bohemian crafters—Lena's past was relatively self-explanatory. You stopped thinking about it the second she was finished telling it. It left nothing to the imagination. Mine, however, was interesting. How did an orphan get *here*? How is an orphan marrying a Walker?

"What does this have to do with their relationship?" Lena asks, ever the overzealous lion protecting her humble cub.

"Shouldn't you be asking about, like, when they moved in together, or how he popped the question or something? Let's move on."

Sarah crosses out a line in her notebook. "I guess we can leave your parents out of it."

I look between the two of them. "Can you tell she works in PR?" I quip to Sarah, laughing, cutting the tension that Lena doesn't notice she inherently creates. Sarah's grateful for the interruption and now I'm posed as the good guy. I'm on *her* side, I *want* to divulge everything, but Lena is so *rudely* interrupting. And how sweet is a girl with an overprotective best friend.

The waiter returns and wordlessly, he picks up the bottle, offers it around, and leaves. Lena must have told him when she arrived that we weren't ordering food and not to bother asking. She knows I wouldn't eat anything—especially after *two* glasses of wine. Though I'd never finish this one. A symptom of not eating is that you get drunk very quickly.

"Now, this is a silly question, but I always ask because I love the answers..." She pauses, presumably giving me time to find this charming. I smile. I cock my head. I lean forward. I do all the things I've learned to do when I'm forced to remain pleasant. "What's your favorite thing about your fiancé— about Graham," she corrects, personalizing it for me. A fool's attempt to claim friendship where there is none.

"He's incredibly generous," I say, pretending to think, though I already had a good answer teed up. "And kind. It was very important to me that he was kind." That word has become more and more empty the more celebrities talk about it in their prematurely published memoirs and Instagram stories. The more the word is used to describe a state of being rather than a series of actions. You can no longer become kind by feeding the homeless or tutoring children or, even, hiding your temper. You're either kind or you're not. You're born with it or you die without it. I wait a beat before continuing, for emphasis. Then, with my gentlest smile, "He's my best friend."

The key to any interrogation like this is not what you say, but what you *don't*. I might not be fooled by a journalist's silence trick, but the jig works both ways. People love to fill in the holes I leave out, and I let them. They can think whatever they want. They couldn't possibly begin to guess the truth.

# EIGHT

---

RUTHIE AND I were on our knees, our hands clasped together, heads bowed, staring down at the gray carpet of the
dorm's hallway, and following Brigid in prayer.

"While we don't dismiss their actions as they each inexcus-
ably violated the Covenant Code," Brigid continued, "we do

pray, oh Lord, for your forgiveness. That you forgive them, and all of us, for the part we played. As a faithful community made in your name, we stand together in sin. We all must learn and reflect on our own actions, as all our friends do with theirs."

As she passed us in her methodical pace up and down the short hallway, continuing to spew prayers, bloated with buzzwords and every synonym for God you could possibly imagine, I felt Ruthie's elbow jab into my ribs. I opened one eye and looked at her. "I get that we're supposed to pray for each other's souls or whatever—" her mouth moved but no sound came out "—but don't they also teach forgiveness? My knees hurt. It's been a month. We're *still* doing this?"

My knees were beginning to hurt, too—we'd been down there on the thin, hard carpet surrounded by Jesus and unidentifiable brown stains older than me for over thirty minutes—but I wasn't sure I was allowed to complain. If I did, I could picture Brigid bending down to my level greeting me with a placating smile and a power grab, and saying, *Jesus was whipped while carrying the cross for our sins. The least we can do is bruise our knees while praying for some of our sinner dormmates. Don't you agree?*

I wouldn't respond—even in my imagined scenario, Ruthie is braver than I am, and would offer some side-eyed comment about how it was unfair that we were constantly expected to compare ourselves and our behavior to the savior of mankind.

A month ago, after Ruthie and I attended our first pseudo party in the woods, we had barely fallen asleep when we were awoken by the most startling scream. The kind of scream that sent goose bumps up my arms before I even realized what it was. Where my instinct was to jump out of bed and make sure our door was locked, Ruthie's was to run into the hall and investigate herself.

"Something exciting is happening," she said, a mischievous smile forming on her face.

I grabbed her arm as she turned toward the door. "We're too drunk for this. This is a bad idea. Being in public is a *bad idea*."

"But what if it's Catherine or Annie? What if they *need* us?" She was out the door before I could tell her that they did not need us. They'd been doing fine on their own for the last three months of school. We were the ones who needed them.

Reluctantly, I followed Ruthie and the commotion down the hall. The yelling stopped as we took the stairs two at a time to the lobby, where we were met by easily a dozen other students in pajamas and with bed head, equally as excited as Ruthie to catch something, whatever it was, in the act.

We moved as a pack toward the West Wing until we opened the fire door and saw Brigid outside room 103, drumming her fists on the metal door like a toddler in a time-out. "Open up! Open up now!" she repeated, her high-pitched voice voiding some of the innate intimidation of an RA banging on your door after midnight. So did her pink smiley face slippers and the white robe over her shoulders with *Ritz-Carlton George-town* embroidered on the chest.

If Brigid noticed her audience, she didn't care because she continued banging on the door until it was opened so quickly by Lucy McCarthy that Lucy almost got two fists straight to the face. One specifically to the perfect button nose that Ruthie was convinced Lucy received as a gift for her sixteenth birthday.

"What's going on?" Lucy said, standing in the center of the open door, her arms folded against her chest. She was wearing glasses and a matching light blue pajama set that made her seem old.

Brigid stepped back, cleared her throat. "I heard noises," she said. "A lot of them."

Lucy shrugged. "Okay…"

"Where's Isabelle?" Brigid asked, referring to Lucy's room-mate, a forty-violation demagogue.

"I'm right here." Isabelle, in a knee-length dress reminiscent of ones my mother wore, appeared behind Lucy, all the edge in her voice of an angry teenager.

From the very corner of the hallway, I could tell they looked disheveled, but not just-out-of-bed disheveled, like the rest of us were. It seemed fake.

The three of them stared at each other like bulls, each waiting for the opportune time to attack. That's when the microwave went off deep in their room with a cavernous ding that seemed to ping-pong through the doorway and around the entire hallway in slow motion. There was a moment of silence, a moment of thinking perhaps Brigid hadn't heard it, maybe we'd *all* imagined it, maybe it hadn't happened. But then, quickly, Brigid burst through the door, pushing past Lucy and Isabelle, the lights inside blinked on, and we all inched farther into the hallway to get a better view. Inside, standing with their backs against the wall like cornered deer, were two junior boys wearing lumberjack Halloween costumes.

"What's going on?" I heard a whisper.

When I looked beside me, Catherine and Annie had joined the crowd, their hair a perfected fake bed head (something they should teach to the rest of us).

"They were coming back from the post–Hell House party," Ruthie said.

Catherine giggled. "Sucks to be stupid," she whispered, before offering me a wink and turning back toward her room, Annie following silently behind her. It took every ounce of self-control I had not to burst out laughing. Because the four of us had done much worse than these people that night. And we weren't even close to getting caught.

As soon as Brigid registered we were there, she shooed us away, telling us to get to bed or else we'd all be written up for whatever Lucy and Isabelle were getting. She did not need to say anything more.

During our next Violation Rotation, Ruthie and I saved the West Wing for last, like the most favorite part of a meal you want to cherish on your tongue. When we finally stopped outside 103, there were two postcards taped to the door frame and I could feel Ruthie's excitement as she bounced down the hall, clawing at them until she had them both in her hands.

One-hundred-and-sixty points. Ruthie nearly fell to the floor.

"This could have been us," I said. Just the thought of it made me throw up a little in my mouth.

"Absolutely *not*," she said. "We're not stupid."

Two weeks later Lucy and Isabelle were expelled and everyone in our entire dorm woke up to one-point violations on our boards. They said it was for association, whatever that means, but I took it as yet another warning. Your actions are important, but so are the actions of everyone around you. If your community messes up, everyone pays.

We've started our mornings praying for them ever since.

"Now bow your heads and close your eyes," Brigid reminded us, still pacing the hallway in front of us. "Let us say the Lord's Prayer for our friends and their sins…"

Everyone began whispering the Our Father, to themselves or to God or to both, the accumulated hush sounding like a waterfall.

For the past week I'd been tacking on an extra Our Father to the end of our session especially for Ruthie and me. For us and our sins.

Because Ruthie and I had acquired a lot of sins.

We had slipped right into our foresty friend group as if we were supposed to be there all along. If you saw the seven of us—in the dining hall, walking to class, sneaking drinks and smokes in the forest—you'd never know Ruthie and I were late additions. We blended right in.

Catherine was right. That was the key to not getting caught. If you play the game—study your lines, look the part—they have no reason not to trust you.

Ruthie and I stopped wearing makeup. We stopped straightening our hair and wearing jewelry, except for my mother's necklace, which we all agreed helped sell our new personalities. I stopped borrowing her clothes—though they were the only ones that fit me at this point—and we *both* started digging through my closet every morning while we were getting ready for the day. Long skirts, tights, sweaters—modest options that took the Covenant Code's dress code five times too seriously.

We almost exclusively ate egg whites and salads with grilled chicken so our numbers on the scale during our weekly weigh-ins stayed the same, even as we drank our weight in Bud Light and marshmallow-flavored Smirnoff a few days a week. When Ruthie and I got back from a jog together to check on our stash in the woods, Brigid greeted us in the lobby with such a massive smile on her face—"You guys work out together, too! You're just a dream roommate example!"—that we started doing it every day. Not to the woods, but around campus and through town. As we started hanging out with the group more often, these runs became my favorite part of the day—unadulterated Ruthie and me time. No distractions. No other people. *Just us.*

We were never late for curfew—or so Brigid thought. We never missed a convocation. We became the students that Covenant University puts on the cover of their brochures, the photos that they handed out to parents and perspective students. We were thin, put-together, happy, God-fearing freshmen. The epitome of the perfect student.

If you want to break their rules, you have to do it from the inside; you have to become one of them.

Friday and Saturday nights were our favorite nights to hang out in the woods, when curfew was later and we didn't need to worry about showing up to class with a hangover. Ruthie loved the drinking and the secrets; I cherished our time after: lying in my bed, going over every single thing that happened the night before. The instant replay of every conversation, every look, every drink. The laughter. The fun.

The whole thing was made tremendously easier after daylight savings time. There's a lot of drinking you can do before curfew when the darkness overcomes campus at 4:00 p.m. It got colder, sure, but that only made us more innovative— bringing blankets from our dorm to warm the forest floor; wearing layers like we were going on a skiing expedition. Occasionally we'd sprint to the edge of the forest and back, hold little races with each other to get our blood circulating, to feel the bitter air biting our lungs, the warm sweat snaking down our frosty backs. I always won.

Andrew even "borrowed" a few Styrofoam coolers from his job in the athletics building and spray-painted them black so we could keep them hidden against the stone wall at our spot. Inside, we filled them with Covenant green gloves and hats and blankets. And alcohol.

If someone found the coolers, they'd never know who they belonged to. It was perfect.

Catherine was the one who procured the drinks. Every week her older brother made a trip to the liquor store for himself and his friends who were over twenty-one and lived off campus, a much tougher place for Covenant to police. Catherine would put in an order with him and, once he'd bought it, he'd wait in his parked car on the other side of the wall until Catherine would get onto someone's shoulders and pop her head over the stones. He would pass the box of beer or handle of vodka or whatever we wanted that week to her, then he'd drive off like nothing happened. I'd never watched it happen, but the thought of it made me laugh. I imagined it looked like someone trying to sneak contraband into a prison.

Ruthie and I had done it. We were having experiences. And we weren't getting caught.

On top of that, no one was dying. None of us dropped dead after taking a sip of vodka. None of us got so high we fell to the floor foaming at the mouth. None of us experienced anything that I'd been told I would my entire childhood. Life went on as usual. But it was way more fun.

As the weeks went on, Timothy and I started getting closer. He was a freshman, too, but he acted much older—he was generally calm and unconcerned, like he was so confident in his decisions he never needed to second-guess anything. He was studying criminal justice—a major you'd think only the RAs and narcs on campus would lean into. Brigid was being primely trained for the job.

I was ever impressed by him and the more I watched him move and listened to him talk, the less my mind focused on what he was doing and saying and the more I thought about what it would be like to be with him.

While he stood in front of the group, acting out a scene from a movie called *My Cousin Vinny* that I'd never watched, I thought about eating pizza with him on a date, laughing at a joke he made about one of his professors. While he pulled my hood playfully over my head and squeezed my shoulders after I said I was cold enough to go home, I imagined going to the homecoming dance with him, then sneaking out here and dancing together, our bodies touching in ways they couldn't in the Covenant ballroom.

While he sat next to me and our knees grazed as he reached

to the cooler to get me another drink, I thought about him in my bed, on top of me, asking me if I was sure I wanted to do this, he'd be gentle, he'd go slow.

I started blushing when I was with him, not because of anything he'd done in real life, but because of the things I'd imagined we'd done together. Things that sent a flash of heat to my cheeks, my chest, in between my legs. An entire life I created in my head with a boy I knew little more about than that he liked to snack on crunchy pickles and, like Ruthie, his parents had sent him to Covenant as penance.

"Tim definitely likes you," Ruthie confirmed one night after she caught me blushing about him. "What's the most you've done...with a boy," she asked.

I thought about what I wanted to admit. I didn't keep secrets from Ruthie, but the story of my first kiss felt like something to strategically leave out. Though was saying I'd done nothing even worse?

"What have *you* done?" I shrugged and turned the question back on her.

I was surprised it took us this long to talk about it. Ruthie told stories—kissing her older brother's friends, skinny-dipping in Lake Erie, making out with a friend named John in her parents' basement. Her retellings seemed anecdotal—lacking substance or feeling or any kind of reflection. But I'd never asked her for more details because I didn't want her to ask me for *any*. Before reading *Cosmo* and *Seventeen*, I had gone my entire life without saying the word *sex* out loud. It was never talked about. And never talking about something—that kind of extreme restriction—just makes you want to binge once you finally have it.

Maybe that's why Ruthie was so obsessed with losing her virginity. Maybe she was less experienced than she made it seem.

"Just hookups," she finally answered, vague. I got the sense she wanted to avoid the question as much as I did. "I've told you about them. First base, second base. A little third. But that was high school. College is more fun." A smile started creeping up her face, like she was trying to hide it. "You should get Tim away from the group. Go for a walk with him or something. See what happens." She paused, then added, "I'm one night away from a home run. Maybe you'll catch up to me."

I didn't know what qualified for each base in her metaphor, but I got the general idea, and I knew I was probably only on first. But I also knew what a home run was. If that's what she wanted, that's what I wanted, too.

Like a small battalion, we changed our spot in the forest every few days; dragging the cooler and drinks deeper into the trees, or farther down the stone wall. Though we were sure we'd never be discovered, we took all the necessary precautions regardless—loosening up any packed dirt formed from sitting for too long, covering our tracks. If we were going to be found out, it wasn't going to be because we were stupid.

When it was Timothy's turn to find us a new spot, I offered to go with him. It was getting colder and darker, and the combined directional knowledge of two people gave us a better chance at remembering where we put everything, so we didn't have another mishap like last week. Ruthie had been in charge and immediately forgot where she set things up after she exited the forest. It took us forty-five minutes to figure it out.

"You've really gotten the hang of the misdemeanor life," Timothy said as we trudged through the trees, a heavy cooler balancing over his left shoulder like a boom box in the movies. I had two handles of Smirnoff clanking in my backpack like a chorus.

"And you've gotten the hang of Covenant campus life," I responded, indicating his church-issued khakis.

He shrugged. "They're not as bad as they look."

"Well, they don't look great," I joked, completely lying and barely hiding it. At that point he could be wearing full pastor robes and I'd still be picturing him naked any chance I got.

"So you grew up in this world?" he asked. "What was that like?"

I could imagine the confusion and judgment on his face as I told him about my parents: my mother, the ever-obeying wife; and my father, the domineering wannabe preacher. No one ever understands, especially not someone who grew up more closely tied to society. In the same way I don't understand how Ruthie grew up having so much freedom.

"It was fine," I said. "Like this but with worse punishments."

He nodded and could probably tell by my tone that I didn't want to discuss it more. "Do you wish it had been different?"

I used to. I used to spend hours at night flipping through those magazines wishing I lived in the same world as those women, that I had the same knowledge and resources. That I had different parents and lived in New York City and had friends I met in school. And once my eyes got heavy and I slipped the magazine back under my mattress, I'd say a little prayer that maybe when I woke up, I could be in a different bed, in a different home, in a different life. But it never happened. So I had to find another way out.

"Sometimes," I said, uninterested in getting into the details; in telling him yes, I'd change everything about my childhood if I could. But no one wants to hear that. "Do you?" I could sense him slowing down so I met his pace, too. "Do you ever regret the stuff you did that got you here?"

He thought about it for a long time. "I don't have regrets," he said finally, something I recognized even at the time as a lofty thing for an eighteen-year-old to announce. "If it was the right thing to do in the moment, it was the right thing. So you take that in stride and move on."

This place was all about regrets—wielding them and antic-ipating them. You'll regret not saving yourself for your hus-band, you'll regret having a drink, you'll regret not obeying your parents and elders. You'll regret eating that pizza, that ice cream cone, that bowl of cereal.

But do you really? I haven't so far. I've enjoyed it all.

Maybe I don't have regrets either.

Timothy stopped walking and the cooler dropped with an echoey thud to the hard forest floor. "This is perfect," he said as we stood in a clearing small enough to fit only our blanket, surrounded on two sides by a thick brush.

He bent down and fluffed the branches, lifting one and scooting the cooler underneath until it disappeared.

When he stood up, he was next to me, our faces only a few inches away. When he leaned toward me, I did the same. When he kissed me, I was grateful I'd had some practice. When he pushed me back against a tree, my lips occupied, my mind racing, my back curdling in pain, I realized I liked it.

"I don't regret that either," he said a moment after he pulled away, half his mouth curled up in a satisfied smile. Before I could tell him I agreed, he was looking around, memorizing this spot so that he could lead everyone back to it later that night.

Then, just to be safe, he pulled a pocketknife from his pants, and carved a cross at eye level in the tree next to the cooler. It's never helped us find our spots—tree carvings blend into the darkness—but it's a fun tradition anyway.

And in a place like this, God forbid you break a long-held tradition.

# NINE

IT WAS ONLY 11:00 p.m., but I returned home buzzed in that way that makes me feel like I'm floating. I'm numb and gravitating an inch above the ground, trusting that my body is moving forward because I'm not consciously telling it to. The kind of buzz I haven't felt in a while. The kind that makes details blurry but un-worrisome in the morning—I'll question how long I waited for the cab, but not whether I lost my phone in the car's back seat. I never get too drunk anymore. Getting too drunk leads to slipups. It leads to saying things you don't want to say.

The cab smells like marijuana, but it's too late for me to get out. I'd already closed the door and we'd started due north before I took a deep enough breath to notice. I have a visceral reaction to that smell now, my cheeks blushing with second-hand embarrassment at my first memory of it.

When I was seventeen, I convinced my mother to drive three towns over to a thrift store. I'd made some money that month de-ticking my neighbor's horse and I told her I wanted a new dress. She dropped me off and gave me twenty minutes to browse while she picked up some groceries. I wouldn't have been surprised if she set a timer.

I stood on the sidewalk outside of Lady Luck Thrifts, watching our white van pull down the street, eventually turning right and disappearing toward the busier boulevard. I waited and stared down the empty road for at least a minute, in case she did a U-turn or decided to come back. But she didn't. I was good to go.

Instead of climbing the narrow staircase to the store, I beelined to the alley beside it, snaking through the small town's backwater passages like a hungry criminal, until I reached the parking lot behind the Sunoco gas station. I stood beside a black dumpster that smelled like onions and urine and watched the cars enter and exit, making sure my mother's wasn't one of them, and that the red Honda mentioned in the Craigslist ad that had been parked three spots from the street wasn't moving.

Craigslist. That's where I'd found it. It turns out it was a lot easier than I'd anticipated to hide my father's cell phone and use it to go on the internet when he was dealing with a "mysterious hole" in the chicken coup. I wasn't sure what I was looking for when I first typed Craigslist into the search bar—just that I'd read something about it in *Seventeen*—but my curiosity took over, clicking this link and that until I found myself in the sex section—people asking for it, people offering it, people writing detailed accounts of their wildest fantasies to see if anyone else's matched.

I knocked on the driver's side of the red Honda and when the darkly tinted window rolled down, a scrawny boy looked up at me, confused, from behind the wheel. Red acne marks cratered his uneven cheeks and his attempt at a Justin Bieber side-swept flick-fringe covered his eyes like Cousin Itt.

"What—" His voice cracked and he cleared his throat, his

cheeks reddening even more than they already were. "What?" he repeated, this time without the lingering hints of puberty.

"I'm here, um…" I wasn't about to say the word out loud; even just standing there next to the car was risky. I was more afraid of my mother finding out than of any potential dangers involved in meeting a stranger next to his running car, in an unfamiliar town, lying to my parents about my whereabouts. Obviously, the Craigslist Killer news coverage hadn't hit *Seventeen* or *Cosmo* yet. "I think you're meeting me?"

"Right," he said, leaning toward the passenger's door and pulling the knob to unlock it. "Get in."

The car smelled like skunk, I thought, as I did what he asked and sunk into the seat. Like a skunk had attacked the gray cloth interior and made a home under the hood.

"You swear you've never done this before?" he asked. I nodded.

The ad was looking for a virgin French kiss. I wasn't sure if it was to French kiss a virgin or to French kiss someone who's never French kissed before, but either way I qualified. The only thing I knew about French kissing was that it involved tongue. How? I wasn't quite sure.

"You have to pay me first."

He pulled the cash out of his jacket pocket, a wad of singles worthy of a bunny at Chicago's Playboy Club and handed it over. "It's all there, I already counted. Sixty bucks."

I had no reason to trust him, but I stuffed the money into my purse without looking at it twice. The Covenant University application fee I knew my parents would never pay. Plus tip.

"So what do we do now—" Before I could finish the question, he grabbed my face and pulled it against his so hard our noses banged together.

We started kissing the way I'd practiced—my lips moving against my hand or against my pillow at night, repeating over and over the motions my body seemed to know how to do instinctually. In real life, it was wet and I could feel the hard acne lining his upper lip as it went in and out, up and down. Then he shoved his tongue into my mouth and just let it sit there, like a dead fish. Every time I opened my eyes, I'd see his, squished closed so tight it was like he was in pain. I couldn't tell how long we'd been doing this, but I got bored quickly. I started thinking about the rest of my day; wondering if this thrift store had anything more interesting than mine; thinking about what my mother was picking up from the grocery store.

When he pulled away, he was out of breath and his face was so flushed it looked like he'd been sitting on a beach in the sun for hours. He stared at me, shocked, seemingly satisfied, catching his breath, then he looked down and I followed his gaze into his lap. In a frantic frenzy, he unzipped his cargo shorts and his penis sprung out, standing up red and veiny. I'd never seen a penis before and I just sat there as he began to touch it, moaning increasingly until he finally let out a squeal and came all over the steering wheel.

The smell of marijuana also reminds me of college, of the woods, of us, but I shove that thought away before I can consider it for too long.

"Can I open a window?" I ask the cab driver, who waves his hand with permission. He's talking into his AirPods in Arabic, not paying me much attention.

I roll the window down just as we climb the ramp onto the FDR. As we speed up, my senses are overwhelmed by the wind and the white noise outside. I'm a dog, my head sticking out the window, my cheeks lapping against my gums, my blowout flattening and knotting with each passing car. But I don't care.

I miss that girl sometimes. The one from Before.

The one who didn't know what was to come.

Danny had the building's thick wooden door unlocked and

opened before I'd exited the yellow taxi. "Eliza, good evening," he says with a knowing smile as I saunter past him, offering an uncharacteristically giggly hello in return. Even he seems thrown off by it and as I enter the elevator, I'm sure he's watching me on the security cameras, making sure I get off on the correct floor and open the correct apartment. Drunk people are a disaster for doormen, I imagine.

Our hallway is dark when I enter, which is unusual for Graham. Some people have husbands who leave the kitchen cabinets open and the toilet seat up. I have a fiancé who can't remember to turn off a light to save his goddamned life.

"Hello?" I call out, flicking the heels off my feet, unaware and indifferent as to where in the hallway they land. "Graham?" The first few barefoot steps are always uncomfortable, as your feet widen and return to their proper shape.

Silence.

I'd be surprised if he didn't wait up for me. I offered him sex for God's sake. He's never fallen asleep if sex was on the table. It's not like we didn't fuck frequently—if the average couple has sex once a week, we are far beyond average. He is essentially *always* in the mood. It's never too late or too early; he's never too tired or too busy. I am the wet blanket in this relationship, pushing him away, or trading it for good behavior rendering me, essentially, a dog trainer.

I turn into the bedroom and the first thing I see is his suitcase: upright, zipped, and—after a slight kick to gauge its weight—packed. He actually did it. He packed for our wedding. Our suitcases are standing beside each other, like he and I would be in just a few days. As embarrassing as that is, I smile at the thought. It's almost happening. We're almost there. And then all this planning will be over.

Graham is in our bed, the navy weighted blanket outlining the shape of his cocooned body. He gave it to me for my birthday a few years ago, an attempt to soothe my lingering insomnia that his mother's therapist once vaguely attributed to "childhood trauma" before handing me her card and offering her six-hundred-and-fifty-dollar-an-hour services if I wanted more information about what those traumas might be. As if I wasn't acutely aware. I never called her, but Graham showed up with this blanket a few days later. "You've gone through so much, maybe this will help," he said as he dragged the fifty-pound box into the bedroom. He loves my vulnerability. He loves trying to fix me. But you can't fix a problem you don't understand.

I lower onto the edge of the padded mattress and silently slide open the bottom drawer of Graham's nightstand. Inside is a pool of pens; a box of ancient condoms; an envelope of dirty Polaroids of me that I'd given him before a month-long business trip to keep him company; and, exactly where I remembered it, a small blackcurrant Grether's Pastilles tin.

I open the box, about the size of the palm of my hand, and pick up the joint inside, my fingers like tweezers lifting it to my nose and taking a long, deep sniff.

"You're back." Graham's raspy sleep voice is barely audible over the sound of him twisting under the heavy blanket to face me. I drop the joint—and the tin—to the floor.

"I didn't expect you to be sleeping," I say, bending to plant a kiss on his prickly cheek. "It's still early."

"I must have been watching Maddow," he says, a joke he makes whenever he needs to justify a nap. I laugh out of obligation. He worms upright, resting on the plush headboard. "How was it?" he asks, meaning *did they miss me?*

"Fine." I pair my answer with a shrug for emphasis. "The writer's excited for Vermont. She's never covered a *forest wedding*. That's what she kept calling it. At least six times."

He laughs. "I mean, that's technically what it is."

"Yeah, but that makes it seem like I'll be barefoot in a flower crown. Not that I paid forty thousand dollars to have a wood floor and fairy lights installed in the middle of a clearing in the woods."

"My mother paid," he corrects with a wink. It's meant to be in jest but it feels demeaning. His family paying for the wedding is something that, they've reminded me time and time again, *is usually the responsibility of the bride's family.* As if money had any value to them. As if paying a few grand to decorate the forest and kill our planet a little wasn't just pennies. Something they write a check for without thinking twice. The rich never fail to make sure the poor feel grateful for their existence.

He reaches his arm around my waist and pulls me closer to him. I shake off my reluctance and relax into his chest, the thick blanket like a much-needed wall between us. "Now, if you look over there—" He raises his voice, like a tour guide at the Capitol, and points toward the corner of the room. "You'll see that I am, in fact, all packed." His hands find their way under my dress, moving toward the back clasp of my bra.

"Where's the suit?" I ask. His body stiffens; his hand drops to the bed. "You're kidding," I say, sitting up.

"It's in the closet," he says quickly.

"You're *kidding*!" I stifle a laugh as he repeats *it's in the closet* and I move back so I can see his whole face. "You forgot it? Seriously?"

"It doesn't count as forgetting if I remember while I'm still in the apartment." I huff playfully in response. "Plus," he adds, "what do you want me to do? I've got to keep it hanging."

I stand up and open the door to our walk-in closet, triggering the automatic lights. Our closet rivals that of Carrie Bradshaw, not only in the original series, but also in the movie where Big proposes. It was *easily* the size of my first apartment's living room. It was almost theatrically empty before I moved in—less than half the hanging space used, only a handful of drawers stuffed, like a sad metaphor for the single, unfulfilled man who occupied it. But when it's all used and organized— each hanger taken, each drawer with a purpose—it doesn't seem as pompous. It seems necessary. Even though it's not.

I return to the bedroom with Graham's suit inside the garment bag hanging limp over my arm and see he's holding the joint, looking at me with a furtive grin.

"Big plans this evening, huh," he asks as I rest the garment bag on top of his suitcase, letting it hang over the sides.

"I'll get it ironed when we get there," I say, ignoring him. "It's fine like this for now."

"Get my light." There's a subtle but familiar force in his voice that never sits well with me. Reluctantly, I pat down the jacket that was thrown onto the velvet chair in the corner of the room until I feel the hard shell of a lighter and throw it to him. "We haven't done this in a while," he says, like we're kids breaking curfew, holding the joint between his lips as he clicks to start the flame. As I open the window next to the nightstand, I realize I'm less enthusiastic about it now than when I was in the taxi ride home. Maybe I'm just less enthusiastic now that it involves him.

Graham has such a virgin-ized PG-13 interpretation of "liking it rough" that we don't even need a safe word when we fuck. It involves a pathetic kind of dirty talk and ass slapping that gets even more dull when he's high. He thinks "I fucking love you" is what I want to hear when he hits my face and throws me against the headboard. "You're so fucking hot," when he pins my arms down and sits on my chest. "You feel so good," when I'm gagging on his dick. I *masturbate* more graphically. But it's cute that that's what gets him hot. That he'll slap my cheek but the second I wince he stops, shaking.

"Oh my God, are you okay, I'm sorry, that was too much," he'll say in one long breath as if I haven't seen worse. As if I didn't want worse.

When we finish—and we *always* both finish; Graham might be tame but that doesn't mean he doesn't know what he's doing—he falls asleep within seconds in that annoying way some people can. He can sleep anytime, anywhere, and I hate him for it. I haven't been able to sleep since college. I hear every noise: every pipe draining is like metal chains dragging on tin; every soft upstairs footstep is a person waiting to pounce. Every move Graham makes—rolling over, yawning, smiling in a dream—numbs my hands and feet in fear and leaves me lying so still, barely breathing, hoping to disappear into the darkness I'm so afraid of.

After an hour, I slip out of bed. I have a routine, you see, silent and effective; a kind of muscle memory doing its job in the darkness.

I keep a clean pair of leggings, a T-shirt, and a Uniqlo thin down jacket hidden in the two-inch gap between the bottom of my dresser and our white Moroccan rug. I can slip everything on in silence—even the jacket's light crackling blends into the night. My sneakers are by the door, where Graham insists we keep all our shoes—so the outside stays outside, or so he likes to say. And within five minutes, I'm out the back door that leads to the service entrance—the one you're supposed to use for dogs and big deliveries. I duck into the stairwell, and the lights turn on with my movement. The cameras on each floor back here are fake, I learned. No one uses the stairs. Especially not anyone on the eighteenth floor.

When I push through the door onto 72nd Street, I waste no time before I begin to run. This is the kind of running I actually enjoy, even when there's no one around to admire my body. The cold air fills up my lungs, even more bitterly when the sun is on the other side of the world. My earlier buzz is gone and I can't get high off two puffs like Graham can and does. *This* is how I get high. This and The Afterward.

I have a route I follow after midnight—down Fifth Avenue to 59th Street, when the apartments begin to make way for hotels and shops and skyscraping offices, then I turn around and work my way north to 90th Street, and then south home again.

Fifth Avenue is littered with doormen in the same way Times Square is with people dressed as Elmo asking for a photo: most buildings have at least two and, on nights like tonight when it's cool and fresh, they're usually standing outside, nodding and smiling as you pass. I remember running this way when I first moved up here, and passing a doorman as he sprinted chest-first from a building to open a cab door for one of his residents. I remember thinking, *I never want to be the kind of person who would make someone else feel that way—like if you don't sprint to serve me, there are consequences.* But I have become that person. I'm marrying that person. When your fiancé grows up in that kind of environment, it rubs off on you. To his family, it's not endearing to thank a doorman for doing his job. *That's what the Christmas tip is for,* they'd say. To them, it makes you look weak; it means you're stooping to the lowest common denominator. So I am that kind of person now.

I like this route because it feels like a controlled risk. I read a Twitter thread once that posed the question to women: What would you do if men didn't exist for a day? Foolishly, I expected answers to involve wearing less makeup or more sweatpants—I know the latest feminist fad is that we dress for ourselves but, I mean, come on…we also dress for men; and in competition with other women to look better for men. No straight women ever strives to be *less* attractive to the opposite sex. Just look at what I'm wearing to run at midnight with no one around. My outfit couldn't be tighter.

But the answers I read were much more real: I'd wear whatever I wanted without the fear of being perceived as "asking for it"; I'd be able to take the subway at night alone instead of spending money on Uber; I wouldn't have to pretend to talk on the phone when taking a cab solo at night; I wouldn't be afraid to run after dark with headphones on.

That's why I liked this route, where you're never more than twenty feet from a doorman, bored and tired, with one eye on the door as he watches *The Office* on his phone. Where you can travel from security camera to security camera without even a blink of static in between. Where something could still happen—anything could happen—but at least someone would hear you scream.

On my way back south, I stopped short on the corner of 80th Street, out of breath as a memory snapped into my head, leaving as quickly as it had arrived: *The wind in my face. The small hairs tickling my forehead. Ruthie's face glowing in the light of the moon.* I pushed back the thought, stuffing it into the far crevices of my brain that I don't have time to visit right now. That's where emotions live. Because emotions create mistakes. The mistakes that keep me awake and running in the middle of the night.

I continue to 72nd Street and sneak into the twenty-four-hour CVS on the corner and walk through the store with tunnel vision until I find a family-sized bag of Cool Ranch Doritos and a box of M&M's ice cream sandwiches. I can't hide my purchases the same way I could when stores still gave out plastic bags. Now I carry them with confidence down the block, one item in each hand, hoping that anyone who sees me—not that there's anyone around—would think I'm buying it for a party or something.

I use my keycard to enter the service entrance, not wanting to bother Danny or let him glimpse The Afterward. I climb up twenty-four flights of stairs, one final requirement to allow what comes next. If, at any point, I can't do it anymore—if my thighs turn to Jell-O, or I can't catch my breath—and I take the elevator, everything I just bought goes straight down the garbage chute. I'm so desperate for this, it feels like I'm itchy from the inside out. Jamming a Dorito into my face is the only thing I can think about as I climb. It takes everything in me not to open the bag right then, offer my body some sustenance to finish the journey up, but I don't.

Finally, on the twenty-fourth floor, I sit on the top step, open the bag of Doritos, open the box of ice cream sandwiches, and wait, completely still, until the motion-sensor lights turn off and I'm allowed to start. *I can still stop*, I think, biting into a chip. *I can control myself. I don't have to do this.* I fist a few more. *I'm going to feel so shitty in the morning.* I lick the prickly spices off my forefinger. You know that feeling of waking up on your side, acutely aware of the way your stomach fat curdles and bubbles as you move? That's how I'm going to feel, the taste of Cool Ranch coating my tongue. In the morning I'll vow to never do it again. That one or two chips is just as satisfying without the self-hatred that comes hours later.

But I know that's not the truth. Nothing is as satisfying as sitting in this darkness, not tasting anything, not feeling anything, but knowing there will be no proof of what I've done. No evidence. *I can cover things up, too*, I think, licking the thick doughy ice cream sandwich remnants off my thumb and forefinger as my other hand reaches for the bottom of the chip bag—for the tiny broken-off pieces that have been sitting in the chemically made flavoring the longest. Maybe it's the self-hatred I actually crave.

When I'm finished, three ice cream sandwiches and only scraps of Doritos left, I toss everything straight down the garbage chute at the foot of our back door. We get a note about once a month reminding residents that food should only be tossed into the trash room if it's in a proper garbage bag. I am the only person who knows that note is for me.

I follow the darkness into the apartment, instinct taking over until I'm in the bathroom, the door shut and locked, the lights still off. I turn the shower on full heat, then lower onto the floor and lean over the toilet. I'm too tired to get my toothbrush so I decide a finger will do. I'm so full I could probably initiate the motion with just a gag, but a finger feels more civilized than dry heaving until something comes up. Anything to make The Afterward feel more civilized and less like a primal reaction to starvation. As the hot steam from the shower starts to build around me, I begin.

When I finish, an exhaustion washing over me like a tidal wave, I shower. The water burns my skin, turning it so red I'm afraid, for a moment, that I'll blister and it will stay that way for the wedding. But the water always needs to be this hot after. I need to come away from this night feeling something. And, at this point, I can only feel extremes.

I slip into underwear and an old sports bra and get back into bed. If Graham noticed my two-hour absence, he doesn't show it. He's curled up in a ball, his hands praying beneath his head. He looks fake, like a black-and-white photo that would come in a frame.

I roll onto my back and stare at the ceiling. Gone was the feeling of exhaustion I had just moments before, replaced by the same chest-pumping fear I had when I left. I close my eyes, trying to breathe through it but I can't, the darkness of my eyelids a welcome respite from the darkness of my bedroom.

If I weren't here, maybe I could sleep.

Because I don't think it's the darkness I'm afraid of.

It's the memories. It's him.

It's her.

# TEN

---

| Twenty-Point Violations** |
| --- |
| **(may include a $150 fine):** |

Falsification of information

Failure to properly identify oneself

Inappropriate personal contact including any state of undress with a member of the opposite sex

Creating a disruption to the community

Interacting with alcohol, including but not limited to: participation in a social gathering where alcohol is served, consumption of alcohol, and/or serving, buying, or possession of alcohol

*\*\*Appeals for 20-point violations are only accepted in limited circumstances within 12 hours of notification. Accepted appeals will be seen before the Student Court of Appeals and a trial of your peers will be had. Following a trial, all decisions—including extended fines and expulsion—are final.*

**WHEN CATHERINE'S OLDER** brother invited us to an off-campus party the weekend before Christmas break, Ruthie couldn't have said yes faster. It was like the word was living on the tip of her tongue just waiting to fly off the second "off-campus" and "boys" were mentioned in the same sentence. She had basically been preparing for this since our first night in the forest, waiting patiently until our party group decided to take the party off the blessed land to somewhere less holy but more interesting.

"This isn't a Covenant party," Catherine had said. "It's with locals. So...don't look like a Covenant student."

Ruthie took that assignment to heart and got us ready in the most scandalous thing we could think of to wear in freezing temperatures: jeans and T-shirts. Ruthie sliced her shirt midway so it seemed to float over her boobs and reveal her belly button, and she pulled mine taut around my newly formed waist and tied it in a flimsy knot that sat against my lower back like a tattoo.

"We look hot," she said, standing beside me in the mirror once we finished getting ready. She was right, we did. I'd lost fifteen pounds at that point. I'd noticed the way my collarbone poked out from my shoulder, the way my cheeks and chin were more defined. The way everyone exalted, congratulating me with every pound gone, like this was the accomplishment of a lifetime. But in my old clothes, all of that was hidden. The only time I thought about it was when my underwear started forming into clumps under my pants, too baggy for my new body, but I was too poor to buy more.

Ruthie pulled her makeup out from under her bed, from the spot it had been sitting and gathering dust ever since we started hanging out with Catherine and Annie. She seemed unconcerned that any of it was expired.

She moved all the wands and brushes and sticks over her face effortlessly, like all of this was muscle memory; she'd done it so many times she didn't need to think. Then she did the same to me—covering my face in foundation, filling my cheeks with blush, lining my eyes with mascara. When she finished, I hardly recognized myself—my eyelashes long and chunky, my eyelids sparkling in brown and gold powder, my cheeks bony and pink.

I could hardly contain my excitement, not just for the party but for Ruthie. There was something about getting ready with her like this—exchanging clothes, making each other look good, smiling side by side in the mirror hanging on the back of the door—that was perfect. Everything was perfect. This was exactly what I'd pictured college to be. And Ruthie was the perfect person to share it with.

"Here." I twisted my hands behind my neck and pulled off my necklace, my initials mocking me with their permanence. The delicate cross on the other side was like one last warning, one last reminder that I was doing this. I was leaving all this behind. "You should wear this," I told her, remembering her compliments from our first day. She took it without question, looping it around her neck and clasping it in one practiced move.

"I love it," she said, her hand lingering over her heart. "Take a picture with me."

She held her camera out, coiling her hands around to attempt to aim the lens at us. We smiled, the flash stinging my eyes for a moment.

She put the camera in her small purse. "I'm going to immortalize this party," she said, uncontained glee oozing from her every word. "Let's freaking do this."

We knew that Brigid would patrol our hallway sometime between 9:45 p.m. and 10:00 p.m., and at 9:48 we heard the heavy fire door open, then the dull shuffle of Brigid's clogs against the carpeted hallway, moving slightly faster than usual. She stopped briefly in front of a few doors, and it was unclear whether she'd heard something or she was innately suspicious. By 9:52, she was gone.

"She moves one floor at a time," Ruthie whispered to me as she peeked her head out our door to double-check we were in the clear. She waved for me to follow her and I turned off the lights and did exactly what she said. We stood against the fire door, peeking through the small glass window until we saw Brigid emerge and disappear down the West Wing staircase.

"Let's go," Ruthie whispered, quickly hopping into the elevator and pressing the down button. It's easy to forget that Brigid is still a student here. She gets weighed in, too. She was probably told by her freshman RA about the benefits of the staircase and hasn't taken the elevator since. Who knew that one note would be so beneficial.

We pushed out the dorm's front doors and into the darkness like we had so many other nights, snaking through the bushes, following our usual routine. But this time there was an excitement to it I hadn't felt since our first night in the woods. This was something new. We were leaving.

We met Catherine, Annie, Andrew, Nicholas, and Timothy in our spot in the woods. When I told Ruthie that Timothy kissed me—running from the spot to our dorm on a mission that afternoon—she didn't quite react the way I expected her to. She cheered me on and we jumped up and down, excited for me to have experienced my first real kiss, to have my first potential boyfriend, to do all the things with boyfriends that we had talked about. But it felt forced. Fake. Like she was doing it to placate me, not because she actually felt that way; not because she was actually happy. She seemed jealous. Like she wished it was her instead.

In the woods, Timothy realized that if we stood on the cooler, we could climb over the stone wall and we wouldn't have to worry about getting caught on any cameras leaving campus late. I wanted to ask how we'd get back without a cooler on the other side, but decided not to worry about it. If they weren't concerned, they probably had a plan. Who was I to question it?

Catherine's brother was on the other side of the wall waiting for us and we squeezed into his car. Nicholas with his broad shoulders sat in the front and the rest of us in the back. Timothy invited me to sit on his lap—I nearly screamed with excitement at the thought—and I could feel his penis against my leg whenever one of us shifted with a bump in the road.

When I looked over at Ruthie, sitting on Andrew's lap, she was staring out the window, her forehead resting on the glass. She was smiling, taking in the promise of the night. With her right hand, she lowered the window. The wind kicked in once we hit the two-lane highway and she closed her eyes, still smiling, dreaming. Her face glowed in the light of the moon.

Catherine's brother parked on the grassy edge of the road, at the bottom of what looked like a full mountain, claiming he didn't have the right tires to trek all the way up and back down if it was supposed to snow, like the forecast suggested. "Plus, his parents don't want all our cars in their driveway," he added.

"His parents are going to be there?" Catherine asked.

"Of course not. But they still have rules, I guess. Whatever. I don't even know them."

Ruthie turned around to face the steep trail through the forest to the house, planks of wood firmly stationed into the cold ground to create steps, their shape uneven and difficult to maneuver, not unlike the Rape Steps on campus.

This was when the first of many uneasy feelings started creeping into my chest, making me wish I'd taken a shot or two in the woods before we left. Something that would help push them away. The anxiety of the unknown sat on my rib cage, making it even more difficult to breathe than it already was as I climbed.

Ruthie sidled up to me on the trail and before I knew it, her camera flashed in our face.

"Dude, what the fuck?" Catherine's brother hissed.

Ruthie giggled like she was already drunk. "Oh, calm down!" she said, continuing up the hill.

I didn't like that I didn't know where we were. I didn't like that our ride home was gone and our access to cell phone service was spotty at best. I didn't like that I didn't have an address or a town or even the name of the owners. It was starting to feel too secluded.

Halfway up the mountain's trail, a light sparked through the trees in the distance, on and off quickly like Morse code as we moved closer.

"There it is," Ruthie whispered, like she'd just found the Holy Land. "There's the party."

I, however, didn't see the light as welcoming. I, like with most things, saw it as a warning. Like the old tin sign that my great-great-grandfather had hammered onto the foot of our property, the point at which the paved street split into our long dirt driveway.

*Trespassers Will Be Shot.*

It wasn't an empty threat.

The house was glass and wood and didn't come into view until we were already in the front yard, blending into the darkness like a Monet painting, so much that it was impossible to tell how big the house was—just that it was big, and dark, and empty. I started to get nervous that we were in the wrong place, or that this was all a trap, until the dull murmurs of talking, the faint bang of a bass, the hushed whooping of cheers, muffled and lost in the surrounding trees, began to reveal themselves.

Ruthie squeezed my arm as we walked around the side of the house, excited beyond words that we were at a college party. Any disappointment she felt over the fact that it took us this long to get invited to one was quickly washed away in anticipation.

"Tonight's the night," she whispered. "It's all going to happen." I looked over and matched my smile to hers, though I wasn't sure exactly what she was talking about.

Behind the house, in the back corner of the property, was an old red barn, the source of the muffled noise we were drawn to like moths to light. It looked like it didn't belong there—the peeling red paint, the hole-filled roof, the broken doors. It looked like my parents' except ours wasn't painted and was filled with hay, not drunk college students.

We followed Catherine's brother as he slipped through the slightly ajar door and the party opened up in front of us. A song about dancing until you die was so loud I was shocked we couldn't hear it from the street where we parked. There were kids everywhere—dancing, rubbing together like they were having sex fully clothed (a thirty-point violation, at least); standing around a folding table covered in a formation of red cups, the same in the scene from the Hell House we'd been to all those months before (twenty points); lingering around the perimeter (twenty points), drinking or smoking or laughing (thirty points). In the back corner of the barn, on a collection of old and frayed leather couches, a couple was kissing, the girl straddling on top of the boy, her legs spread over his lap (thirty points).

It was like everywhere I looked, a little button popped out of the air, tallying how many points everyone would be accumulating throughout the night. At first it freaked me out and, for the briefest moment, I contemplated leaving—if I left now, I could still make it back before curfew. I'd be safely tucked into bed and zero points would be written on the dry-erase board next to my door when I woke up in the morning.

But Ruthie would never let me. She'd been waiting for this for months. If I left this party, I'd lose her. There was no question about it. So, in that moment, I took a deep breath and decided to stay. And if I was going to stay, if there was even the slightest chance that this night would lead to hundreds of points and a one-way ticket to my parents' less-than-welcoming arms, well, it was going to be the best night of my life.

A flash brought me back as Ruthie took another photo, though this time, in the light of the barn, it didn't leave me with white circles under my eyelids. And no one else seemed to notice at all.

Two guys—possibly two of the hottest boys I have ever seen—greeted Catherine's brother with an excited "Yooo!" as we snaked through people toward the drinks. A girl I could only describe as absolutely beautiful followed them closely, a fake smile on her face as she watched the two boys' attention divert from her to us.

"See?" the taller boy said to the shorter, "I told you he'd bring girls!"

Their fangirl stopped in her tracks then, shook her head, and walked away.

They stood in front of us, looking each of us up and down in the least subtle way I'd ever seen. They weren't trying to play it off as hello, either—they were undressing us with their eyes. Little did they know how easy we'd made it for them compared to our usual outfits.

I tugged at my shirt once the taller one's eyes met mine. I suddenly felt naked, like he could see right through my T-shirt and jeans and borrowed The North Face jacket. It felt like he was bypassing the abs that had more definition than I'd ever known possible or the arms that were toned just for Jesus, and focused straight on my real body, the virgin body. The guys were like golden retrievers: happy, excited, and staring at us, waiting for us to play with them.

"Are you going to get us drinks or what?" Catherine finally said, breaking the drunken silence.

The guys turned and led us to a Gatorade cooler in the back—I recognized it from convocation. There was always a stack of them on the sidelines as Dr. Felix Chastain spoke from his makeshift altar in the center of the football field once a week.

The shorter boy pulled some red cups out of a stack and held them under the cooler's spout. He handed one to me as he began to fill another and when I looked inside, I was disgusted by a fluorescent pink liquid. I watched as everyone else received their glasses and no one questioned why our drinks looked radioactive, so I didn't either. If everyone was drinking it, it wouldn't kill us all, right?

Ruthie sidled up to me, holding her cup to mine. "This is going to be the best night of our lives," she said. "Cheers."

I didn't think. I just drank. I knew that if I let myself truly taste—or even smell—whatever shit was in this cup, I'd vomit, so I put it to my lips, opened my throat, and didn't take another breath until I banged the cup against the side of the barn, empty, (thirty points), and Ruthie flashed her camera in my distorted face.

"Well fuck me," Timothy said, staring at me and the cup in disbelief.

It was worse than any sips of moonshine I'd ever stolen from my father's stash. But I was done. And I was going to get drunk.

As my eyes moved around the room, I realized how fake the entire thing seemed. The barn was barren and seemed like the only purpose it served was for parties like these. The room was filled with normal teenagers—kids who weren't waiting until marriage, or taking creationism classes, or taught that drinking and drugs and touching a boy will send you straight to hell.

I took Ruthie's arm. "Let's dance!" I said, pulling her onto the dance floor, which was really a clearing of hay in the center of the room. We dropped our empty cups somewhere along the way so we could swing our arms in the air and move to a song I'd never heard before.

Maybe the alcohol was hitting me, or maybe this was God's radioactivity beginning to strike me down, but it felt like Ruthie and I were the only ones in the barn. I could barely hear the music anymore. I couldn't see or feel anyone around us. It was only her.

Flash.

Her brown hair, in salty untamed waves, flung around her head in every direction like a lion's mane. Her eyes were a stunning purplish blue. Like the sky during magic hour. Captivating and calming all at once. When she closed them to hear the music, her smile got so big she looked like she'd never been happier. Like this truly was the best moment of her life.

This is how I try to remember her. This is the Ruthie I wish I could have known forever.

"I love you!" Ruthie yelled, not to me, or to anyone really. Into the ether. Into the night. Into the song.

"*I* love *you*!" I yelled back to her, and her alone, wrapping my arms around her neck.

"Let's get another drink!" she said, once the song she liked faded into one she didn't. I could have danced with her forever. I could have stayed in that moment forever.

I liked the weightless feeling I got from the pink drink. The way my forehead felt detached from my body, my brain acting on its own accord.

We drank another cup.

Then we danced. Catherine and Annie popped in here or there. Then the two hot guys who invited us. Then Catherine and Annie again.

We drank another cup, and time was nonexistent. I had no clue where in the night we were. I hadn't seen Ruthie in ages. Or had I? Had we just been dancing? Or was that hours ago? How many drinks had I had? Did any of it really matter?

"Ruthie?" I knew I said it—loud, I think—but I couldn't hear the words actually come out of my mouth. I was looking around, my lips moving the way I told them to, when I felt hands around my waist.

"You look amazing."

Timothy was standing behind me, his chin pressing into my shoulder a little too hard, too much of his weight pulling me down.

I turned and before I could even fully register that it was him, his thick hands cupped my lower back and he started kissing the side of my neck. It felt, and sounded, like a suction cup; like he was pulling my skin into his mouth and then popping it back into place. His five-o'clock shadow felt scratchy but I stopped noticing when I realized his hands were moving down my body, from my back to my butt to between my legs. I could feel the heat building there, a sensation I'd only experienced to this degree once before. In a car, in a gas station parking lot, looking at a strange boy's contorted face as he orgasmed for the first time.

"Kiss me on the mouth," I told him, surprising even myself. I could feel him get hard at my demand and I pressed my knees together to get rid of the tingle, sucking in like I had to pee. He pressed against me even harder as he started to kiss me, with tongue, without tongue, his mustache scraping my upper lip. The pins and needles I'd felt in the car—the same I had when Timothy pushed me against the tree a few days ago—started to fade as we stood in the center of this barn, his hands gentle, careful, nervous even. I started to get bored and my mind started wandering to Ruthie—what was she doing? Was she seeing this? Or, even better, was she kissing someone, too?

He stepped back and took my hands in his. "Want to go outside?" he asked.

"It's pretty cold out there…" I said.

He smiled. "Come on…" He pulled me close to him and my boobs squished against his chest. He wanted to go outside to be private, I realized. To have sex. He wanted to have sex with me.

*He* wanted to have sex with *me*.

My article Rolodex started spinning on overdrive: *Ten Moves to a Guaranteed Orgasm—Blow Jobs for Dummies—Positions to Make Him—Condoms 101—*

"Do you have a, um…" I started to ask then stopped myself. Everything I'd ever learned about sex cascaded into my brain until it felt like it could explode. Condoms were bad. Sex is for procreation and condoms prevent procreation. But condoms are good. Sex is for pleasure and condoms prevent unwanted procreation. Blow jobs are bad. Sex is for procreation and blow jobs have nothing to do with procreation. But blow jobs are good. Sex is for pleasure and foreplay is important. Sex is bad. Sex before marriage is bad. Sex with someone you don't love is bad. But sex is good. Sex is so mouthwateringly good.

He took my hand and I followed him outside, unable to process all my learned contradictions. Everything I'd read belied everything I'd been taught. The only thing I knew for certain was that since I arrived at Covenant, everything I'd been told was a grave sin—something for which I'd never be forgiven—seemed small and unimportant. I'd been doing some of these things for months and I was still alive. We all were. So what was the big deal?

I was drunk, but I was sober enough to say yes. I was sober enough to take his pants off. I was sober enough to put his penis in my mouth and then take my pants off and then lean against the outside of the barn while he put it inside me. I was sober enough to know it felt bad and then it felt good.

As I pulsed back and forth, our bodies moving in tandem as he moaned and repeated "you're so hot, this is *so hot*," I became quickly uninterested and, frankly, found the whole thing boring. He was touching my boobs under my shirt, and I was looking at his face, contorted with each pulse until finally he moaned so loud, I was afraid someone was going to hear us, and he fell on top of me.

"Holy shit," he said, out of breath. "That was amazing."

"Yeah," I agreed, panicking for a moment that I'd been so bored I'd forgotten to fake an orgasm like *Cosmo* had told me to. But my panic was relieved when I realized he didn't even notice.

"Was that good? For you?" he asked.

I nodded and kissed him, more out of obligation than desire. "So good," I said, playing it off though I probably didn't need to. He wasn't thinking about me anymore.

Once he caught his breath he stood up and pulled the condom off, tossing it with a flick of the wrist. It landed in the cold dirt about an inch away from my face and I felt a wash of relief that he'd put one on in the first place. I had been too caught up in all the other unknowns to notice.

He was standing over me, pulling his pants on, staring at me with an exhausted smile. "You're seriously so hot," he said. "It's wasted in those stupid Covenant clothes."

The more he said it the less meaning it held. It was just a temperature, really. It meant almost nothing anymore.

He kissed me again, only for a second, like a thank-you, and then walked back into the party, leaving me lying there half naked, dirt covering my back. But I was grateful to be alone. To make sure I was okay. I reached for my face, felt my cheeks, hollower than usual but still there, my eyes, my nose, my ears. I felt my shoulders and elbows, my breasts and belly button and hip bones. Nothing had changed. The forest was exactly as it was before, silent and still. The barn was exactly as it was before. I was exactly as I was before. I looked down at my underwear, looped around one ankle like a Hula-Hoop. The same.

It wasn't the romantic moment I had pictured—slow and gentle with kisses and whispers asking if I was okay. It all happened so fast. And then he was gone. It seemed more function than form. We were no longer virgins. We helped each other cross that mighty uphill bridge. And now that we were on the other side, we could just have sex without worrying about whether anyone will know how inexperienced we were; whether there will be proof. I became just a girl. A non-virgin girl.

I stood up slowly and pulled on my underwear, then my jeans. Then I waited, again, to give God one more chance to strike me down. But nothing happened.

Once my head cleared, the fog of fear washing away with every moment of inaction, I remembered an article I'd read: *Why You Must Pee after Sex, from a Gyno!*

Pee after sex, I reminded myself.

I made my way around the side of the barn, to the open sliding doors, and was stopped in my tracks the second I spotted Timothy, next to the Gatorade cooler, pouring himself another drink and talking to Andrew and Nicholas. They were laughing and I could feel myself blush, my face was hot, stinging almost. Were they laughing at me?

The image of Timothy's contorted face, his eyes bulging and the vein in his neck popping out as he collapsed on top of me flashed in my mind and I immediately felt my shoulders drop from my ears. I almost started laughing, too. If anyone had been inhabited by the Devil this night, it was surely him, in that moment, with that wild face.

Then I thought about Ruthie. I needed to find her. I needed to tell her everything. Every. Single. Detail. I couldn't wait to see her face—how excited she'd be for me, how we'd laugh together about what a big deal we both made it. *It really doesn't hurt*, I'd tell her, assuaging my own concern. I did kind of feel like a different person—but in the same way you might after a milestone birthday. Nothing has actually changed, it's just another day, but I felt oddly wiser. Like I finally had an experience Ruthie didn't. I had something *she* could ask *me* about.

I turned and walked out the door through which I'd entered. I wasn't sure if Timothy had seen me, but I didn't care. First stop was the bathroom—peeing was either supposed to prevent STDs or UTIs or pregnancy, I didn't remember which, but I wanted none of those. Second stop was Ruthie.

Torches lit a long path from the barn toward what looked like some kind of pool house—a small structure beside the covered pool with a kitchen and bathroom inside. It had started snowing—the thick kind of flakes that melt the second they touch the earth—and when I reached the pool house door I leaned my head into the sky, feeling the snow land gently on my face before turning into water.

As I twisted the doorknob, I felt familiar hands wrap around me. "Where have you beeeeen!" Ruthie sang, her head bobbing around mine, her breath sour in my ear.

She pushed me into the pool house bathroom and was sitting over the toilet, pants off, before I could even lock the door. "Oh my gosh, I have so much to tell you." She tried to speak over her river of pee, but it came out as shouts. I was sure everyone within five miles could hear us.

"I hooked up with one of the guys—the one with the brown hair, the super freaking hot one. Oh my God, he's so hot. It was *so hot*." She wiped and stood and zipped and went to the sink, repeating how hot he is, how great of a kisser he is, how she wants to see him again.

I listened impatiently, not remembering whether there was a time limit for how close to sex you have to pee for it to work. Two minutes? Five minutes?

"And he's older than us. He obviously doesn't go to Covenant because he *knows what he's doing*." She turned from the sink and nodded at me for emphasis as I took my turn. Then she grimaced. "Eww don't sit on that toilet. You should always squat in public, has no one taught you that?"

"I had sex," I blurted out, trying to balance as my butt hovered an inch over the seat. "I had sex."

If you didn't know Ruthie, you wouldn't have noticed the way her face changed. It looked like she was psyched, the way she was leaning toward me, eyes wide and thrilled. "I'm sorry. What?" She had on a smile now, a big, shocked smile. But in the millisecond it took her to register what I said, she was not smiling. She was not excited. She was angry.

I finished peeing and stood up, desperately reaching for the wall next to the toilet to stay balanced. It felt like all the blood rushed to my head, and then rushed away as I pulled my pants on.

"With who—"

There was a heavy bang on the door. Then another.

"Open up!" Annie yelled.

"We know you're in there," I could hear Catherine adding a little farther away.

I didn't want to talk to them. I didn't want to tell them. I wanted to talk to Ruthie. But she clearly did not want to talk to me.

She reached for the door but I grabbed her arm—"Wait, I want to"—but she twisted the lock and the door pushed open before I could finish. Before we could have a moment. Before I could see her face again.

Catherine and Annie stood at the threshold, staring at me, heads cocked, sly smiles widening on their drunken faces, holding the camera. Flash. The zzzzzz sound as they twisted the shutter. Flash.

"You're a woman now," Catherine said.

"Tim," Annie added, a statement of fact. With one word, she was telling me she knew everything. They both did. More than I was able to tell Ruthie before they burst in.

Annie grabbed my arms and pulled me out of the pool house bathroom and into the cold. It was snowing more outside now, sticking to the dirt and the shriveled grass. As we walked back toward the barn, the ground felt cold through my sneakers, and my brain fixated on it.

Annie was going crazy with Ruthie's camera. Flashes darting into the darkness like lightning. Flash. Flash. Flash.

"You're a woman," Catherine repeated, sidling up to my other side and entangling her arm in mine. "How do you feel?"

I could feel Ruthie lagging behind and I tried to turn to look at her, to make eye contact, to tell *her* how I felt, not them. But they pulled me forward, kept me moving.

"The same, I guess," I finally said. "It all happened so fast."

I could feel myself blushing as I talked about it, not because I was thinking about the moment or the intimacy, but because I felt an embarrassment start to curdle in my chest. I'd never felt it like this before—like I wished I could go back and not tell anyone. Not have sex in the first place. Keep this as a memory for only me, like I had done with my first kiss.

Why did I do that? If I had just stopped and thought about it with a clear head—would I have still agreed? If I took a second and realized that I was about to have sex on the dirty ground outside a barn in the freezing cold at a stranger's house, would I have done it? Or would I have asked him to take it slower? To just kiss me. To be my boyfriend first.

My head felt hot and I was getting dizzy. I felt like a slut. How did that happen? An hour ago I was the most prudish virgin they'd ever met and now, just one spin around the clock later, I'd had sex? They were asking *me* how I felt?

Not okay. I didn't feel okay.

I don't know why I did it.

I wished I could go back. I wished I could blink, and we'd be back at school getting ready, or in the car, Ruthie's hair blowing in the freezing wind. I wished I never came here. I wished I never met any of them.

Back inside the barn, we walked up to the boys and Timothy handed me a drink with a wink that made me gag a little. I hated that I'd let him do that. I hated that he'd let me do it.

Flash. Flash. Flash.

I turned to Ruthie, who was standing next to me, staring into her cup like she was trying to figure out once and for all what alcohol was actually inside.

"Ruthie, can we—" When she looked up at me, she wasn't smiling anymore. She wasn't trying to seem interested or happy. She looked emotionless. Dead.

Something about that look—her stagnant eyes, her bleak expression—made me want to rip her head off. This was not right. She was my best friend. Fuck her if she's going to make me feel guilty for something I wanted to do. Something I had been more excited to talk to her about than anything else in my life.

She was the one who brought me to this party. She was the one obsessed with finding our party group, becoming party people. She was the one excited—desperate, even—to meet boys, to lose her virginity. Why was she acting like I shouldn't have done the same?

"Come with me," I yelled, grabbing her arm and swinging us both toward the barn door. Catherine and Annie started to follow but I stuck my hand out at them—"Not you, only Ruthie"—and they stayed put.

Outside, she stood there staring at me, thick snowflakes getting stuck in her hair as she waited. "What is wrong with you?"

She took a long sip from her red cup, finishing whatever was left in there, and then tossed it to the floor between us.

"I'm just surprised, I guess," she finally said.

"Surprised by what?"

She shrugged.

"What's wrong with you?" I repeated. "I was so excited to tell you about this. *You* were the one who thought Timothy liked me. *You* were the one who told me to get him alone. What did you think was going to happen?"

I was right. I knew I was right. I just wanted her to acknowledge it.

"Good for you," she said, placating me with a smile. "Glad you got over the hump. Hopefully God doesn't find out."

She turned away from me again, but I grabbed her by the shoulders, the cup in my hand falling to the ground, spraying our feet with sticky pink liquid. This wasn't like her. Maybe it was the alcohol—we were certainly drinking more than we normally did at our weekly jaunts in the woods—but it felt like more than that. Like maybe the alcohol was giving her the liquid courage she needed to say how she actually felt. Naive, silly little me did something first. And she hated it.

"You're jealous," I realized.

She shrugged my hands off her shoulders. "Don't be ridiculous. I—"

"You're jealous that I did it first. I've one-upped you and you can't stand it."

"I'm not—"

"—you're mad because someone wanted to have sex with me and no one wants to have sex with you."

She took a step back, and I did, too. Her face was shadowed, the moon only lighting her forehead and nose, but I could tell she was just as shocked as I was. Her jaw was tight, her eyes slim and harsh. Then her face lowered, looking down at the ground. The snow had accumulated at our feet in thick, uneven clumps, bumpy like the dirt below it.

My necklace was shining on her chest, like it was trying to remind me who I was talking to. *It's Ruthie. You gave her this. You love her. What are you doing?*

"I'm sorry, Ruthie. I—"

She turned away before I could finish but I immediately moved to follow her. I didn't mean it. This was all a mistake.

"Ruthie—" I called after her, but once we were back inside the barn it was no use. The music was too loud; the talking and excited yelling overtook all my attempts to get her attention again.

I figured she was getting Catherine and Annie, and we were going to go home. She was done with this party, and honestly, so was I. But she walked right past them, not acknowledging Catherine's overuse of her camera, and instead ended up at the Gatorade cooler. She snatched a cup from the stack and filled it. Then she put her head back and gulped the entire thing, throwing the cup onto the floor as she finished. She seemed for a second like she was going to throw up—mouth pursed, her eyes watering—but I think it was just a burp instead.

She turned her back to the cooler and looked around the room and when she spotted whatever she was looking for, she took a deep breath, pulled at her shirt, at the necklace around her neck, and then walked silo-visioned to a group of guys standing in the center of the barn, not dancing but not standing still either.

She tapped one on the shoulder—the taller of the two guys who greeted us when we first got here. I think the one she said she'd hooked up with, but I couldn't tell the difference. Everything was blurry—from alcohol, from anxiety, from anger. When he turned around, she pulled him by the collar and kissed him. Hard. Sloppy and messy and hard. I could tell Ruthie didn't like it, but she kept going, letting her hands get caught in his hair, letting his roam down her back.

When they finally parted, Ruthie smiled and wiped her mouth with the back of her hand and then got on her tiptoes to say something into his ear. He smiled, wide, then nodded and took her hand.

As he led her out of the barn, out the back exit I used with Timothy, Ruthie turned back and looked at me. She didn't seem excited or happy. She didn't seem like she wanted this at all. She seemed vengeful. She looked like she hated me.

And then they were gone.

I ran after her. I ran to the barn door and pushed it open. I wanted to say I was sorry. Tell her not to do this unless she wanted to. Make sure she knew I didn't mean it. I didn't mean any of it.

When I got outside the snow was really coming down. Thick white flakes reflecting the moon as they sprinkled the entire world, falling on my hair and my shirt and my nose.

She wasn't out here. She was in the woods.

They were gone.

And I never saw Ruthie again.

# ELEVEN

THE FLIGHT FROM New York to the private airport in Stowe, Vermont, is a short one-hour hop over two and a half states, but for some reason today's journey feels more exhausting than it usually does and we're not even at the airport yet. I try to push the fatigue back, not give value to the anticipatory anxiety growing in my chest. But the closer we get to Vermont—to the wedding—the more my chest starts to feel heavy, my eyes weary, my head foggy. Though that's normal. It's just prewedding jitters. It's all just prewedding jitters.

Graham takes my hand in the back of the Uber and squeezes it, smiling like someone *would* on the way to their wedding, and I remind myself to take a deep breath and do the same. One step at a time.

When we arrive at Teterboro, the Walker family's preferred airport because of its proximity to Manhattan and strict privacy rules, Graham hands our passports through the back seat window to a stocky Port Authority officer who looks comically oversized in the small security booth. We arrived five minutes earlier than expected thanks to my flying anxiety.

Anytime I hand over identification, I get inexplicably nervous. As if I haven't done my research. As if my identity wasn't a life in the making. But I brush it off by the time the man hands our documents back and wishes us a safe flight. As if we can control that.

The glass double doors of the terminal part like the Red Sea before us and a man who looks like Harrison Ford but sounds like Cyndi Lauper appears, flanked by two tall associates in black suits. "Welcome, welcome, welcome," he sings, snapping his fingers at the men, an instruction for them to collect our suitcases from the trunk. God forbid we lift a pound of our own things.

I've met him many times—nearly every single time I've taken this trip with Graham, which turns out to be at least once a year—but I can't remember his name. Louis, maybe? Pronounced the French way—Louee? I'm sure Graham knows. He remembers everyone's name—a business habit his father taught him: remember their name and they'll feel important, and if you're in a position to make an equal feel important, you have the upper hand.

Harrison/Cyndi stops a foot away from us and firmly shakes Graham's hand, then takes mine and puts it between his. The most professional version of a hug this man is allowed to give. "We are just so thrilled to be even the smallest part of your special day," he says, holding just a second too long before freeing my fingers. The worst part is that he means it. He will genuinely be thinking about us for the next five days, smiling at the thought of our cocktail parties and cake towers and handwritten vows. But we won't think about him again after this moment. Hell, I've met him at least five times and I can't even remember his fucking name. That's how much space this man occupies in my mind.

From the corner of my eye, I catch one of Harrison/Cyndi's

Men in Black flunkies pulling my white garment bag out of the trunk like it's a piece of gum stuck to the bottom of his shoe.

"Oh, that one stays with me," I say pleasantly, trying to sound nonchalant and not like a worker at Williams Sonoma whispering *they break it they buy it* to the mother whose children are playing hide-and-seek in the glassware section. "This one gets its own seat," I joke, overcompensating, of course, as they place the white bag in my outstretched arms.

This dress cost more than they make in a year, and I love every single fucking stitch.

I had the dress picked out before Graham and I even started officially dating—a silk masterpiece with a high neck and a back so low no underwear is possible. It was the kind of dress that looks like a cheap Zara slip if you have even *one* extra pound on your waist. But me, right now, the only thing protruding from the silk will be my hip bones, wiry and ossified, precisely what the dress was made to highlight. Just what God would want, right?

The week after Graham proposed, Lena made an appointment at the boutique in Greenwich Village—where Emmy Rossum is purported to have browsed before her nuptials—and we bought the dress. I didn't try it on in the moment because I knew it was fruitless. My bingeing was back and strong, and it wasn't until buying this dress that I realized I needed to supplement my binges with something that could get me to the skin and bones I was expected to look like at my wedding. That night, after Lena and I celebrated with martinis and veggie burgers (in lettuce wraps, not buns, obviously), I stabbed my tonsils with a finger to throw up for the first time.

During the final alterations three weeks ago at the tailor I'd hired to come to Vermont and tighten as needed, Graham's mother insisted on joining me to see the dress in person for the first time. I'd never even shown her photos and she recognized that, in not paying for it, she didn't technically have a right to see.

She sat next to Lena on the white velvet couch, a judgmental smile tucked onto her face as she pretended to sip Moët—champagne has too many calories for her. Even in the Village's most sought-after wedding boutique, Cheryl was acutely aware that she was the most expensive thing in the store.

When I came out of the changing room and stood on the small pedestal, the dress—an inch too large now—softly tucked with clips at my hips, I watched Cheryl's face carefully. She and Graham have the same expressions, so once I learned his, she became easy to read. As she looked at me, listening to the seamstress explain where the dress would be tailored, her usually unemotional face from the Botox and fillers had a layer of something else to it. It wasn't until I got home a few hours later that I recognized what it was: impressed. Not by the dress or the way I looked in it—she called it "lovely" which in Cheryl means *not what I would have chosen*—but impressed by my successful manipulation of the system to get exactly what I wanted.

Between the gown and the expected alterations, I'd put down the better part of my salary for the dress of my choice, but I knew that was the only aspect of our wedding I was paying for. And I insisted on paying for it for that exact reason: to get what I wanted. I didn't give a shit about the flowers or the cake or the band or the table settings. Graham's mother could dictate those items entirely. But if I was going to be immortalized in photographs and a *New York Times* feature, if this wedding was going to be the talk of the town and my photo the token image to go along with it, I wanted complete control over what I was going to wear.

Past security, after we've retrieved our things, we're escorted to a sitting area that looks more like a hotel lobby than an airport gate. Brown and white couches and chairs are organized into small groups, so you never have to share a side table or an outlet with someone you don't know. This isn't the kind of place you usually wait for long. Since the private plane can't leave without you, there's no need to be more than a half hour early. But I was nervous this morning, last-minute unpacking and packing at 4:00 a.m., double-checking we have our passports and marriage license at 5:00 a.m. By the time Graham woke up, I was dressed with two coffees and an Uber scheduled for that afternoon. Thus, our plane wasn't ready for us, despite us being ready for it.

"I apologize for the wait, Mr. Walker," the man said to Graham as I sat down. "It should only be a few more minutes as they finish up the inspection." Outside of gushing about the wedding or asking if I need anything, I'm not the one people address here. It's not my account, it's not my money, no one needs to suck up to *me*.

"Thank you, Clarke," Graham says, shaking his hand one last time. *Clarke.* I would never have guessed that.

"If there's anything we can do to make this an even more special weekend, please don't hesitate," Clarke says with a smile so big you'd think he was talking about his own wedding. *"Anything,"* he emphasized. What does he expect us to say? He's a concierge at a private airport. There's one job he can do and he's already doing it.

There are many differences between flying private and flying commercial, but the one I most appreciate is how peaceful the waiting area is without the constant overhead announcements and overtired children. In fact, there are only five other people here: an older couple reading the *New York Times* and drinking coffee from *Best PopPop and Best Grandma* to-go mugs from home, and three men sitting in separate couch circles, probably traveling for business judging by their suits.

As I position my dress on the empty couch, carefully laying it over the cushions like a dead body, Graham takes a phone call—his mother, no doubt, asking for our ETA.

"We're a little early, so we'll probably leave a little early," I can hear Graham tell her as he paces across the floor-to-ceiling windows looking out on the tarmac. I count five planes behind him and there are seven people here. It always intrigues me how inexplicably different the plane-to-human ratio is in a place like this.

Graham is one of those men who looks sexier in a cashmere sweater and jeans because everyone's used to seeing him in some variation of a suit or workout clothes. It's not that *he's* sexier when he's more casual, but the feeling I get knowing I'm one of very few people who get to see this side of him—that exclusivity—that's what I find very sexy. I also feel it when I call him at work, telling his secretary to please pull him out of that meeting, only to say that a special outfit he's going to want to take off me arrived from NET-A-PORTER, and I'll have to try it on for him later.

Based on the paparazzi shots of the Kardashian sisters that littered every magazine I could steal growing up, I always thought that being rich meant ostentatious silver Gs on your belt buckle, dresses with "Balenciaga" running up and down the sleeves, sandals screaming "CHRISTIAN DIOR" on the leather toe strap. It wasn't until I moved to New York that I realized there are multiple layers of rich, in the same way there are multiple layers of poor. Two-white-collar-parents-in-debt-from-their-McMansion poor was different from single-mom-who-buys-groceries-at-the-dollar-store poor, which was different from homeschooled-on-a-farm-in-a-religious-cult poor.

What I saw in magazines was New Money Rich. The kind of rich when you've recently—often quickly and hastily—lifted your status in the world and want everyone to know it. That's when you plaster "GIVENCHY" on your chest but still pronounce it Give-in-chee not Zhee-vaah-shee. That's when you buy the Aston Martin with the doors that open like a spaceship just to keep it in your driveway because you can't afford the insurance. When your house has more rooms than you can afford to furnish.

But that's not Walker rich. Walker rich is two-hundred-and-fifty-dollar sweaters so plain you could have bought them at the Gap. It's five-hundred-dollar white sneakers you lightly scrub with a toothbrush after each wear. It's four-hundred-and-twenty-five-dollar raincoats that only have a label on the inside tag.

That's what I'm marrying into. They wouldn't stand out in a crowd for anything other than looking perfectly pressed and put together, but their clean and uncomplicated outfits probably cost more than your average mortgage. That's the point, I've learned time and time again. Blending in so as not to be a target. But blending in is a much more arduous task than standing out. It takes considerably more effort to look like you belong than to intentionally go out of your way not to.

The plane ride was so steady my dress only swayed on the hook in the closet as we took off and landed. In between, we floated through the clouds, the blue sky around us and the world below us.

Graham is asleep across from me, snoring just low enough that it blends in with the engines. His small sinuses don't allow him to sleep sitting up—he's a fragile man—but he refuses to get comfortable on any kind of transportation, regardless of whether it's just the two of us. His shoes stay on, feet planted firmly on the floor, his seat only slightly reclined. I used to be the opposite—I'd slip my shoes off, sit cross-legged as I looked out the window, my coat or a blanket draped over my legs, the same way I'd be sitting if I were on the couch at home.

But on our second flight to Vermont, when we were in our seats waiting for his parents to join us for what they called a "carpool," Graham leaned in like he was about to kiss my cheek but instead moved toward my ear and whispered that I looked unprofessional. We had a status to maintain, even at thirty thousand feet. I didn't realize until a few minutes later that our appearance was for his parents, not the airline.

The Walkers aren't the *pick you up at the airport* kind of family. They'd rather pay absurd amounts of money for car services to alleviate the inconvenience of greeting their son as he arrives. Instead, we'll show up to the house and Oskar, the family's "house manager"—a title invented by rich white people to make themselves feel less guilty for having a full-time maid—will tell us what time to meet for dinner and we will retreat to our bedroom to "freshen up" until then.

It's an hour drive from the airport to the house, winding down familiar roads, passing through small one-block towns filled with Victorian mansions brilliantly posed on the edge of a stream or inlet, so delicate that as quickly as you approach the town, you're exiting and watching it blend into the trees until it completely disappears behind you. That's why this place is divine. The trees. The most beautiful treescape you'll ever see—green, copper, gold, and rust leaves radiate off the mountains like a bright acrylic painting. The entire place is an Instagram filter in itself, encapsulating the cottage-core, cabernet-by-the-fire vibe that twentysomething New Yorkers pay sixty dollars in Metro North fares to feel on some mountain "upstate" that's littered with so many people it may as well just be Harlem Hill in Central Park.

I didn't do much for this wedding, but I did pick the season. October. When the foliage is pornographically alluring, calling me into it like a shadow in the night. I've always had a thing for that kind of shit.

As we arrive at the base of Walker Mountain, where the main two-lane road meets the skinny one that snakes up to the family's several homes and yet-to-be-developed plots of land, Graham asks the driver to stop. He pulls to the side and before he's even pushed the gear to park, Graham has the door open and a foot out on the muddy ground.

"Sorry, just one minute," I explain to the driver who nods and shrugs, nary a concern on his face. He's getting paid whether we're moving or stopped. What does he care about Graham's weird tradition?

Above the road hangs an arched wooden sign, cracking and stained from years of snow and rain. It's barely visible now, but branded in a plain serif font is *Walker Mountain*, the two words separated in the center by the family's crest involving a coyote and a maple tree. It's one thing to be a part of a family with its own crest, but it's another to have the crest on a sign, and printed on lowball glasses, and embroidered on the chest of Oskar's uniform. I hate this fucking family.

On the forest green poles flanking the road, supporting the sign above us, Graham finds a spot and begins to write his initials and the date with a black marker he keeps in his carry-on for this reason and this reason alone. He and his brother each have a pole and, ever since they moved out, they record every day they return to the mountain. Graham said it was born out of a competition to see who visited their parents more when they were both at Yale. Reed stopped adding to his years ago, but Graham continues, again unable to break a tradition.

When he got back in the car, the bitterly cold air sneaks in with him and sends shivers up and down my arms. He reaches his phone screen out toward me and smiles. On it is a picture of his initials and the date, and next to it a poorly scribbled heart that looks more like a drunken tattoo someone would pay good money to remove from their ankle. "The next time we're up here, you get to put your name on it, too." He's beaming at the thought, expecting from me the kind of excitement I'd feel if he were gifting me a house.

Once in our early days of dating, we were lying in bed, talking about our families for the first time. I told him about how tragically my parents passed away, offering the occasional look away and rub of the eyes to really sell the vulnerability. He nuzzled his face into my neck and whispered, "I'm sad you don't have traditions of your own. But one day, you'll have mine."

I smile back at him as he closes the car door. "I can't wait," I say, letting him kiss me.

Then he turns to the driver. "Okay, we're ready," he says. But I don't think I'll ever be. My heart beats in my ears, and I start to feel light-headed as we pass under the sign and begin to climb the mountain.

The road gets thinner and steeper as we approach the peak and it feels, for half a mile or so, like the trees are closing in on us and the mountain could, at any moment, swallow me whole. It is an odd claustrophobia I only feel here, surrounded by sky and nature, but never in Manhattan, where even the most normal thing—a bedroom, a street, a park—was made to squish in as many people as possible. But maybe it's the opposite of claustrophobia—whatever you feel when there's too much space, too much silence, too much darkness. When you can sleep with the windows wide open and hear nothing in the night. When there's nothing connecting you to the outside, to people. When you're in a place where no one could hear you scream.

At the crest of the hill, the road opens onto a flat and green meadow, overlooking layers and layers of mountain ranges in every direction, the closest textured with swaying leaves, getting lighter and smoother until the farthest is merely a thin blue line that almost blends into the sky. The sun is setting slowly behind the farthest mountain, painting the sky pink and orange, like a watercolor in a hotel lobby. It's the kind of endless horizon that makes me feel small and grateful for the mansion we were about to park in front of; something stable and close I could grip onto, something cementing me to the ground. Somewhere I could hide.

We round the circular cobblestone driveway and the house emerges before us, like a man-made mountain hidden atop the peak. Tall, angular lines formed by metal and concrete shaped the house, while exposed wooden accents were taken from the trees that used to live on this land, whose roots are now dead and buried under the foundation. It's a multimillion-dollar modern log cabin built to be an extension to the surrounding forest, with so many massive un-curtained windows you can watch the sunrise while you shit. I never understood the curtainless style in a place like this. I'd live in a windowless black box if I could. Sure, the view is beautiful, but every time I look out on it, I'm afraid of what could be looking back in.

I pull my sweatshirt sleeves all the way down and put on my coat as the car parks and we step out into the brisk October air, so fresh it smells like nothing.

"My Grahmmy boy!" An old woman, petite and rotund, lumbers down the front steps, her arms outstretched as wide as her chubby smile. The family insignia faded and worn on the chest of her too-tight polo shirt.

"What are you doing here!" Graham jumps out of the car and embraces her in a way I've never seen him apply to the help. If thanking them makes one look weak, what does hugging them do to your marble reputation?

I climb out of the hulking car and stand beside the open door, watching them hug like a third wheel. She starts rocking him back and forth, mumbling in Spanish.

"Where's Oskar?" I finally ask to no one in particular. Just something to say, out loud, to remind them I was there. Graham certainly seemed to forget.

"Vacation," she says. "I had to come out of retirement for this very special weekend."

Graham untangles himself from the woman's grip and steps beside me, resting his hand on my lower back in the way he does when he's about to show me off, like a falcon he's trained to land on his gloved arm. "This is Eliza," he says, excitedly, more so than when he was introducing me to his mother for the first time. "My fiancée."

The woman steps back and cocks her head to the side, examining me like a piece of meat at the butcher. I don't like being looked at that way—studied. It feels intrusive. So I do it right back at her, offering her the same puzzled stare she was giving me. The longer this lasts the more I start to feel like she does look familiar. Maybe I met her before, though I doubt it considering the way Graham introduced me. Maybe it's just that she looks like an older Melissa McCarthy.

"Babe, this is Lorraine—" He continues to say something else about her, but I can't hear anything. My ears start ringing like I'd spent the past twenty-four hours front row at a Metallica concert, and I feel so light-headed I think I could realistically pass out right here on the uneven cobblestones.

I have seen her before, I realize. I most *definitely* have seen her before. And I don't like the way she's looking at me.

"It's so good to see you," she says, further shoving my heart into my throat. Had she been trained to greet people that way, just like I trained myself to? In that way all rich people do, as if they meet so many people it's hard to keep track, so let's just assume I've met everyone. Or did she truly remember me?

"It's great to finally meet the living legend," I manage to say, each word taking extreme concentration to get out of my mouth. Graham used to talk about Lorraine the way someone would talk about their mother or a doting aunt. She started her tenure as the Walker house manager when Graham was two years old, and didn't retire until he was in college. I'd only heard about her, but Graham always implied they'd lost touch after she was replaced by Oskar and she stopped serving a purpose. Growing up in a household that was cold, where family dinners were more like mandatory business transactions, Graham cites Lorraine as the only person who ever showed him affection; the only person who wanted to hear about the boys' day and learn what they did in school. Once, in the early morning hours on a Saturday when we first started dating, when we'd wake up and fuck and then lie on the terrace watching the late sunrise in a carnal daze, Graham said he wished Lorraine was his mother.

She stretches her hands out, palms up, and I rest mine inside them, feeling her cold and dry fingers coil around mine. "You're going to be the most beautiful bride," she says with a smile that, maybe I imagine this, seems to fade and turn into something else as she drops my hands and looks behind us, at the driver unloading our luggage from the trunk to the front door.

She faces Graham, doting on him like he's her own son. "Your mother's at her facialist, your father's in his office. Your brother and Veronica took Henry into town. Everyone will be here for supper in two hours." She glances down at her watch—a gold Cartier I wasn't expecting to see twisted on her dimpled wrist. "One and a half hours," she corrects.

She looks at me one more time—as if she wants to memorize my face—and I smile politely, pretending I'm not bothered by any of this, like I have no idea who she is, nor she, I. She shakes her head, like she's pushing away the same memory I am, and, without another word, I watch her turn and disappear into the house.

Fuck.

This was not part of the plan.

# PART TWO

# TWELVE

"NAME."

The woman behind the boxy glass desk didn't look at me when she asked. Instead, she stared behind me, toward the double doors that opened gracefully onto Madison Avenue, as if she was waiting for someone more important to show up.

"Eliza Bennet," I responded, forcing from her, finally, eye contact.

"Like—"

"Yes," I said, cutting her off. It had been seven years since I first heard that reference, and I no longer found it charming. I go by Eliza now. Not as lace-veil, silver-cross as Elizabeth the Mother of Mary, but still a tribute to that girl; to a part of my life I couldn't forget. No matter how hard I tried.

The woman focused on her computer and while she searched for my name in their database, I scanned the sign-in sheet on top of the glass. It wasn't unlike the one in Willits—a line of printed names beside a line of messy signatures.

"Here you go," the woman said, handing me a paper sticker with my name printed on it. I almost affixed it to my chest before stopping myself—thank God. People like us don't put stickers on our one-hundred-and-fifty-dollar cashmere sweaters. *That's not something people like us do*, I reminded myself then. And many times after.

Ashleigh and Brittany waited for me at the entrance to the fifteenth-floor office suite, like overly enthusiastic hostesses at a bad restaurant.

"Eliza!" Brittany squealed as the elevator doors opened. I put on a smile and approached them kindly, despite wondering how long they'd been standing there and how many people had fallen victim to their misguided excitement before I showed up.

"We're thrilled to have you join the team!" Ashleigh said, shaking my hand like she was trying to be the professional one in their relationship. A good cop/bad cop kind of thing. It was about as trustworthy as a handshake in an interrogation room.

Once I was at my desk and told to "sit tight" until my boss Hilary arrived, the room began to fill quickly. One fashionable white girl followed by another fashionable white girl in their cool ripped jeans and bodycon dresses and oversized blazers.

Lena stood out amongst the rest, like a bull in a Lilly Pulitzer store. She wore a black dress that floated over her bones-only body like she was always walking in the path of the wind or a perfectly placed invisible fan, and white sneakers. They were platform, making her usual five foot nine seem more like five foot eleven, but they were sneakers. And I bet it needled at Brittany and Ashleigh.

Lena didn't stop to greet me as she passed my desk on the way to hers, as so many others had. Instead, she glided down the aisle of white desks like it was her wedding and she didn't have a care in the world. I'd looked her up, obviously—I'd looked everyone up—but she was *the one*. Lena Cunningham. Twenty-seven. Graduate of the Yale School of Drama.

Wrote an award-winning play that dramatized William Carlos Williams's poem "The Red Wheelbarrow." She and her ex-boyfriend were arrested two years ago for getting drunk, ripping down a stop sign on Lafayette Avenue, and then attempting to install it onto the top of a police vehicle in protest. She donates to three abortion rights organizations, grew up in SoHo, and lives in the West Village.

When I was researching this PR agency and I saw her photo online, smizing like she'd invented the form, I immediately recognized her. She'd help me live in this world. She'd help me become one of them.

When I moved to New York, I got an apartment in the East Village, a hole-in-the-wall studio on the second floor above a Chinese food place with a Roman bath in the back room. It was a piece of shit—holes the size of my fist stuffed with browning mouse filler, roaches under the oven that had been dead for decades, a radiator that screamed bloody murder in the middle of the night. It wasn't what I had pictured for myself in the Big Apple, but it was all I could afford—I scraped together all the money I'd made in college and after to pay for it until I got the PR job. It would do for the moment.

And it was all mine.

The exterminator I called was my first friend in New York. He was a broad, ghoulish man named Fyodor who was bald and looked like he might have a side hustle as one of the gargoyles on the side of St. Patrick's Cathedral. Every Sunday morning at 7:15 a.m. he'd knock on the door yelling "exterminator" as if I didn't already have our weekly date scribbled into my calendar. As if I hadn't started looking forward to it. Week three I had coffee waiting for him on the counter. He took it with heavy cream, which I kept on hand for this purpose only. Week four, he brought me a greasy bag of paczki his wife made fresh that morning.

"Why do you live here?" he asked week five, after we found a golf ball–sized hole in the back of the closet that hadn't been there two weeks prior. He had been so frustrated when it appeared behind my rain boots that he slammed his workbag against the wood floor so hard that whatever was inside the hole squealed. "This is a piece of shit apartment. Piece of shit. They rob you to make you pay for this."

"It's cheap, Fyodor. *You* want to pay my rent for a high-rise in SoHo? Then I'll move tomorrow."

He laughed loud, from his gut, like a roar. "You need to find a rich man, Miss Eliza. Very rich."

I thought about that Cher quote, "My mom said to me, 'You know, sweetheart, one day you should settle down and marry a rich man.' I said, 'Mom, I am a rich man.'" That's how a good feminist would have responded: *I don't need a rich man, I'll make it big in New York City all by myself. I'm a strong independent woman.*

"I'm working on it," I told him, instead.

I was *really* working on it.

I interviewed for the job at the Brit & Ash Agency from my mattress on the floor while I watched a roach slowly suffocate to death between my double-paned windows. I told them I was out of town, that I would *love* to interview, but that I wasn't going to be able to do it in person. Thankfully it was before video chats were the norm, so I could get away with wearing underwear and the coffee-stained Hanes T-shirt I got in a pack at the bodega for eleven dollars, while slurping down my fifth ramen noodles of the week and proffering my passion for writing press releases for high-end designers.

I'd done my research to know exactly what they wanted me

to say. I spent hours at the Tompkins Square Library googling until I found Lena, then Brit & Ash, then the opening for a senior account executive. It was no surprise to me that two days after my interview they offered me the job. I'd made sure I was the perfect candidate.

I just couldn't see them in person until I confirmed I had a job. Because I couldn't see them in person until I could buy the kind of clothes I needed and to do that I had to make sure I'd have a salary to pay off the Nordstrom Rack credit card debt.

It was three weeks into the job that Lena and I first spoke. I had just plucked a transparent glass mug from the cabinet in the kitchen and was holding it up to the light to see if the edge was actually clean. The top-of-the-line dishwasher in our office's kitchen had nothing on all the Tom Ford reds and Armani purples.

"They burned the coffee today," Lena said, standing in the doorway, leaning against the arched entrance like she was modeling her tailored jeans and strappy white bodysuit. "Let's go across the street."

I couldn't see my boss Hilary at her desk from the kitchen, but I could hear her. She typed like she was angry at her keyboard for betraying her, like she had lead strapped to the tips of her fingers. The sound had become so annoying I'd convinced myself it was performative; that she wasn't actually busy but pretending to be.

"She'll literally never know," Lena said, sensing my hesitation. "She hasn't looked up from her computer once in the last hour."

We took the hallway and elevator in silence, but it wasn't awkward, and I didn't feel the need to fill the space with the sound of my voice. I felt like whatever I wanted to say around Lena needed to be important; I needed to think about it and have it fully conceptualized in my own head before I could speak. She wasn't the kind of person who befriended just anyone, and I wanted her to befriend me. I needed her to.

She was cool, but not in that "cool girl" male gaze kind of way that had become so popular—the one who knows football players by jersey number and drinks Bud Light and wears her hair up to bars; the one that men have deemed approachable because "she's one of us." Lena was cool in the female gaze. Which meant she wasn't approachable at all, but incredibly intimidating. She was the kind of woman other women hated. Because they want to be her. But they didn't know how. I did.

I had some practice shadowing someone until I became her. Until I blended right in.

This wasn't that different. But the stakes were a lot higher now.

Outside our building, Lena stepped off the curb confident there were no cars coming before she even attempted to glance to her left and right. This, I learned, is a New Yorker instinct. No one here waits on the sidewalk—you walk as close to the approaching cars as possible. They might be busy, but you're busier. And they'll never hit you. Because they'll go to jail. Sure, you might die in the process, but there's also consequences for them. It's a kind of nihilistic revenge that would only be fulfilling in a place like this.

She began to move across the street before the light turned red and before the cars passed, getting closer and closer but walking so confidently I'd believe even the drivers trusted what she was doing. I followed boldly behind her, standing up straighter, making myself bigger, by association. It was her attitude, that was the key. The gives-no-shits confidence she imbued—whether she felt it inside was irrelevant. The New Yorker shrugging things off. *There's nothing we haven't seen and nothing we won't do. We're New Yorkers. We're a different breed.*

I expected to walk into the Starbucks across the street from the office where I was first introduced to the concept of people willingly spending seven dollars and fifty cents a day on ten ounces of slightly burned coffee, often just for the ambiance of bringing that paper cup to their mouth. I'd been there once before with Hilary—I got a Pike Place Roast and she got a soy latte—and when I asked for regular milk, instead of a nut variety, she looked at me like I'd just admitted to being the Son of Sam.

"I don't do chains," Lena said, walking past Starbucks's stone entrance, a line of suited men and bloused women inside. "Shop small, and all that."

Instead, we turned the corner and headed south on Fifth Avenue.

"What are you really doing here?" Lena asked. For a brief moment, I felt myself stop in the center of the street, my feet pausing over a white crossing line like they were stuck in concrete quicksand. She couldn't possibly... "—in New York," she continued. I put one foot in front of the other without skipping a beat, without her realizing that just a millisecond before my head was spinning. "There are PR firms everywhere. Why here? What's your New York City Romance?"

"My what?" I asked.

"Your New York City Romance. Everyone has some movie that sent them here, romanticizing the city so it seems more approachable."

It was like a light went off in my brain; suddenly that old Rolodex, the one that had been acquiring dust since freshman year of college, was awakened, pulled out of an old filing cabinet in the back of my brain and ready to get back to work. Magazine headlines I hadn't thought about in years flew across my line of vision like a tennis ball in the US Open: *Classic Romances Everyone Needs to See. Tips for a First Date from These Five Classic Romances. Meg Ryan's Take on—*

"*You've Got Mail,*" I said, hoping she didn't ask for one plot detail.

"Interesting..."

We rounded the corner of 18th Street and stopped outside a glass-walled shop; a four-inch coffee cup epoxied to the glass door was the only thing letting you know it was a café.

"I would have pegged you for *The Devil Wears Prada* or *Working Girls,*" Lena said as she opened the door and we walked inside. "But *You've Got Mail* is a classic, I guess."

"I'm not a big movie person," I said, nodding at my confession. That was a fine thing to say. Vague, but admissive. Not something that would put me in any category Lena wouldn't approve of.

"Me neither, honestly," she said. "But I'm always curious. You can tell a lot about a person by their New York Romance."

"What does *You've Got Mail* say about me?" I asked as we approached the counter.

She looked at me for the first time in this entire conversation, straight into my eyes. It was worse than being read. It felt like I was being analyzed, like she was looking for one crack in my story.

"I haven't decided yet," she finally said.

When she looked away from me, she ordered a matcha latte with oat milk, and asked what I wanted as she pulled out her black Amex. "Next round's on you."

While we walked back to the office, I realized I never asked what her movie was. I wanted to know what it said about her, as much as she wanted to know what mine said about me.

"Oh." She laughed after I asked. "I grew up in the city. This place has never been romantic to me. That's what's great about New York. We all hate it here, but no one will ever leave."

I didn't understand the concept at first. I hadn't romanticized this place at all; even that wasn't something I could afford to do. It was hard to think this was the city of dreams when my closest friend was an exterminator and I had to give myself cold-shower facials once a day to counteract the bloating from my salty but cheap ramen noodle diet.

She was right about one thing: I didn't come here for the job. I came to the job for her.

It was easy for me to learn from Lena. Every item of clothing—from jeans to a wool coat—should be tailored, so I found a woman named Wendy on Avenue A. Never leave the apartment without styling your hair, so I bought a blow-dryer and a straightening iron and a curling iron and some spray Lena uses that smells like perfume and is supposed to protect you from heat. Fresh flowers—on your desk and in your living room—from a bodega where you're on a first-name basis with the owner and the cat are essential. Wear heels no matter how tall you are. Walk fast whether or not you're in a rush. Never look up.

That one I actively disobey.

I often walked home from work to save the two-dollar-and-seventy-five-cent subway fare and to get in a free workout. Though I told Lena I belong to the Equinox on Broadway and the Tracy Anderson on 59th, a gym was a luxury I couldn't afford yet. When I walk, I watch strangers' apartments like their windows are TV screens into an HBO drama. The couple eating dinner on their four-by-two balcony are trying to get pregnant and just had yet another disappointing negative test. The bright cartoon emanating from the fourth-floor corner are two kids being distracted by a teenage babysitter whose boyfriend is coming over later to fuck her in the rich couple's bed. The twinkle lights on a penthouse's terrace belong to a lonely woman reading Elin Hilderbrand and waiting for her husband to return from a business trip.

I wondered what people thought about me—the girl sitting on her fire escape every night, drinking from an eleven-dollar bottle of wine, swiping through Lena's Instagram like she was a celebrity I was desperate to one day meet.

I'd been nervous that my *You've Got Mail* selection put a wrench in the friendship I hoped would have blossomed after our coffee date. She did say that I was paying for the next round, which meant there would *be* a next round, a shrivel of hope that kept me going when two weeks passed without Lena saying more than a handful of words to me. She said good morning once, but Kelsi, my bootlicker desk mate whose phony smile was plastered on her face even when I caught her crying in the bathroom, responded before I could. Lena complimented my Golden Goose sneakers as she passed my desk once, but she was gone before I could come up with a catchy way to say thank you. I wore those shoes every day after that.

I wanted to keep my head down, give her space, not seem like a needy follower desperate for her friendship, but it was hard. I couldn't tell if I needed to initiate the next interaction since she instigated the first. Lena seemed like the kind of person who was always in charge, who led the group and made the reservations and decided who her friends would be.

I had started to wonder if maybe those are traits she likes in a friend, too, until one day at 7:00 p.m. Lena moseyed over to my desk and asked to grab a drink.

"There's a new bar opening in SoHo," she had said, standing over me. "A friend from college is the mixologist and there's a soft opening tonight."

I'd go wherever she needed me to. Especially when that thing involved college friends.

"I would not have picked this name," Lena said as we were greeted by a bouncer outside the new bar. He took our IDs like he suspected we might be underage, which was not yet a compliment, but still annoying; a way for this city to make you feel like a child despite paying for yourself to be here.

I looked up at the sign above the door, a raw-edge wooden plank swinging gently off the brick building.

"'Doll's Eyes,'" I read.

She shrugged as she took her ID back. "If you ask me, that's the name of a Halloween haunted house, not a craft cocktail bar."

"It's a poisonous berry," I said, remembering the way their striking color—white berries with a black dot, clustered on a long red stem—stood out amongst the fall foliage like something from another planet.

The first time I saw them, on a branch in the back near the sugarhouse, I was a kid, attracted to them for their strangeness. When I reached out to touch one, my brother William grabbed my arm so hard it ached for days.

"If Mom and Dad don't grow it, then don't touch it," he told me. I snuck back out there two days later—I wanted to lick it, see how my body would react to poison—but the stems were gone.

"That makes it a little more interesting," Lena said as we walked past the bouncer and into the bar.

Inside was crowded and too dark, like they had forgotten to turn on one of the chandeliers. The decor made me feel a familiar kind of dizzy—wooden dining chairs hung from the ceiling, a collage of paintings of sixteenth-century women with their breasts out sat crooked along one wall, the wood floor was uneven like you were always on the verge of tipping over. The whole thing was a bit of a mind-fuck and made me feel confused in the same way I would get as a kid when we were punished and forced to stay inside for weeks on end. If the sun doesn't touch your face for long enough part of you starts to question whether the sun still exists.

Lena and I posted up in the center of the bar, where two seats opened for us. Normally I would have assumed that was a coincidence, but I soon realized that's just what happens to Lena. It would eventually be something that happened to me, too.

A bartender with a handlebar mustache and blue eyes that looked painted onto his face greeted us, the nose ring in his septum shifting slightly as he smiled. Lena never begged for attention. All she had to do was put her butt in a stool and her elbow on the counter and smile, the bartenders would be fighting to serve her.

The drinks were all named for other poisonous berries, a theme I appreciated because it was as subtle as you wanted it to be. Only girls who grew up on a farm would recognize it. Girls like me, though that was not something I was going to admit to Lena. I had my backstory laid out by this point and growing up in a religious cult was not part of it.

I'm twenty-six, from Providence, Rhode Island, a place I visited for research and determined to be the most innocuous but interesting New York–adjacent city to claim residency. Everyone seems to know *someone* from Rhode Island, but most people haven't been there themselves, thus removing the risky conversation starter: *Oh, I love that bar on that road with cobblestones, what's it called again?* Though, I memorized my way up and down the modest winding streets, so I'd probably be able to keep up. I have no siblings, no parents—no relatives to speak of—a guaranteed conversation-*stopper*. No one wants to ask for more details from an orphan who doesn't want to talk about it.

I knew that part of my backstory needed to involve an Ivy League school, a place that would be unabashedly accepted by this elite crowd. But not one as dull as Harvard that would raise eyebrows. People from Harvard don't apply for jobs at the Brit & Ash Agency. I figured I could just fake it—put whatever school I wanted down on my resume—but I had a brilliant idea after watching an episode of *Law & Order: SVU*. I started calling the less exclusive schools—UPenn, Columbia, Cornell, Brown—claiming I was from a grad school admissions office looking for the missing transcript for Elizabeth Bennet. I was hoping I'd get lucky. Perhaps there was an Elizabeth Bennet whose experience I could borrow. I struck gold at Brown.

"Hmm, Elizabeth Bennet," the admissions assistant at Brown hummed when I called. I could hear the click clack of her keyboard aggressively typing in the background. "I don't see anyone with that name, I'm sorry."

I'd gotten used to that answer—prepared to pull my usual *no problem, I must have the wrong number, so sorry for the inconvenience!* that I'd offered to all the other schools I'd already called. But before I could respond, she said, "Oh wait, maybe you mean Eliza Bennet? Class of 2014?"

That could work. I was the Covenant University class of 2013, but I could pretend to be one year younger. People pay good money for doctors to send their faces back in time; turns out all you need to do is claim the identity of a younger person.

"Yes," I said quickly. "You know what, my apologies, it's absolutely Eliza Bennet. That's what I meant. Can you fax over her file?"

I liked the name Eliza immediately. It seemed to suit me better than Elizabeth ever did. And it absolutely seemed to suit New York. Eliza Bennet. That's me.

"I'll have the Black Lotus," Lena said to the bartender after scanning the menu for less than a few seconds. She knows what she likes to drink, what cocktails suited her, got her the perfect kind of tipsy. I didn't have that in my arsenal yet. I had no idea what to order.

"Surprise me," I told the bartender, leaning in confidently so it came off as flirting and not as stressed indecision. "I trust your taste." I locked eyes with him like I was supposed to and smiled. Then looked away bashfully, like I was hiding a blush.

"I've got the perfect thing," he said, walking away.

This was the kind of guy I'd been taking home since I moved to New York City—a bearded beatnik who wanted nothing more than to eat me out and then fuck me while I clawed at his tattooed chest. This guy seemed like he'd choke me if I asked for it. And he wouldn't be bothered by the fact that my apartment consisted of a mattress on the floor, three cooking pots, a Thanksgiving-scented candle, and a computer charger. He'd call it art.

I found them easy to find and easy to get rid of. An unemotional need-based desire-filler. Ever since that night, that was all I wanted sex to be. Detached. Fun. On my terms.

"You continue to surprise me, Eliza," Lena said when we got our drinks back and Handlebar Mustache had written his number on my napkin.

"I want to see what that mustache can do," I told her, slipping the napkin into my bra. I wouldn't call him later, but I wanted Lena thinking I would.

"Until you've had a woman between your legs, you'll never know how good it can really get," she said, taking a sip. I'd argue that true pleasure came with a ball gag and a couple slaps across the face, but this seemed like a hill she was willing to die on, so I'd let it rest. She dated around, I saw that on her Instagram—pictures of her kissing a guy, naked on vacation with a woman. I liked that about her. Sex was just sex. It didn't carry any baggage. No matter how much I tried to rid myself of mine, it was always there, lumbering over my back.

"Oh. My. God." Lena put her drink down on the bar and looked past me to the back, where leather booths lined the narrow walls. "I went to college with those guys. That's—oh shit…" She stood up and snagged her drink and purse in one motion. "We have to say hi. These guys are better flirts than the bartender anyway."

I took a deep breath as she started to move past me. This was it. It was happening.

"Is that Graham Walker," I heard her say as she approached the table. The sentence echoed in my head for days after that, bounced around inside my brain until I was light-headed, until I couldn't quite see straight.

When I turned around, Graham's sweet face appeared from behind a banister, smiling and carefree, and I blacked out for a moment. I couldn't think or speak. But I felt myself moving toward him like a magnet, until I was standing beside Lena as they hugged. This was it. My life here was finally about to start.

I shook his hand, soft and thick as Lena introduced us. "This is my coworker Eliza," she said. "It's literally a Yale reunion in here." She moved on to the next person, but Graham's eyes stayed on me.

"It's nice to meet you," he said. "Here—" He slid down the booth as I slipped in next to him, feeling small and fragile next to his rower's frame, the muscles I could tell existed underneath his effortlessly cuffed button-down. I sat on the edge of the booth, half my butt perched off it for fear of getting too close to him.

Lena ordered tequila shots to celebrate their college reunion and they all reminisced about the epic rugby house parties and getting laid in the stacks and that one professor who got fired for having an affair with a student even though everyone knew it wasn't his first—"or last," Graham joked.

With each drink Graham and I drew closer, gravitating toward each other like it was inevitable—and it was, I'd made sure it was—until our legs were touching. Until the hair on his arms tickled mine. Until he told me he worked in finance. Until he told me he was from Vermont. Until Lena mentioned I wanted to fuck the bartender. Until I noticed Graham stiffen, uncomfortable with the thought. Until I brushed my hand against his thigh, long enough for him to realize it wasn't an accident. Until he put his hand on my bare knee. Until he and I locked eyes when I stood, my heart racing, knowing exactly what I needed to do to lock him in. He likes a bad girl. I am a bad girl.

I didn't wait in the single-person bathroom more than thirty seconds before the door inched open just enough for him to slip inside and lock it behind him. We stood a foot apart, staring at each other, my heart rate rising with each pulse, the sensation between my legs exploding as I looked at him.

When we kissed I felt it over my entire body.

When he slipped his hand into my pants, my knees almost gave out.

When I came, the image of our wedding was the only thing I was thinking about.

# THIRTEEN

**WE WERE SUMMONED** for dinner exactly as Lorraine planned at a prompt 7:15 p.m. when a buzzer went off inside our bedroom and Lorraine's voice materialized over the intercom. "Dinner is ready," was all she said, like a fork in fucking *Beauty and the Beast.*

Fucking Lorraine.

I had spent the last hour and a half unpacking and thinking about her. I hung up my dress and Graham's suit and wondered why she had looked at me for so long in the driveway. I laid out my makeup and toiletries in our bathroom while replaying her greeting—*it's nice to see you*—and studying my memory of her face.

Then I started self-soothing. She was looking at me normally. I was imagining it all. There was no weird pause or unwanted lingering. She greeted me the same way I greeted Lady Gaga when I met her at a fundraiser. It doesn't mean I'd ever met Lady Gaga before.

I imagined the moment. I imagined all those moments. I didn't know this woman. And this woman does not know me.

She's simply come out of what is surely a luscious retirement to be there for her little boy Graham on his big day. It was nothing more than meeting her favorite kid's fiancée for the first time. The woman he was about to promise to spend the rest of his life with. It was as simple as that. I couldn't think about the other possibility, because that would mean Lorraine could ruin everything.

"You ready?" Graham asks at the door.

I roll out of bed and slip into the white minidress and heels waiting for me and take Graham's hand.

We walk slowly down the hallway from the north wing of the house—consisting of our suite and Reed and Veronica's suite—to the south wing, where the common spaces, offices, and Oskar's lodging are spread out over eleven thousand pristine square feet. Getting anywhere in this house involves at least five minutes and several walks down dimly lit hallways. At home, Graham leaves all the lights on all the time. It is by far his most annoying domestic trait, and I'm talking about a guy who buys his underwear from a boutique in London. But here, it's like his parents hide the light switches to force you to walk around in the dark, feeling for walls, desperate for a way out, trying to sense if someone is there watching you.

I tug on Graham's hand a little tighter and push that claustrophobic feeling away. The one I always get in the dark that always gets worse when I'm here. The feeling like I'm going to be swallowed whole into the night.

"You're late," is the first thing Mr. Walker says to us—well, to Graham—when we enter the dining room. He is not a man who has time for pleasantries, so his greetings are usually insults or instructions.

Graham fears his father more than I fear his mother. Though maybe *fear* isn't the right word. I'm not afraid of her. I'm afraid she can see under my carefully crafted costume. I could distract Graham with my body, and Mr. Walker and Reed with fantasies of my body, and Veronica with the fake closeness she thinks we have, but Mrs. Walker has the power to see right through me. If anyone was going to figure out I was a fraud, it would be her. And she'd kick me out of this family faster than Graham could say *but Mom, I love her...*

Graham's fear of his father is forged from lack of affirmation. Mr. Walker knows all he needs to do is tell Graham that he did a good job. But Graham will never get it. That would mean Mr. Walker acknowledging that someone he raised might have turned out better. Graham is better looking. Graham is more successful. Graham is marrying someone hotter. Graham has it all. So Mr. Walker holds all Graham's flaws over his head, letting them drop in the most convenient moments.

"You told us 7:15," Graham says, releasing my hand to look down at his watch, an early wedding present I gave him last week. Everyone but Graham recognizes the irony in that— me getting him a two-thousand-dollar watch with his own money and calling it a "gift"—but he loves it. "It's 7:16. Give me a break."

Mr. Walker approaches me slowly, looking me up and down with an approving smile that sends some vomit up my throat behind my oh-so-lovely grin. I love being objectified by my sixty-five-year-old father-in-law. It's not only like he's taking my clothes off with his eyes, but also snapping a picture of my naked body so that he can think about it the next time he's having sex with Cheryl.

I know I look the part. Lena and I spent two months finding white outfits appropriate for all the evenings leading up to the aisle. A strappy minidress for the family dinner. A white jumpsuit for the cocktail party. A lace white calf-length dress for the rehearsal dinner. A silky white pajama set. A white wool coat and white shawl and a furry white option if I don't like the shawl. If I weren't going straight to hell, I'd have enough clothes for every possible event in heaven.

For this tradition-obsessed old-school family, our courtship happened fast and our engagement even faster. Anything I could do to paint myself as the picture of a perfect bride, I would do, until they were obedient dogs in my Pavlovian experiment. Eliza. Bride. Eliza. Bride. Eliza. Bride.

"You look beautiful," Mr. Walker says, taking my hands and giving me a kiss on both cheeks like he was the Prince of Wales and I should be honored to be in his company. It's not entirely far off.

The Walker family is an institution in this town, where the median income is four hundred thousand dollars but theirs is far greater. They aren't the mayor or the owner of the local market chain or the purveyor of the ski-in-ski-out resort a few mountains over, no. But they know all those people. They're great friends with the mayor and the governor and the vice presidential candidate who lives a half hour away. They have monthly dinners with the lieutenant governor. Douglas golfs with the attorney general and Cheryl organizes three fundraisers a year with the police commissioner's wife. The chief justice of the Vermont state court is Graham's godfather. The Walker family is an unbreakable, untouchable institution. And I'm about to join it.

"Thank you, Mr. Walker," I say. "You look very handsome yourself." I pretend to fix his tie, as if it was anything but perfectly straight already. I pause when I am supposed to, leaving him just enough of a gap to step in—*please, call me Douglas, I've told you that. You're family now.* But it never comes. He likes the patriarchal power of it. He's the head of this family. He gets what he wants. So I call him Doug in my head to spite him. Even though he'll never know it.

Cheryl is on the other side of the room, standing at the bar and stabbing three olives with a toothpick before drowning them in her vodka martini. "You look lovely, dear," her prickly voice says, though she has yet to look in my direction once. She's wearing an off-white frock eerily similar to the jumpsuit I am planning to wear tomorrow. Of course the mother of the groom is wearing white. She always has trouble giving up the spotlight. Mine looks better, of course. Mine is lower cut to show just enough cleavage for Graham's friends to be jealous, and just enough protruding rib for my friends to be jealous. Hers is a little, well, matronly. Like something on a mannequin at Neiman Marcus.

Graham pulls a chair out for me, and I lower into it, waiting for him to sit in the seat beside me before tucking myself a little farther under the table. All of these habits, from sitting down for dinner to choosing the fork to wiping my mouth properly, have been engraved into my brain by this point. But it only comes out when I'm here, when Graham sits up straighter and smiles less and eats even though his father's disappointment makes him lose his appetite. It's important for people like them to maintain these arbitrary traditions, like where your fork and knife go on your plate when you're finished eating. It perpetuates the division between us and them. Between those with and those without.

"Where's Reed?" Graham asks when the seats across from us remain empty, the prodigal son and his inane other half apparently even later than we are.

No one acknowledges Graham's question. Instead, Cheryl takes a sip of her martini, and her lipstick tags the edge of her glass like she is marking her territory. Her makeup, as usual, is subtle but expensive and it's caked slightly around the crow's feet that peek through the Botox. You'd only notice if you were looking for it, and I always was. "How was your flight?" Cheryl asks, finally breaking the silence.

"Smooth and easy," Graham says, unfolding his napkin and gently placing it on his lap as I do the same. "Nick says hello," he adds, referring to our pilot this morning. He is the son of one of Doug's coworkers. Doug is the one who got him the pilot gig after he graduated from his flight training program. Usually, jobs working with this prestigious level of clientele take years to climb up the ladder toward. But not for a friend of the Walkers.

"Travel days are always exhausting, I find. Even for such a short flight," I add. I'd heard Veronica say that unironically once after flying from New Jersey to their place in Southampton and I never forgot it. There couldn't be anything less stressful than a private jet. We could not have been less troubled. But rich people see everything as a personal inconvenience.

"I feel the same way," Cheryl expounds, like I'd just articulated something she'd been unable to put into words all these years. "Why don't I see if I can get Marta or Louis up here tomorrow for a little massage? Lorraine!"

Lorraine marches in from the kitchen, moving faster than a woman her age probably should, an apron twisted around her middle and a salad bowl in each hand. She places one down at Doug's seat first, then Cheryl's as she offers to call into town tomorrow and schedule something for the morning.

"We're meeting the caterer in the morning," I say to Lorraine without thinking. I didn't say it aggressively or with the tone of an order like Graham and Doug would have—like she should already know our schedule—but I immediately analyze her pause, the way she stands beside Cheryl looking at me. Is it a look or a *glare*? Is it a *glare* or a moment of recognition?

I offer a smile, kind and apologetic. *I'm just stressed.* It's just *so fucking stressful* to be a bride.

"I'd love for you to be there, but I understand if you're too busy," I say to Cheryl. "You've already done so much."

"In the afternoon, then," she corrects. She looks at me, placating and pitiful, like I need a massage now more than ever. "Of course I'll be there."

Most of this wedding is Graham's mother's fever dream—the kind of thing she would have chosen for herself if her mother-in-law weren't so heavily involved in the same way she is now in mine. She picked a florist—the son of a former conservative congressman friend—and decided on chocolate cosmos in a bed of greenery. She found a caterer—the most sought out for their Southampton parties—and compiled a menu of filets and salmons. She tagged a bakery—the midlife crisis of the police chief's wife—and chose the vanilla naked cake and apple cider doughnuts. And she had the final say on the venue: a plot of land she and Mr. Walker are gifting us to build our very own mountainous castle.

This is fine with me because I don't give a shit. About any of it. My only three requests were a ceremony in Vermont in October, a dress of my choosing that I would pay for, and to have the *New York Times* Vows writer and photographer in attendance. She could have whatever band she wanted and invite whatever attorney general her black heart desired.

"Sorry we're late," Reed says, gliding into the room like he's being pulled on one of those airport moving staircases. Separately, Graham is one of the hottest people I've ever laid my eyes on. However, I learned during my first visit here, when you put him in the same room as Reed—if they stand too close or get caught in a picture together—it suddenly looks like each of Graham's features are just one centimeter off in some way. Separately, Graham's head is the perfect size. Together, he looks like a bobblehead. Separately, his eyes are the most stunning blue I've ever seen. Together, they're gray like dirty bathwater.

I hated that Veronica had that on me. That in our wedding

photos, she'll be married to the hotter Walker. What gets me through is knowing that Graham will have the hotter wife.

The 2008 sauv blanc is taunting me in the glass at my seat. It is making my head spin, I want it so badly. Here, in this house with these people, I can't outwardly be on my wedding diet. I'm not about to eat a grilled cheese with French fries, but I have to eat what I am served. With my friends in New York, everyone knows you can say the words *wellness* or *gluten free* or *intermittent fasting* and it means you're dieting in one of the many socially acceptable capacities. Here, food is the biggest topic of judgment. If they knew the diet I'm on, the amount of restricting and bingeing and puking I do daily, Veronica and Cheryl would look at me with their heads tilted, small smiles escaping their lined lips—*How sad for you that to look like us you need to* diet. But if I ate whatever I wanted, gave in to every salty or sweet craving my mouth watered for, then I'd get the *Oh, you're having another one?* or *Didn't you just eat?* or *Are you sure you* need *that?*

So I drink the wine. And, yes, Cheryl, I do fucking need it.

Veronica enters a few seconds behind Reed, always. An eighteenth-century tradition they don't even realize they're following. She's tall and thin and is the kind of put together that probably made her look thirty-five when she was twenty-two, a trait that comes with family money. Sometimes when I look at her, I think about how in different circumstances—in a different life—we probably could be friends. She was the first family member I met. We got a bottle of rosé at Café Cluny when Graham and I first realized this was serious; that we were moving fast and on the same page about it. We sat at a table outside one cool spring afternoon, when the temperature was chilly but the sun was hot like summer on your face. Every few minutes I'd bring the glass to my lips and let the liquid sit there, cold and sweet, barely seeping through into my mouth. Then I'd put it down.

"Do you not like the wine?" she'd asked when her glass was empty and mine was still full. "We can get a different bottle."

"I love it!" I said before she could call the waiter over. "This is my second glass!" I lied. "You've got to catch up." She blushed as I refilled her.

Then refilled it again. And again.

When she was drunk enough—one bottle had turned into two and it might as well have been an IV straight to her head—she leaned in, wobbly and giggly, like a happy child. "You don't have to do this," she said. "You really don't."

"Do what?" I asked, charmed by her drunkenness.

She was silent for a moment, but then her face turned serious, her eyes thinned and she was suddenly alert, like the booze had disappeared from her body with the breeze. "The Walkers are... They know everyone. They're important. Once you know their secrets, you won't ever be able to leave."

Then she leaned back and hiccupped, giggling at the sound like what she had just said was already a memory she wouldn't have tomorrow.

I knew the Walkers had secrets. So do I. That's the point.

"Thanks for gracing us with your presence," Graham says to the two of them as they sit across from us, their salads dressed and getting soggier each moment they aren't eating them.

"Oh, chill out," Reed says.

"Are you going to be late to the ceremony too?" Graham asks. "Make me stand up there by myself for a half hour?"

Graham likes being told to *chill* as much as a woman likes being told to *calm down*. There is something about that word that's inherently offensive.

"You waited fifteen minutes. You survived."

"I don't—" Graham keeps glancing at Doug, waiting for

him to be as ticked with Reed as he was with us. If Doug is paying attention, he doesn't show it.

"That's enough. Just eat," Cheryl commands, shaking her head. She looks between Veronica and me, like she is still trying to keep up appearances, as if we both hadn't experienced worse from our chosen men. "Boys will be boys." She laughs.

Yours sure will.

After dinner, Graham suggests a walk. He says it inconspicuously, with a sly smile only I would catch. It was the weekend of arbitrary traditions so why not pile another one on top of the stack?

I'd spent the last hour eating grilled chicken and sautéed vegetables and talking about nothing. The Walkers are good at that—talking about nothing. Skimming the surface without actually saying anything of importance. The appearance of care was there, knowing just enough to have a response should Doug's coworker ask about the wedding or Cheryl's Pilates instructor ask what Henry got for his birthday, but it was absent of any interest. Like they were afraid to divulge too much to one another. Like saying the wrong word would be held over their heads for the rest of their lives.

I'd witnessed cracks in this indifferent foundation twice, which led me to believe that there was a time before me when they actually cared. And seeing the presence of that love, however fleeting, made me think about what must have happened to break it.

The Walkers' fifteen acres sit on the peak of the mountain, surrounded by views to the south and lush color-changing trees to the north, east, and west. Graham likes to go on walks into the wooded part of the property, around the lake that sits peacefully on the edge of their land, remote and unbothered. Probably eight of the fifteen acres they have are woods, and those are Graham's favorite parts. Not the house or the pool or the hot tub or tennis court. The woods.

"There are bears around here but I'll protect you," Graham had said during our walk the first time I ever visited the compound. He put his arms around my shoulders like that was all it would take to ward off a hungry beast. The animal would be so intimidated by Graham's flexing biceps that it would run in the opposite direction.

In reality, I'd be the one protecting him. Or feeding him to it. That just depended on the day.

I'd been face-to-face with a black bear before. Everyone knows they're more afraid of humans than humans are of them. Being attacked by a black bear would be rarer than getting attacked by a cow. Only one of the two allows you to die with a little dignity, though.

We had black bears around the farm when I was growing up. Once a week, my mother would fill a spray bottle with cayenne pepper and water and make me walk the perimeter of the land, spraying the ground and the lower half of the trees. It was mostly to keep them from scavenging for food out of the compost and the garden and the chicken pen. When I was eight or nine, I was kicking a rock along the path, spraying in the line of the rock's passage, and I looked up to see a bear, not three feet from me, the rock underneath its paw like a soccer ball. If I hadn't looked up, I would have bumped right into it.

We were both frozen still, staring at the other. All I remember thinking was *stop, drop, and roll*, instructions for if you're caught on fire, not for when you're close enough to a wild bear to see its pupils dilating. *Stop, drop, and roll.* But that was stupid fucking advice.

"Go away," I said, matter-of-fact, like I was reasoning with one of my brothers over who should get to use the bathroom first. "GO AWAY!" I yelled it a second time, my voice echoing through the trees to sound like two or three people were demanding the animal leave. But it worked. It scurried away so fast, I was sure it wasn't coming back.

But I'd let Graham protect me. Sure. My little Manhattan-bred fiancé. The idiot would probably stop, drop, and roll.

"Do you want me to come tomorrow? To the caterer?" Graham asks as we round the bend away from the house toward the passage to the lake. His arm was wrapped around my shoulders in that way it was the first time.

"If you want," I say, knowing he wouldn't. I didn't want him there either way. He was so uninvolved in the whole planning process that when he decides to show up, it just confuses things. It's like trying to have an opinion on something you've never thought about before in your entire life. "But I think your mom and I have it handled if you want to make other plans."

"I think the guys start arriving around noon, so I want to be around when they get here."

"Then you should stay," I say, as if this entire conversation wasn't just an excuse to get me to allow him to hang out with his friends guilt free. They'd be drunk before I got home from the meeting, I knew it. They didn't have anything to say to each other, so instead they drink to fill the silence. I'm really looking forward to walking into *that* room.

I spin around and walk backwards a few feet in front of him, watching him watch me.

"We're almost there," I say, smiling wryly.

He adjusts himself and continues walking, watching me like a bear stalking its prey.

I see the small patch of poisonous berries—the red kind that Graham reminded me three times never to eat, as if I had a penchant for plucking food from the wild and sticking it into my fucking mouth. Graham's favorite tree was three feet away from the berry bush. "Go for a walk" was Graham speak for "Let's have sex at my favorite tree." I had a favorite tree growing up, too, but this was never something I imagined doing against it.

As we approached the tree, I lifted the back of my coat and dress so my thong was visible and I let him slap my bare ass so hard I was sure it would bruise.

The tree had formed around the corroded stump of another tree and the way the tree's bark enveloped the stump made it look like an asshole. Like a naked butt was squatting. Graham really knows how to get a girl in the mood.

Graham picks me up and I wrap my legs around his waist until he bangs me up against the tree, pulling at his belt buckle like if this didn't happen right now he'd explode.

"I love you so much," he says as we start fucking, which I roll my eyes at behind his back. He gets off on the fact that I'm into this shit. That I'll have sex whenever, wherever, and we both come every time. But I get turned on not by him but by the show. The idea that someone could be watching us. His brother, his father. My first time—and *our* first time—was in public, and I never quite got over that rush of getting away with something you shouldn't. I thrived on it. I came on it.

I also liked the way the tree felt against my back as we moved up and down against it. The way the bark embedded into my skin, scratching my shoulder blades and my back, painful and delicious. Something my makeup team will have to cover up in the morning, but that's a thought for another day.

We walk back to the house silently but enveloped in each other. His jacket is draped on my shoulders, his arms around me, my head resting on him, our sides and hips pressed together so close I could smell the salty sweat of our sex.

"Can we take the shortcut?" I ask. "I'm freezing."

He rubs his hands up and down my arms. Sex was a momentary release from the cold, but afterward it was worse; not even my coat could protect me from the cold air clinging to my sweat, sending chills up my spine and my back.

The shortcut was walking along the road instead of through the trees. It was a more direct path that was already cleared and would lead us to the front door in ten minutes instead of thirty.

When we reach the edge of the woods, Graham stops and lets me jump onto his back. I couldn't walk the gravel in heels, and I couldn't walk it barefoot. So, a piggyback ride up a steep mountain it is.

"You weigh less than a feather," Graham says after a few minutes. "If you weren't breathing on my neck, I wouldn't even know you were there."

I let out a long warm puff directly into his ear and then kiss him just below it. I could feel him shivering.

"We've got a hot shower in our future," he says, pretending to be less breathless than he is.

I rest my head on his shoulder and close my eyes. If I let myself think about this place too long, I can feel the panic start to grow, from the hole in which it usually resides in my chest to my neck and stomach and my face and my knees. But sometimes if I close my eyes, I can forget, for just a moment. Forget about everything.

"What the fuck—"

I'm dropped to the floor before I realize what's going on, landing so hard on my feet I'm not sure I'll be able to walk tomorrow. The sharp rocks hit my soles and send strikes of pain up my entire body until my knees give out and I fall to the ground.

When I look up, Graham is standing in front of me, staring straight into the woods beside us. His hands are at his sides, balled into fists so tight his white knuckles are reflecting the moonlight.

"A bear?" I ask, slowly getting back on my feet. But when I stand next to him, fully prepared to reason with this animal the same way I did the one at home, I'm speechless. "What is this?" I ask.

Stapled onto the trees in front of us, right on the edge of the gravel road, are posters—dozens of them:

MISSING: BERNADETTE WARD

Beneath that is a photo of a smiling blonde girl. It looks like an oil painting; she is so perfect, her hair so straight, her eyes so blue.

They don't look like the kind of missing posters I'd seen on *Law & Order*. They don't have any details, no age or height or weight, no date she was last seen, no description of her clothes. The more I stare at her, the more it looks like she is staring at me, watching me, pulling me closer and closer until my face meets hers. I reach forward and gently tug the paper off a tree, wanting to get a closer look at her.

"Don't fucking touch that," he says.

"Who is she?" I ask, her face smiling up at me like a hopeful child's.

"I said don't touch it." He slaps my hand, hard, until the paper falls out of it and onto the cold ground. Then he rips another poster off another tree. He crumples it up in his hand as he reaches for the next. Then the next. He starts pulling them off two at a time, getting farther and farther into the dark forest as he does it, pulling each and every one off the trees so violently little paper slivers stick to the staples and wave at me in the wind.

"What is this about?" I ask. "Do you know her?"

Graham appears a few moments later, white-knuckling the posters like if he squeezed hard enough they'd disappear. Just like her, I guess.

"It's an old case," he says. "I don't know anything about

her. This makes our neighborhood look unsafe. And with everyone coming up here tomorrow—" He starts walking up the mountain toward the house, leaving me standing there by myself, the tough gravel maiming the bottoms of my feet. But I know better than to call him back. I know better than to ask any more questions.

I pick the last poster up from the ground and look at her. MISSING: BERNADETTE WARD.

I fold up the paper and slip it into my bra.

Then I follow him up the mountain in silence.

# FOURTEEN

**A WEEK AFTER** that night with Lena, Graham and I went on our first date. We met at Ludlow House, a place where neither he nor I were members, but at which he had the clout to get a prime reservation anyway. When he texted me the details for our date, I couldn't tell if he was expecting me to be more impressed than I let on. I didn't know members-only clubs like this existed. It wasn't until I was seated at the bar, waiting for Graham to arrive, when two celebrities I'd never heard of were escorted through the back door to a table labeled *Reserved*, that it clicked.

The woman was bony and gorgeous, wearing five-inch heels she had no trouble walking in and an outfit so ugly only a celebrity could claim it as *fashion*. The man had a cutesy salt-and-pepper look to him, and wore a gray suit and pink shirt that accentuated it. No one was taking pictures of them, or really acknowledging them in any way, but that was the key; that was what they were paying for. To enter a public space and feel normal again.

When the bartender approached with my drink, a glass of

pinot so dry I almost choked as it slid down my throat, I asked who they were.

He looked at me like he was a youth minister and I had just rolled my eyes at the "Pizza and Purity" event he'd spent months planning. "Seriously?"

I shrugged and took a sip.

"Sarah Jessica Parker and Andy Cohen," he said. "They're in here all the time."

"Are they actors?"

"I mean… I guess. *Sex and the City… Watch What Happens Live…*" He waited for a gasp of realization from me that never came. The embarrassed *oh my gosh, of course, duh* that I stopped offering years ago when I realized it didn't actually work. If you don't know something when it's first mentioned, you don't know it and it's pathetic and fruitless to try to cover your tracks.

When Graham walked through the main door, I had to do a double take. The way he glided toward me, the way he captivated the women at the tables around him, the way people stared, wondering who he was. He could have been the third in their famous trio.

His only tell was that he was staring at me like I was the only person in the room. And this was when I still had some baby fat around my cheeks and stomach, when I'd watched hundreds of hours of makeup tutorials but always looked 20 percent worse because I could only afford the CVS versions, when I didn't know who Sarah Jessica Parker or Andy Cohen were and didn't have the wherewithal to fake it from the get-go.

I knew after our meeting at the bar that I was a magnet he couldn't stay away from. It was love at first sight, or so it seemed to him and everyone around us. I'd played the part he needed me to play—the bad girl who looks like a good girl, the one who can make his friends jealous, who can have his kids but still get dirty with him after they're in bed, who will fit in perfectly with his family but shit talk with him after they're gone.

I knew everything about him already. Graham Walker, twenty-eight. Graduated from Yale with a BA in finance and then an MBA. He works at BlackRock, where he'd managed to move up a hundred times faster than anyone else who graduated with him. He seems like a smart guy, but there's no way that kind of rise comes without Daddy's help.

From what I could tell, he's basically dated three women. First, Tori, a brunette with a nose ring he messed around with in college. She posted more pictures of the two of them than he did—most of them involved her sticking her tongue out at the camera while holding a beer at a party. Then there was Caroline, an intern who started his first few months of work—young, cute, perky. Then Meg, a bartender trying to be an actress who'd inherited a Lower East Side loft in her parents' messy divorce.

What I gathered from all of his past relationships was that he needed one thing: spontaneity with the appearance of stability. He needed to feel like he was living out his best years while appearing like he had it all together. Someone who could have fun with him, while wearing the appropriate clothes to walk in and out of his expensive building. Someone who could fuck him in a bathroom and then fit right in with his friends and family.

He needed someone younger, someone he could get validation from *teaching*; but someone on his level in other ways. Someone in his class.

On one hand, Lena was probably Graham's perfect girl. I just got there first. The student surpasses the teacher, as they say.

"You look great," Graham said, smiling at the black jeans and strappy black top I decided would show off my body best, but not so much that he thought we'd traipse to the bathroom again. I was going to go home with him this time.

I stood from the stool, keeping one eye on my drink, as always. "Thank you," I said. "So do you."

"Shall we?" Without pausing, Graham took my drink and led us to our table, also labeled *Reserved*, directly next to Sarah and Andy's. In this place, with this person, the four of us were equals. Everyone knew who they were and wondered, by association, who we were. Who I was. But out of jealousy, though not because I didn't fit in. I made sure I looked like I was exactly where I belonged.

Up close, and put-together, Graham didn't look quite how I expected him to. He was arguably the hottest man I'd ever met, but he seemed to contribute to that status less than I thought he would. His clothes fit him but weren't fitted to him. His hair was brushed but not styled. He smelled swoony of soap, not expensive aftershave. He just looked like this. He didn't have to force it. It was just the way he existed. He had quite a set of genes.

"How are you liking New York?" he asked. "Lena mentioned you just moved a couple months ago."

"It's been...fun," I responded. "I could see myself staying here long-term."

New York, I learned after moving there, was not *like a character* in the way *Cosmo*'s articles about movies made it seem. New York was a *Main Character*. *The* Main Character. New Yorkers love shitting on New York—the trains never work, there are rats everywhere, the rent is insane—but the second you join in, they turn as defensive as a lion protecting a smelly-ass cub: *The trains never work but at least we have the largest public transportation system in the world.*

*There are rats everywhere, but they're basically just squirrels. Unsocially-acceptable squirrels. Honestly, justice for rats!*

*My rent is insane but I'm paying for the opportunity. And my kitchen is so big I can open my fridge and oven at the same time!*

*How do you like New York?* and *What do you do?* were the two questions I'd most received since I'd been here. All anyone seemed to care about on the surface were how you felt about their city and what you did to afford to live there.

"Already?" he asked. "It usually takes a few years to picture long-term."

I was incapable of thinking past my five-year plan. A plan that involved Graham. I'd live here at least until that happened. After that felt like another life. One I couldn't conceptualize quite yet. I'd be a different person in five years; just as I was a different person now than I was five years ago. That Elizabeth doesn't exist anymore. And this Eliza won't exist then.

A woman in a suit named Zena stopped at our table and took our drink orders with the attitude of someone very happy to be here, but slightly pissed that she wasn't serving the big celebrity tippers at the table over. I ordered a second glass of wine so quickly I was afraid she didn't hear me properly. I was too nervous to be completely sober. When she turned to Graham he ordered a club soda.

"I don't drink…" he said, as she marched off.

I immediately felt like a deplorable alcoholic. "Oh shit, I'm sorry. I should have waited." I turned to get Zena's attention. "Let me see if I can order something else—"

"No, no, no." He reached across the table for my arm, touching it so gently he might as well not have been holding it at all. It was electrifying. "Have all the wine you want. Seriously." When I turned back, he was looking at me like an earnest child, afraid he'd offended me in the same way I feared I'd offended him. How, in all my research, did I not learn he was sober? I knew his fucking social security number—I couldn't have somehow put together that in all his recent social media pictures he's the only one of his friends not holding a beer?

It made me nervous for what else I could have possibly missed.

"I'm not an alcoholic or anything," he clarified, pulling his hand back to his side of the table. "I stopped drinking in college. Had one *really bad* night, you know..."

I knew.

"Everyone's got that one night," I said, brushing it off. "So you were a partier in college, I gather?"

His eyebrows rose and fell with a laugh. "I was *stupid* in college," he corrected. "I thought keg stands and body shots would impress girls."

"Did it?"

"Maybe if I knew how to do it right," he said. "I was more like the one varsity athlete in my frat who could only drink during off-season and overcompensated."

"Wow." I laughed as Zena dropped off my wine and his seltzer. I found myself blushing even though I didn't want to. I blamed it on the wine. "That was one subtle flex you did just there."

He smiled. "I know what impresses girls now. I've learned from my mistakes." That last sentence hung there and I was tempted to probe—what other mistakes have you learned from? How have you learned, exactly? But I kept quiet. I was actually enjoying myself and part of me didn't want to ruin it.

"What was your collegial trope?" he asked. "You went to Brown, right?"

I nodded as I swallowed slowly, gifting myself some more time. I was an inexperienced, prudish, naive, questioning Christian, who finally escaped her parents' overbearing arms and considered her college experience an opportunity to course-correct everything that was so fucked-up about her childhood. I became someone else entirely. And I never went back.

"What do you *think* I was?" I asked.

He studied me carefully, as if anything about my current self would hint to who I was back then. I was too well trained to let any of that come out. Even if it did, that wouldn't matter. His answer was just a reflection of what he wanted to see, regardless of who I was. Helpful for my research.

His eyes slimmed and one side of his mouth curled up with wry amusement. "You look more innocent than you really are," he said. "I bet you could get away with anything in college." He paused, like he was deciding whether or not to say the rest. "And now, too, probably," he added, his smile morphing into something else, something that turned him on. "Am I right?"

I pretended to think about it for a moment. I learned early on that the most convincing lies are cloaked with half-truths, sprinkled with things to help you remember so you're never caught in your own mistake. "You're not far off," I replied. Though, with his family and his background, I'd argue he'd know how to get away with things best.

My entire four-story walk-up (arbitrarily named The Theodore so whoever lives there can pretend to be pretentious) could fit into Graham's apartment. Entering the lit hallway, I felt both like I was faking it—like I didn't belong, and I would never belong—and also like it was working, whatever I was doing was working. Graham held my hand, leading me in, and I wondered how often he did this; how often he brought a woman home to make her horny with hope for their future. That one day she could be roasting a chicken in that signature Wolf stove. That she could replace the god-awful abstract acrylic in the living room with something that didn't look like it belonged in a hotel elevator bank. That she could gossip and drink martinis with her jealous friends on that terrace. The easiest way to get into a woman's pants is with an apartment like this.

The sex was bland, but that's what happens when you're fucking on two-hundred-dollar sheets in a room with views of Central Park compared to the last time when you were in the bathroom of a bar with sticky floors and *God Loves Dick* subtly engraved into the brand-new molding. That's what happens when you whitewash the sexy filth.

Graham fell asleep almost immediately, spooning my naked body like he was afraid if he let me go, I'd disappear. I didn't expect him to be so affectionate. He seemed like the kind of guy who would roll over, falling into the kind of deep sleep that allowed him to forget I was there and wake up a little surprised. *Oh…hi!*

Once he was snoring in my ear, his chest heaving up and down with every breath, I snaked out of his heavy grip carefully, making sure not to shake him or the bed too much. I don't sleep. I haven't since that night Ruthie didn't come home and I especially couldn't here, in a strange bed with a strange man. If I let my guard down who knows what he would do.

I pulled a thick gray robe off the back of Graham's closet and slipped into it as I snuck out of the room, shutting the door behind me so I'd have some audible warning if he were to wake up and come looking for me.

I walked around the room, turning off all the lights that Graham left on in our haste to get to the bedroom. I wanted to be in the dark. The best sleuthing happens in the dark, when I feel removed from time, like it could be 10:00 p.m. or 4:00 a.m. and I wouldn't know.

I started in the bathroom. Under the sink: Clorox, the Laundress laundry detergent—*his mom bought that, for sure*—a four-pack of bamboo toilet paper—*environmentally conscious*—a plunger. On the counter: an electric toothbrush, whitening toothpaste, mouthwash, hand soap. *He cares about his teeth.* I saved the best for last, the medicine cabinet: a half-finished Kiehl's facial cream—*he moisturizes, interesting*—a slew of shaving accessories, some toothbrush head replacements, deodorant—*Degree Men Sport, just like every man I've ever met*—a comb with no hair in it, a box of Band-Aids, a box of Icy Hot patches, face wash, Epsom salts—*athletic*—gummy vitamins, and…prescriptions… Zoloft, Prozac, Lexapro, Celexa. *Anxiety. Severe anxiety.*

In the living room, I took my phone out of the purse I'd dropped on the floor on my way to the bedroom. A few messages from Lena asking about the date. A few emails from work I won't open.

I browsed the photos on the built-in bookshelves flanking the television. A line of graduates—as hot as him, as rich as him—standing in their black caps and gowns, smiling in their accomplishments.

A baby Graham, I could tell by the eyes, he had very striking eyes, sitting on his mother's lap, her hair and outfit reminiscent of the '80s, back when they had a lot of money, but not *this much* money.

A photo from a ski trip, Graham and his family completely anonymous underneath their helmets and gaiters and orange goggles.

I made my way slowly into the kitchen, running my fingers over the soft marble counters, the white cabinets, the black knobs. One plate was in the sink—crusted with yellow egg yolks and brownish-green avocado. *He cooks.* I pulled the garbage out from underneath, a brand-new bag in the trash, a bottle of Stella in the recycling. *Hmm.*

On the refrigerator were two wedding invitations—Lynn & Jack, Kate & Clarissa—and next to them a family picture. It was recent—Graham looked the same. Candid around a fire in the dark—his mother, uptight even in the way she sat; his father, cross and stern; Graham, smiling because he was told to do so; and his brother. Reed.

My phone in one hand, I dialed the number I'd memorized all those years ago and listened to it ring. It always rang. Like the ringing would never stop.

*"Hi, it's me, leave a message. Or don't. Love ya!"*

Beeeep.

*Oh, I miss your voice.*

*I wish you were here.*

Then I did something I hadn't done in years. I opened the fridge, pulled out the first thing I saw—a half-finished bag of fresh four-cheese ravioli—and fisted the cold chewy cubes into my mouth until the bag was empty and I could remember how this felt. The moment before the dread sinks in. Before the nausea and panic and calorie counting. A moment, so brief, of pure unrestraint. A moment I could finally relax.

Freedom.

# FIFTEEN

————

**MOLLY HOLDS THE** fork in her fist like a vengeful woman in an Oxygen Network true crime reenactment finding out her husband cheated with their twenty-four-year-old babysitter. When she stabs the slice of cake with it straight through, handing the golden plate to my future mother-in-law, she smiles like it's as much a game to her as it is to me.

"I know it's strange," Molly assures us as Cheryl reluctantly takes the plate from her hands, staring bewilderingly at the fork that stands erect from the cake's brown belly. "But it's a real crowd-pleaser. I want the food and presentation to combine the edge of the couple, with the raw wilderness we'll all be surrounded by on the big day."

She sounded like my yoga teacher, Feather, but with less body hair.

"I guess it ensures the utensils won't fall to the ground when the cake is being handed out," I offer, a sign of peace between the two women.

"A well-trained waiter would ensure that as well," Cheryl

says under her breath, pulling the fork from the cake like King Arthur.

Molly came on strong this morning when Cheryl and I arrived for our meeting, which I only somewhat appreciated. Less is always more with the Walkers. I thought I had mentioned that on one of our preliminary phone calls: Veronica is fake gluten-free; can we have a dairy-free option at the dessert buffet; the Walkers aren't impressed by anyone, but want you to always be trying. Yes, I definitely mentioned it.

Molly is incredibly confident, that's her problem. No shaky hands, no nerves when presenting her outside-the-box, Instagram-worthy creations. She knew we were getting what we asked for—a picture-perfect event created by someone who specializes in picture-perfect. She had nothing to be nervous about.

The problem: Cheryl is intimidated by confident women. They make her feel weak. That's why Veronica and I are always acting so overly pleasant around her, smiling gracefully, standing behind our Walker men, letting ourselves be wrong in friendly arguments even though we know we're right. We bow down to her, our matriarch. Or, at least, she needs to think we do. After all, without her, this family would cease to exist as we know it.

I'd been planting the seed to use Molly for our caterer since the first time I met Cheryl, when we were drinking cocktails in the sitting room, and I first introduced her to the concept of specially designed charcuterie. Molly's company was a household Hamptons name by then and Cheryl's friends would be *positively offended* if Cheryl didn't know her personally in some way. "You know everyone," I'd said, "I'm shocked she's not a friend of a friend!" I knew Molly wasn't, but I liked playing this game with Cheryl. Molly started out too low-brow to be the daughter of a Walker acquaintance. She was self-made. Another thing the Walkers feared.

I feigned surprise when Cheryl called two weeks after my engagement to Graham to say she had hired Molly as the caterer. My light suggestion had worked. "We should count ourselves lucky," she began. "She only does a select handful of weddings a year, so she squeezed us in." It was the presumptuous *so* that made me laugh out loud, nearly spitting out the LaCroix that had been bubbling in my mouth while she spoke. As if Molly had been anticipating our engagement, holding a special slot open for the fateful day Cheryl Walker would ring and ask for her services.

"Everyone recommends her," Cheryl continued. "Carol at the club tried to get her for their anniversary party last summer but she was booked solid all year."

"Well, I guess we *are* very lucky, then," I responded.

Molly Bell is the founder and CEO of Say Cheesed, a cheese board empire—and I don't use that ridiculous combination of words lightly. Just out of college she started a charcuterie business, boxing up premade boards for Avon ladies' nights on Long Island and Hamptons-adjacent bachelorette parties that requested their brie in the shape of an uncircumcised dick. Turns out, Amy Schumer had been at one of those bachelorette parties and drunk-posted a video of herself pretending to give the dick-shaped cheese head.

*Say Cheesed* went superviral. In her first year, Molly made two million dollars selling cheese boards. Beyoncé used her for Blue's birthday party; Ramona Singer and Bethenny Frankel had a screaming match while standing over Molly's salami in the shape of a rose; Stanley Tucci called her honey dippers "inventive."

She designed a Super Bowl–themed board on Rachael Ray's show. She offered charcuterie basics on Colbert's Thanksgiving special. She even got invited to Chrissy Teigen's house to teach charcuterie arranging for her blog.

Seven years after her first Instagram post, Molly has become the most sought-after caterer in New York City, the Hamptons, and Los Angeles. She's not a chef—her specialty is not cooking. It's appearance control. Social media. It's in creating shareable moments through food. At least, that's what her tagline says. And that's what the Walkers want. When you know all the most important people in the state, you then become responsible for impressing the most important people in the state.

"Is Graham all right?" Cheryl asks, leaning into me so it is clear who the question is directed toward. As if Molly would think to field a question about my fiancé. "He was acting strange in the kitchen earlier. Jumpy."

It was clear to me that Graham hadn't told his mother about what happened last night—the eerie barrage of posters on the edge of the woods. He'd gone to bed so quickly I didn't even know what he'd done with all the papers he'd ripped down and stuffed into his pockets. It's possible they're still in our bedroom, or that he flushed them down the toilet or something. It wasn't my place to say anything—of course, I didn't even know about this *old case* that Graham so quickly dismissed. But I had hoped in the night I'd feel him stirring. I'd pretend to be asleep as he slipped out of bed, into his slippers, and out the door to knock across the hall and tell his brother what he'd found. The person I'd hoped he'd tell. But he slept as soundly as ever.

"He's just excited," I say. "Sometimes his excitement materializes as nerves."

"I know that," she says, always defensive when it comes to who knows the most about her precious son. "Good," she adds, a period on our conversation before turning her attention back to Molly. "You know the *Times* will be attending the wedding."

Molly turns around and looks up at me and offers an impressed nod. She has long hair, blonder now, remnants from the summer sun, that falls effortlessly into beachy waves around her face. She seems like the kind of person who washes her hair maybe twice a week, and, when given the opportunity, will tell you about the months of "hair training" that went into the routine. *But it's totally worth it, look at me now.* She is wearing a white chef's coat with *Say Cheesed* written in a pleasant cursive, over jeans that show off her lean running thighs.

"That's amazing," Molly says, unexpectedly proud. "Good job."

"Good job?" Cheryl pushes the cake toward Molly, signifying we're finished and ready for whatever part of the tasting menu she has next. "It's not like you've never been mentioned in the *Times* before. They're your biggest fan."

Molly shakes her head, seemingly shaking away a memory, and turns her attention from me to Cheryl. "Sorry," Molly says, moving around the long wooden raw-edge table to the side opposite us. "I just meant that it's great. Very exciting."

Cheryl sits up straighter in her seat at even the slightest hint of submission from Molly; of confidence weakening.

Molly takes the cake plate and returns it to the station behind her. I wasn't finished but I guess I should be. It was physically painful for me not to attack the cake, to stuff the entire slice into my mouth with my hand, licking the vanilla frosting off each finger like a leopard devouring every inch of a gazelle. But I can't. Because I'm here. That's not behavior conducive to a Walker Woman. Walker Women are controlled. I am controlled. I plant my feet firmly on the cold ground and remind myself where I am, letting my skinny heels sink into the grass of Graham's land, the land on which there were hundreds of people actively prepping for us to wed. The land on which everything will change.

I take a deep breath and the sharply cool air feels good as it goes into my lungs.

"And now for the main course," Molly says. From her station she pulls a long hot stone, displaying sizzling filet mignon, buttery lobster, and blackened tofu. The heat is coming off the meat like it is blacktop in the middle of July. That is all I'll think about for the rest of the day. Tonight, I'll eat, I tell myself as she puts the stones in front of us, the smell of oily, salty goodness wafting straight to the part of my brain that controls impulse, anger, desire. The part of my brain that would stuff four pounds of this into my mouth later tonight and then throw it up after. The part of my brain that makes sure I'm never satisfied. Not even when I know Molly is here and the wedding is just around the corner.

The willpower it took not to eat at the tasting sent me straight back to our room to nap so deeply I didn't hear Graham knocking on the door. I was having one of those dreams that seemed real despite how strange it was. Molly and I were at college—my real college, not this Brown bullshit—and Ruthie was there, too. We were sitting in a circle in the quad, Dr. Felix Chastain leading us in prayer. But he wasn't actually saying words. He was just making animal noises—a pig, a goat, a hyena. Everyone but Molly and I seemed to understand him and follow along. We were looking around, confused, pretending to pray—our hands in the right spots, our heads bowed—until we made eye contact. Once we realized we were together, she looked at me the same way she had when Cheryl told her about the *Times*. Then—poof—Dr. Felix Chastain was gone and Ruthie was standing in his place, dressed in a bloody wedding gown; not mine, but the kind you get at a David's Bridal sale. She was staring at me as a blue-and-purple line bloomed on her neck, growing thicker and darker. She didn't even blink.

I had been staring into her huge blue eyes when Graham's knocking started to penetrate the dream. With every bang, the students around the circle clapped. Ruthie stared at me. Everyone clapped. I stared at Ruthie. Everyone clapped.

When I wake up, I'm so disoriented I don't recognize what room I'm in. I look at the white walls, the plants in the corner, the floor-to-ceiling window out back, where the sun bursts into the room so brightly you'd think it is shining only for me.

"Babe..." I can hear Graham outside now. That was his frustrated *babe*. The one that sounds like more of an exhausted huff than a loving pet name for his future wife.

Finally, once I get my bearings, I stand and open the door. "Sorry," I say. "Fell asleep."

He gives me a kiss before passing over the threshold and entering the room. "Why'd you lock the door?"

I think about Ruthie standing on the pedestal in the center of our circle on the quad. Pale and bruised. Wearing pure white no more.

"Just habit, I guess," I say. "Sorry."

He gets close to me, his face maybe an inch from mine, his breath a mix of minty toothpaste and fried over easy egg with hot sauce. "Stop apologizing," he says. "It's all good."

He kisses my forehead, leaving a stinging circle where his lips were, like an itchy bug bite. It's hard to kiss him when I'm thinking about her. And I always think about her up here. There's something in the isolation that's equally terrifying and riveting. It always brings me back to that night. Losing my virginity on the side of a red barn two minutes before Ruthie hoped to do the same. What happened to her could have happened to either of us. It was a toss-up which girl wouldn't survive the night.

"You okay? You look so pale, babe. Can Lorraine make you something to eat?"

When I look up from my hands, Graham is standing in the doorway of the bathroom, a stark white towel tied around his waist, my toothbrush sticking out of his foamy mouth.

The Walkers are always taking things that aren't theirs. Like they think their money and their notoriety gives them permission to take whatever they want.

"That's my toothbrush," I say.

He pulls it out of his mouth, looks at it like it's a strange object that has yet to be identified by man, and shrugs before sticking it back between his lips. "Oh," was all he could say. And barely that since his mouth was full of whitening tooth-paste. He walks back into the bathroom and turns the shower on, the steam greeting me like a facial I didn't want.

I lie back down on the bed, staring up at the ceiling, a crack from the heat forming directly above my head. If I'm lucky, the whole house will fall on top of us all.

Seeing Molly this morning was surprisingly tough. It made the whole thing real. It felt like she'd put my cold feet into blocks of cement, fastening me to this place until this ordeal is over. Until the wedding passes and I can move on.

"What time is it?" I ask Graham when he gets out of the shower, clean and dewy and hot.

"It's almost six. Everyone's starting to arrive at the hotel, so they'll be heading up here soon. Lorraine said she'd help Molly's team, since everything's running a little early."

"No!" I sit up far too quickly, sending a surge of dizziness through my brain, like a cartoon who just got hit on the head with a meat tenderizer. "What I mean is, Molly can be ready early. That's what we're paying her for." I swing my legs off the side of the bed. "Lorraine should enjoy the night. She's not working, she's a guest."

Not a bad argument for something pulled straight out of my ass, like a stray hair in the shower. Graham even seems impressed by my selfless suggestion. How thoughtful of his future wife to insist his old, retired nanny be treated as a human instead of hired staff they're no longer paying.

"That's very thoughtful," he says, kissing my forehead. Then he stands and I unconsciously lean my hands on his thighs, moving my weight from one to the other like a bad massage, until he pulls away and walks into the closet.

When he reappears, he's already dressed in his blue suit, tailored to his every inch, and a shirt so white it would reflect the sun. The top button is undone and, for a moment, I want to undo the rest, let him get a little wrinkly as I feel him up. I hate how attracted I can be to him. It helps, sure, but the way he can make me melt, lower my guard, it's disarming sometimes. The thought makes me even more light-headed.

"You look good," I say, and he smiles, always aware of that. He's not a *hot and doesn't know it* kind of guy.

As he turns to leave, he lifts the back of his suit jacket and shakes his butt at me, and I can't help but laugh. At him, at me, at this house—at the entire situation, really.

But when he closes the door, and I hear enough footsteps to ensure he's not coming back, I lock the door and laugh again.

In the closet, I find my outfit: a white deep-V jumpsuit and silver heels. It hangs next to Graham's big-day tux, perfect in its polished, expensive newness. He's worn tuxes before—we go to enough black-tie events for him to own one and me to own multiple accompanying gowns—but this one's different.

I reach my hand into the jacket pocket of his tux until I feel the thick envelope, satisfied that it's still there. Everything I need is still there.

I delicately pull my jumpsuit off the hanger and drape it over my arm, careful not to wrinkle it. Then I look at his tux one last time. It reminds me of that Hemingway six-word story—"For sale: baby shoes, never worn."

For sale: wedding tux, once worn.

The south wing of the house has been transformed into the cocktail party of Cheryl's dreams. Lights dangle down the banister and oversized vases house branches of balsam trees so fragrant you could light a match and the air would burn. Bokhara rugs overlap in the dining room, the table gone and replaced with a full bar that matches so well it might have been permanently installed while I was in the shower.

I creep down the staircase, late to my own party, hoping no one notices me until I have a drink in my hand, preferably something with vodka and zero calories, though that doesn't exist. Everyone seems to be dressed in jewel tones, like that was a secret message written in invisible ink on the back of the invitation. *Dark reds, dark greens, and dark blues only, please.* They float around the room like leaves falling on the mountain outside, everyone meandering without a true purpose there, unsure exactly where they are going until someone stops them with an awkward icebreaker like *We're wearing the same color,* or *Bride's side or groom's side?* as if I have anyone here.

I pluck a blood orange martini off a waiter's tray as he passes—even the drinks are in the jewel tone family—and down it in two gulps before I can even remember I am wearing white and thus need to stick to clear drinks only.

I lean back against the bar and scan the crowd, smiling at everyone who passes. Most of them I've never met before, and I can tell as they scan me and smile that they are only 90 percent sure I am the bride. There is a 10 percent chance I am an out of touch plus-one in a white outfit.

Normally, I think, a gathering two days before the wedding like this would be with family and the bridal party only—a quick thing that let everyone get to know each other so that by the rehearsal dinner and ceremony, everyone was familiar enough to dance and get drunk together. But we don't have a bridal party. Lena and Reed were technically asked to stand up beside us on our wooden altar but we didn't make them coordinate tie and dress. They were both hot and would somehow match without any kind of prior discussion the way hot people often do. Neither Graham nor I were interested in a bridal party—we both agreed that it was a little trivial for the wedding of a twenty-nine-year-old and thirty-two-year-old. Big bridal parties with matching blue/gray chiffon dresses are something that you enjoy when you're twenty-four. There comes an age when you don't want to put your friends through that because you don't want *them* to put *you* through it in return. There also comes an age when you don't have many friends willing. Or at all.

Ruthie was the only person I wished was here. I wished she was wearing a forest green silk dress, her hair long and in the kind of natural curls people pay good money for. Though, if she were here—on earth, I mean, not at this party—my life would probably be entirely different. Who knows what decisions I would have made—*we* would have made—if she came home that night.

"You look incredible." I feel Graham's arm slide across my back and down my waist before I see him sidle up to me and pull me against him. Hard. Suspiciously hard.

I swallow the memory of Ruthie. I'm here. She's not. She'll never be.

"Sorry I'm late." He smiles and eyes me like he wants to pull me into the nearest closet and rip my jumpsuit right off.

"Worth it."

I squirm out of his grip and give him a kiss, long and deep, tasting him to see if my hunch was right. I break it off when an embarrassing and pathetic *aww* reverberates through the crowd from anyone within walking distance. We're not Duggars. This was hardly the most exciting or passionate thing we've done.

The second I step away, looking up at my fiancé with the doe-eyed smile everyone in the room expects me to be wearing, I know I was right. He'd been drinking. I could tell from the second he touched me—a little too confident, too possessive, something only I would notice—but I needed the confirmation from a kiss. I could taste the bourbon. He didn't even try to hide it.

"Where have you been?" I hear Ruthie's voice echo in the back of my mind, the darkness of the small, cold bathroom creeping over me like a hurricane, slow and steady, until Lena crashes into me with a hug, and I realize it was she who'd said that, not my dead best friend in my own mind.

Lena, of course, looks better than I ever could. Lena is effortless. She doesn't even look like she washed her hair but it falls in wispy strands around her face and down her back like someone who just paid two hundred dollars for a blowout. I fucking hate her for it.

"Eliza, this is Jess," Lena begins, stepping aside for her girlfriend to appear, hand out and ready to shake. "Jess, this is Eliza."

Jess is exactly Lena's type in the same way I'm exactly Graham's. She looks like the best of every single person Lena's ever dated for as long as I've known her. She's tall with long legs like the girl Lena dated who somehow orgasmed in a British accent, and she's softball-player-strong with arms like the girl Lena fucked because she wanted to see how adult braces felt.

"Thanks for having me," Jess says. The crooked smile on her face feels like home. "You look beautiful."

"Oh, thank you. I'm happy you could make it," I reply, another phrase I learned from the Walker Family Dictionary. "It's great to finally meet you. Lena has said…almost nothing about you, so I will be watching you two carefully all week-end." The three of us laugh, Lena harder than expected, and I finish my champagne.

"This place is unforgettable," Jess says, glancing from the wood beams to the floor-to-ceiling windows, the darkness like a black wall outside.

"It sure is." I remember having that thought the first time, too. I'd never seen a house so big, a property so expansive. The place could be heaven if a bunch of assholes didn't own it.

Jess smiles at me again as Lena lowers her hand down Jess's backless dress in that way you do when you just want to feel your person next to you. Jess seems agnostic about the whole thing.

When they inevitably break up—Lena and her people *always* break up—Lena's going to be heartbroken.

"I have to make the rounds, but I'm thrilled to see you," I say. Then, to Lena, "This is a giant bore. I'd rather be drunk on your couch watching *Real Housewives*."

Lena laughs and shrugs. "The price of getting married, hun."

Quite a price.

I excuse myself and snake through the crowd, managing a soft smile as people acknowledge me, congratulate me, tell me I look *stunning* or like a *blushing bride*, whatever that means.

I sneak past Reed and Veronica, only just now arriving.

I pass a few of Doug and Cheryl's friends I know I've met but whom I don't remember—they're all old and white and dress in excessive tweed like they're daughters and sons of the American Revolution. I wave and smile at some of Graham's cousins and neighbors, their faces all blurring into one the more of them I see, until I'm standing at the bottom of the stairs, a spot from which I can see almost everyone in the room.

I look for Graham and find him standing by the bar, giving Reed an overenthusiastic hug and a pat on the back so rough I'm surprised it doesn't make Reed choke on his old-fashioned. Then Molly crosses my eye line, walking toward Graham with a rocks glass and a tray with one lone antipasto skewer left. She stops and hands the glass to Graham, which he gleefully accepts despite the full one on the bar beside him. Reed notices this, too, but he doesn't try to take the glass or make a scene. Instead, he takes the meat and cheese skewer and plops it into his mouth in one bite, dropping the toothpick back on the tray as Molly continues toward the kitchen.

Reed watches Graham take a big sip until Lena and Jess arrive to distract him. Jess stands there defiantly as Lena gives Graham a hug so long you'd never guess he hated everything about her except her body, the one thing that would never be his.

Following Lena, a few other college friends join their group—kids from Yale who all look vaguely familiar. It's their laughing that really gets to me. Watching the group of them, heads falling back, banging on each other's shoulders. Even if you've never met them, it's impossible not to assume they're laughing at you.

I walk toward the kitchen and, without stopping, from a prep table near the back, I snag an overloaded tray of mac and cheese balls and make my way seamlessly up the back stairs. I drift down the hall, quickly but not rushed, past the sitting room, the library, Reed and Veronica's suite, until I'm in our bedroom, the door locked behind me.

I can still hear the music downstairs, the clanking of Waterford glasses. But in this pitch-black room it feels like I'm on another planet. I feel light-headed, like I'd had fifteen more drinks than I really did, and the familiar claustrophobia begins to set in, sinking over me like fog rolls over the mountains. I try to take a few deep breaths but I can't—the jumpsuit is too tight, like a corset pulling my ribs so close together they'd morph and I'd never be able to take a deep breath again.

I claw at the side zipper until it's at my waist, and I can let this stupid costume fall off me—all of it, the outfit, the hair, the spray tan, the eyelash lift, the lipstick, the contour. I want it all gone. And the Brown, the English major, the orphan, the origin story. I close my eyes and pretend, for a moment, that all these things are lifted off me until I'm back in the forest on the edge of campus, squeezing next to Ruthie for warmth. In my khakis, my Aéropostale T-shirt, my borrowed faded Converses, my hand-me-down winter jacket with holes in all the pockets.

She can't be here. She can't be anywhere.

Naked, I slide down the wall to the hard floor and spread my legs like I'm about to stretch after a world-class workout. Instead, I bring the tray between them, the perfect spot to grab all the crumbs that fall out of my mouth as I begin.

I eat all thirty-eight mac and cheese balls in nine minutes. I count because knowing the exact numbers makes me feel worse about myself. At this point, good or bad, I'll do anything to feel something.

# SIXTEEN

AFTER OUR FIRST date, things took an unexpected turn when I didn't hear from Graham for weeks. I'd texted him the next morning, the classic *I had a great time, we should do it again* that always leads to a second date. I even left a pair of socks, clean and nicely folded, on the floor just under the side of the bed I slept on. I figured if nothing else, the next time Patricia, his six-foot-five hockey-playing cleaning lady vacuumed, she'd pick them up—white with *BOMBAS* written in pink— and leave them on the end of the bed. *You left your socks here*, Graham would inevitably text. *No wonder my feet have been so chilly*, I'd play. *I can warm them up for you*, he'd respond coyly.

Instead, I sat at my desk or on my mattress or at a bar stool, waiting. There's nothing more desperate—even suspicious— than a girl overzealous for a second date. And Walkers don't do desperate.

I'd fielded texts from Lena—and others—asking how the date went, when we were hanging out again, if I slept with him, and it was hard to play it cool. To shrug it off. To tell them, *He'll come to me, I'm irresistible*, when I felt incredibly far from it.

Truthfully, going on that date was one of the scariest things I've ever done. There was an odd permanence to it that I'd never felt before because I'd never really dated anyone before. Not in the same way. From the moment I saw Graham in the bar, I felt my life shift on its axis. My five-year plan was starting. And once you're on that train—once you're spending your days with him, your nights with him, moving in, getting engaged, planning a wedding—there's no getting off. There's no going back. I was in or I was out.

And I needed to be in.

"I'm in the mood for a margarita," I told Lena, sidling up to her in the kitchen after the longest and most boring client lunch-and-learn I'd ever attended. "Tonight?"

She rolled her eyes, seeing through me immediately. "Graham went home for the long weekend," she said. I swallowed the need to defend myself, to tell her that's not why I was asking. She knew it and there was no sense convincing her otherwise. Plus, she reveled in the power she had over me. I might have sucked Graham's dick, but *she* knew his weekend plans, *she* has reactivated their college group chat, *she* needed to introduce *me*.

"He might be at that gallery opening on Monday, though, if that's of interest." She dropped a dollop of soy milk into her coffee and left me there to think about it.

I'd done all my research, I knew I was the exact woman he was looking for, so why wasn't he answering me back? For the love of God, why was this taking so long?

That weekend, I stayed at home, lying naked on my mattress for most of the day, unwilling to install my own window AC unit for fear of it falling and killing whoever happened to be walking out of the Chinese food place below me at that moment. That would be a horribly embarrassing way to go, and I decided I would not contribute to that narrative. So instead, I opened the windows, let the stuffy still air fill my stifling apartment, and I found Veronica's Instagram account again.

It wasn't that I was stalking him—or any of them—it's that I knew what needed to happen: we needed to go out again, I needed to be with him. I'd do whatever it took. Waiting for someone else to get on the same page is as exhausting and frustrating as waiting for your own death.

As I was lying there, my phone extended precariously over my nose, a new photo popped up on her page. It was Veronica, an effervescent smile slapped across her face, standing next to Reed, the brother, who was beaming at his wife in a way that made my throat hot with bile. In their hands, pointed toward the camera, was an ultrasound. *I've got a troublemaker on my hands!* the caption read, paired with blue heart and baby bottle emojis.

They were having a baby. Bringing a child into the world. A boy.

We didn't need any more boys like them in the world. We didn't need them teaching sons their ways, setting a moral code, establishing right and wrong.

Nausea overcame me and I rolled over just fast enough to throw up on my sweaty pillowcase.

After I caught my breath, I tossed my phone across the room and stood to start stripping the sheets. I didn't have a second pair so I'd either have to go to the Laundromat tonight or sleep on a bare mattress. I couldn't stand the smell of throw-up.

As I pulled the pillowcase off the bed, an anticipatory fizzle of anxiety hit my chest.

*Well, at least Graham will respond to me soon*, I thought. *Nothing pressures someone to get a girlfriend like a sibling's baby announcement.*

★ ★ ★

The gallery opening in Chelsea was filled with the kind of people I was trying to be friends with—people like Lena but less interesting. It's a strange crowd, where straitlaced Harvard business money meets Oberlin girls with pierced nipples and arm tattoos. Though I guess it's often Harvard business money that *breeds* Oberlin girls with pierced nipples and arm tattoos. If you're twenty-three, with an art show, Daddy's paying for it somehow.

Lena took my hand and floated around the room, introducing me to everyone she laid eyes on. "This is my friend Eliza," she'd say, a step up from when she'd call me a coworker, or worse, give me no attribution at all.

I must have been visibly disappointed when, halfway through the night, Graham was nowhere to be found because Lena eased up to me, so close—and after a few glasses of champagne— that I thought she might try to kiss me, and she whispered, "Get over him. There are so many hotter guys here anyway. He's not worth it."

I took a deep breath and smiled, nodding like she was right. Like I was being pathetic, and I needed to shake myself out of it. If there was one person besides Graham that I didn't want to look desperate in front of, it was Lena. She was too carefree to ever give a fuck about anyone. I bet *she'd* never been ghosted like this. I bet she did the ghosting and her partners probably felt honored to have ever been in her presence in the first place.

But she had no idea what she was talking about.

To ease her mind, I plucked a glass of champagne off a passing tray and ambled toward a guy in a dark suit standing alone, admiring what looked to me like a piece of fabric covered in staples then tacked to a wall and called "art" by a rich person with little taste. But what did I know, the walls of my apartment were bare.

"Beautiful piece, isn't it?" he said once he noticed I was there, his voice more gruff than I would have expected. Something I'd find at the farm, not at an art show.

"So emotional," I said, convincingly, taking a sip of champagne. The art world is subjective to the point of being both brilliant and obsolete. Everyone can have an opinion and no one can say you're wrong. I learned from Lena that *emotional* or *textured* or *moody* were easy buzzwords to stick to when trying to impress someone and seem like you know what you're talking about and care.

He stepped closer to the fabric, his head cocked, eyes squinting. "In what way?" he asked, resting his pointer finger on his bottom lip like flirting with the painting would help him critique better.

I wasn't expecting a follow-up.

"Well, the way the curvature of the…*staples* represents the downfall…of democracy…" I trailed off, hoping that it would feel like I was so overcome with emotion I couldn't even finish the thought. It was staples on a canvas—what the hell?

"Hmm," the man began, backing away from the *art*. "That's so—"

"—interesting." When Art Critic and I turned, Graham was standing on my other side, a knowing smile on his face. "It's so fascinating you see that," he said. "The piece is called *Spears*. The artist—Franny, she's right over there—" he motioned toward an older woman, with gray hair and a floor-length black cotton dress and at least ten oversized necklaces hanging around her gaunt neck "—she loves expressing architecture through industrial art. If you look at it this way—" he moves to the right and we both follow until we are looking at the canvas at an angle "—it's a skyline."

I could see it now—the way the staples formed buildings and skyscrapers, jutting into the canvas like their spears jut into the sky. But only half of me believed Graham. The other half believed I'd see whatever he told me to see.

It's not unlike what I was doing with my own cover story. Graham would believe me because I told him to.

"Wow, what an insight," I said. "You're a natural."

He motioned away from the painting, leaving Art Critic there to really think about Graham's interpretation.

"I could tell you were struggling," he said, stifling a laugh. "I figured I'd save you."

I shrugged and took a sip. He likes being the hero. Interesting. I should have known he was that type—the savior, the helper, the one pulling his woman away from danger. Maybe it was some kind of personality penance from a different life. I could play into that. I could be the damsel in distress. He could save me.

"I'll be honest," I said. "I really hate this stuff. I find it terribly boring."

He smiled, politely at first, someone ready to disengage at the first opportunity, but then he started laughing—hard—like I should have my own Netflix special. "Want to get out of here? There's a great pizza place around the corner."

"For the love of God, yes," I said, feeding into this.

We stopped for slices at Prince Street Pizza, where the tiny pepperonis contort into little cups holding all the gooey oil, and then just walked, aimlessly, for hours. We talked about everything and nothing. I recited my story as memorized, the dead parents part adding some unexpected color now that I knew his triggers. Who better to save than a little girl with no family to speak of?

He didn't tell me anything I didn't already know, but I feigned interest. In his professional career. In his crew career.

In his IPA tasting, his traveling, his green juices, his sober life, his parents, his brother. Vermont. The soon-to-be nephew I pretended I knew nothing about; the one that surely *isn't* the reason we're here. The reason he needs to find a girl like me. And fast.

He offered to walk me home, but I refused. He couldn't know I lived in a four-story walk-up in the East Village and didn't own a couch or a lamp. If I could help it—and I could— he'd never come over. We'd date at his place, we'd sleep at his place, we'd live at his place. My life before would be a perfect mystery.

"Let me at least get you a cab," he insisted. "It's late."

He wasn't insisting on bringing me home, which meant he wasn't interested in sleeping with me tonight, which meant that there was a chance this would turn into last time and I wouldn't hear from him for months. That could not happen again. I refused to keep waiting.

I watched him move onto the street and look down the block, waiting for a lit-up medallion to speed our way before sticking his hand into traffic.

"So are you going to respond to my texts or do I have to accompany Lena to another bougie event just to see you again?"

His shoulders rose with a laugh, and he turned around. "Can I make it up to you?"

"You can try."

He walked to me, stopping just an inch or two away, and I craned my neck to look him in the eye. He smelled good. I hated it.

"Can I make you dinner?" he asked. "Friday, maybe?"

Two dates in one week was a good sign. A very good sign.

"I think I can make that work."

He got closer. "Yeah? You can pencil that in?"

Closer. "Probably."

Closer. A half smile. "Good."

Then he kissed me. It wasn't a stuff-your-face kiss, where our hands roam and people pass on the sidewalk and think *get a room*. It was a long-term kiss. The kind of kiss that comes after love. The kind of casual kiss reserved for people you're sharing a life with. Or those you plan to.

My anxiety didn't set in until I was in the cab. Until I was in the back seat, riding the few blocks home, listening to too-loud club music coming in staticky from the radio. I closed my eyes and tried to ride the waves, let myself ebb and flow until the current took me away completely and I either drowned or could peacefully float on my back.

I took some deep breaths. I could see the cab driver's license taped to the back of his seat, the leather glasses case someone forgot at my feet, the stoplight turning red in front of us. I could hear the music, people laughing outside, the wind. I could feel my toes throbbing in my shoes, my forehead itchy as my hair blew into my face, my butt squished against the leather seat.

"Right here is fine," I said, desperate to get out. He pulled over and I paid and I slammed the door harder than I meant to and I walked into the Chinese food place and ordered General Tso's chicken and rice and brought it upstairs and sat in the dark staring at the plastic bag, heat wafting out of its crevices.

I hated that I was doing this again. I hadn't binged like this since I left Covenant, since it was the only way to calm the anxiety of not having a best friend anymore. I didn't need to do this. I could get myself out of the blurriness with breathing and thinking. With focusing on the five-year plan. The plan that would officially bring me out of the life I'd been trying so hard to never think about again. I'd never have to go back there—to the farm, to the school, in life or in memories—if

I could make this thing with Graham work. I could finally forget everything.

I didn't need to do this. I took another deep breath, my diaphragm heaving forward and back, desperate to fill every inch of my lungs with the stuffy air.

I could see the bag, the light coming in from the window, the closet door. I could hear the people on the street talking about the sky, the door across the hall struggling to close, the movements of animals in my walls. I could feel my eyelids getting heavy, the sweat dripping under my breasts, my shoulders relaxing.

*This is all part of the plan*, I told myself. *Everything's going exactly to plan.*

Before I let myself think too much, I took the bag of Chinese food and threw it, full and unopened, into the garbage under the sink, stuffing it as deep as my arm could go. I didn't need to do this.

As I closed the cabinet—if I took some melatonin and fell asleep, the need to binge would go away, it had to—my phone lit up on the counter in front of me.

Graham. This is the Vermont house I was telling you about. Maybe fourth-date material?

The house was exactly as I pictured it—dauntingly expansive, claustrophobically large.

I could see my phone on the counter, I could see the counter, I could see—

I pulled the food out of the garbage and clawed at the plastic bag and then the paper bag and then the black container until I was bringing pieces of chicken to my mouth with my fingers.

Can't wait, I responded, sauce staining my phone screen as I ate.

Graham and I sat in Sheep Meadow at sunset, the sky a bright orange after clearing up from a late-day storm. We'd decided to run the six-mile loop of Central Park, ending at the Whole Foods in Columbus Circle where we'd bought a six-pack and charcuterie to picnic in the park until the sun went down—or until maintenance workers in golf carts started kicking everyone out, whichever came first. This was my idea of a perfect date. One that involves exercise to balance out the food.

I'd needed to start getting creative with our dates and this was my most recent attempt to do something that wasn't just get drinks or get food and go back to his place.

It turned out the first month of our relationship was essentially a microcosm of the first year. I never would have pegged Graham for a lazy boyfriend—the guy who made no plans, just followed them; who would ask *What do you want to do today?* and mean *Figure out what we're doing today.* I guess I should have known—as someone who has had everything done for him his entire life, why would dating be any different? Why would he treat me, his girlfriend, any different than he treated his mother or his childhood nanny? That's the culture he grew up in—women make the plans, do the housework, take care of everything; men follow, often performatively rolling their eyes.

He wasn't a bad boyfriend—he treated me exceptionally well, never made me pay for anything, gave me free rein of his apartment, and wanted to have sex anytime I said the word. But it was a lot of work for me.

I'd hoped that once we met I would be able to sit back and follow his lead. That he'd take the reins and I could seamlessly transition into the role of his girlfriend by doing everything he planned for us to do. But I'd been wrong. It fell to me to plan everything. And the research was unmatched. It was exhausting. I studied Lena's Instagram photos, searching for any location tags or hints in the background that would tell me where she was—what restaurants and bars and museums had received her approval. Where do rich people go to brunch? Where do rich people take three-day weekends? Where do rich people hang out on Saturday nights?

I was also the one initiating any kind of serious conversations that could speed up our timeline. I brought up kids and he said he wanted two. I brought up locations and he said he'd like to stay on the Upper East Side. I brought up money and he said married couples should always have joint accounts. I had molded myself into the person he needed and I could be the person quickly. I'd make sure we didn't need to date for long; that we could get this party started.

The thing I was the most nervous about—that could have eventually become the downfall of our relationship—was if he pushed me about my past. There were only so many lies my little brain could hold—common ones floated to the top: my name, my memorized elevator pitch of my history, my favorite shoe brand, my favorite restaurant in the city—but most were so deep I only brought them out if I was specifically asked. Those were the ones I got nervous about, the questions so uncommon I started to second-guess my own answers. The ones that only came up when you were talking to your partner, the person in it with you for life. I was sure when we started dating there were lies I hadn't even realized I needed to tell yet.

However, after a few months I realized Graham was uninterested in learning about my past because he didn't want to discuss his own. I knew all about it—his parents and brother and college escapades and Vermont upbringing—but he never shared any of it with me. It was from all of my research. It was like it was a fresh start for both of us—an opportunity to be the people we wanted, little baggage, little history.

One thing I did know about him, and confirmed with almost all of our dates, was that this hero concept he lauded—the prince on a white horse saving the damsel in distress—was his kryptonite. And once I learned that, I could get away with anything.

"Do you want to come look at an apartment with me?" I asked him one Sunday morning. I knew he'd never accept, but I scheduled a viewing under Lena's name at a place I could never afford in TriBeCa. The problem with having a passive boyfriend was that it took forever to move things along, to hit the milestones that I needed to be hitting faster. When we were a year in and he still hadn't asked me to move in with him, I decided to take matters into my own hands.

"Why are you looking at an apartment?" he asked.

"My lease is up. I can't be homeless."

He asked me to move in with him two hours later.

"I have something for you," he said, as I sat on his couch moments after canceling the viewing on his insistence. He presented me with two closed fists from which to choose a fate.

An old memory flashed into my mind before I could push it away like I made sure to do whenever I was with Graham, whenever I was living this life I'd made for myself now. My brother Will and me, sitting on the ground in the backyard, dirty and in need of a deep scrub. His fists were held out, white-knuckling whatever was inside. I tapped the right. When he opened it, it was empty. Then he opened the left. Before I could scream at what I saw, he was throwing it at me. A baby mouse, stiff, pale pink, and dead, landed in my lap as delicately as a dollop of cream in my father's coffee. As Will walked away, laughing so hard he had to bend over every few steps to catch his breath, I dug a meager hole in the dirt with my fingers. It was easy to bury something that small.

I looked up at Graham, his smile slightly fading with each

second I wasn't responding. I took a deep breath and told myself to play along. I had to play along.

"If I choose the wrong one, do I not get the surprise?"

"With proper negotiation you can have whatever you want."

I looked at his fists, hairless and smooth from the moisturizer he applies ritualistically. Every night over the sink like Lady Macbeth except instead of blood it's La Mer. For something that appeared so innocent, they were capable of such harm if they wanted to be. In one swift move, he could reach for me, twist his fingers around my neck, and squeeze until he'd emptied me of my last inch of life. Like a pale pink baby mouse. Their money could bury me as easily as I had buried it.

Graham had gotten into fights before—most notably the one in college that left his right nostril a little smaller than his left. For a man who prides himself on self-control—whose respect for me increases threefold every time I turn down a third glass of wine or a piece of predinner bread—I'd been shocked to learn he'd ever put himself in a position to lose his balance so much, to drink so much that he would punch and get punched back. That felt more like a move his brother would make than him.

I made fun of him for it once—when his parents visited and we all met for dinner at Elio's, his parents' favorite place on the Upper East Side. His father almost choked on his honey chipotle salmon when I said I was grateful our kids couldn't inherit Graham's college fight nose. He cleared his throat, staring at Graham like if it weren't for the table between them, he'd have him up against the wall, his hands gripping Graham's collar. I never brought it up again. Clearly the behavior was so unbecoming of a Walker that it need not be mentioned in public. That should be the least of their worries, as far as I was concerned.

I tapped Graham's waiting right fist.

"Interesting choice…" he mumbled. When he unraveled his fingers, I braced myself, but inside he revealed a key, resting in his palm. I smiled. I gasped. I threw my hand against my mouth and looked at him like I'd never been happier in my life.

It felt like he was offering me the bullet I needed to shoot myself. Like his hands around my neck were tightening and tightening. *This is all part of the plan*, I thought. I knew this was coming. I wanted this. I needed this.

So I made sure the smile stayed plastered on my pathetic face.

"A key to your heart?" I asked, ever the charmer.

He laughed and took my hand and the warm metal squished between our palms. "My heart and my apartment."

Obviously. What else would it be for? A storage unit in Astoria where he keeps dead bodies?

"You never even lock the door," I said.

He laughed and sat next to me, planting a kiss on my lips before I could object. "It's symbolic. A gesture."

I took the key from his hand and moved it between my fingers and the heat of suffocation began to fade into calm. Slowly, I could breathe again. My chest could move up and down without me having to remind it to do so. Because this was all part of the plan. And this meant it was going well.

I moved into Graham's apartment a week later with only four suitcases—one of mine and three I borrowed from him—and a *New Yorker* tote bag stuffed with underwear. Graham offered to help, but I turned him down swiftly each time he brought it up. I'd told him—and Lena and anyone else who asked—that the reason they could never come over, the reason I couldn't host a dinner party, the reason Graham didn't have a toothbrush in *my* bathroom, was because the building was under construction. "It's loud, it's dusty… I'm better off at yours." This person, Eliza, was made to live in a penthouse-adjacent twenty-fourth-floor suite in a prewar luxury building on the Upper East Side. My old apartment—with its holey floorboard and cockroach motels around the sinks; with its water-stained bathroom ceiling and yellowing kitchen caulk—was the last strand of Elizabeth in my life. The part that couldn't afford things. The part that would never have been welcomed into the Walker clan in the same way Eliza was about to be.

Graham was never going to see that part. I worked hard to ensure that.

When I stood in my empty apartment, four suitcases and one tote bag in the center of the room like a woman about to embark on a two-week vacation to Greece, I found myself saying a prayer for my old life. I hadn't prayed in years. Since school, really. Since the night I stopped believing. But I was suddenly praying all over again. Asking God—or *someone*—to please let this work. Please help me. So Ruthie—and I—can finally have peace.

I left four keys and two envelopes on the one foot of counter space my kitchen allotted. The first was for my landlord, Sun Lee, with the last month's rent and a note to keep the bed if he wanted it. And the second was to Fyodor, my first friend in New York. *I found my rich man*, I wrote. *Our conversations were delightful.*

It felt like a suicide note.

I had one more thing to do before I left.

I walked over to the armchair in the corner, which used to live in the office of the Chinese food place downstairs before it was gifted to me; I've counted stains from at least five different kinds of chicken on it. I got down on the floor, turned onto my back, and shimmied beneath the chair like a mechanic under a humming Mustang. I pulled the zipper—there for easy removal and reupholstering—around the perimeter of the bottom of the chair to reveal an open crevice with a hole in the center, the perfect hiding spot.

I flipped through the cash on the counter like a drug dealer, the uneven bills moving through my hands—twenties, tens, fives, singles. All the money I'd accumulated throughout my time in New York. Every cashed Brit & Ash paycheck, every dollar I found walking Alphabet City, every penny I didn't include as a tip to the barista. It was an old life's habit I couldn't quite quit. My father kept all his money in three places: a box with a four-digit lock in the ceiling above the kitchen pantry, my parents' horsehair mattress (which they stuffed themselves after each of Rudolph's clippings, way before you could buy the same thing for a paltry two hundred thousand dollars), and in a cutout under the armchair in the living room. His entire life's savings was scattered around our home, as he was always suspicious the government would somehow take it or tax it if he put it in a bank. A different version of Douglas Walker's account in the Seychelles, honestly.

I parsed out one thousand dollars and packed it into Fyodor's envelope—a sad goodbye to the only person I ever invited over—then I put the rest back into its pouch and stuffed it into the *New Yorker* tote until it sunk below the layers of underwear—the sexy lingerie, the comfortable lace, the period panties—and hit the bottom.

For me, this wasn't a ruse to get out of taxes or keep the "government's sticky fingers" out of my pocket. This money was a safety net. A way out. Just in case I needed one.

As the Uber approached Graham's apartment—well, *our* apartment now, I guess—Reed was standing outside, smoking a cigarette carelessly close to the building and talking to Danny, who seemed less than intrigued. I rolled down my back seat window, just an inch, and could hear him explaining, "They are moving quite fast, but, I mean, I guess when you know you know…"

I recognized Reed immediately. We'd never met before—

as far as he was concerned—but his gruff face was smiling on too many photos around Graham's apartment for me to not know, in detail, what he looked like. I'd had his first-notice features memorized for a while—his thick eyebrows, blue eyes, quaffed brown hair—but I also knew the less noticeable parts. The cowlick in the back right of his head, the dimple that shows up on his chin if he gains five pounds, the worry lines on his forehead that seem to be deeper than his age would require. He didn't look unlike Graham, they were almost interchangeable if you saw them separately, but they had bitterly different personalities. Where Graham's general ease and quick humor softened his edges, made everyone fall in love with him as quickly as I seemed to, Reed's arrogance and white-man-failing-up confidence only served to sharpen his.

I didn't like him before move-in day, and I liked him even less after.

"Welcome home," Danny said as he opened my door, offering me a hand to step out of the Uber driver's Chevy Suburban.

"Eliza," Reed said, stubbing out his cigarette and walking toward me like we were business associates meeting for the first time. "It's great to see you." When he got close enough, his hand transitioned from a shake to a hug, and he wrapped his arms around me gingerly like I was an old girlfriend he didn't expect to see. I reminded myself to take a deep breath. *I'm Eliza now. I'm in charge.*

"I feel like I already know you," I said, mustering all the confidence I had to keep my shoulders straight and strong under his grip. His breath smelled like Listerine and smoke in my ear, a nauseating combination. "Thanks for coming! I'm afraid there's not too much for you to do, though."

He stepped back and moved toward the suitcases that my Uber driver and Danny were coordinating from the sidewalk to the bell cart like a game of real-life *Tetris.*

"That's it?" Reed asked as Danny positioned the last suitcase on the cart. He looked at me, then the pile of bags containing every single thing I owned, and forced a confused smile. It seemed almost skeptical in its rigidness. Like I'd poked a hole in my own cement-sealed cover by not owning a dresser or a Peloton.

"There's more than you think," I said. "I'm a good packer."

There was a long pause before he muttered, "Clearly," and grabbed the trolley by the wrong end to begin pushing it inside. "You should talk to my wife about minimalist living," he added. "She could learn a lot from you, apparently."

Danny followed us like a concerned parent surrounds a child who just learned to walk. "I can do that, Mr. Walker, really. Here—let me—" He continued until we reached the elevator, satisfied that as long as Reed wasn't moving, he couldn't jerk the trolley in the wrong direction and break something.

When the elevator doors opened on the twenty-fourth floor, Graham was standing there like an aide awaiting the queen's arrival.

"I told you to tell me when you got here," he whined, repeating the promise I made when I left my apartment. "Danny probably thinks I'm a terrible boyfriend."

I squeezed out of the elevator and kissed Graham's cheek. "I don't think Danny thinks about you at all, babe," I said.

Inside, a bottle of Veuve was chilling in a marble slate on the kitchen island, with three champagne flutes anxiously awaiting their time to shine.

"Unpack later," Graham said, "let's celebrate."

It was a sweet gesture. That's how they get you, these boys. They charm you with their perceived thoughtfulness even though I knew for a fact he ordered this bottle via an app on his phone from the liquor store two blocks down and only had to walk from the couch to the door thirty seconds before

I arrived to accept the delivery. But I guess it's the thought that counts. And the expense.

Graham popped the bottle carefully and poured three glasses as Reed slowly approached, his gaze jumping from Graham to me.

"You're drinking?" Reed asked him.

He gave up drinking after that college bar fight, but sometimes I'd find an empty cabernet or Stella in the recycling when I was sneaking a midnight binge. They'd be hidden under a bottle of lemon-lime seltzer or jar of pickles, the same way I'd hide the chip wrappers and never bring it up. It's better to keep things like this close to the vest until you figure out how to use them.

"Just on special occasions," Graham said, taking a defiant sip. Reed seemed unconvinced. "It's just a glass of champagne," he continued. "It's fine."

That night, after Reed left, Graham and I continued celebrating with another bottle of champagne followed by some shower sex and kitchen counter sex and outdoor patio sex to consummate the move and make it all official, as if we hadn't been fucking on every surface of the apartment this entire time.

I lay in bed, listening to Graham snore, louder and more congested from the drinking and the sodium-filled Chinese food dinner, and I had a hard time getting Reed's face out of my head. The skeptical look he gave me when he saw my few belongings. The way it seemed like he was already convinced I didn't belong. *You just seem so familiar* replayed over and over again.

My suitcases lay still on the bedroom floor, untouched since I got home. Graham decided the actual moving-in part was the least exciting thing to do on move-in day, so instead we just drank and ate and fucked. I'd become a master of slipping out of bed unnoticed and managed to do just that even after half a bottle of champagne.

I picked up the tote and rummaged around my underwear until I pulled out the envelope, still thick with all my cash. My entire life's savings. All that was necessary to get out. I needed to put it somewhere Graham would never find it. While my underwear drawer was a good option, it seemed a little too risky for someone who had as many opinions about my lingerie as Graham did.

I opened the closet doors, quickly closing them behind me so the automatic lights didn't stir the prince in his sleep, and I looked around. What's something Graham never touches? A drawer he never opens, a clothing item he never wears?

That's when his suit popped out at me, beetling out of the back rack like a fully glammed Kardashian at a Whole Foods. The suit he's never worn since we've been together, but that he insists was a good investment. The one he'll probably wear for our wedding.

I felt the material up and down until I found the flap pocket. The envelope fit perfectly inside. It was noticeable, the cash creating a bulge, but it was hidden for now. As hidden as it needed to be.

Just like me.

# SEVENTEEN

GRAHAM'S SNORING SOUNDS like the ferry's horn as it leaves the Wall Street station on those days after work when Graham and I would take a spontaneous trip to our favorite restaurant in Vinegar Hill. On the way back, we'd walk the Brooklyn Bridge with mini bottles of champagne for dessert. It always felt like the most New York thing: to take a boat to another borough because we liked the pork chops. We only did it a handful of times, but it never got less exciting. It was a rare moment when I could forget the five-year plan and just be.

I try to ride the wave of that feeling now, lying in bed next to Graham, in a room so dark you'd think there was no moon outside. So dark your pupils could take over your entire iris and still find nothing to lock onto. But the feeling fades as quickly as the memory until I feel stuck again, my eyes bloodshot, my throat hot and stinging with acidic bile, my teeth brushed so many times my gums are raw.

If Graham was with someone who actually slept, he would have gone to a somnologist at this point; she would have put him on a CPAP machine to shut him the fuck up. But I found the snores comforting, a kind of white noise in the background of my night; and a surefire way to know if he was awake and I was about to get caught.

By the end of the cocktail party, Graham was mildly drunk but hid it well. Probably because Reed kept such a close eye on him, guiding him away from risky conversations, not letting him kiss me for that long, following him around with a constantly refilled glass of ice water. Graham's drunkenness made Reed vulnerable. Too many boyhood secrets ready to be revealed at any moment—all it takes is one too many Jack and Cokes. It was fascinating to watch.

I roll out of bed without trying too hard to stay quiet and rummage through the dresser drawers until I find the sports bra and leggings I snuck into my suitcase. Graham had insisted while I was packing that I wouldn't need or want to work out during our wedding weekend; "There won't be time, and plus, you already look amazing, that won't change." He put his arms around my waist and his hands paused on my belly and he said something about how I'm basically nonexistent I've gotten so thin, and normally that would be a compliment but for some reason in that moment, as I was packing to marry him, the thought of being nonexistent was alarming. Because that was how I felt. Like the wedding had taken over and I didn't fucking exist anymore. I was no longer Eliza. And I had left Elizabeth far behind.

So I stuffed four days' worth of workout clothes into my bag like I was smuggling drugs into Vermont straight from Colombia.

I put on the sports bra and from the hole in the side, where those useless cups normally sit deformed and annoying, I pull out the folded piece of paper. MISSING: BERNADETTE WARD with her shining eyes smiling at me like nothing was wrong. That girl had no clue what was coming to her, the devastation and torture she was about to endure. That girl was still alive. Her life had yet to be defined solely by her death. Or disappearance.

I fold the paper up again, this time smaller and more gingerly, and put it back in my bra. For some reason I don't want to leave her in that room alone. I don't want him to find it.

The hallway is speckled with night-lights, lining the wood paneling every couple of feet like an airplane aisle during an emergency evacuation. *This way. This way, please. You're going the right direction.* As if when you're cascading to your death at five hundred miles an hour, you'll be thinking, *Thank God my demise will be well lit.*

The gym is in the furnished basement, in a room next to the pool table, a second bar, and a guest bedroom bigger than my first apartment. It's covered in floor-to-ceiling mirrors and one large window at just the right height that you can look out into the darkness of the backyard while on the treadmill. You can stare at the mountains during the day, but I'm never here during the day.

The delicate hum of the treadmill is like white noise to me. I always need sounds now. Maybe it's from living in Manhattan for a few years, or from having lived in silence for so many before that. But if it's too quiet, if things are so still the loudest sound is the ringing in my own ears, I start to feel suffocated. I start to see things and hear things. I start to have daydreams about people coming in the night, breaking into the house and killing all of us. I do the math for how long it will take until our bodies are found. This weekend's events are an exception, but normally it's just the family here. It could be weeks before a neighbor knocks on the door. Would the smell of our bodies be the first thing she notices—our rotting flesh wafting into her face the second she comes inside? Or would she notice the cars—*hmm, they haven't moved in a while, that's strange.* Or maybe it would be longer than that. Months. My body would begin to decompose in that bed right next to Graham's. Maybe we'd die spooning. Or naked. Blowflies and flesh flies and skin beetles crawling over my no-longer-tanned-and-toned body. Entering my mouth, biting at my eyes.

I hit the emergency stop button in the center of the treadmill's console and nearly fall backwards when the machine abruptly stops. It keeps humming in my ears as I stand there, drenched in so much sweat I'd drizzled all over the thing's base, and try to catch my breath. Four miles goes fast when you're thinking about dead bodies. About Ruthie. About Bernadette.

I can feel the paper burning a hole in the pocket of my bra, pressing down on my chest, slowly suffocating me.

On the way back to our bedroom, I stop outside Reed and Veronica's door. In the darkness, it would be easy for me to hide there, sidle up to the wood paneling until I felt like I was sinking into it, waiting. I think to that day in the apartment when Reed attempted to help me move. I think about him standing beside my suitcases, skeptical.

I think about Graham insisting he pick up Chinese food from the best place on the Upper East Side, leaving me alone in my nightmare. I retreated to the closet—"I have to find my pajamas"—and sat down on the floor. It was the first time I realized there was a rug in there. A rug in the closet. That's the kind of rich I was moving into. The kind that buys a rug to make sure my feet are comfortable when I'm picking out a shirt.

I closed my eyes and took a deep breath, reaching for my phone in my pocket, not to call anyone but to know that I could. I didn't hear the closet doors opening until Reed spoke, but I didn't stir. I opened my eyes slowly and looked directly at his fucking face. At this point very few things scared me, but he was on the list as one of them.

"Do I know you?" he asked, his head cocked like a puppy confused about why his supposed treat tasted like medicine.

"What?" I said, trying to muster the attitude of a pleasant but slightly ditzy girlfriend. That's what *he* needed me to be. Since I'm prettier than his wife, he needs to think I'm at least equally as stupid.

"You just seem so familiar." He was staring at my face like he was calculating it, running my nose and eyes through the Rolodex in *his* head—probably of women he'd fucked. The multitudes this man went through only to be domesticated by Veronica because his mother told him to be. The only true way to remedy someone's fuckboy reputation is to get him husbanded and fathered as soon as possible.

"Maybe in pictures from Graham?" I offered, knowing that wasn't remotely convincing.

"No, that's not it. It's not your face. Just your...vibe."

He said it like a Mormon expat living in Hawaii who just discovered surfing, coconut milk, and premarital sex. "My *vibe*?"

"Just something about you..." he said. I reminded myself to smile, to loosen my shoulders, to laugh it off. *He doesn't know me*, I told myself. *He knows nothing about me.* "I definitely recognize you from somewhere."

I lean my ear against the hard wooden door of Reed and Veronica's room, listening for any motion inside. Were they trying for Baby Number Two? Then I look down at the Apple Watch draped onto my wrist. 4:18. They wouldn't be awake or moving. Only I'm up at this hour.

The truth is he does know me from somewhere. He hasn't been able to figure it out since that day in the closet, but I live in constant fear that he'll wake up one morning and it will pop into his memory with the same clarity of what he ate for dinner the night before. I hate that he has something over me but he's too stupid to know it. I hate that I'm here and that he's here. I hate that he has a wife and a kid. I hate that there's not much stopping me from bursting through the door, plucking Veronica's stiletto off the cold floor, and jabbing it into his neck.

Instead, I pull the missing poster out of my bra. I unfold it, carefully. I run it back and forth over the door frame's trim to get out the creases.

I look at Bernadette one more time. Her eyes. Her mouth. The way some hair falls whimsically around her temples. Is this how she'd want to be remembered? Or was this just the photo her parents decided to use?

I wonder what photo Graham would use if I went missing—the one of us together at the firepit? Or our engagement photo from Carl Schurz Park? But then I realize I wouldn't get missing posters or a search party of friends and family calling my name in a line through the woods. With his family's reach, I'd get the FBI. My face would be plastered on every TV station from here to Thailand. They'd find me if they wanted to. If I wanted to be found.

I slip the poster under the door frame so Bernadette's face can greet him in the morning the same way it's been haunting me.

# EIGHTEEN

**A FEW MONTHS** after I moved in, Graham proposed. It was simple, really, and quite nice. Probably what my dream proposal would be in very different circumstances. We ate dinner outside, watching the sunset and listening to sirens, betting two dollars on whether it was an ambulance, police car, or fire truck before someone leaned over the banister to check. When it was dark, and the fairy lights flickered on, I looked over to Graham, sitting beside me on the couch, and he kissed me. It was a moment—one of very few—that felt almost unadulteratedly blissful. Sometimes, when I let my guard down, I would find myself getting used to this life—the spoils of being with someone like Graham, who thinks you deserve the world and has the money to prove it.

He leaned into me and for a second I thought he was going to put his head in my lap, but when he leaned back I realized he'd pulled a ring box out of his pocket. My first thought was how uncomfortable it must have been for him to be sitting on it all night, like the pea in the mattresses in that story my mother used to tell me.

Inside the navy blue box was a piece of Walker history: his mother's engagement ring, which she inherited from Douglas's great-grandmother. A kite-set diamond, on a delicate gold filigree band. If I were to be honest for a moment, this is exactly the engagement ring I would have wanted.

"Marry me…"

He said it in a way that was difficult to define. It was not a question. He did not ask me if I wanted to marry him, or give me an opening for a yes-or-no answer. It was more of a statement. Less harsh than a demand, but something deceivingly close.

"I've been waiting for you to ask," I finally said, letting him slide my three-carat fate onto my finger. I hugged him and didn't let him go until I could muster a few happy tears and make sure a believable smile was plastered onto my face.

For years I felt numb. Hollow. Like I was just going through the motions, resigned to my fate. But, for the briefest second, as my face nuzzled into Graham's neck, still smelling of chlorine from a recent workout that made my head spin, I felt a strike of excitement in my chest. It lasted a millisecond, like lighting on the Freedom Tower, but it was there. And it was exactly what I needed to step back, look at my fiancé, and kiss him.

I didn't want an engagement party, but I knew it was part of the process. Like a sweet sixteen or quinceañera or debutante ball, announcing us and our intentions to the world. We'd send out invitations (*come celebrate with us!*) that would no doubt occupy a top spot on countless strangers' refrigerators; we'd find a venue, hire a caterer, bring in a band. It was like a prewedding; a party for the locals to give you a taste of how great the actual wedding will be. And Veronica volunteered her Walker party planning expertise.

"What about all of Doug's Vermont cronies?" I had asked,

the day Veronica came over to order everything online, using the address book from their engagement party as a baseline— it's not like I had anyone to invite. I'd insisted all the invitations only refer to me as Eliza. Not Eliza Bennet. *Not* Elizabeth. But just Eliza. *I'm already more of a Walker than I ever was a Bennet*, I'd explained, staring into Graham's eyes the way everyone expected me to when saying something like that.

"Just locals for the engagement party," Veronica explained. "Everyone gets the wedding invite, though. Get ready for an onslaught of Doug's important friends. And their checkbooks."

"If you don't have anything nice to say," I began, "write a check instead."

She laughed, but I'm not sure she understood the joke.

Three months after we got engaged, I was standing on a rooftop in Midtown, a place Veronica loved but couldn't book for her own engagement. It looked like a tight and trim Versailles garden, with paths between tidy shrubs surrounding the perimeter of a grassy center, all in twenty-five hundred square feet of Rockefeller Plaza. However, instead of a golden palace where a war was ended towering behind us, we got a hulking St. Patrick's Cathedral, looming over me like an abusive boyfriend, lit from below as the sun went down to give the same air of menace I was feeling. Like the church was watching us, counting our sins one by one. An unbelievably apt and twisted mind-fuck that Veronica wasn't clued in enough to know she'd planted.

Maybe that's why my mother kept popping into my head that evening. I did not think about my parents—or my brothers or the farm—often. At first I was afraid that would be my downfall, that being here with these people would force out of me a longing for my old life—a life that was simple, but difficult in other ways. Money couldn't buy us out of all our problems; instead my parents believed we could pray our way out of them. Pray for guidance, pray for a solution, pray for it all to go away.

That shit never worked for me.

"You need another?" one of the waitstaff asked, hovering beside me with a tray of empty glasses, a rainbow of lipstick stains scattered on the surfaces like an advertisement for Sephora. She couldn't be older than eighteen and if she was, I needed to know her skincare routine. I was immediately jealous but not enough to ask. She smiled kindly. "I've been told to keep a special eye out for you and…him," she said with a wink, as if I didn't know I'd get special attention at my own fucking engagement party.

She nodded toward Graham, who stood near the entrance greeting Jim and Ellis, two friends from work. They all came up at BlackRock together. Though none of them are self-aware enough to discuss it, I'm sure they were also subconsciously drawn to each other as three men who only work in finance to please the whims of their overbearing and undercaring fathers.

Graham looked especially good today. He'd come home from work a few days before with a bag from Carson Street Clothiers and the excitement of a child anxious to tell me everything he just bought.

"It's apparently what *all the celebs are wearing*," he said in the prim voice of Charles, the man who always styles him. He spun around in the navy blue suit, paired with a plain white T-shirt and brown wing tips and he looked hot. An understated sophistication that, I knew, would go perfectly with the light blue floral maxi dress I had decided to wear. The dress made me feel like a carefree wife who goes to 10:30 a.m. Pure Barre classes and always has perfectly beachy curls and shops down Madison Avenue on a Tuesday afternoon. But it also reminded me of my mother's church dress, the one she made herself out of a similar blue floral-patterned fabric that had been donated to the church office. She'd worn it every single Sunday as long as I could remember, and hand-washed it in the bathtub with the kind of slow tenderness I think about sometimes when I'm doing dishes.

I like to think I looked like what she could have been in another life. I do have her eyes.

"He doesn't drink…" I told the waitress, slipping my empty vodka soda onto her tray and staring at the three of them as they laugh in anxiety-inducing harmony. I could feel her staring at me, probably processing the two or three old-fashioneds she'd already served him this evening. I could taste the whiskey on him an hour ago.

When I finally turned to her, she'd lost whatever Jergens glow she had on her face before and her mouth was agape in that unattractive way it falls if you're not paying attention. *A bug is going to fly into your mouth*, I wanted to tell her, a line my mother repeated to us whenever we opened our mouths or cried in public.

"Just kidding," I finally said, a gentle smile on my face, the kind that merely lifts your cheeks but doesn't touch your eyes. "I *would* like something else, actually. Perhaps a sauv blanc?"

She nodded and turned before responding any further, no doubt desperate to get the fuck out of here before I could play with her anymore, which is always a satisfying power. The only power I had that day, it turned out.

My dress blew ever so slightly with the wind, and I was thinking about my mother again. I kept imagining her here, walking around in that graceful way she did, like she was floating—a stark contrast from my father's lead feet stomping around the rickety house, always like he was on a mission. It was a trait we only became thankful for once we appreciated it for what it was: a warning.

I imagined my mother, in her church clothes, greeting Graham. He'd tower over her bony five-foot-two-inch frame. She wasn't allowed heels and got skinnier and skinnier with each child, like all her excess anything went into us from birth. Her forehead was creased with years of worry, her crow's feet deep from a lifetime of planting in the sun. She always had dirty hands and soil-filled nails, except on Sundays. She'd stand at the kitchen sink, yelling for us to hurry up, while scrubbing her skin raw with a brittle brush. She kept a tin of O'Keeffe's in her nightstand, always working it into her hands and elbows to try to undo the damage.

I think, on the surface, she'd be disappointed in my relationship; marrying an agnostic banker, living with him in sin, taking birth control so I could fuck him whenever I wanted. More than that, I think she'd hate that I'd become dependent on Graham—his money, his family, his success. I didn't need *him*, but as far as this life went, the life I'd gotten used to, the second he was gone, it was gone—the roof over my head, the clothes on my back, any kind of security I felt. Right now, he and his money served all my basic needs. That was part of the plan, of course, but as far as appearances went, she'd be unimpressed I couldn't live this life myself.

My parents met at a church singles' night, got married in a joyous ceremony with a dry after-party at my grandparents' farm. My mother even had a job for a brief period in the beginning—a secretary at the elementary school in town. That is, until she got pregnant and it was deemed inappropriate for a pregnant married woman to work; until they had moved hours away from her family, from town, from any kind of normalcy, because he found a good deal on an expansive Christmas tree farm near a church far more extreme than the one my mother had grown up in. Until he was in control of her money, her chores, her reproductive system. Until *she* became *them* and my mother turned from Grace into the woman I knew. Into someone's wife.

But under those layers of fear, so deep-seated I'm not sure anyone would be able to exhume it, I think she'd be proud of me. For doing what she said. For taking the scariest leap and leaving them and the farm. For getting an education and a job that pays more money than my parents have ever seen. For reading whatever books and wearing whatever clothes and doing whatever activities—not only because I could afford it but because I had freedom. I had autonomy. I had everything.

I think that would thrill her.

She never wanted what she got. And she especially didn't want it for me. I was their only daughter. She used to call me her second life.

*Don't think of us*, I remembered. *Do not*—

"Here you go." A glass of wine so clear it almost looked like water was dangling in front of me and I took it from the waitress's streaky tan hand quickly, nodding a thank-you I couldn't quite get out of my mouth.

At least, I like to think my mother would be proud. But part of me wonders if she's even still alive. If she received the brunt of the repercussions when I never came home. Someone had to, and my father would absolutely assume a female conspiracy. I haven't talked to them since the day I left for school. Communication wasn't exactly easy considering the only phone my family had was hidden around the house at my father's will and used for emergencies only. But I could have tried—I could have called the church, asked them to send a message to my mom. I could have left messages on the phone, updated them on how I was doing, what classes I was taking. I could have told them about Ruthie.

But all of those things felt like an opportunity to be taken away; an excuse for my father to assume I was doing badly, making poor decisions, hanging out with the wrong people. It started to feel like the less I reminded my father that I was there, the more likely he'd forget about me entirely. Leave me alone. Let me get out.

So I never called. I never went home. I never spoke to them again.

*Don't think of us*, my mother told me the day I was leaving for school. The last time I saw her. She had just put my necklace in my hand and told me to hide it in my bra until I was on campus, away from them, away from my father. *Don't think of us*, she said, her eyes shining at me. *Do not—*

My father walked in then, barreling through the front door and into the creaky foyer, annoyed that I wasn't sitting in the car waiting for him. Bringing me to school was an inconvenience. It meant he had to be sober enough to drive.

I never found out what my mother was going to say just then. Before she could finish, I was pulled by my hair to the loaded car and thrown into the passenger's seat so hard I thought I might have bruised my hip.

*Don't think of us*, she said. Then, after that? I like to think she was going to say *do not come back*.

"Can I do the same, please?" I looked up to see Lena standing next to me, sending the waitress away with another order before the girl could try to invade my personal space again. "Nice party."

I was grateful for the distraction. I didn't want to think about my mother anymore. Not now.

"Thanks to Veronica," I said, lifting my glass toward the center of the garden where my future sister-in-law party planner, wearing an off-white dress a little too bridal for me to not be somewhat offended, bent down in her four-inch heels to whisper something to Reed.

Lena and I leaned into each other with a cheek-to-cheek kiss greeting, the kind of affection rich people save for when they don't want their makeup to smudge. But then I go rogue and wrap her into a hug, my wineglass moving gingerly around her as I bring her in close.

"This is...nice..." she said into my ear, confused but not uninterested in the affection. Or the attention that some affection from the bride brings.

Behind her I could see a few people watching us, but my eyes moved quickly past them to the bartender—a lanky woman in a suit and tie with a bob of dark hair and arms that seemed thick underneath her formal black jacket. I smiled at her. She nodded at me.

"Sauv blanc," the waitress said, handing Lena her drink after I released her from my selfish grip.

We both thanked her properly this time and Lena clanked my glass surreptitiously, like our celebration was different from the one for which everyone else was here.

"Engaged," she said, more to herself than to me. I could have sworn she side-eyed my ring. But I'd gotten so used to people gazing at it that I didn't think about it anymore. It was just a five-figure addition to my hand. "I'm honored to have introduced you."

I took a sip of wine to stop myself from rolling my eyes. She loved bringing that up. As if I hadn't planned the introduction all along.

"Now I'll return the favor..." I leaned back against a decorative light pole. "Don't look now, but the bartender has been eyeing you."

She looked, of course, but in the inconspicuous way I expected her to, never moving too quickly, taking a deep breath before doing anything, always in control. She doesn't operate in a manner that would get her caught for looking. She's too composed for that.

"She's cute," Lena said when she turned back to me, satisfied.

"You should go for it."

"Yeah?" She looked back at the bartender intentionally this time, staring at her for long enough to establish interest. It was like they were having sex with their eyes across my engagement party. She'll definitely be Lena's guest at the wedding.

Lena was about to say something when glasses started clanking around the garden, the sound bouncing off the buildings around us, and Veronica approached.

"Toast time," she sang, tugging at my arm and pulling me toward the center of the party where Graham was waiting and a circle had begun to form, everyone gently tapping forks or knives or spoons against champagne flutes that had mysteriously appeared in everyone's hands.

"I'd like to make a toast..."

Reed's voice echoed around me like the precursor to an avalanche as he climbed onto a chair. The impossibly short, silent, eerie beat before everything begins to crumble.

Graham put his arm around my waist and turned me to face Reed and I reminded myself to smile, to show teeth, to exude joy from my stance and my eyes. The more you look like you're actively laughing, the harder it is for anyone to decipher what's actually happening underneath.

"I'm the groom-to-be's brother, for anyone here who doesn't know. Actually—" he scanned the room quickly "—*is there* anyone here who didn't know that?"

From the bar in the back, Brittany and Ashleigh and a few of my colleagues raise their hands and cheer like we're at a talk show and the host mentioned the small town in Missouri they grew up in. Judging from the way Brittany's skinny strap kept falling over her shoulder, I'm guessing she was at least two drinks in and, no doubt, discussing how she wished Reed weren't married.

"Eliza doesn't have a lot of family, that's what I'm told. At least not family she's introduced us to—" He motioned toward himself and his parents. "She could have a secret second life no one knows about…" The crowd laughs and I do, too. Because it was a joke, of course. "We always thought that was kinda strange. A girl we know almost nothing about—I mean, she had five suitcases when she moved in with my little brother. Her entire life in *five suitcases*. And she just walks in here and takes Graham for all he's got." He looked at Veronica, who was sitting at the table in front of him gushing like a mom at her kid's first ballet recital. "At least no one's questioning how quickly we got married, babe. This was *way* faster."

The crowd offered a few uncomfortable laughs.

"The day I met Eliza was the day she moved in with those five suitcases. I was there to help them unpack but there was nothing for me to do. Literally nothing. She's the first female minimalist to ever exist."

All the women in the room laugh, to make Reed feel less bad about offending us, in that charming way we care about other people's emotions before our own. I look up at Graham, who's smiling but cautiously, like concern might be bubbling in him the same way it was in me.

"And I knew the second I saw her that she looked familiar. I told her that—I said *I feel like we've met before*. I was convinced we had. I mean, look at her—" All our guests turned toward me, looking me up and down. I smiled back believably, but it was only believable because just two people there knew me well enough to read through it. "She doesn't exactly have a face you forget," Reed continued, once he got everyone's attention again. I felt myself get rigid in Graham's arm. Was this really going to happen here? At my engagement party? The gig was going to be up after all this? I was so close.

"I started racking my brain, you know, trying to come up with places we would have met. Did we grow up together? No, she's from Rhode Island, we're from Vermont. What about college? No, she went to Brown, we went to Yale. That semester we studied in Spain? No, she was in London. Then I had the sudden panic that, well…maybe we'd hooked up…" The room exploded in guffaws loud enough to break the stained glass windows of the church behind us. I felt like I couldn't breathe. I felt like Graham's hand on my waist was getting too tight, my dress was shrinking. If there was ever a moment in my five-year plan that I wanted to run, this was it.

"I'm kidding," Reed continued, laughing, his hands out to the crowd apologetically. "We never hooked up. Don't worry. Wouldn't want to start a rumor here—"

"—she's too good for you," Graham yelled, squeezing me tighter against him as the crowd bloomed in laughter again. Talking about me like I wasn't standing right next to him. Like every time he wobbled in his buzzed happiness, I wasn't the one keeping him stable.

I kept a smile plastered on my face like I thought this was charming. *Just boys being boys*, and all that other bullshit. I scanned the crowd and saw Veronica, still staring at her husband with stars in her eyes. There were Jim and Ellis, slapping their knees and taking a sip of scotch from the old boys' club. There were my coworkers, by the bar, laughing only because they were grateful for a break from talking to one another.

Then I saw the bartender, the woman who was inevitably going home with Lena tonight, standing next to the caterer, both staring at Reed with the kind of straight face reserved for funerals and boring subway rides. Finally, someone who was allowed to look the way I felt. Bored, unenthused, and, honestly, ready to go home. At least *they* were getting paid to listen to this shit, I guess.

Reed finally calmed the crowd down by saying, "The faster I'm finished, the faster we can get back to drinking," which was so déclassé I could physically feel Cheryl shaking with embarrassment from across the room. "This is all to say," Reed continued, red-faced both from the gin and from the satisfaction of making an entire room laugh, "I guess she looked familiar because she's always been my sister. I just didn't know it yet."

The room *awwed* and I pretended to wipe a tear from the corner of my left eye. Emotional didn't look good on him. It looked pathetic. Like he was trying too hard. Like maybe he was playing some kind of game, too.

After Graham and I hugged him and the entire room cheered and drank to our union, I excused myself and slowly made my way to the bathroom. I was about to open the door when I realized what I really wanted was the employees-only bathroom, one where no one could find me and touch me and congratulate me. *Congratulations for what?* I always want to say back. *For proving I'm lovable?*

I snuck into the kitchen, where only a few suit-clad waiters stood delicately placing prosciutto-wrapped honeydew and mac and cheese balls on metal trays and followed a WR arrow down a steep staircase and onto a platform.

When I pushed through the heavy door, the automatic lights flickered on like a bad horror movie. It took three blinks of darkness before they stayed lit, fluorescent and slightly blue, reflecting off the white tiled floor and walls like fake daylight. The room was cold and damp and I felt uncomfortable in how out of place I was. I hadn't peed in a bathroom without complimentary deodorant and Q-tips in over a year.

I sat on the toilet in one of the stalls unsure if I needed to throw up or pass out. Neither would relieve the nausea that speech had brought on. My head was spinning with the thought of being recognized, of the conversation in the closet, of the night we met. God, I fucking hate him. I hate everything about all of them.

The door whispered open, and I steeled myself, preparing for someone to recognize my shoes under the janky gray stall and realize I didn't belong here. *I'm sorry*, they'd apologize, as if *they* were invading *my* space. As if *I* hadn't prevented *them* from relieving themselves comfortably.

I heard two sets of practical shoes pulse against the tile floor until they were standing at the sink, still. They turned the faucet on and let the water run, probably staring at a sign that says *Employees Must Wash Hands* while washing their hands. The sound of water running was helpful, distracting, a much-needed separation from my own thoughts. I sat there and breathed deep, healing breaths, breaths a doctor or yoga teacher would be proud of, until the nausea subsided, and I started craving another drink. My last, probably until the wedding. The conversation about which wedding diet I was planning to undertake had already started. And none of them allowed drinking your calories.

I stood up and pretended to re-dress and flushed the fresh toilet water down the drain.

When I opened the stall door, the caterer and the bartender were there, no longer leaning over the sinks but standing still, hands clean and dripping wet onto the floor, the water still running like a wasteful noise machine.

I moved to the sink in between theirs and they watched me wash my hands, just standing there, silently, watching like prison guards untrusting I wouldn't take my own life or the life of another. I rubbed my hands in boiling water like my mother had done each Sunday. It felt like they'd never be clean.

The caterer pulled a paper towel from a stray roll sitting damp and crusted on the countertop and handed it to me. I pulled back from the sink and took it, gently patting my hands so they wouldn't get irritated and bleed from the hot water on my dry skin.

"You okay?" the bartender asked.

I nodded.

Neither of them seemed satisfied with that answer. They continued to look at me through the mirror. Did they think I was floundering? Having second thoughts? Cold feet before the wedding planning even started?

I stood up straight and let out a deep breath. Then I turned off my sink, then the other two, until the room was so quiet you could hear the heartbeat of the party happening two floors up.

"Everything's going fine," I said. I looked at the two of them, feeling more at home with the help than my guests. They stared, more unconvinced by the minute. "We're good," I repeated. "It's all good."

I tossed the paper towel into the bin and walked out.

# NINETEEN

**THE SUN RISES** on the other side of Walker Mountain, painting the sky a deep orange and shadowing me in tall black trees. I look out on the western view—the lake, the water-colored leaves, the layers of blue mountains reflecting the orange, getting lighter and lighter until they recede into the background and fade into the sky, disappearing altogether.

I clutch the envelope, thick with bills, in my hand like it's the world's most expensive stress ball. After my run last night, I slipped it out of Graham's wedding suit and lay with it under my pillow until it was time to get up again. I felt comfort in knowing it was there, within reach. But now as I stand here, it feels less like a life jacket and more like an anchor. A reminder that I don't have to do this—I can leave, I can become someone else, I can disappear into the sky, too. This envelope allows me to leave right now, or leave later. After.

Now I have to choose.

From where I'm standing, in the center of the grassy knoll on which Graham and I are to be married tomorrow, I can just barely see the collection of lights in a valley on the closest mountain range. Once the sun finished rising, it would be gone, blending into daylight and hiding under the surrounding forest. But for now, it's there, and I stare at it until I have to squint to focus.

I wonder if anyone in that valley is looking this way. Can they see my speck of a figure standing in the open plain? Would they wonder what I'm doing here in the same way I'm wondering what they're doing there?

All of this is because of you, I'd tell the place if I could.

I think about the night in our dorm that we sat on the floor, shuffling through your iPod listening to NSYNC songs I'd never heard. I think about when we drank marshmallow-flavored Smirnoff and snuck back into the dorm by telling Brigid you were sleepwalking with the light of God and then stuffing our faces with leftover lasagna from the dining hall. I think about the time you taught me about your throwaway party shoes—cheap ones that can get ruined as they're dragged along the floor of a sticky bar or house—and didn't think less of me when I said my entire wardrobe was throwaway party shoes.

All of this is because of you.

All of me is because of you.

I close my eyes and straighten my shoulders and open my feet and rest my hands on my hips, just like you taught me to. I take a deep breath and then let it out slowly. I look at the mountains one last time.

Then I begin to jog down the stony road, toward the end of all of this.

Revenge is one sweet son of a bitch.

"Did you have a nice run?" Graham asks when I walk into the kitchen. I unzip my tight blue jacket, letting it fall loose around my body, cooling myself off. Running up and down a mountain is impossibly hard even when all you do is run.

"It was—" Graham doesn't look up for an answer so instead of elaborating, I just say "yep" to cater to his lack of genuine interest. He's sitting at the kitchen island, hunched over the *Burlington Free Press*. He loves this newspaper. He says it's the only paper in the world that prints mostly good news, which is stupid and inaccurate. Personally, I think a newspaper that chooses *Essex Woman Grows Largest Radish* over *The End of Roe v. Wade?* is useless.

I go to the sink and wash the mulch off my fingers. Evidence down the drain. Once I'm dry, I move around the island to where Graham sits and snag a blueberry off his plate, one of the off-colored squishier ones he'd left uneaten on the side, and I kiss his cheek. It's more stubbly than I'd like for the day before our wedding, but I don't care enough to say anything. His mother will do that for me, I'm sure.

"How are we feeling this morning?" I ask, pressing my chin into his shoulder the way he likes. "You had a couple drinks last night."

He stares down at the paper, but I can tell he's no longer reading. "It's a special occasion," he says. He's trying to sound pleasant and unbothered by the question, but the way he's white-knuckling the real estate section is giving him away.

I kiss his cheek again. "It's totally fine, babe. We're getting married tomorrow. Can you believe it?"

That seems to loosen him up, hopefully get him ready to have a couple more later, and he looks up at me for the first time in this conversation. He looks tired, light blue bags peeking out under his eyes, his eyelids heavy with each blink. But he looks happy. Or, more than that, content. Like this—him reading a newspaper, me scratching his back and stealing blueberries off his plate—is how he wants to spend the rest of his life.

He leans his head against mine, so our cheeks barely touch.

"You have to get your stuff out of our room before people get here tonight," I remind him.

He nods, scraping me with his stubbly face.

"Are we really doing the whole *can't sleep together the night before the wedding* thing?" he asks, rolling his eyes like the thought is exasperating.

I take his face in my hands and turn it toward me so I can look him straight on. "Are you asking me to break a long-held wedding tradition? When I'm marrying into a family that's, dare I say, *obsessed*, with tradition?" He laughs. "I'll let you have that conversation with your mother."

He huffs disappointedly and turns back to the woman in the paper with the ten-pound radish. "Fine. I'll get my stuff after breakfast."

Satisfied, I kiss his cheek, then move to the counter to pour a cup of coffee into my favorite mug—a ceramic disaster Veronica bought from an artist in town that Cheryl hates so much she keeps it buried deep inside the cabinet. I'm the only one who uses it and every time I bring it out Cheryl dies a little inside.

"Just be grateful for your nice little brotherly sleepover. I'm stuck spooning with fucking Veronica."

Graham laughs empathetically, probably imagining the two of us at fourteen, sharing a pillow, whispering about boys we like and girls we think are prettier than us. In reality, I'll probably sneak some Benadryl into her drink so she passes out by ten.

"Speaking of...any sign of life in this house besides us?" I ask, a seemingly innocuous question. What I want to know is: *Have you heard anything from your brother? Any movement behind those thick bedroom walls?*

Graham is the dictionary definition of a morning person. The kind of person who thinks you've wasted your day if you wake after nine; who mocks you with *morning, sunshine* or *thanks for joining us* when you come downstairs after him. His body clock is rigidly set and there's nothing that can stop him from excitedly opening his eyes at six thirty on the dot every day and that makes him better than all of us. So, as expected, I've become a morning person, too. And, because I don't ever do anything half-assed, I've become another thing he can brag about—*My fiancée has already run three miles, what have you done with your day?*

"Mom and Dad went into town for breakfast. Nothing from Reed and Veronica yet..."

I thought about the missing poster. How they may have reacted when they saw it on the floor—Bernadette's face staring up at them as they left to get coffee or water or something equally innocent. I wish I could have seen it.

I turn to ask Graham another question, but stop when I notice Lorraine, standing near the breakfast nook in the corner, hiding in the shadow of the open pantry door, sipping coffee and watching us. She stands so still she could blend in with the wallpaper behind her. She doesn't seem charmed by our banter, by my kisses and thoughtfully placed touches. She seemed wary, her eyes thin, eyebrows raised, her mouth unmoving. Normally I'd call it Resting Bitch Face but I recently decided I hated that term. Not smiling doesn't mean she's a bitch.

She blinks a few times when she notices I'm looking at her. Since we arrived, she's made herself generally scarce, only coming out of her old quarters to eat. I would have forgotten her presence entirely if I wasn't sleeping with the president of her fan club and didn't have her anguished face burned into my eyelids. The way she looked at me when I first arrived. That moment of recognition. I still don't know if it was real or imagined.

"Good morning," I finally say to her, offering as genuine a smile as I'm capable of.

Graham looks up and sees her, seemingly for the first time. "Oh, hi," he says, waving slightly. "I didn't realize you were up. Good morning."

She smiles through a sip of coffee. "I'm always up," she says. It sounds less like a fact and more like a threat.

I take my coffee to go and make my way to the bedroom, climbing so slowly you'd think each step was a hurdle of Everest proportions. I'm already exhausted and the day hasn't even started yet, but I guess that's what happens when you don't sleep. When you spend nights on a treadmill or staring at a wood-paneled ceiling next to someone snoring so loud it's like he's bragging about how fantastic a night's sleep he's getting. How peaceful he's allowed to be here. How much this place warms his sad little heart.

I follow my own footsteps back to Reed and Veronica's door. It's not as menacing in the light of day—the bookshelves and console table in the vestibule are warmer, the cushioned window seat even welcoming. Frankly, I'm shocked I didn't get caught last night—the hiding places were nonexistent. Though I guess there was no one awake to catch me.

The poster was the first time I had to take our meticulous plan into my own hands. Based on his harsh reaction, I assumed Graham would share the woodland discovery with his brother, someone he could talk to about it. But I guess their relationship was even more fractured than I thought it was.

For the briefest moment, I close my eyes and listen, standing so still in the hallway anyone who passes might think I've fallen asleep. It's like every floorboard creak and door hinge whisper has a microphone. Like the house itself is trying to offer warnings. But warnings to whom, I'm unsure.

That's when I hear some stirring. An old bed creaking as

someone turns. The floorboards waking up. Shoes slipped on. Glasses slapped out of their case.

"How're you doing in there, babe?" Veronica's voice is raspy, like the words had to claw their way out. "Need anything?"

I hear a moan from the bathroom, then the door slowly creaking open.

"How are you not sick?" Reed asks slowly. "I think I'm dying."

"You're not dying," Veronica responds. I could feel the eye roll. When Graham's sick his entire world shuts down. He can't work, can't cook, can't move off the couch. The *rub some dirt on it* mentality was lost in the Walker blood. "You just have food poisoning," she continues. "Not surprising with this trendy caterer she hired."

Nice dig.

"I'm going to get some coffee." I hear some feet padding on the floor. "Do you want s—" a pause "—what the fuck is this?"

Then everything goes bitterly silent.

I move a few steps farther down the hallway, my back to the wall between us. I'm just around enough of a bend that if one of them comes storming out of their room, I wouldn't be seen. Not that Reed seems in any physical position to *storm* anywhere, but I have to be careful. When adrenaline kicks in, even the sickest can't feel pain anymore.

I close my eyes again, listening. When one sense is gone the others are heightened, after all.

"Where'd that come from?" Reed asks, from farther into the room, maybe on the bed or the chair in the corner.

Silence.

"Where the fuck did that come from? Where did you—"

I hear a gag, then running, then the bathroom door slamming so hard it jostles the bedroom door. I can hear him vomiting through the wall. Surely he'll want Molly fired.

Any good caterer knows better than to leave any evidence. He's the only one sick, after all. We all ate the same things.

I expect the door to open, for Veronica to come out, leaving the paper on the nightstand for Graham to deal with. But no sounds come. No more talking, no more shuffling.

Instead, I smell the fireplace in their room turn on—that gaseous warmth that comes with a remote control–operated fire.

I could have sworn I heard the crinkle of the paper as it began to burn.

"There she is!"

Sarah Keens's voice echoes through the foyer, rippled with pride like she's an old friend I haven't seen in years and not a reporter from the *Times*. She stands at the bottom of the stairs, drowning in a faux fur jacket far too warm for an average October night, and smiling like we're doing one of those stupid first looks and she's the awed groom.

Sarah *New-York*-fucking-*Times* Keens.

"I'm so sorry we're late," she says as I descend. "It's hard to find this place in the dark, huh? We must have driven past the gate three times. It gets *very* dark up here. Like, spooky dark. I'd never..." She continues but I zone her out, instead centering on her photographer, a twenty-three-year-old named Rufus Hunter, standing behind her. I knew this would be a picture-perfect moment and I let him immortalize it with his camera: me Cinderella-ing myself down the gorgeous mahogany staircase in my strappy lace dress, red lips turned up ever so slightly in a wry smile. The smile means nothing to anyone right now, but when this picture graces the pages of the *New York Times* with Sarah's exclusive feature about everything that will go down tomorrow, my face will have everyone wondering how much I knew.

The answer: everything.

"So good to see you. We were just sitting down for dinner." I reach my hand out and receive her limp one in return, like shaking hands with a dry dead fish.

I switch gears to Rufus who, in his jeans, T-shirt, and bomber jacket looks like someone who lives in Bed-Stuy and is a vegan because *it's the single greatest way I can reduce my carbon footprint.*

"Eliza Bennet," I say, shaking his hand, warm in mine. This is a grip more appropriate for someone who works at the *New York Times.* Thank God Sarah's highest-stakes interview is a bridezilla wearing couture, not someone like President Obama or even a Real Housewife.

"Thanks for having us," Sarah interjects, moving in front of Rufus like a dog establishing dominance. "Your in-laws have such a beautiful home."

"Thank you," I say, looking around like I'm admiring it, too. I always feel strange accepting a compliment for something that has nothing to do with me. "They've actually given us a plot of land on the mountain to build our own snowy escape. It's where we'll be having the ceremony tomorrow." It took everything in me to say that with a straight face. Pleasantly smiling. Voice an octave higher than usual. *Snowy escape.* It feels like I'm reading from a Lifetime movie script.

Sarah's gasp of excitement was only matched by Rufus's stare of pure boredom. "I *love* that," she says. She opens her overwhelmingly large purse, digging through it until she finds her notebook, and then repeats the process for a pen. It's painful to watch but I smile as if I'm not embarrassed by the whole thing.

"Well, if you're ready…" I begin as she finishes scribbling my statement on a coffee-stained page. "We can join everyone outside."

In the expansive backyard, a clear tent is set up, lit only by floating candles in the centerpiece and the moon. Cheryl's idea, of course. I join Graham at the head of the table and watch as everyone finds their spots—finally able to sit now that Sarah and Rufus have graced us with their presence. Cheryl was less than pleased with the tardiness of the honored guests her husband reluctantly allowed.

She sidled up to me a half hour ago, one dirty martini in: "Being late means you don't respect someone's time, and I don't make it a habit of associating with people who don't respect my time," she remarked, as if I'd never heard that before. I had thought she'd be pleased with the feature, throw her hands up and kiss the air around my cheeks in celebration, but she was surprisingly as uninterested as Graham when I presented the plan to her. *Are you sure this is a good idea?* she'd asked, sitting at the kitchen counter, nursing a cup of coffee that might have had a shot of something more fun in it. *Seems like needless attention.*

That's the point, Cheryl.

Sarah and Rufus introduce themselves around the room as Lena approaches me offering a glass of wine. "We don't want an article about a bride on a wedding diet," she reminds me, as if the article would have anything to do with my meal selection for the weekend.

"Feeling good about tomorrow?" Lena asks.

"I feel fine," I say, perhaps unconvincingly. "Ready."

I don't know if I'm one hundred percent there, but I have no choice. I've made it this far; just one more day and then I can put all of this performative bullshit behind me and get back to real life. I've missed real life. Though I'm not even sure I know what that is anymore.

Just as I say it, Jess appears next to Lena, snaking her arm around her waist.

"I feel good," I repeat. "I'm a little stressed about the slide-show, but I'm sure—"

"A slideshow?" Lena steps closer to me. "That's a little tacky."

I could see Jess nail Lena hard with an elbow to the rib cage. "It's a great idea," she compensates, trying to mute Lena's *fuck, babe* as she rubs her side.

Lena takes a deep breath, hardening herself to say the word *slideshow* again. "Sorry," she says. "That's not what I meant. I just—"

"It's fine." I laugh. "It's another family tradition. They've been putting on slideshows at Walker weddings for decades."

"What do you need?" Lena asks. "We'll help."

I look between them, Jess as eager to ease the bride's worries as Lena. *Helpful* isn't exactly Lena's natural disposition. Especially when *helpful* is not for her own gain.

"I don't know… Reed and Veronica are taking care of it."

"You sound alarmingly unconfident."

I bring the wine to my lips, letting it rest there for a moment, as if I'm drinking.

"It's not a big deal—it'll play on the lot while guests arrive tomorrow to keep them occupied during our first look. I'm just nervous about what kind of pictures he'll include because he thinks they're funny. He has some less-than-flattering ones of Graham in his arsenal. But he and Veronica won't let anyone see it. They're refusing. Want it to be some big surprise. Even Cheryl's in the dark, which never happens."

Lena looks at Jess, who offers a nod, then at me. "She can hack into it."

"What?"

"She does computer shit." Lena looks at her partner, who's standing there like she's embarrassed to accept these humble brags. "Right?"

Jess glances around the room as she scratches her neck. A nervous tick?

"I guess. If I'm on his device, I can try. What do you want me to do, though?"

"Just scan for inappropriate pictures and delete any bad ones," Lena answers for me, nodding proudly. "Do you know his password?" she asks me.

"One hundred bucks says Veronica's birthday or the name of his favorite porn star," I respond, getting a laugh out of both of them. "It's in his room. The computer."

Jess offers an understanding smile. "You know what," she says to Lena, "I'm not feeling great. I think maybe I'll sit inside for a moment, get my bearings." She starts backing away.

"Problem solved," Lena says, as we watch her exit the tent. "Now, drink up, baby."

When it's time to eat, Graham and I take our seats behind little wooden letters labeling us Mr. and Mrs. that Molly had carved from the stash of firewood in the garage. Really going the extra mile, this one.

Cheryl and Doug are the closest to us, sipping martinis and snacking on bruschetta until the food arrives. Beside them are a few cousins—Marty and Margarita, unfortunately married and kitschy about it; Elliot and his wife, Lauren, who are sharing the title of officiant only because Graham wanted Elliot but I didn't trust him to not write a speech entirely about drinking at Yale together, so I got Lauren involved. Then Lena, in her black velvet suit with only a lacy dark purple bralette underneath, next to an empty place setting.

"She's not feeling great," she explains to Veronica on her other side.

"You know what," Veronica begins, leaning too close to Lena, "Reed was throwing up all morning. I wonder if they ate something strange?"

Lena feigns consideration, looking past her new companion and toward Reed, definitely paler than usual. "Maybe. That's a good point... I didn't eat anything last night. Not in that dress."

Veronica smiles approvingly.

Opposite us, on the other end of the table, are Sarah and Rufus, drinking a glass of rosé and a beer, respectively, and looking a bit like summer renters in the Hamptons—they don't officially belong but they'll try their best to look it.

I make eye contact with one of the waiters, a man with a thin face standing near the dining room's exit, and point to my empty water glass. "Can I have another?" I mouth, barely finishing the last word before he is off, catering to my every whim as he is probably grossly underpaid to do. I'd mentioned to Molly after my first glass of wine that I didn't want to drink anymore tonight—I need to stay sharp—but I didn't want anyone to know it.

A glass of ice water with a lime performatively balancing on its edge is delivered but a minute later, as if they had a tray of them in the kitchen, waiting for me to summon them one by one. My old glass disappears as the new one replaces it, like it was never there in the first place. A vodka-soda-appearing drink is perfect. I take a slow and shallow sip, holding the icy water against my impenetrable red lips until they begin to go numb.

I hate everyone at this table except for Lena—and Rufus, whom I know the least and to whom I have not spoken one full word the entire night. He seems like the one person who isn't gob-smacked by this family, their wealth, their connections. He seems grounded in a way no one I've met in a while has been.

For most of the evening I watch Sarah make the rounds, charming everyone with her soft giggle and wild enthusiasm for everything. It's sweet, to be that easily excited, to be so carefree that the world can amuse you that much. It also helps that she's hot—an Alexa Chung type.

She asks Cheryl about her first impression of me—"I knew immediately that she was the one"—and presses Veronica for a quote about our relationship—"She's the sister I never had." She lingers between Reed and Doug, asking them about work. She seems genuinely fascinated by the hierarchy of Vermont, and where Doug's spot is, right at the top. He might not be the governor, but he has the governor's ear whenever he wants. And his money means that what Doug wants, Doug gets.

Reed is not receptive to Sarah's questioning. He's quiet all night. At one point I catch Veronica reaching her hand to touch his arm but he brushes it away, so subtly if you weren't looking for it, you wouldn't notice. But I do. He's distracted—obviously, but he keeps staring at Graham with fervor. Like he's reciting a monologue about how much he hates his brother in his head. I wish I could goad him into saying it aloud, encouraging it. The more you say, the more Sarah can use, after all. *So say it all, you son of a bitch.*

When the meal comes, everyone is served their selection of chicken, fish, or vegetarian, except for Reed, who asks for a bowl of grits instead. "My stomach isn't completely back to normal," he insists, letting the implication that Molly caused all this sit with us just as we're all about to chow down.

He looks like a child, sitting there spooning the mushy beige into his mouth. The only thing that would have made it stranger is if he was drinking, but he's still watching Graham drink instead. Careful observation that starts to sway more *1984* Big Brother than normal Reed Big Brother.

Just then, Lorraine walks in, sneaking through the tent's plastic entrance and whispering something into Reed's ear, and my light-headedness comes on. That happens up here. Graham says it's the high altitude and that I don't drink enough water, but I know it's not. It's the memories. It's her. It's them.

It's the fact that, for the last hour, I'd completely forgotten about Lorraine. I've been keeping track of everyone out here, ensuring that Jess had the house to herself, could do whatever she needs in peace. Meanwhile, where has Lorraine been? What did she catch? What does she know?

And what is she telling Reed?

She's watching me again, just like she did at breakfast this morning, and when we first arrived. In fact, the more I interact with her, the less I'm convinced I'd made it all up. The more it seems that the recognition is real. That somewhere buried deep in her subconscious, she remembers me.

I lean into Graham—"I need some air," I say. "Be right back."—and stand before he can protest that it's too cold or that I'll be fine if I just have a sip of water. I'm not even sure he heard me. He's too busy listening to his mother talk Sarah's ear off about the night she and Doug met for the first time. The more she convinces herself this article can be about her, the more accepting of our reporter guests she'll become, so I let her have it.

I feel like if I don't get out of the tent soon, there's a high probability I'll projectile vomit all over the entire table. It wouldn't be the *New York Times* article I'd envisioned—*Bride Vomits All Over Family at Rehearsal Dinner*—but it would be equally as memorable, I guess.

Outside the tent, it's cold, bitterly so, and I feel goose bumps growing on my arms and legs immediately. But I like it. It's a good feeling. A clean feeling.

I walk over to the porch and sit on the edge of the lowest wooden step, slightly damp from the cold air. I've never gotten over how dark it is out here. The ground blends into the trees, which blend into the sky. It's the kind of darkness where my imagination goes wild. Anything can be in those woods, standing just behind the tree line, watching me, watching us. The fear, I guess, isn't that you're alone in the dark, but that you're not alone.

"Hello, Eliza." I look up to see Lorraine standing over me, a silhouette of a person backlit by the soft light from inside the house. "Can I join you?"

I motion toward the step beside me, *be my guest*, and she sits down. Her legs are short and stubby, folding at the knee like two thick Twizzlers.

"I'm listening for Henry tonight," she says, lifting the monitor in her hand. "He was fussing but he's back to sleep now. A good self-soother." I let out a deep breath, relieved that that's probably what she was reporting to Reed, not that Jess was hacking into his laptop as we speak.

"I get light-headed sometimes," I explain to her, pleasantly. "Graham says it's the elevation."

She nods a few times, clawing her hands on her knees and looking back and forth from me to the tent. Only half her face is lit, an orange glow coming in and out like a fire, and I think back to the reflection in the window. The shadow of a woman looking out at us from the dark living room. And then how that person disappeared right when I needed her.

"My parents used to have horses," she says. "Three of them. Baboso, Chamba, and… George." She laughs and looks at me, anticipatory, so I laugh, too. "My nephew named them," she continues, clearly still charmed by it. She is looking straight ahead, into the woods, like a camp counselor telling a ghost story to kids who're probably too young to understand how scary it really is.

"There used to be a barn over there, you know," she says then, nodding toward the back corner of the yard. At night it was indistinguishable in the darkness, but in the right light of day, you can still see a slight discoloration in the grass, a barely perceivable perimeter of where the barn used to be. "The roof on my parents' barn—where we kept the horses—collapsed a few years ago. Maybe eight or nine. Everything was fine, we went to bed, and then we woke up on Sunday morning and the back half of the barn had just collapsed. Like someone pushed the legs out from under it, you know."

I nod, but I can't tell where she is going with this. For all the years I've known Graham and the family, no one ever mentions the barn. It seems, actually, like an unwritten rule that it is never to be brought up. It never existed. Not here, not anywhere.

"The horses were fine," she goes on. "They jumped their corrals and were all standing in the front by the food. Thank God." She pauses, and I realize it's for me to agree.

"Thank God," I murmur. I haven't said those words out loud in years. Even now, it feels like I didn't say them. Like I'm watching myself from a few feet away. Like I'm removed from all of it.

"We didn't know what we were going to do. We couldn't afford to fix it, we were sure about that. We had shitty insurance, too. They said it was caused by foul play and refused to cover it. Which was ridiculous. We were all asleep. There was no chance. But we couldn't argue. We were ready to put the horses up for sale. But then, the very next day, Mr. and Mrs. Walker offered to give us their barn. The one that used to sit right over there. I couldn't believe it."

I remember the barn clearly. The chipped red paint. The hay floor. The feeling of the slimy wood paneling.

"I didn't know you could gift someone an entire barn," she continues. "But the Walkers, they figure out how to do everything. And two days later, they had the old barn removed, they had the site dug up. They even paid for someone to add wash stalls and a feed room and all that. And then the barn was just there. It fit like a glove. Like it had been there all along." She shook her head and took a deep breath, her hands pressing against each other on her lap. "The horses went from a Motel 8 to a Ritz-Carlton in a week." She laughs to herself. "You know why they did that?"

I twist my body to the left so I can face her straight on, look her in the eyes for the first time in this entire conversation. I need to see her face.

I did know why they would do that. I did know why they'd get rid of the barn. Why they'd want it far away, claimed and settled somewhere else. Someplace where it looked like it belonged all along. They needed to hide the evidence. There was no party if there was no barn. And there was no Ruthie if there was no party.

I never knew how they got rid of it so quickly.

I could run down the mountain and grab the envelope from its hiding spot. I can pack my things quickly. Call the girls from the road. I can take Sarah and Rufus's car; I'm sure the keys are in the purse she left in the foyer with her ridiculous jacket. I can get out of here. I can kill Eliza right now.

Or I can kill Lorraine. That would keep her mouth shut and allow our plan to continue unscathed. I can bury Lorraine in the woods, create a mass graveyard and add her to where Reed probably buried Ruthie. After the party in the barn. After he took her into the woods and only one of them returned.

The night she never came home.

"They're good people," Lorraine says, answering her own question. "Really good people."

She stands and looks down at me, her eyes filled with judgment, not recognition. That's what it's been all along. She didn't remember my face, but she saw me for what I was. A fraud. A fake. A liar.

"Don't marry him if you're not a good person, too," she says. "He deserves better."

Before I can respond, she walks away coolly, smoothly, back toward the tent. Like trying to end her favorite child's marriage was just a day in the life. Nothing to see here.

She didn't even realize she'd given me answers to questions I started asking long ago.

Before I have time to stand, to figure out what to do with this new information, how to use it, two figures round the tent and start walking toward me, slow and steady, not unlike Lorraine, who just joined the crowd inside.

Molly and Jess appear in the light, their features curious but cautious.

"The slideshow is ready," Jess says. "All the photos we took that night are loaded to play. As long as he opens his computer tomorrow when you meet with him, I'll be able to get remote access and can get everything projected."

"Good," I say, feeling slightly nauseous.

"Are you sure you don't want to see the pictures? I have the file. I can—"

I shake my head. I had found Ruthie's camera stuffed into the side of one of those worn leather couches in the back of the barn that night. Annie had squirreled it in there for safe keeping and forgot. But I couldn't leave without it.

I never looked at the photos. I couldn't do it. I kept the camera inside a sock in a bathroom cabinet or couch cushion or glove compartment, moving it around with every failed attempt to print the photos. I couldn't fathom looking at a picture of us dancing or smiling or feeling invincible, while knowing what would happen next. It would feel like peeping into someone else's life. A kind of happiness, innocence, sincerity I'd never feel again.

"Did you look at them?" I ask.

"A couple. Not everything."

"And?"

She nods, considering it. "I think this is going to work."

She puts her hand on my shoulder and I rest mine over it.

"I left posters in their room, too," Jess says, lightening the mood. "Molly had a few left over from the trees, figured we shouldn't waste them."

"Good idea…"

"The idiot thinks he's so smart ordering grits," Molly adds. "I can put those berries in there just as easily as I did his appetizer last night."

They laugh together, thinking of Reed growing paler and paler as the night went on, eventually running upstairs with his hand over his mouth, barely making it to the bedroom before vomiting everywhere. I didn't laugh, though. I couldn't. Something was bugging me about what Lorraine said. They gave the barn to her the day after Ruthie disappeared? *The day after?*

They look at each other, then back at me. "You okay?"

"I found the barn," I say. "I know where the barn is."

# PART THREE

# TWENTY

**COVENANT UNIVERSITY'S ONE-YEAR** reunion banners littered the town of Eden, Vermont, like clumps of trash on the beach. They were hanging on fences above overpasses next to homemade and faded *Welcome Our Troops Home* flags and padlocks that overzealous virgins carved their initials into.

The signs were dangling from light posts down Main Street, advertised on full pages of the local newspaper, and handed out as fucking coasters at the diner where I was sweating my ass off working, making sure some fat fuck with a motorcycle helmet got his coffee and feta egg scramble on time.

After Ruthie disappeared, I took most of her clothes, stuffing them into my plastic mattress cover to hide them from her mom and stepdad when they came to campus to collect her things. They were convinced she'd simply run away. *She's done it before and she'll do it again*, her stepdad kept saying, unsuccessfully assuaging her mother's frustration. *She's desperate for attention*, he told Brigid, who oversaw their move-out—shoulders back, stomach in, like a drill sergeant disappointed in her trainee's inability to shut up and take it.

But Ruthie wasn't coming back. I knew it. She would never leave me. She knew that if she went anywhere, I would go with her.

When I came back to campus after curfew alone, I tried to tell Brigid what happened—"Ruthie's gone, we have to go get her. Can you drive?"—but I was promised a violation and a fine and then stuffed into my room to think about how Jesus would feel that I was out so late. As if I wasn't already thinking about how Jesus would feel that I wasn't a virgin anymore. This man needed to mind his own fucking business.

Then I tried to convince Dr. Theresa Bregg, the head of Covenant's Office of Equity and Inclusion. Her windowless office was located in the basement of the Student Center, underneath the main dining hall so it smelled like oregano and burned cheese, and while she and I sat at a conference table discussing Ruthie, debris occasionally fell from the ceiling tiles, spraying us with powdery insulation every time a football student ran toward the pizza line upstairs.

I told her we went to a party. That Ruthie and I snuck out, drove to a mountain with a big red barn, drank radioactive pink alcohol, and that she followed a boy into the woods and never came out. I tried searching for her. I yelled her name until my throat ached and my toes were numb in the snow. I ran up and down the forest, trees grating against my body, puncturing holes in my jacket, scraping my face, until I wasn't sure which way was out. Until I was so deep in the evergreens, I couldn't see the moon. Until it was so dark, I wasn't sure whether my eyes were open or closed.

When I found my way back to the barn, it could have been an hour later, I had no idea, everyone was inside, dancing to a Lady Gaga song I'd never heard before but would never be able to forget. All but two of the boys were there, talking to that dark-haired annoyed girl, drinking like nothing happened.

I stormed up to them and slapped the red cup from one of their pale hands. "Where are your friends?" I asked. "The ones who live here?"

The kid looked around at his friends, like I was joking, like he was waiting for them to start laughing so he could, too. But the laughter never came. They were all too shocked by the bloody scrapes on my face.

"Where's Ruthie?" I asked. "Where is she?"

"I don't know who you're talking about," he said.

"Where are the other two?"

He shook his head again. "I don't know who you're talking about." He laughed to his friends, uncomfortably, stiffly.

"She's wasted," the girl said to her friends. "That's really embarrassing," I heard her add as I walked away.

Dr. Bregg's pen moved furiously over her notebook while I spoke, like she was writing down every single word I said, a record of the night, step-by-step, that we could use to call the police, to find Ruthie. To figure out what happened to her. To get her back.

When I was finished, explaining that I tried to talk to Brigid but was stonewalled, she capped her pen and sat up straight. She glanced down at her notebook, still cradled against her chest like a small child. Then she looked at me.

"You're aware that parties go against the Covenant Code?" she asked.

I sat back in the chair and let out the kind of breath that makes you light-headed. Fuck.

"And you were drinking?" she continued. "How much did you have to drink?" She sighed, disappointed in *our* behavior. "This is a wily accusation, Elizabeth. That your roommate, who had also been drinking, is in danger. Do you think it's possible she just went home? That she needed some time to think about the violations she'd committed? Drinking, pre-marital sex, being alone with a member of the opposite—"

"She didn't go home. Her parents don't know where she is," I started to yell. "Something happened to her."

Dr. Bregg put her notebook on the table and leaned over it, toward me. She knew exactly what to do to make me think she cared—get on my level, speak softly, calmly. If I didn't hear what she was saying, by the looks of this meeting, I'd think it was going well.

"I understand you're concerned for your friend. But I need you to understand that by filing this report, by getting the university involved, you could be found to have broken the Covenant Code yourself. We'll have a proper trial, of course, like we do for every large-scale violation, but by making this report official...well, you remember what happened to Lucy and Isabella? They were in your dorm, right? And I believe you and your dormmates were also penalized for their trans-gressions?"

I might have nodded but I couldn't tell. It was like my en-tire face was numbed by her unwarranted reaction.

She leaned just an inch closer. "If you're found guilty, you could lose your scholarship or, more likely, be expelled. Ruthie as well. And obviously your parents would be notified of... *everything.*"

I didn't know what to say, so I said nothing. I pictured my father, intercepting the letter from the school, then slapping my mother across the face with it until she was cowering on the floor, her nose bleeding down her apron. *How dare you encour-age this?* he'd repeat over and over. *How dare you encourage her?*

I looked at Dr. Bregg, the way her eyebrows scrunched in the middle, as if she was genuinely concerned. As if she'd heard my every word.

When she finally leaned back and I could see the contents

of her notebook, the only thing in it was a write-up of accrued violations, like an algebra problem showing all her work.

Two days later, I tried to convince Dean Gerwig. I ran to his office Wednesday morning, waiting outside the speckled glass doors for him to stroll in without a worry in the world at 10:15 a.m., a giant iced coffee in hand, telling someone via Bluetooth headphones that his assistant will send the papers over this afternoon, thank you for your donation, Doug.

"Can I help you?" he asked.

He towered over me, swishing his iced coffee around like it was part of a fucking symphony. "My roommate is missing," I said. It had been seventy-two hours. She'd missed three days of classes, three days of homework, three days of curfews. She missed a convocation. She missed breakfasts and dinners. She was gone.

After waving off his assistant, and two other concerned office workers—he invited me to take a seat in his office, in one of the tall leather chairs opposite his gargantuan mahogany desk. The room was covered in floor-to-ceiling amber bookshelves, filled with leather-bound classics and an entire shelf dedicated to all three hundred translations of the Bible. As if this stupid man could speak anything other than English.

I explained to him exactly what I told Dr. Bregg. We snuck out. We went to a party. It was on a mountain. I don't remember the address, but I'd memorized everything about it that night and on the drive home. I could take him there by memory. The windy street, the wooden sign hanging over the entrance to it, near where we parked our car. It was a big house with glass walls and a firepit. There was a lake, I think, I could hear water moving when I was deep in the woods, her name echoing off each tree as I said it over and over again. Behind the house was a big red barn. It was the only thing on the entire mountain.

He put his coffee down and leaned back into his chair, resting his hands behind his head like he was getting comfortable to watch a movie.

"I believe I know the house you're talking about," he said, calmly. "I'm friends of the family. Douglas Walker and I went to Yale together. That's where his boys go. They're good kids, the two of them. And I know for a fact that they were away on a family trip to Beaver Creek this week. They're still there, in fact. I received this picture of them this morning."

He pressed some buttons on his computer and flipped the thin screen around to face me. Four people were in the photo, covered from head to toe in black-and-white ski gear—orange goggles, beanies, gaiters—standing next to a sign, listing three black diamond courses: Spider, Cataract, Keller Glade. Not an inch of skin was visible. They could have been anyone.

"Actually," Dean Gerwig continued, "I know their house very well. I've been there many times for fundraisers and sponsor dinners. Things of that nature that the Walkers are generous enough to host for the school. And I don't believe there *is* a barn in the back, as you've described, Elizabeth. They don't have any animals or cattle. Never have." He pulled his computer back, clicked a few more buttons, then turned it around. The picture now enlarged on the screen was of an expansive yard. In the daylight, it was hard to connect it to what I remembered. The evergreens looked the same in the back corner, but they would anywhere, I guess. It was just the snowy grass and trees. No barn. No hay. No Ruthie.

He turned the computer back, then leaned toward me. "I encourage you to take a day or two and rethink this accusation, Elizabeth. There are consequences for both of you if you come forward. Especially when your memory has clearly been affected by your inebriation." He nodded toward the computer, toward the photos that seemed to debunk everything I knew for sure. "Seriously think about that."

I'd thought about it every day for over four years since.

At the diner, I still wore Ruthie's clothes. I gained thirty pounds so the Abercrombie T-shirt was stretched to the point of breaking at the seams, and I used a large safety pin to get her jeans closed around my waist. The Eden Diner apron covered it all anyway with its red-and-white horizontal stripes, something Ruthie would have told me never to wear, especially now. Horizontal stripes were a fashion faux pas, she'd say, and I'd have pretended to know that, too.

I didn't want to celebrate the one-year reunion at a college I hated. One that I barely graduated from, but for some reason couldn't leave. I couldn't go back to my parents' farm; I knew my ties with them were broken, unrepairable. And frankly I didn't want to return home. I knew from the day I left that I'd never see them again. I wanted to move to New York City, create the life for myself that Ruthie had always dreamed of. But as much as she would have pushed me, encouraged me to get as far from here as possible, she was also pulling me back, tying me to this place like a rope around my neck.

The more the years passed, the less I remembered the details of her face, of our time together. One morning I woke up and couldn't recall her smell anymore. Frantically, I ran to my dresser and pulled out her perfume, the bottle of Victoria's Secret's Very Sexy Now, the name still duct-taped over from when she hid it in our room in college, and pressed the snuffer cap against my nose until I started breaking out in a rash.

If I had brownouts in my memories of her here, it would only get worse if I moved away.

The ding of the diner's bell pulled me back, as two women entered, ignoring the *Please Wait Here to Be Seated* sign and claiming a booth against the window.

They looked different, but not different at the same time. It's incredible what one year in the real world can do. Catherine's hair was long and blonder now, in perfect beachy curls around her thin and blushed face. Annie wore a black beanie and dark eyeliner that accentuated her thick eyebrows and blue eyes. They looked like adults. Like people with real jobs in real cities who had forgotten everything that happened here and built new lives for themselves.

They weren't in my section—I was assigned to the counter today, waiting on mostly regulars and very few alumni, for which I was grateful. I wasn't ready to talk to them yet, so I just watched. I stood at the counter as Lisa took their order—an omelet with home fries, blueberry pancakes with extra syrup—and I found myself jealous that they could eat like that in public. I was still delicately crunching on arugula whenever I was in front of anyone, keeping the real food for after. They didn't recognize me at all, I was sure of it. I hardly recognized me either.

After that party, we fell out of touch. I stopped talking to almost everyone. I got a new roommate, a soccer player named Inez who created a cloud of body odor in our room every day after practice. I became reclusive. I went to class and back, that was it. I stopped seeing Timothy or answering his calls. When I spotted him a few weeks later walking with his arm around another girl I felt relieved. Maybe we could pretend that losing my virginity never happened. Maybe if I could have that night back, Ruthie could, too.

I didn't answer Catherine's and Annie's texts. I didn't open the door when they knocked to invite me to dinner and eventually the knocks stopped coming. I didn't meet them in the forest one more time. Instead, I lofted my bed and created a childish fort underneath, pulling my sheets over the wood siding until I could sit on the floor unseen. Down there, I'd eat fistfuls of Doritos and drink queso straight from the jar.

I'd let ice cream melt in the gallon and then lap it up like a cat with milk. I'd buy family-sized bags of caramel M&M's and eat them one by one until my jaw was throbbing, until I'd counted every single piece.

God didn't exist. I didn't care about looking good for Him, about treating my body like a temple, like something He created in His likeness. I didn't want anything to do with this place, these people, this religion.

Ruthie was the only person I wanted to see. The only person I wanted to talk to.

But she was gone. And no one would listen to me.

I'd taken a double shift at the diner that day, figuring it was better to have something to do as all my former classmates strolled back into town. I didn't leave until after 2:00 a.m., when we closed for a few hours so a cleaning crew could come in and scrub the grease from the floor. I locked up quickly— it's routine at this point, transferring the cash from the register to the safe, making sure appliances are off, the freezers are shut, the lights dimmed. Then I stopped just inside the door and looked at the poster on the community bulletin board, which I also did every night. MISSING: BERNADETTE WARD. I noticed the one-year reunion poster hanging next to it and tore it down, letting it crumple to the floor and get swept up with all the day's other garbage.

I walked outside with two to-go containers filled with enough chicken tenders, French fries, and onion rings to last a normal person four or five days, but that I would eat in the span of fifteen minutes, until my belly was protruded and bloated, until I'd wake up in the middle of the night so full with food I couldn't roll over. So full with shame I'd start to cry.

When I rounded the corner into the parking lot, I stopped short when I saw Catherine and Annie there, sitting on the trunk of the navy Suburban I bought for five hundred dollars from a Craigslist ad, the only car left in the diner's lot.

"Hi," they said in unison, like two people possessed.

"Hi," I responded, walking the gap between us like a plank.

Catherine looked me up and down, a disaster covered in ill-fitting clothes and grease stains. I could see her reading my name tag, staring at it on my chest for too long.

"You still go by Elizabeth?" she asked. It wasn't judgmental, just surprised. Like she assumed I'd want to leave that world behind. But I couldn't. It was all Ruthie knew.

I nodded and shrugged.

"My real name is Molly," she said. "I don't do the saint's name thing anymore. It was kind of bullshit, if you ask me. A way to strip us of our identities, create new God-fearing personas—"

"—that's enough." Annie nudged her and Catherine—*Molly*—stopped talking. "Sorry," she said. "We're just—I'm Jess. In real life."

Of course, I already knew their real names. I'd been following them since graduation. Molly moved to New York and created a cheese board business on Instagram, which didn't sound like a real job but according to *Forbes*'s "30 Under 30," her net worth was over half a million dollars. And Jess was a lesbian now. She'd discovered herself at NYU while getting her masters in computer engineering. She calls herself an Ethical Hacker on her LinkedIn.

I shook their hands and it felt like a reunion with strangers.

"That poster in the diner—" Molly nodded toward the entrance, as if I didn't know where it was. "Got any more?"

I waved them off the trunk and they jumped down, standing next to me as I push the key into the cylinder and open it up.

I printed out ten posters every morning. Sometimes I'd find

ten places to put them, scattering them around town so everyone has as hard a time forgetting as I did. Sometimes I'd find they'd been ripped down or graffitied on, or had crumpled in a rainstorm, so I replaced them, good as new. But sometimes I didn't and they ended up here. In my trunk. Like having three hundred Ruthies staring up at me.

"Bernadette..." Molly muttered, taking a poster in her hands. "I wouldn't have pegged her for a Bernadette."

"I wonder if she ever had a nickname," Jess posited. "Betty or Bernie or something." I didn't answer her, but I wasn't sure she was speaking to anyone but herself anyway.

"Want to take a ride?" I asked, instead.

We arrived at the edge of the mountain thirty minutes later, and I parked the car on the side of the road, the same place we had been dropped off all those years ago, and we trudged up the wooded mountainside, avoiding the one paved road in case anyone from the house was home.

I'd been watching this family for almost four years now. I'd drive up here, stake out the spot in the woods where I kept a Styrofoam cooler painted black and stuffed with blankets and binoculars and a Nikon D810 Full-Frame DSLR. And I'd sit there for hours, watching them. The parents, Douglas and Cheryl, ate dinner in the dining room on opposite sides of the long table, with large glasses of wine. The younger son, Graham, brought home girl after girl, introducing these brunette bombshells to his parents, who seem disinterested at best, fucking them with the windows open in his second-floor bedroom, leaving the lights on as he fell asleep. Then the older one, Reed. He hardly ever came home. But when he did, he was angry about it, putzing around the yard, walking in circles around the firepit as he talked on the phone with his girlfriend, Veronica. He never wanted to be there.

And I understood why.

I led Molly and Jess through the woods the long way, around the house and yard and lake. Though the Walker family always goes on vacation this time of year, the risk of taking a shortcut wasn't worth it.

We moved in silence until we reached my spot, a slight valley in the woods where my cooler sat camouflaged by branches I'd broken down. I pulled the cooler to the edge of the woods, to the place Ruthie disappeared into. To the last place I saw her.

"They all said there wasn't a barn here, but look at that." I pointed to the grass in the nearest corner of the yard, still slightly yellowed and flattened four years later. "It was more obvious in college. But what was I supposed to say? That a barn mysteriously disappeared? And I realized because I was trespassing?" I took a photo of the progress then, as I had every single time I stood there. "And look at what else—" I opened the cooler and pulled out a large freezer bag filled with smaller baggies. "These are fibers from my jacket that night. I found them on the trees. They match the holes perfectly. And this—"

"Is that a—"

"It's the condom from when I lost my virginity. Timothy threw it on the ground and I didn't think about it again until I came back here a few weeks later. The barn was gone, but there was the fucking condom. It must have been covered in snow that night. That's probably why they didn't trash it."

I stuffed everything back into the cooler. "I've searched this mountain for four years looking for her..." I turn to face them, my back to the house and the memories. "I know she's dead. But if they buried her in these woods, I would have found her by now. I would have—"

"Someone's in the house." I looked at Molly, who was staring behind me, completely frozen. "There's someone in the window."

I spun around quickly, just as the shadow of a petite woman disappeared through the swinging curtains. How long had she been there for? How much had she seen?

"We have to go."

There's a hill five miles off campus called Covenant Landing. It's rumored to have been where seniors used to go to make out. That is, until Dr. Felix Chastain got word of it and started having security patrol the area for students' cars. Now it's just an abandoned lot, covered in overgrown trees and weeds breaking through the gravelly ground.

Molly, Jess, and I sat on the hood of my car, drinking Bud Light and looking over campus as the sun set. For what it's worth, Covenant is a campus straight out of a movie—brick buildings covered in green ivy; pristine lawns and quads, not one piece of mulch out of place. From the outside it was the perfect school, a small haven cut out of a gorgeous forest. But from the inside...

"You know Tim still lives up here, too?" Annie said. "We still talk sometimes. His real name is Gregory. Greg. I think I'm going to see him tomorrow."

I hadn't spoken to him, but I looked him up online a few times. Gregory Greene. Engaged. A police officer. Living thirty minutes outside of town in a trailer on a lot where he was building his own house, stone by stone. He'd figured it out. He'd moved on. They all did.

"Have you been in touch with him at all? Seen if he can help?" Catherine asked.

"He can't. They're impenetrable," I responded, about the Walkers. "At first, I just figured they were big donors to the school, that's why Gerwig didn't do anything. And why

Bregg convinced me not to file a report. But then the more I researched… They know everyone. Literally everyone. And every single person helped them cover it up. I just don't know how. Finding a barn in Vermont is worse than finding a needle in a haystack."

I threw my empty bottle onto the dirt and slid another from the six-pack beside me, opening it with my apartment key in one swift move.

"Maybe you need to think about getting out of here. This place wasn't good for any of us, Elizabeth. Maybe you need to start over, too."

"I can't bring myself to leave," I finally admit. "I feel like leaving Eden is leaving Ruthie. And I just… I'm the reason she went in there. I have to get her out. I have to make this right."

I looked down at the campus, getting brighter as the sun slowly fell behind the mountains and the sky went from blue to orange to purple to black.

"I also have this…" I stood up and moved around the car to the passenger's seat, sticking my hand through the window and into the glove compartment until I pulled out a green fuzzy sock covering a digital camera.

"Oh shit," Molly said when I handed it to her.

"Is this real?" Jess moved it around in her hand like it was a technological relic. Which, at this point, just four years later, it kind of already was. "Do you know what's on it?"

"Pictures of us climbing up to the party," I said. "Those are all I remember taking."

"And some in the pool house bathroom," Molly added.

"Can I take this?" Jess asked.

"I don't want it anymore," I said. "I never should have kept it in the first place."

They say you can see Covenant University from a satellite in space. That's something the student tour guides brag about when walking prospective families around. Our campus is so brightly lit, so safe at night, that astronauts can use it as a guide to tell which hemisphere they're looking down on. *Nothing bad happens here, because there's no darkness*, they'd claim. *You can see our prayers from space.*

Well, prayers don't mean shit if they're not followed by action.

"Okay then," Molly said, standing between me and campus, looking at me with a wry smile on her face. "It's settled. If you want to bring them down, you have to become one of them. We all do."

# TWENTY-ONE

**NOTHING AND EVERYTHING** makes sense at the same time.

I tell them what Lorraine told me: that her barn collapsed. Mysteriously. Out of nowhere. Coincidentally. The night of the party. "And the Walkers, the *heroes* that they are, gave her family theirs."

"They just gave them the barn? The whole thing?"

"Cleared the old site. Dug it up to size. Plopped a barn right… on top…"

They look at me, then each other. "What's going on?" Molly asks, but I ignore her.

The barn where the party was still existed. The barn that, even at its best, was circumstantial evidence, yet was still too damning for them to keep has just been out in the world this whole time. And I missed it. I'd searched for it for years—through college, the whole year after when I was working at the diner. I bribed every dump officer within a fifty-mile radius to tell me if someone ever dropped off a suspicious amount of red painted wood. I searched random hauling sites, lumberyards. I even drove around aimlessly just in case my memory of that night was so skewed I had the wrong house, the wrong family, the wrong targets.

This whole time it was at their fucking now-retired nanny's house. How did I never think to check up on her, to follow her home one weekend and scope out her situation? If I had done that, just once, I would have figured it all out. Maybe I could have avoided this entire play I'd been putting on for years. Maybe Eliza would never have existed. Maybe I could have actually lived a life that was mine. Maybe—

I stop my own thoughts short. I never found Ruthie's body. I searched every end of the woods on the Walker property, looking for soil that was recently touched, ground that was recently interrupted. Nothing.

But she was never on the Walker property, was she?

"That's why I never found her body," I tell them, so softly I second-guess whether it actually came out of my mouth. "It was never here. It was always with the barn."

It was always with the barn.

"That's why they offered to dig up the site," Molly realized aloud. Just as we all did.

"Why would they do that?" Jess asked. "Why wouldn't they just get rid of it? Fill a body bag with cement and put her at the bottom of the lake?"

"If there was a chance someone would keep looking for her... Lorraine was their scapegoat. They didn't know how her parents would react. Her friends. Me. If someone got too close and they got wind of it...just one anonymous tip and the police would find her body and Lorraine would go down for it. It was an easy out."

I stood up, finally on eye level with my partners in this wild game we'd been playing for years. This hoax to get Reed to confess what he'd done. The retribution we deserved. That Ruthie deserves.

"I'd bet my entire fake life that she's still under there."

"If that's true," Jess began, "we could get the entire family. We could bring them all down."

Molly nodded, then looked toward the pool house, where we used the bathroom all those years ago, where Ruthie and I started our fight.

Where, in a closet, the gardeners kept their tools. Their shovels. The things you'd need to dig up whatever's left of your best friend's body.

"You have to stay," Molly said. "But we don't."

Jess met her gaze and smiled. "Let's go get Ruthie."

# TWENTY-TWO

━━━━━

**I SIT AT** the vanity in our bedroom, staring at myself in the mirror. Half a dozen people have been scampering around me for hours. Massaging my face with oils. Soaking my feet in warm water. Filing my heels and soles. Painting my nails the subtlest of nudes. My hair has been washed and dried and straightened and curled and pinned up and let down. My face has been peeled and ice rolled and moisturized and masked and unmasked.

I've stood in the center of the room on a life-sized lazy Susan pedestal, completely naked while a petite blonde slipped my dress onto my body, spinning me in circles as she sewed the final seams and buttoned the last buttons.

And now I'm sitting here, looking at myself, finally alone.

I'm different now than I used to be—I've gotten older and have begun covering up the first sign of worry wrinkles, just like every other twenty-nine-year-old. I am tanned and I have fake lashes and makeup made to look like I'm not wearing any, merely just glowing in the light of the sun. I'm a different person. I'm not really a person at all.

I'm a doll. I've spent the last five years embedded into a plan that forced me to change everything about myself—my name, the way I look, the clothes I wear, the words I choose to use. And now that it's almost over—now that I can be free—I don't know who I am anymore. I don't know what I am without this. I hardly feel like my real name.

"Eliza?" There's a knock on the door and I call them to come in.

Sarah Keens's head pops through the gap, smiling at me like a child successfully walking in on her mother getting ready for something special. "Can I come in?" she asks, as if half her body hadn't already entered.

"Of course." I wave her farther into the room, and she shuts the door silently behind her. "Here, take a seat."

She lowers onto the edge of the bed, and I spin in my vanity chair to face her.

"You look incredible," she says, an obligatory compliment I've heard so many times this weekend it had started voiding itself.

"There's been a slight change of plans I wanted to make you and your photographer aware of," I begin. "We're doing a slideshow for our guests as they arrive—just a couple photos of us throughout the years... I'm sure you've seen this before, I don't have to tell you." She nods pleasantly. "It might be nice to get a few photos of that for your article—of Vermont's elite blushing over how cute we are." I add a laugh at the end, like I was in on the joke of how silly that sounded. "That will happen just before the first look. I'm actually seeing Graham's brother before Graham, to make sure that's all sorted out. It's always risky to put brothers-in-law in charge."

We laugh together like lifelong girlfriends.

"We've also added a slightly modified first look. Instead of just Graham and me, we're going to include his whole family and my maid of honor, Lena."

"Oh, interesting. What made you decide that?"

I shook my head. "You know, we just figured there are so many people here—so many friends of Mr. Walker and the family, that we really wanted a more intimate, private moment. Everyone else can see me for the first time when I'm walking down that long aisle," I said, knowing—and grateful—that we'd never get that far.

"This is all so great to know. I promise we'll make ourselves scarce. You'll never know there's anyone but family there."

"I appreciate that," I said. "I think there's a good chance you'll get your cover shot then."

A very good chance.

# TWENTY-THREE

**MY PHONE BUZZES** in my hand as I slowly follow my entourage of photographers and videographers and makeup artists down the long hallway on the second floor, my footsteps—and my head—feeling lighter and lighter as we get closer to the end.

I glance around as I answer, reminding myself not to say anything revealing. We've made it this far. Don't want to spoil the surprise now, do we?

"Yes?" I say, garnering a sideways glance from my hairstylist. *Who would dare call the bride this close to her wedding? And why would the bride answer?*

"We found something," Molly says, her voice distant and harsh. "Greg is on his way to you. We'll be there soon."

I hang up without another word.

# TWENTY-FOUR

**AT SIX O'CLOCK,** I am where I need to be.

Almost there, was the text from Molly a few minutes ago. After all this time, we finally found Ruthie. And now it is time to close the door on this chapter of our lives; to find a new normal; to finally live.

I'm in the reception tent, prepared for the confrontation disguised as first looks. It was a first look at something, but not the dress. At the evidence.

Reed is set to meet me in ten minutes, which is more perfect timing than I could imagine. Sarah and Rufus are waiting outside the tent. Everyone's in their spots.

I move toward the entrance, out of view of the ceremony area across the cobble street where people are beginning to gather, bused in from a meeting spot in town. We are safe hosts, making sure no one is drunk driving up or down this winding road.

Governor McCallester and his wife, Heather, have just arrived. Rumor has it they're beginning an exploratory campaign for president. They sit behind Robert Joliet, the lieutenant governor, and his wife, Emory, a teacher at the local high school. There's Dr. James Farthy, the mayor, talking to Police Commissioner Thomas Edwards. Of course, Graham's godfather, Lawrence O'Brien, the chief justice, and his wife, Laura, are sitting in prime third-row spots, just behind the designated family seats.

I'm about to head to my spot when I see, exiting a bus in a tailored gray suit, Dr. Les Gerwig followed immediately by Dr. Bregg, stepping onto the grass like the kings and queens they think they are.

Seeing them now, even all these years later, sends a shiver of nausea through my entire body. Suddenly I'm eighteen and I'm back in those offices, trying to convince them that Ruthie's gone. That we need to do something. I'm not crazy, I'm not drunk, I'm not PMSing. My best friend wasn't coming back. They told me to give up but I wouldn't. I would never give up.

I gag a little when the next bus pulls up and Dr. Felix Chastain struts off. He looks exactly the same. Aged backwards, even, like Jennifer Aniston or Anne Hathaway. The only thing that gives his age away is that I am older, too; his eyes are a little saggier, his shoulders more hunched. But he has money, a lot of money, more than the Walkers could probably dream of, and so all of the other tells have been fixed. He gifted us a weeklong stay at his ski-in ski-out cabin in Beaver Creek, Colorado, for a post-wedding trip. I started laughing when we received his card.

Dr. Felix Chastain doesn't recognize me. None of them do. My name—the name famous from a novel everyone loved bringing up at the time—goes completely unremembered all these years later. My time at Covenant is just a blip in their memory, Ruthie and I apparently undeserving of more time and space in their brain.

I was taught from an early age: "Do unto others as you would have them do unto you." The Golden Rule. We even gave it to my parents as a Christmas gift—Will carved it onto a plaque to hang on the front porch. My father repeated it often, sometimes to himself, sometimes to us, sometimes to no one in particular. Do unto others as you would have them do unto you.

As an adult, my thoughts on the Golden Rule have evolved: do unto others the way they deserve to be treated. Give people what they've earned.

And if they've murdered your best friend, they've earned public humiliation.

"Wow."

When I look up Reed is standing there, admiring me in a genuinely brotherly kind of way. Like he's proud of me and proud of Graham for locking me down. Like he's happy I'm about to join their family.

"Eliza, you look, I mean—" He takes my hand and spins me around. I go along with it to buy myself time; to let myself take a deep breath—a few of them—and gear up. To finally get myself out of here. And to give him what he deserves.

"Do you have your computer?" I ask. "Half the crowd is already here, so…we should get it started."

From under his arm, he slips his laptop out of a brown leather case and puts it on one of the unfinished tables. "Happy Wedding Day," he says, resting his thumb on the fingerprint recognition button like he, too, was presenting me with an all-inclusive vacation to Colorado. "Um…" He types his password into the space and judging by the movement of his fingers, he was *not* typing June 4, Veronica's birthday. "I'm not sure—"

He can't get into his computer. That means someone else did. That means Jess was close and that, if her calculations were correct, I should be hearing shocked gasps from the crowd in three…two…

"What the fuck is going on?" Doug storms into the tent, his face so red it looks like it might pop right off his body. He beelines straight to the computer and tries, as a seventy-year-old man does, to unlock it—to no avail, obviously. "This is not funny, Reed. Turn it off."

"I don't know what—"

*"Turn it fucking off!"*

Before he can finish, he and Reed are stomping out of the reception tent and across the cobblestone street as I follow, coolly from behind, one step at a time. I can't help the smile forming on my face. It's like watching an actor break on *SNL*. Trying to hide it is fruitless so you're better off pulling a Bill Hader and turning it into a character trait.

Everyone at the ceremony is standing at their seats, staring at the projector hanging from the wooden archway where Graham and I are meant to say "I do" in less than an hour.

Doug and Reed blend right in with them once we reach the crowd, standing and staring like they are completely overcome by what they are seeing.

"What's going—" Cheryl and Graham approach and stop short behind us, their eyes darting toward the screen.

First, a photo of teenage me and Ruthie and Catherine and Annie smiling, giddy, in the forest on our way from the car to the property. Catherine's brother yelled at Ruthie for taking it—claiming the flash would be the thing that got us caught. Then a photo of Catherine and Annie, their faces pressed so hard against each other. A photo of the party crowd, the hay floor, the red painted barn, the orange Gatorade cooler. A photo of Catherine's brother and Reed and Graham, holding their red cups, looking toward us, toward the camera, ambush predators scoping out their prey.

"I thought we should include some photos from the night I met you," I say, softly, pointedly, at Reed. "Here. At your house. At that party."

A photo of me and Catherine dancing with a few unrecognizable strangers.

"What are you talking about, babe?" Graham asks, stepping toward me. He reaches his hand out for my waist, but I pull away before he can get it. I don't want to be touched right now.

"You know the one," I say to Graham before turning my attention back to my prime target. To Reed. "In the big red barn. The night you killed Ruthie."

He is impossibly still then, they all are. It seems like the entire state of Vermont might have stopped moving with the Earth's orbit. Like everyone is holding in their last remaining breath.

I could hear Sarah and Rufus approaching, Rufus's camera already ticking away.

"Oh, I'm sorry." I shake my head like a silly girl who forgot to buy the eggs on her shopping list. "We called her Ruthie at school. At Covenant University. We used different names there. Saint names. Some Evangelical controlling bullshit." I glance behind Reed at Chastain and Gerwig and Bregg, moving into the center aisle. Maybe they recognize me now. "I think you know her as Bernadette."

After an impossibly long silence, Reed takes a step toward me like he might reach for my neck but then stops himself when he remembers we have witnesses. Approximately three hundred and fifty of them, if my seating chart is correct. Two of whom were from the *New York Times*.

"I figured it all out," I tell them. "It wasn't hard—you may have a lot of people covering for you, but that doesn't change what happened. What *was* hard was deciding what to do about it. How to touch the untouchable. How to prosecute people above the law."

He looks behind me toward his family—at Graham and Doug and Cheryl.

"They can't help you," I continue. "It's over. I figured it out. I figured it all out. They've dug out the barn." He seems to grow pale at the thought. "Where we drank your jungle juice and I lost my virginity and you killed my best friend. The barn you guys donated to Lorraine the second the lovely Covenant University staff told your father I started talking. How incredibly generous of your family to offer to renovate it for her. A convenient spot to hide a girl's body, huh?"

"You're fucking crazy," he spits.

"Get her out of here—" Doug grabs my arm—hard—and when I pull away his nails dig into my skin.

"Do not fucking touch me," I tell him, loud, determined. "What happened that night, Reed?" I ask, moving forward, pushing him toward the altar—the sacred place meant for my vows. "What was it? She didn't want to fuck you? She kissed you and pulled you outside but when it came down to it, she didn't want to fuck you? You felt your dick shrivel up a little, embarrassed you couldn't get *everything* you wanted? So you killed her? Or did you fuck her anyway? Did you cover her mouth while she screamed for help into your disgusting face. While she—"

Behind him a new photo comes up. At first glance it's just the party crowd again, the Gatorade of radioactive liquid, the dancers and the kids making out on a worn leather couch in the back. But there, in the corner, that's what catches my eye. It's Ruthie. The moment she walked out of the barn. The last time I saw her.

And she was holding Graham's hand.

I feel like the air has been knocked out of my chest.

"It was you!"

I spin around to face my fiancé.

"What are you—"

I rack my brain for memories of that night—of Graham and Reed. Of Ruthie and me. I think back to all our interactions, to everything I knew about these two men. I was so meticulous. So thoughtful. How could I possibly have been so wrong? How could I possibly have chosen the wrong brother?

I look at Graham's face. The man I've been touching and fucking and loving for years. The man who touched me and fucked me and loved me, too. The man I slept beside. The man who kept all the doors unlocked and all the lights on. The one with the twisted smile and touchable hair and stunning blue eyes. The right cheek dimple and the curved nose. The curved nose.

I take his nose in my hand. I could break it with one easy move but I won't. I'll let the other prisoners do that for me. "I had it all wrong. It was you. She left with you. And there's a photo to prove it."

He shoves me off him, but no one is able to move.

"She decked you across the face, didn't she? She was fighting and she hit you and broke your fucking nose. And then you killed her. How did you do it? How did you—"

Before I can blink, he has my neck in his hands; his face is so close to mine that I'm sure he's going to kill me, too. At least Ruthie would be waiting for me wherever we ended up.

I can feel Doug and Cheryl and Reed tugging at Graham's arms. I can feel the crowd begin to close in on us, try to separate us, try to get both our heads on straight. But all I can see are Graham's eyes. The eyes of a man who is getting what he deserves.

"Is this how you did it?" I feel his fingers cage around my neck. Getting tighter and tighter. "Is this how you did it?" The words scratch at the back of my throat, one by one, barely making their way out, but I have to keep trying. "Is this… how…you…killed…"

"Shut the fuck up," he says to me so softly I'm sure no one else heard it. "She was a fucking tease who deserved what was coming to her."

The next thing I know, I'm falling onto my back on the hard ground, and Graham is being pulled away from me by two sheriff's deputies. The brown uniforms that normally help them blend into the background make them stand out here.

The sound of my own coughs erupts in my ears as I try to catch my breath, but I can hear Graham yelling. He's struggling to get out of their grip, kicking and trying to push their thick hands off him. "She's fucking crazy," he screams. "She has no idea what she's talking about."

Sarah appears next to me, pulling me up to my feet.

"I got it all," she whispers, the recording device beetling out of her pocket. "Holy shit."

When I'm back on my feet the entire crowd is surrounding us closely—every guest and plus-one and family member stare at us in silence, watching like they know they should run but can't get their feet to move. Every person involved in this cover-up is right here. They are all about to be hung, too.

"Graham Walker," begins the taller police officer. Greg. Who we called the night we made this wild plan after I brought Jess and Molly to the lookout. Who told us it would never work. But who showed up today because it did.

"Get your hands off him," Doug says, stern but steady, like he's negotiating a hostage situation. "There's been a mistake. This is absurd. We don't even know who—"

Cheryl erupts into tears at that point, a comically contrasting reaction to her husband, who couldn't be calmer. Veronica and Lena twist their arms to steady her and her screams.

I'll never forget Lena's face, staring at me, mouth wide open, startled and shocked for the first time in her whole fucking life. For a moment I see an image of teenage Lena, of her desperate laughter at the party as she called me wasted, embarrassing. Her dismissal of a woman in trouble because she felt threatened by us. We took the attention away from her.

I flash her a quick smile and she looks away. *You should be ashamed. What is it you always say? "Girls have to stick together"?*

Graham steps two feet away from the officers, rubbing his wrists like they'd been zip-tied too tightly. "You are under arrest for the murder of Bernadette Ward," Timothy says.

Hearing those words feels surreal. I'd pictured this day for years—though Reed was the one in handcuffs, not Graham. My sweet, sweet Graham.

I thought I was the only one making up stories.

I could hear Cheryl and Doug beginning to talk—to me, to Graham, to the officers—but I can't hear their words. I'm completely siloed in my own head.

I picture Ruthie, then, standing next to me, still in that Abercrombie shirt and jeans from when we met. I picture her curled up next to me on a blanket in the woods, sharing vodka mixed with pineapple juice from the dining hall. Sitting on her bed in the middle of the night, a flashlight pointed at her face from below, her mouth moving to tell me that Riley Klein from her American history class got a boner when they started talking about Martha Washington. Ruthie on her last day, dancing with me like we were the only two people on earth.

"There must be a mistake." Police Commissioner Thomas Edwards parts the crowd, holding out his badge to the sheriff's deputies. Graham smiles and visibly loosens up like it's the get-out-of-jail-free card he's been waiting for. "Now, look, clearly there's been some kind of miscommunication. These are the *Walkers*. This is his wedding day. These are good people." He stands between Graham and the officers now, feet planted firmly on the floor like a man who always gets what he wants.

Doug joins him. A united front for getting away with murder. "Let's all calm down and discuss this like adults."

"The body of Bernadette Ward was found this morning in

the yard of your housekeeper, Lorraine Sakara," the shorter officer says to Doug. "She was strangled with what looks to be a chain or a necklace."

A necklace.

"Lorraine? Okay. Why aren't you talking to *her*? Why isn't she—"

"—and your son just confessed in front of all these witnesses."

Greg and the other officer take Graham by the shoulders and begin walking him to their convoy on the cobble road.

"What? He didn't—"

"—I recorded it—" Sarah says.

"—you have no right—"

My necklace.

"—you are all going to be fired and sued—"

*My* necklace.

The entire crowd follows Graham and Doug and Cheryl. They can't believe this is happening. They can't believe they're witnessing this. They *just can't believe it*.

I, instead, snake out the other direction in my wedding gown and four-inch heels. I find my very familiar path in the forest, and begin to descend to the road the same way I did all those years ago. But now it's over. It's all over.

The bottom of Walker Mountain still has an 8,891-foot elevation. It's still above everyone else. I can still see campus, a ball of light in the valley as the sun sets. The place where I met Ruthie. The place where this all started. The place I'll never be able to forget.

As a blue Suburban begins to slow on the street beside me, I kneel next to the green pole holding up the *Walker Mountain* sign and, with my hands, dig through a thin layer of mulch before I find the envelope, exactly where I left it yesterday morning during my run. Beside it is a black marker.

I stick the envelope under my arm, the dark dirt staining the silk of my dress, I'm sure.

I uncap the marker, and just above the ground, where no one will be able to see it, I write *Bernadette Ruth Ward*.

Then, beside it, *Alexandra Elizabeth Bennet*.

The car comes to a stop and the passenger's-side door opens, and I jump inside as we begin to hear the sirens wail their way down the mountain.

Molly, Jess, and I don't speak.

Instead, I roll the window down and let the cool air hit my face, blowing away the last eight years. I close my eyes and can feel us speeding up, turning with the mountains, and moving away from this place. From these memories. These people.

I don't know what's next. I didn't plan that far ahead. But that's okay with me. I like not having a plan. I feel free. It's the first time in years I can be whomever I want.

In the far distance, like a flash of home, I can hear a gunshot, tinny and cold. A hunter preparing for the season, like they always do this time of year. As the echo gets farther away, eventually fading into the wind, an overwhelming silence follows.

I can rest my head.

I can take a deep breath.

I can close my eyes.

I can finally feel peace.

★ ★ ★ ★ ★

# ACKNOWLEDGMENTS

First, I want to thank you, the reader, for picking up this book. I also want to thank everyone who read my first book, *Smile and Look Pretty*. Thank you for every purchase, every post, every library request, every photo, every like, every review, every message. It is because of your support that I'm able to do the job that I love. I hope you like this book, too.

Thank you to my literary agent, Liz Parker. Thank you for always championing me and my writing, for giving the absolute best advice, and for knowing exactly what to say during my stressed calls and emails. I still can't believe what started in the slush pile has turned into two novels I'm incredibly proud of. I'm so grateful to be on this wild journey with you.

Thank you to my editor, Laura Brown, for taking this book under your wing and loving it like one of your own. This book is so much better because of your patience, brainstorms, and gimlet-eyed edits. And you were so right about the title. Thank you, Natalie Hallak, for seeing the promise in this idea very early on. Thank you to everyone at Park Row Books and

HarperCollins—especially Justine Sha and Nicole Luongo—for your incredible support.

Thank you, Chris Lupo, Anne Sawyier, and the whole team at Verve; Delaney Morris, Matt Rosen, and the whole team at Grandview. Thank you for always working to give my books a second life and for pushing me and my writing career.

Thank you, Jake, Tess, Dorian, and Richard Froelich and Shevaun Stigers for your hospitality and for the inspiration behind the Vermont setting. I wrote the first sentence of this book at your home there, and I'm so grateful to have had a place to sit in the brisk October air with a glass of wine and a fire and plot out this book.

To Bernadette, my freshman year roommate, who complained there was no one named after her in my first book… how's this?

Thank you, Erin, Maggie, Brynna, and Steph, four of my all-time favorite people, for your very early reads, thoughts, notes, and answers to my constant "okay, question about book 2" texts.

This book is dedicated to my parents, who I simply cannot thank enough. For this, for everything, I love you.